ACCLAIM FROM AROUND THE WORLD:

'Wow...Blockbuster perfection...An exhilaratingly brainy thriller. Not since the advent of Harry Potter has an author so flagrantly delighted in leading readers on a breathless chase'

NEW YORK TIMES

'Brown's novel adroitly blends the chase-scene stuffed thrillers of Robert Ludlum and the learned romps of Umberto Eco...For anyone who wants more brain-food than thrillers normally provide'

SUNDAY TIMES

'Exceedingly clever...Both fascinating and fun... a considerable achievement'

WASHINGTON POST

'A gripping bestseller...Brown has cracked the bestseller code'

GUARDIAN

DAN BROWN

is the author of *The Da Vinci Code*, one of
the most widely read novels of all time, as well as two
other international bestsellers featuring Harvard symbologist
Robert Langdon, *The Lost Symbol* and *Angels & Demons*.
Langdon also stars in his new novel, *Inferno*. He has written
two stand alone thrillers, *Deception Point* and *Digital Fortress*.
He lives in New England with his wife.

www.danbrownofficial.co.uk

THE BOOKS:

Digital FORTRESS

An impossibly complex code threatens to obliterate
the balance of world power forever...

Angels & DEMONS

An ancient secret brotherhood launch a devastating
new weapon against an unthinkable target...

Deception POINT

An apparently miraculous scientific discovery might
change the future of the planet if its truth is revealed...

The Da Vinci CODE

A quest almost as old as time itself for an object thought
lost forever becomes a deadly race against the clock...

The Lost SYMBOL

A breathless chase through Washington's dark history and
into a shadowy, mythical world of Masonic secrets...

DAN BROWN

Digital FORTRESS

CORGI BOOKS

TRANSWORLD PUBLISHERS
61–63 Uxbridge Road, London W5 5SA
A Random House Group Company
www.transworldbooks.co.uk

DIGITAL FORTRESS
A CORGI BOOK: 9780552169981
9780552169998

First publication in Great Britain
Corgi edition published 2004
Corgi edition reissued 2009, 2013

Addresses for Random House Group Ltd companies outside the UK
can be found at: www.randomhouse.co.uk
The Random House Group Ltd Reg. No. 954009

The Random House Group Limited supports the Forest Stewardship
Council® (FSC®), the leading international forest-certification organisation.
Our books carrying the FSC label are printed on FSC®-certified paper. FSC is
the only forest-certification scheme supported by the leading environmental
organisations, including Greenpeace. Our paper-procurement policy can be
found at www.randomhouse.co.uk/environment

Typeset in Palatino by Falcon Oast Graphic Art Ltd.
Printed and bound by CPI Group (UK) Ltd, Croydon, CR0 4YY

2 4 6 8 10 9 7 5 3 1

For my parents . . .
my mentors and heroes

A debt of gratitude: to my editors at St Martin's Press, Thomas Dunne and the exceptionally talented Melissa Jacobs. To my agents in New York, George Wieser, Olga Wieser, and Jake Elwell. To all those who read and contributed to the manuscript along the way. And especially to my wife, Blythe, for her enthusiasm and patience.

Also . . . a quiet thank you to the two faceless ex-NSA cryptographers who made invaluable contributions via anonymous remailers. Without them this book would not have been written.

PROLOGUE

PLAZA DE ESPAÑA
SEVILLE, SPAIN
11:00 A.M.

It is said that in death, all things become clear; Ensei Tankado now knew it was true. As he clutched his chest and fell to the ground in pain, he realized the horror of his mistake.

People appeared, hovering over him, trying to help. But Tankado did not want help – it was too late for that.

Trembling, he raised his left hand and held his fingers outward. *Look at my hand!* The faces around him stared, but he could tell they did not understand.

On his finger was an engraved golden ring. For an instant, the markings glimmered in the Andalusian sun. Ensei Tankado knew it was the last light he would ever see.

CHAPTER 1

They were in the Smoky Mountains at their favorite bed-and-breakfast. David was smiling down at her. 'What do you say, gorgeous? Marry me?'

Looking up from their canopy bed, she knew he was the one. Forever. As she stared into his deep-green eyes, somewhere in the distance a deafening bell began to ring. It was pulling him away. She reached for him, but her arms clutched empty air.

It was the sound of the phone that fully awoke Susan Fletcher from her dream. She gasped, sat up in bed, and fumbled for the receiver. 'Hello?'

'Susan, it's David. Did I wake you?'

She smiled, rolling over in bed. 'I was just dreaming of you. Come over and play.'

He laughed. 'It's still dark out.'

'Mmm.' She moaned sensuously. 'Then *definitely* come over and play. We can sleep in before we head north.'

David let out a frustrated sigh. 'That's why I'm calling. It's about our trip. I've got to postpone.'

Susan was suddenly wide awake. 'What!'

'I'm sorry. I've got to leave town. I'll be back by

tomorrow. We can head up first thing in the morning. We'll still have two days.'

'But I made reservations,' Susan said, hurt. 'I got our old room at Stone Manor.'

'I know, but—'

'Tonight was supposed to be *special* – to celebrate six months. You *do* remember we're engaged, don't you?'

'Susan.' He sighed. 'I really can't go into it now, they've got a car waiting. I'll call you from the plane and explain everything.'

'*Plane?*' she repeated. 'What's going on? Why would the university . . . ?'

'It's not the university. I'll phone and explain later. I've really got to go; they're calling for me. I'll be in touch. I promise.'

'David!' she cried. 'What's—'

But it was too late. David had hung up.

Susan Fletcher lay awake for hours waiting for him to call back. The phone never rang.

Later that afternoon Susan sat dejected in the tub. She submerged herself in the soapy water and tried to forget Stone Manor and the Smoky Mountains. *Where could he be?* she wondered. *Why hasn't he called?*

Gradually the water around her went from hot to lukewarm and finally to cold. She was about to get out when her cordless phone buzzed to life. Susan bolted upright, sloshing water on the floor as she grappled for the receiver she'd left on the sink.

'David?'

'It's Strathmore,' the voice replied.

Susan slumped. 'Oh.' She was unable to hide her disappointment. 'Good afternoon, Commander.'

'Hoping for a younger man?' The voice chuckled.

'No, sir,' Susan said, embarrassed. 'It's not how it—'

'Sure it is.' He laughed. 'David Becker's a good man. Don't ever lose him.'

'Thank you, sir.'

The commander's voice turned suddenly stern. 'Susan, I'm calling because I need you in here. Pronto.'

She tried to focus. 'It's Saturday, sir. We don't usually—'

'I know,' he said calmly. 'It's an emergency.'

Susan sat up. *Emergency?* She had never heard the word cross Commander Strathmore's lips. *An emergency? In Crypto?* She couldn't imagine. 'Y-yes, sir.' She paused. 'I'll be there as soon as I can.'

'Make it sooner.' Strathmore hung up.

Susan Fletcher stood wrapped in a towel and dripped on the neatly folded clothes she'd set out the night before – hiking shorts, a sweater for the cool mountain evenings, and the new lingerie she'd bought for the nights. Depressed, she went to her closet for a clean blouse and skirt. *An emergency? In Crypto?*

As she went downstairs, Susan wondered how the day could get much worse.

She was about to find out.

CHAPTER 2

Thirty thousand feet above a dead-calm ocean, David Becker stared miserably from the Learjet 60's small, oval window. He'd been told the phone on board was out of order, and he'd never had a chance to call Susan.

'What am I doing here?' he grumbled to himself. But the answer was simple – there were men to whom you just didn't say no.

'Mr Becker,' the loudspeaker crackled. 'We'll be arriving in half an hour.'

Becker nodded gloomily to the invisible voice. *Wonderful.* He pulled the shade and tried to sleep. But he could only think of her.

CHAPTER 3

Susan's Volvo sedan rolled to a stop in the shadow of the ten-foot-high, barbed Cyclone fence. A young guard placed his hand on the roof.

'ID, please.'

Susan obliged and settled in for the usual half-minute wait. The officer ran her card through a computerized scanner. Finally he looked up. 'Thank you, Ms Fletcher.' He gave an imperceptible sign, and the gate swung open.

Half a mile ahead Susan repeated the entire procedure at an equally imposing electrified fence. *Come on, guys . . . I've only been through here a million times.*

As she approached the final checkpoint, a stocky sentry with two attack dogs and a machine gun glanced down at her license plate and waved her through. She followed Canine Road for another 250 yards and pulled into Employee Lot C. Unbelievable, she thought. *Twenty-six thousand employees and a twelve-billion-dollar budget; you'd think they could make it through the weekend without me.* Susan gunned the car into her reserved spot and killed the engine.

After crossing the landscaped terrace and entering

16

the main building, she cleared two more internal checkpoints and finally arrived at the windowless tunnel that led to the new wing. A voice-scan booth blocked her entry.

The armed guard looked up. 'Afternoon, Ms Fletcher.'

Susan smiled tiredly. 'Hi, John.'

'Didn't expect you today.'

'Yeah, me neither.' She leaned toward the parabolic microphone. 'Susan Fletcher,' she stated clearly. The computer instantly confirmed the frequency concentrations in her voice, and the gate clicked open. She stepped through.

The guard admired Susan as she began her walk down the cement causeway. He noticed that her strong hazel eyes seemed distant today, but her cheeks had a flushed freshness, and her shoulder-length, auburn hair looked newly blown dry. Trailing her was the faint scent of Johnson's Baby Powder. His eyes fell the length of her slender torso – to her white blouse with the bra barely visible beneath, to her knee-length khaki skirt, and finally to her legs . . . Susan Fletcher's legs.

Hard to imagine they support a 170 IQ, he mused to himself.

He stared after her a long time. Finally he shook his head as she disappeared in the distance.

*

As Susan reached the end of the tunnel, a circular, vaultlike door blocked her way. The enormous letters read: CRYPTO.

Sighing, she placed her hand inside the recessed cipher box and entered her five-digit PIN. Seconds later the twelve-ton slab of steel began to revolve. She tried to focus, but her thoughts reeled back to him.

David Becker. The only man she'd ever loved. The youngest full professor at Georgetown University and a brilliant foreign-language specialist, he was practically a celebrity in the world of academia. Born with an eidetic memory and a love of languages, he'd mastered six Asian dialects as well as Spanish, French, and Italian. His university lectures on etymology and linguistics were standing-room-only, and he invariably stayed late to answer a barrage of questions. He spoke with authority and enthusiasm, apparently oblivious to the adoring gazes of his star-struck coeds.

Becker was dark – a rugged, youthful thirty-five with sharp green eyes and a wit to match. His strong jaw and taut features reminded Susan of carved marble. Over six feet tall, Becker moved across a squash court faster than any of his colleagues could comprehend. After soundly beating his opponent, he would cool off by dousing his head in a drinking fountain and soaking his tuft of thick, black hair. Then, still dripping, he'd treat his opponent to a fruit shake and a bagel.

As with all young professors, David's university salary was modest. From time to time, when he needed to renew his squash club membership or restring his old Dunlop with gut, he earned extra money by doing translating work for government agencies in and around Washington. It was on one of those jobs that he'd met Susan.

It was a crisp morning during fall break when Becker returned from a morning jog to his three-room faculty apartment to find his answering machine blinking. He downed a quart of orange juice as he listened to the playback. The message was like many he received – a government agency requesting his translating services for a few hours later that morning. The only strange thing was that Becker had never heard of the organization.

'They're called the National Security Agency,' Becker said, calling a few of his colleagues for background.

The reply was always the same. 'You mean the National Security *Council?*'

Becker checked the message. 'No. They said *Agency*. The NSA.'

'Never heard of 'em.'

Becker checked the GAO Directory, and it showed no listing either. Puzzled, Becker called one of his old squash buddies, an ex-political analyst turned research clerk at the Library of Congress. David was shocked by his friend's explanation.

Apparently, not only did the NSA exist, but it was considered one of the most influential government organizations in the world. It had been gathering global electronic intelligence data and protecting U.S. classified information for over half a century. Only 3 percent of Americans were even aware it existed.

'NSA,' his buddy joked, 'stands for "No Such Agency."'

With a mixture of apprehension and curiosity, Becker accepted the mysterious agency's offer. He drove the thirty-seven miles to their eighty-six-acre headquarters hidden discreetly in the wooded hills of

Fort Meade, Maryland. After passing through endless security checks and being issued a six-hour, holographic guest pass, he was escorted to a plush research facility where he was told he would spend the afternoon providing 'blind support' to the Cryptography Division – an elite group of mathematical brainiacs known as the code-breakers.

For the first hour, the cryptographers seemed unaware Becker was even there. They hovered around an enormous table and spoke a language Becker had never heard. They spoke of stream ciphers, self-decimated generators, knapsack variants, zero knowledge protocols, unicity points. Becker observed, lost. They scrawled symbols on graph paper, pored over computer printouts, and continuously referred to the jumble of text on the overhead projector.

```
JHDJA3JKHDHMADO/ERTWTJLW+JGJ328
5JHALSFNHKHHHFAFOHHDFGAF/FJ37WE
OHI93450S9DJFD2H/HHRTYFHLF89303
95JSPJF2J08907IHJ98YHFI080EWRT03
JOJR845HDROQ+JTDEU4TQEFQE//OUJW
08UYDIH0934JTPWFIAJER09QU4JR9GU
IVJP$DUW4H95PE8RTUGVJW3P4E/IKKC
MFFUERHFGVDQ3 94IKJRMG+UNHVS90ER
IRK/0956Y7UDPOIKIOJP9F876DQWERQI
```

Eventually one of them explained what Becker had already surmised. The scrambled text was a code – a 'ciphertext' – groups of numbers and letters representing encrypted words. The cryptographers' job was to study the code and extract from it the original message, or 'cleartext.' The NSA had called Becker because they suspected the original message was written in Mandarin Chinese; he was to translate the symbols as the cryptographers decrypted them.

For two hours, Becker interpreted an endless stream of Mandarin symbols. But each time he gave them a translation, the cryptographers shook their heads in despair. Apparently the code was not making sense. Eager to help, Becker pointed out that all the characters they'd shown him had a common trait – they were also part of the Kanji language. Instantly the bustle in the room fell silent. The man in charge, a lanky chain-smoker named Morante, turned to Becker in disbelief.

'You mean these symbols have multiple meanings?'

Becker nodded. He explained that Kanji was a Japanese writing system based on modified Chinese characters. He'd been giving Mandarin translations because that's what they'd asked for.

'Jesus Christ.' Morante coughed. 'Let's try the Kanji.'

Like magic, everything fell into place.

The cryptographers were duly impressed, but nonetheless, they still made Becker work on the characters out of sequence. 'It's for your own safety,' Morante said. 'This way, you won't know what you're translating.'

Becker laughed. Then he noticed nobody else was laughing.

When the code finally broke, Becker had no idea what dark secrets he'd helped reveal, but one thing was for certain – the NSA took code-breaking seriously; the check in Becker's pocket was more than an entire month's university salary.

On his way back out through the series of security checkpoints in the main corridor, Becker's exit was blocked by a guard hanging up a phone. 'Mr Becker, wait here, please.'

'What's the problem?' Becker had not expected the meeting to take so long, and he was running late for his standing Saturday afternoon squash match.

The guard shrugged. 'Head of Crypto wants a word. She's on her way out now.'

'*She?*' Becker laughed. He had yet to see a female inside the NSA.

'Is that a problem for you?' a woman's voice asked from behind him.

Becker turned and immediately felt himself flush. He eyed the ID card on the woman's blouse. The head of the NSA's Cryptography Division was not only a woman, but an attractive woman at that.

'No,' Becker fumbled. 'I just . . .'

'Susan Fletcher.' The woman smiled, holding out her slender hand.

Becker took it. 'David Becker.'

'Congratulations, Mr Becker. I hear you did a fine job today. Might I chat with you about it?'

Becker hesitated. 'Actually, I'm in a bit of a rush at the moment.' He hoped spurning the world's most powerful intelligence agency wasn't a foolish act, but his squash match started in forty-five minutes, and he had a reputation to uphold: David Becker was never late for squash . . . class maybe, but *never* squash.

'I'll be brief.' Susan Fletcher smiled. 'Right this way, please.'

Ten minutes later, Becker was in the NSA's commissary enjoying a popover and cranberry juice with the NSA's lovely head cryptographer, Susan Fletcher. It quickly became evident to David that the thirty-eight-year-old's high-ranking position at the NSA was no fluke – she was one of the brightest women he had ever met. As they discussed codes and code-breaking, Becker found himself struggling to keep up – a new and exciting experience for him.

An hour later, after Becker had obviously missed his squash match and Susan had blatantly ignored three pages on the intercom, both of them had to laugh. There they were, two highly analytical minds, presumably immune to irrational infatuations – but somehow, while they sat there discussing linguistic morphology and pseudo-random number generators, they felt like a couple of teenagers – everything was fireworks.

Susan never did get around to the real reason she'd wanted to speak to David Becker – to offer him a trial post in their Asiatic Cryptography Division. It was clear from the passion with which the young professor spoke about teaching that he would never leave the university. Susan decided not to ruin the mood by talking business. She felt like a schoolgirl all over again; nothing was going to spoil it. And nothing did.

Their courtship was slow and romantic – stolen escapes whenever their schedules permitted, long walks through the Georgetown campus, late-night cappuccinos at Merlutti's, occasional lectures and concerts. Susan found herself laughing more than she'd ever thought possible. It seemed there was nothing David couldn't twist into a joke. It was a welcome release from the intensity of her post at the NSA.

One crisp, autumn afternoon they sat in the bleachers watching Georgetown soccer get pummeled by Rutgers.

'What sport did you say you play?' Susan teased. 'Zucchini?'

Becker groaned. 'It's called *squash*.'

She gave him a dumb look.

'It's *like* zucchini,' he explained, 'but the court's smaller.'

Susan pushed him.

Georgetown's left wing sent a corner-kick sailing out of bounds, and a boo went up from the crowd. The defensemen hurried back downfield.

'How about you?' Becker asked. 'Play any sports?'

'I'm a black belt in StairMaster.'

Becker cringed. 'I prefer sports you can win.'

Susan smiled. 'Overachiever, are we?'

Georgetown's star defenseman blocked a pass, and there was a communal cheer in the stands. Susan leaned over and whispered in David's ear. 'Doctor.'

He turned and eyed her, lost.

'Doctor,' she repeated. 'Say the first thing that comes to mind.'

Becker looked doubtful. 'Word associations?'

'Standard NSA procedure. I need to know who I'm with.' She eyed him sternly. 'Doctor.'

Becker shrugged. 'Seuss.'

Susan gave him a frown. 'Okay, try this one . . . "kitchen."'

He didn't hesitate. 'Bedroom.'

Susan arched her eyebrows coyly. 'Okay, how about this . . . "cat."'

'Gut,' Becker fired back.

'Gut?'

'Yeah. Catgut. Squash racquet string of champions.'

'That's pleasant.' She groaned.

'Your diagnosis?' Becker inquired.

Susan thought a minute. 'You're a childish, sexually frustrated squash fiend.'

Becker shrugged. 'Sounds about right.'

It went on like that for weeks. Over dessert at all-night diners Becker would ask endless questions.

Where had she learned mathematics?

How did she end up at the NSA?

How did she get so captivating?

Susan blushed and admitted she'd been a late bloomer. Lanky and awkward with braces through her late teens, Susan said her Aunt Clara had once told her God's apology for Susan's plainness was to give her brains. A premature apology, Becker thought.

Susan explained that her interest in cryptography had started in junior high school. The president of the computer club, a towering eighth grader named Frank Gutmann, typed her a love poem and encrypted it with a number-substitution scheme. Susan begged to know what it said. Frank flirtatiously refused. Susan took the code home and stayed up all night with a flashlight under her covers until she figured out the secret – every number represented a letter. She carefully deciphered the code and watched in wonder as the seemingly random digits turned magically into beautiful poetry. In that instant, she knew she'd fallen in love – codes and cryptography would become her life.

Almost twenty years later, after getting her master's in mathematics from Johns Hopkins and studying number theory on a full scholarship from MIT, she submitted her doctoral thesis, *Cryptographic Methods, Protocols, and Algorithms for Manual Applications*. Apparently her professor was not the only one who read it; shortly afterward, Susan received a phone call and a plane ticket from the NSA.

Everyone in cryptography knew about the NSA; it was home to the best cryptographic minds on the planet. Each spring, as the private-sector firms descended on the brightest new minds in the workforce and offered obscene salaries and stock options, the NSA watched carefully, selected their targets, and then simply stepped in and doubled the best standing offer. What the NSA wanted, the NSA bought. Trembling with anticipation, Susan flew to Washington's Dulles International Airport where she was met by an NSA driver, who whisked her off to Fort Meade.

There were forty-one others who had received the same phone call that year. At twenty-eight, Susan was the youngest. She was also the only female. The visit turned out to be more of a public relations bonanza and a barrage of intelligence testing than an informational session. In the week that followed, Susan and six others were invited back. Although hesitant, Susan returned. The group was immediately separated. They underwent individual polygraph tests, background searches, handwriting analyses, and endless hours of interviews, including taped inquiries into their sexual orientations and practices. When the interviewer asked Susan if she'd ever engaged in sex with animals, she almost walked out, but somehow the mystery carried her through – the prospect of working on the cutting edge of code theory, entering 'The Puzzle Palace,' and becoming a member of the most secretive club in the world – the National Security Agency.

Becker sat riveted by her stories. 'They actually asked you if you'd had sex with animals?'

Susan shrugged. 'Part of the routine background check.'

'Well . . .' Becker fought off a grin. 'What did you say?'

She kicked him under the table. 'I told them no!' Then she added, 'And until last night, it was true.'

In Susan's eyes, David was as close to perfect as she could imagine. He only had one unfortunate quality: Every time they went out, he insisted on picking up the check. Susan hated seeing him lay down a full day's salary on dinner for two, but Becker was immovable. Susan learned not to protest, but it still bothered her. *I make more money than I know what to do with*, she thought. *I should be paying.*

Nonetheless, Susan decided that aside from David's outdated sense of chivalry, he was ideal. He was compassionate, smart, funny, and best of all, he had a sincere interest in her work. Whether it was during trips to the Smithsonian, bike rides, or burning spaghetti in Susan's kitchen, David was perpetually curious. Susan answered what questions she could and gave David the general, unclassified overview of the National Security Agency. What David heard enthralled him.

Founded by President Truman at 12:01 A.M. on November 4, 1952, the NSA had been the most clandestine intelligence agency in the world for almost fifty years. The NSA's seven-page inception doctrine laid out a very concise agenda: to protect U.S. government communications and to intercept the communications of foreign powers.

The roof of the NSA's main operations building was littered with over five hundred antennas, including two large radomes that looked like enormous golf balls. The building itself was mammoth – over two million square feet, twice the size of CIA headquarters. Inside were eight million feet of telephone wire and eighty thousand square feet of permanently sealed windows.

Susan told David about COMINT, the agency's global reconnaissance division – a mind-boggling collection of listening posts, satellites, spies, and wiretaps around the globe. Thousands of communiqués and conversations were intercepted every day, and they were all sent to the NSA's analysts for decryption. The FBI, CIA, and U.S. foreign policy advisors all depended on the NSA's intelligence to make their decisions.

Becker was mesmerized. 'And code-breaking? Where do *you* fit in?'

Susan explained how the intercepted transmissions often originated from dangerous governments, hostile factions, and terrorist groups, many of whom were inside U.S. borders. Their communications were usually encoded for secrecy in case they ended up in the wrong hands – which, thanks to COMINT, they usually did. Susan told David her job was to study the codes, break them by hand, and furnish the NSA with the deciphered messages. This was not entirely true.

Susan felt a pang of guilt over lying to her new love, but she had no choice. A few years ago it would have been accurate, but things had changed at the NSA. The whole world of cryptography had changed. Susan's new duties were classified, even to many in the highest echelons of power.

'Codes,' Becker said, fascinated. 'How do you know where to start? I mean . . . how do you break them?'

Susan smiled. 'You of all people should know. It's like studying a foreign language. At first the text looks like gibberish, but as you learn the rules defining its structure, you can start to extract meaning.'

Becker nodded, impressed. He wanted to know more.

With Merlutti's napkins and concert programs as her chalkboard, Susan set out to give her charming new pedagogue a minicourse in cryptography. She began with Julius Caesar's 'perfect square' cipher box.

Caesar, she explained, was the first code-writer in history. When his foot-messengers started getting ambushed and his secret communiqués stolen, he devised a rudimentary way to encrypt his directives. He rearranged the text of his messages such that the correspondence looked senseless. Of course, it was not. Each message always had a letter-count that was a perfect square – sixteen, twenty-five, one hundred – depending on how much Caesar needed to say. He secretly informed his officers that when a random message arrived, they should transcribe the text into a square grid. If they did, and read top-to-bottom, a secret message would magically appear.

Over time Caesar's concept of rearranging text was adopted by others and modified to become more difficult to break. The pinnacle of noncomputer-based encryption came during World War II. The Nazis built a baffling encryption machine named Enigma. The device resembled an old-fashioned typewriter with brass interlocking rotors that revolved in intricate ways and shuffled cleartext into confounding arrays of seemingly senseless character groupings. Only by having another Enigma machine, calibrated the exact same way, could the recipient break the code.

Becker listened, spellbound. The teacher had become the student.

One night, at a university performance of *The Nutcracker*, Susan gave David his first basic code to break. He sat through the entire intermission, pen in hand, puzzling over the eleven-letter message:

HL FKZC VD LDS

Finally, just as the lights dimmed for the second half, he got it. To encode, Susan had simply replaced each letter of her message with the letter preceding it in the alphabet. To decrypt the code, all Becker had to do was shift each letter one space forward in the alphabet – 'A' became 'B,' 'B' became 'C,' and so on. He quickly shifted the remaining letters. He never imagined four little syllables could make him so happy:

IM GLAD WE MET

He quickly scrawled his response and handed it to her:

LD SNN

Susan read it and beamed.

Becker had to laugh; he was thirty-five years old, and his heart was doing backflips. He'd never been so attracted to a woman in his life. Her delicate European features and soft brown eyes reminded him of an ad for Estée Lauder. If Susan's body had been lanky and awkward as a teenager, it sure wasn't now. Somewhere along the way, she had developed a willowy grace – slender and tall with full, firm breasts

30

and a perfectly flat abdomen. David often joked that she was the first swimsuit model he'd ever met with a doctorate in applied mathematics and number theory. As the months passed, they both started to suspect they'd found something that could last a lifetime.

They'd been together almost two years when, out of the blue, David proposed to her. It was on a weekend trip to the Smoky Mountains. They were lying on a big canopy bed at Stone Manor. He had no ring – he just blurted it out. That's what she loved about him – he was so spontaneous. She kissed him long and hard. He took her in his arms and slipped off her nightgown.

'I'll take that as a yes,' he said, and they made love all night by the warmth of the fire.

That magical evening had been six months ago – before David's unexpected promotion to chairman of the Modern Language Department. Their relationship had been in a downhill slide ever since.

CHAPTER 4

The Crypto door beeped once, waking Susan from her depressing reverie. The door had rotated past its fully open position and would be closed again in five seconds, having made a complete 360-degree rotation. Susan gathered her thoughts and stepped through the opening. A computer made note of her entry.

Although she had practically lived in Crypto since its completion three years ago, the sight of it still amazed her. The main room was an enormous circular chamber that rose five stories. Its transparent, domed ceiling towered 120 feet at its central peak. The Plexiglas cupola was embedded with a polycarbonate mesh – a protective web capable of withstanding a two-megaton blast. The screen filtered the sunlight into delicate lacework across the walls. Tiny particles of dust drifted upward in wide unsuspecting spirals – captives of the dome's powerful deionizing system.

The room's sloping sides arched broadly at the top and then became almost vertical as they approached eye level. Then they became subtly translucent and graduated to an opaque black as they reached the floor – a shimmering expanse of polished black tile that shone with an eerie luster, giving one the unsettling sensation that the floor was transparent. Black ice.

Pushing through the center of the floor like the tip of a colossal torpedo was the machine for which the dome had been built. Its sleek black contour arched twenty-three feet in the air before plunging back into the floor below. Curved and smooth, it was as if an enormous killer whale had been frozen midbreach in a frigid sea.

This was TRANSLTR, the single most expensive piece of computing equipment in the world – a machine the NSA swore did not exist.

Like an iceberg, the machine hid 90 percent of its mass and power deep beneath the surface. Its secret was locked in a ceramic silo that went six stories straight down – a rocketlike hull surrounded by a winding maze of catwalks, cables, and hissing exhaust from the freon cooling system. The power generators at the bottom droned in a perpetual low-frequency hum that gave the acoustics in Crypto a dead, ghostlike quality.

TRANSLTR, like all great technological advance-ments, had been a child of necessity. During the 1980s, the NSA witnessed a revolution in telecommunica-tions that would change the world of intelligence reconnaissance forever – public access to the Internet. More specifically, the arrival of E-mail.

Criminals, terrorists, and spies had grown tired of having their phones tapped and immediately embraced this new means of global communication. E-mail had the security of conventional mail and the speed of the telephone. Since the transfers traveled through underground fiber-optic lines and were never transmitted into the airwaves, they were entirely intercept-proof – at least that was the perception.

In reality, intercepting E-mail as it zipped across the Internet was child's play for the NSA's techno-gurus. The Internet was not the new home computer revelation that most believed. It had been created by the Department of Defense three decades earlier – an enormous network of computers designed to provide secure government communication in the event of nuclear war. The eyes and ears of the NSA were old Internet pros. People conducting illegal business via E-mail quickly learned their secrets were not as private as they'd thought. The FBI, DEA, IRS, and other U.S. law enforcement agencies – aided by the NSA's staff of wily hackers – enjoyed a tidal wave of arrests and convictions.

Of course, when the computer users of the world found out the U.S. government had open access to their E-mail communications, a cry of outrage went up. Even pen pals, using E-mail for nothing more than recreational correspondence, found the lack of privacy unsettling. Across the globe, entrepreneurial programmers began working on a way to keep E-mail more secure. They quickly found one and public-key encryption was born.

Public-key encryption was a concept as simple as it was brilliant. It consisted of easy-to-use, home-computer software that scrambled personal E-mail messages in such a way that they were totally unreadable. A user could write a letter and run it through the encryption software, and the text would come out the other side looking like random nonsense – totally illegible – a code. Anyone intercepting the transmission found only an unreadable garble on the screen.

The only way to unscramble the message was to enter the sender's 'pass-key' – a secret series of characters that functioned much like a PIN number at an automatic teller. The pass-keys were generally quite long and complex; they carried all the information necessary to instruct the encryption algorithm exactly what mathematical operations to follow to re-create the original message.

A user could now send E-mail in confidence. Even if the transmission was intercepted, only those who were given the key could ever decipher it.

The NSA felt the crunch immediately. The codes they were facing were no longer simple substitution ciphers crackable with pencil and graph paper – they were computer-generated hash functions that employed chaos theory and multiple symbolic alphabets to scramble messages into seemingly hopeless randomness.

At first, the pass-keys being used were short enough for the NSA's computers to 'guess.' If a desired pass-key had ten digits, a computer was programmed to try every possibility between 0000000000 and 9999999999. Sooner or later the computer hit the correct sequence. This method of trial-and-error guessing was known as 'brute force attack.' It was time-consuming but mathematically guaranteed to work.

As the world got wise to the power of brute-force code-breaking, the pass-keys started getting longer and longer. The computer time needed to 'guess' the correct key grew from weeks to months and finally to years.

By the 1990s, pass-keys were over fifty characters long and employed the full 256-character ASCII alphabet of letters, numbers, and symbols. The number of different possibilities was in the neighborhood of 10^{120} – one with 120 zeros after it. Correctly guessing a pass-key was as mathematically unlikely as choosing the correct grain of sand from a three-mile beach. It was estimated that a successful brute-force attack on a standard sixty-four-bit key would take the NSA's fastest computer – the top-secret Cray/Josephson II – over nineteen years to break. By the time the computer guessed the key and broke the code, the contents of the message would be irrelevant.

Caught in a virtual intelligence blackout, the NSA passed a top-secret directive that was endorsed by the President of the United States. Buoyed by federal funds and a carte blanche to do whatever was necessary to solve the problem, the NSA set out to build the impossible: the world's first universal code-breaking machine.

Despite the opinion of many engineers that the newly proposed code-breaking computer was impossible to build, the NSA lived by its motto: Everything is possible. The impossible just takes longer.

Five years, half a million man-hours, and $1.9 billion later, the NSA proved it once again. The last of the three million stamp-size processors was hand-soldered in place, the final internal programming was finished, and the ceramic shell was welded shut. TRANSLTR had been born.

Although the secret internal workings of TRANSLTR were the product of many minds and were not fully understood by any one individual, its basic principle was simple: Many hands make light work.

Its three million processors would all work in

parallel – counting upward at blinding speed, trying every new permutation as they went. The hope was that even codes with unthinkably colossal pass-keys would not be safe from TRANSLTR's tenacity. This multibillion-dollar masterpiece would use the power of parallel processing as well as some highly classified advances in cleartext assessment to guess pass-keys and break codes. It would derive its power not only from its staggering number of processors but also from new advances in quantum computing – an emerging technology that allowed information to be stored as quantum-mechanical states rather than solely as binary data.

The moment of truth came on a blustery Thursday morning in October. The first live test. Despite uncertainty about how fast the machine would be, there was one thing on which the engineers agreed – if the processors all functioned in parallel, TRANSLTR would be powerful. The question was *how* powerful.

The answer came twelve minutes later. There was a stunned silence from the handful in attendance when the printout sprang to life and delivered the cleartext – the broken code. TRANSLTR had just located a sixty-four-character key in a little over ten minutes, almost a million times faster than the two decades it would have taken the NSA's second-fastest computer.

Led by the deputy director of operations, Commander Trevor J. Strathmore, the NSA's Office of Production had triumphed. TRANSLTR was a success. In the interest of keeping their success a secret, Commander Strathmore immediately leaked information that the project had been a complete failure. All the activity in the Crypto wing was supposedly an attempt to salvage their $2 billion fiasco. Only the

NSA elite knew the truth – TRANSLTR was cracking hundreds of codes every day.

With word on the street that computer-encrypted codes were entirely unbreakable – even by the all-powerful NSA – the secrets poured in. Drug lords, terrorists, and embezzlers alike – weary of having their cellular phone transmissions intercepted – were turning to the exciting new medium of encrypted E-mail for instantaneous global communications. Never again would they have to face a grand jury and hear their own voice rolling off tape, proof of some long-forgotten cellular phone conversation plucked from the air by an NSA satellite.

Intelligence gathering had never been easier. Codes intercepted by the NSA entered TRANSLTR as totally illegible ciphers and were spat out minutes later as perfectly readable cleartext. No more secrets.

To make their charade of incompetence complete, the NSA lobbied fiercely against all new computer encryption software, insisting it crippled them and made it impossible for lawmakers to catch and prosecute the criminals. Civil rights groups rejoiced, insisting the NSA shouldn't be reading their mail anyway. Encryption software kept rolling off the presses. The NSA had lost the battle – exactly as it had planned. The entire electronic global community had been fooled . . . or so it seemed.

CHAPTER 5

Where is everyone? Susan wondered as she crossed the deserted Crypto floor. *Some emergency.*

Although most NSA departments were fully staffed seven days a week, Crypto was generally quiet on Saturdays. Cryptographic mathematicians were by nature high-strung workaholics, and there existed an unwritten rule that they take Saturdays off except in emergencies. Code-breakers were too valuable a commodity at the NSA to risk losing them to burnout.

As Susan traversed the floor, TRANSLTR loomed to her right. The sound of the generators eight stories below sounded oddly ominous today. Susan never liked being in Crypto during off hours. It was like being trapped alone in a cage with some grand, futuristic beast. She quickly made her way toward the commander's office.

Strathmore's glass-walled workstation, nicknamed 'the fishbowl' for its appearance when the drapes were open, stood high atop a set of catwalk stairs on the back wall of Crypto. As Susan climbed the grated steps, she gazed upward at Strathmore's thick, oak door. It bore the NSA seal – a bald eagle fiercely clutching an ancient skeleton key. Behind that door sat one of the greatest men she'd ever met.

Commander Strathmore, the fifty-six-year-old deputy director of operations, was like a father to Susan. He was the one who'd hired her, and he was the one who'd made the NSA her home. When Susan joined the NSA over a decade ago, Strathmore was heading the Crypto Development Division – a training ground for new cryptographers – new *male* cryptographers. Although Strathmore never tolerated the hazing of anyone, he was especially protective of his sole female staff member. When accused of favoritism, he simply replied with the truth: Susan Fletcher was one of the brightest young recruits he'd ever seen, and he had no intention of losing her to sexual harassment. One of the senior cryptographers foolishly decided to test Strathmore's resolve.

One morning during her first year, Susan dropped by the new cryptographers' lounge to get some paperwork. As she left, she noticed a picture of herself on the bulletin board. She almost fainted in embarrassment. There she was, reclining on a bed and wearing only panties.

As it turned out, one of the cryptographers had digitally scanned a photo from a pornographic magazine and edited Susan's head onto someone else's body. The effect had been quite convincing.

Unfortunately for the cryptographer responsible, Commander Strathmore did not find the stunt even remotely amusing. Two hours later, a landmark memo went out:

EMPLOYEE CARL AUSTIN TERMINATED FOR
INAPPROPRIATE CONDUCT

From that day on, nobody messed with her; Susan Fletcher was Commander Strathmore's golden girl.

But Strathmore's young cryptographers were not the only ones who learned to respect him; early in his career Strathmore made his presence known to his superiors by proposing a number of unorthodox and highly successful intelligence operations. As he moved up the ranks, Trevor Strathmore became known for his cogent, reductive analyses of highly complex situations. He seemed to have an uncanny ability to see past the moral perplexities surrounding the NSA's difficult decisions and to act without remorse in the interest of the common good.

There was no doubt in anyone's mind that Strathmore loved his country. He was known to his colleagues as a patriot and a visionary . . . a decent man in a world of lies.

In the years since Susan's arrival at the NSA, Strathmore had skyrocketed from head of Crypto Development to second-in-command of the entire NSA. Now only one man outranked Commander Strathmore there – Director Leland Fontaine, the mythical overlord of the Puzzle Palace – never seen, occasionally heard, and eternally feared. He and Strathmore seldom saw eye to eye, and when they met, it was like the clash of the titans. Fontaine was a giant among giants, but Strathmore didn't seem to care. He argued his ideas to the director with all the restraint of an impassioned boxer. Not even the President of the United States dared challenge Fontaine the way Strathmore did. One needed political immunity to do that – or, in Strathmore's case, political indifference.

Susan arrived at the top of the stairs. Before she could knock, Strathmore's electronic door lock buzzed. The door swung open, and the commander waved her in.

'Thanks for coming, Susan. I owe you one.'

'Not at all.' She smiled as she sat opposite his desk.

Strathmore was a rangy, thick-fleshed man whose muted features somehow disguised his hard-nosed efficiency and demand for perfection. His gray eyes usually suggested a confidence and discretion born from experience, but today they looked wild and unsettled.

'You look beat,' Susan said.

'I've been better.' Strathmore sighed.

I'll say, she thought.

Strathmore looked as bad as Susan had ever seen him. His thinning gray hair was disheveled, and even in the room's crisp air-conditioning, his forehead was beaded with sweat. He looked like he'd slept in his suit. He was sitting behind a modern desk with two recessed keypads and a computer monitor at one end. It was strewn with computer printouts and looked like some sort of alien cockpit propped there in the center of his curtained chamber.

'Tough week?' she inquired.

Strathmore shrugged. 'The usual. The EFF's all over me about civilian privacy rights again.'

Susan chuckled. The EFF, or Electronics Frontier Foundation, was a worldwide coalition of computer users who had founded a powerful civil liberties coalition aimed at supporting free speech on-line and educating others to the realities and dangers of living in an electronic world. They were constantly lobbying against what they called 'the Orwellian eavesdropping capabilities of government agencies' – particularly the NSA. The EFF was a perpetual thorn in Strathmore's side.

'Sounds like business as usual,' she said. 'So what's this big emergency you got me out of the tub for?'

Strathmore sat a moment, absently fingering the computer trackball embedded in his desktop. After a long silence, he caught Susan's gaze and held it. 'What's the longest you've ever seen TRANSLTR take to break a code?'

The question caught Susan entirely off guard. It seemed meaningless. *This is what he called me in for?*

'Well . . .' She hesitated. 'We hit a COMINT intercept a few months ago that took about an hour, but it had a ridiculously long key – ten thousand bits or something like that.'

Strathmore grunted. 'An hour, huh? What about some of the boundary probes we've run?'

Susan shrugged. 'Well, if you include diagnostics, it's obviously longer.'

'How *much* longer?'

Susan couldn't imagine what Strathmore was getting at. 'Well, sir, I tried an algorithm last March with a segmented million-bit key. Illegal looping functions, cellular automata, the works. TRANSLTR still broke it.'

'How long?'

'Three hours.'

Strathmore arched his eyebrows. 'Three hours? That long?'

Susan frowned, mildly offended. Her job for the last three years had been to fine-tune the most secret computer in the world; most of the programming that made TRANSLTR so fast was hers. A million-bit key was hardly a realistic scenario.

'Okay,' Strathmore said. 'So even in extreme conditions, the longest a code has ever survived inside TRANSLTR is about three hours?'

Susan nodded. 'Yeah. More or less.'

Strathmore paused as if afraid to say something he might regret. Finally he looked up. 'TRANSLTR's hit something . . .' He stopped.

Susan waited. 'More than three hours?'

Strathmore nodded.

She looked unconcerned. 'A new diagnostic? Something from the Sys-Sec Department?'

Strathmore shook his head. 'It's an outside file.'

Susan waited for the punch line, but it never came. 'An outside file? You're joking, right?'

'I wish. I queued it last night around eleven thirty. It hasn't broken yet.'

Susan's jaw dropped. She looked at her watch and then back at Strathmore. 'It's *still* going? Over fifteen hours?'

Strathmore leaned forward and rotated his monitor toward Susan. The screen was black except for a small, yellow text box blinking in the middle.

TIME ELAPSED: 15:09:33

AWAITING KEY: _____

Susan stared in amazement. It appeared TRANSLTR had been working on one code for over fifteen hours. She knew the computer's processors auditioned thirty million keys per second – one hundred billion per hour. If TRANSLTR was still counting, that meant the key had to be enormous –

over ten billion digits long. It was absolute insanity.

'It's impossible!' she declared. 'Have you checked for error flags? Maybe TRANSLTR hit a glitch and—'

'The run's clean.'

'But the pass-key must be huge!'

Strathmore shook his head. 'Standard commercial algorithm. I'm guessing a sixty-four-bit key.'

Mystified, Susan looked out the window at TRANSLTR below. She knew from experience that it could locate a sixty-four-bit key in under ten minutes. 'There's got to be some explanation.'

Strathmore nodded. 'There is. You're not going to like it.'

Susan looked uneasy. 'Is TRANSLTR malfunctioning?'

'TRANSLTR's fine.'

'Have we got a virus?'

Strathmore shook his head. 'No virus. Just hear me out.'

Susan was flabbergasted. TRANSLTR had never hit a code it couldn't break in under an hour. Usually the cleartext was delivered to Strathmore's printout module within minutes. She glanced at the high-speed printer behind his desk. It was empty.

'Susan,' Strathmore said quietly. 'This is going to be hard to accept at first, but just listen a minute.' He chewed his lip. 'This code that TRANSLTR's working on – it's unique. It's like nothing we've ever seen before.' Strathmore paused, as if the words were hard for him to say. 'This code is unbreakable.'

Susan stared at him and almost laughed. *Unbreakable? What was THAT supposed to mean?* There was no such thing as an unbreakable code – some took longer than others, but every code was breakable. It was mathematically guaranteed that sooner or later TRANSLTR would guess the right key. 'I *beg* your pardon?'

'The code's unbreakable,' he repeated flatly.

Unbreakable? Susan couldn't believe the word had been uttered by a man with twenty-seven years of code analysis experience.

'Unbreakable, sir?' she said uneasily. 'What about the Bergofsky Principle?'

Susan had learned about the Bergofsky Principle early in her career. It was a cornerstone of brute-force technology. It was also Strathmore's inspiration for building TRANSLTR. The principle clearly stated that if a computer tried enough keys, it was mathematically guaranteed to find the right one. A code's security was not that its pass-key was unfindable but rather that most people didn't have the time or equipment to try.

Strathmore shook his head. 'This code's different.'

'Different?' Susan eyed him askance. *An unbreakable code is a mathematical impossibility! He knows that!*

Strathmore ran a hand across his sweaty scalp. 'This code is the product of a brand-new encryption algorithm – one we've never seen before.'

Now Susan was even more doubtful. Encryption algorithms were just mathematical formulas, recipes for scrambling text into code. Mathematicians and programmers created new algorithms every day. There were hundreds of them on the market – PGP, Diffie-Hellman, ZIP, IDEA, El Gamal. TRANSLTR broke all of their codes every day, no problem. To TRANSLTR all codes looked identical, regardless of which algorithm wrote them.

'I don't understand,' she argued. 'We're not talking

about reverse-engineering some complex function, we're talking brute force. PGP, Lucifer, DSA – it doesn't matter. The algorithm generates a key it thinks is secure, and TRANSLTR keeps guessing until it finds it.'

Strathmore's reply had the controlled patience of a good teacher. 'Yes, Susan, TRANSLTR will *always* find the key – even if it's huge.' He paused a long moment. 'Unless . . .'

Susan wanted to speak, but it was clear Strathmore was about to drop his bomb. *Unless what?*

'Unless the computer doesn't know when it's broken the code.'

Susan almost fell out of her chair. 'What!'

'Unless the computer guesses the correct key but just keeps guessing because it doesn't realize it found the right key.' Strathmore looked bleak. 'I think this algorithm has got a rotating cleartext.'

Susan gaped.

The notion of a rotating cleartext function was first put forth in an obscure, 1987 paper by a Hungarian mathematician, Josef Harne. Because brute-force computers broke codes by examining cleartext for identifiable word patterns, Harne proposed an encryption algorithm that, in addition to encrypting, shifted decrypted cleartext over a time variant. In theory, the perpetual mutation would ensure that the attacking computer would never locate recognizable word patterns and thus never know when it had found the proper key. The concept was somewhat like the idea of colonizing Mars – fathomable on an intel-lectual level, but, at present, well beyond human ability.

'Where did you get this thing?' she demanded.

The commander's response was slow. 'A public sector programmer wrote it.'

'What?' Susan collapsed back in her chair. 'We've got the best programmers in the world downstairs! All of us working together have never even come *close* to writing a rotating cleartext function. Are you trying to tell me some punk with a PC figured out how to do it?'

Strathmore lowered his voice in an apparent effort to calm her. 'I wouldn't call this guy a punk.'

Susan wasn't listening. She was convinced there had to be some other explanation: A glitch. A virus. Anything was more likely than an unbreakable code.

Strathmore eyed her sternly. 'One of the most brilliant cryptographic minds of all time wrote this algorithm.'

Susan was more doubtful than ever; the most brilliant cryptographic minds of all time were in her department, and she certainly would have heard about an algorithm like this.

'Who?' she demanded.

'I'm sure you can guess,' Strathmore said. 'He's not too fond of the NSA.'

'Well, that narrows it down!' she snapped sarcastically.

'He worked on the TRANSLTR project. He broke the rules. Almost caused an intelligence nightmare. I deported him.'

Susan's face was blank only an instant before going white. 'Oh my God . . .'

Strathmore nodded. 'He's been bragging all year about his work on a brute-force-resistant algorithm.'

'B-but . . .' Susan stammered. 'I thought he was bluffing. He actually *did* it?'

'He did. The ultimate unbreakable code-writer.'

Susan was silent a long moment. 'But . . . that means . . .'

Strathmore looked her dead in the eye. 'Yes. Ensei Tankado just made TRANSLTR obsolete.'

CHAPTER 6

Although Ensei Tankado was not alive during the Second World War, he carefully studied everything about it – particularly about its culminating event, the blast in which 100,000 of his countrymen were incinerated by an atomic bomb.

Hiroshima, 8:15 A.M. August 6, 1945 – a vile act of destruction. A senseless display of power by a country that had already won the war. Tankado had accepted all that. But what he could never accept was that the bomb had robbed him of ever knowing his mother. She had died giving birth to him – complications brought on by the radiation poisoning she'd suffered so many years earlier.

In 1945, before Ensei was born, his mother, like many of her friends, traveled to Hiroshima to volunteer in the burn centers. It was there that she became one of the hibakusha – the radiated people. Nineteen years later, at the age of thirty-six, as she lay in the delivery room bleeding internally, she knew she was finally going to die. What she did not know was that death would spare her the final horror – her only child was to be born deformed.

Ensei's father never even saw his son. Bewildered by the loss of his wife and shamed by the arrival of what the nurses told him was an imperfect child who probably would not survive the night, he disappeared from the hospital and never came back. Ensei Tankado was placed in a foster home.

Every night the young Tankado stared down at the twisted fingers holding his daruma wish-doll and swore he'd have revenge – revenge against the country that had stolen his mother and shamed his father into abandoning him. What he didn't know was that destiny was about to intervene.

In February of Ensei's twelfth year, a computer manufacturer in Tokyo called his foster family and asked if their crippled child might take part in a test group for a new keyboard they'd developed for handicapped children. His family agreed.

Although Ensei Tankado had never seen a computer, it seemed he instinctively knew how to use it. The computer opened worlds he had never imagined possible. Before long it became his entire life. As he got older, he gave classes, earned money, and eventually earned a scholarship to Doshisha University. Soon Ensei Tankado was known across Tokyo as *fugusha kisai* – the crippled genius.

Tankado eventually read about Pearl Harbor and Japanese war crimes. His hatred of America slowly faded. He became a devout Buddhist. He forgot his childhood vow of revenge; forgiveness was the only path to enlightenment.

By the time he was twenty, Ensei Tankado was somewhat of an underground cult figure among programmers. IBM offered him a work visa and a post in Texas. Tankado jumped at the chance. Three years later he had left IBM, was living in New York, and was writing software on his own. He rode the new wave of public-key encryption. He wrote algorithms and made a fortune.

Like many of the top authors of encryption algorithms, Tankado was courted by the NSA. The irony was not lost on him – the opportunity to work in the heart of the government in a country he had once vowed to hate. He decided to go on the interview. Whatever doubts he had disappeared when he met Commander Strathmore. They talked frankly about Tankado's background, the potential hostility he might feel toward the U.S., his plans for the future. Tankado took a polygraph test and underwent five weeks of rigorous psychological profiles. He passed them all. His hatred had been replaced by his devotion to Buddha. Four months later Ensei Tankado went to work in the Cryptography Department of the National Security Agency.

Despite his large salary, Tankado went to work on an old moped and ate a bag lunch alone at his desk instead of joining the rest of the department for prime rib and vichyssoise in the commissary. The other cryptographers revered him. He was brilliant – as creative a programmer as any of them had ever seen. He was kind and honest, quiet, and of impeccable ethics. Moral integrity was of paramount importance to him. It was for this reason that his dismissal from the NSA and subsequent deportation had been such a shock.

Tankado, like the rest of the Crypto staff, had been working on the TRANSLTR project with the understanding that if successful, it would be used to decipher E-mail only in cases preapproved by the

Justice Department. The NSA's use of TRANSLTR was to be regulated in much the same way the FBI needed a federal court order to install a wiretap. TRANSLTR was to include programming that called for passwords held in escrow by the Federal Reserve and the Justice Department in order to decipher a file. This would prevent the NSA from listening indiscriminately to the personal communications of law-abiding citizens around the globe.

However, when the time came to enter that programming, the TRANSLTR staff was told there had been a change of plans. Because of the time pressures often associated with the NSA's antiterrorist work, TRANSLTR was to be a free-standing decryption device whose day-to-day operation would be regulated solely by the NSA.

Ensei Tankado was outraged. This meant the NSA would, in effect, be able to open everyone's mail and reseal it without their knowing. It was like having a bug in every phone in the world. Strathmore attempted to make Tankado see TRANSLTR as a law-enforcement device, but it was no use; Tankado was adamant that it constituted a gross violation of human rights. He quit on the spot and within hours violated the NSA's code of secrecy by trying to contact the Electronic Frontier Foundation. Tankado stood poised to shock the world with his story of a secret machine capable of exposing computer users around the world to unthinkable government treachery. The NSA had had no choice but to stop him.

Tankado's capture and deportation, widely publicized among on-line newsgroups, had been an unfortunate public shaming. Against Strathmore's wishes, the NSA damage-control specialists – nervous that Tankado would try to convince people of TRANSLTR's existence – generated rumors that destroyed his credibility. Ensei Tankado was shunned by the global computer community – nobody trusted a cripple accused of spying, particularly when he was trying to buy his freedom with absurd allegations about a U.S. code-breaking machine.

The oddest thing of all was that Tankado seemed to understand; it was all part of the intelligence game. He appeared to harbor no anger, only resolve. As security escorted him away, Tankado spoke his final words to Strathmore with a chilling calm.

'We all have a right to keep secrets,' he'd said. 'Someday I'll see to it we can.'

CHAPTER 7

Susan's mind was racing – *Ensei Tankado wrote a program that creates unbreakable codes!* She could barely grasp the thought.

'Digital Fortress,' Strathmore said. 'That's what he's calling it. It's the ultimate counterintelligence weapon. If this program hits the market, every third grader with a modem will be able to send codes the NSA can't break. Our intelligence will be shot.'

But Susan's thoughts were far removed from the political implications of Digital Fortress. She was still struggling to comprehend its existence. She'd spent her life breaking codes, firmly denying the existence of the ultimate code. *Every code is breakable – the Bergofsky Principle!* She felt like an atheist coming face to face with God.

'If this code gets out,' she whispered, 'cryptography will become a dead science.'

Strathmore nodded. 'That's the least of our problems.'

'Can we pay Tankado off? I know he hates us, but can't we offer him a few million dollars? Convince him not to distribute?'

Strathmore laughed. 'A few million? Do you know what this thing is worth? Every government in the world will bid top dollar. Can you imagine telling the President that we're still cable-snooping the Iraqis but we can't read the intercepts anymore? This isn't just about the NSA, it's about the entire intelligence community. This facility provides support for everyone – the FBI, CIA, DEA; they'd all be flying blind. The drug cartels' shipments would become untraceable, major corporations could transfer money with no paper trail and leave the IRS out in the cold, terrorists could chat in total secrecy – it would be chaos.'

'The EFF will have a field day,' Susan said, pale.

'The EFF doesn't have the first clue about what we do here,' Strathmore railed in disgust. 'If they knew how many terrorist attacks we've stopped because we can decrypt codes, they'd change their tune.'

Susan agreed, but she also knew the realities; the EFF would never know how important TRANSLTR was. TRANSLTR had helped foil dozens of attacks, but the information was highly classified and would never be released. The rationale behind the secrecy was simple: The government could not afford the mass hysteria caused by revealing the truth; no one knew how the public would react to the news that there had been two nuclear close calls by fundamentalist groups on U.S. soil in the last year.

Nuclear attack, however, was not the only threat. Only last month TRANSLTR had thwarted one of the most ingeniously conceived terrorist attacks the NSA had ever witnessed. An antigovernment organization had devised a plan, code-named Sherwood Forest. It targeted the New York Stock Exchange with the intention of 'redistributing the wealth.' Over the course of six days, members of the group placed twenty-seven nonexplosive flux pods in the buildings surrounding the Exchange. These devices, when detonated, create a powerful blast of magnetism. The simultaneous discharge of these carefully placed pods would create a magnetic field so powerful that all magnetic media in the Stock Exchange would be erased – computer hard drives, massive ROM storage banks, tape backups, and even floppy disks. All records of who owned what would disintegrate permanently.

Because pinpoint timing was necessary for simultaneous detonation of the devices, the flux pods were interconnected over Internet telephone lines. During the two-day countdown, the pods' internal clocks exchanged endless streams of encrypted synchronization data. The NSA intercepted the data-pulses as a network anomaly but ignored them as a seemingly harmless exchange of gibberish. But after TRANSLTR decrypted the data streams, analysts immediately recognized the sequence as a network-synchronized countdown. The pods were located and removed a full three hours before they were scheduled to go off.

Susan knew that without TRANSLTR the NSA was helpless against advanced electronic terrorism. She eyed the Run-Monitor. It still read over fifteen hours. Even if Tankado's file broke right now, the NSA was sunk. Crypto would be relegated to breaking less than two codes a day. Even at the present rate of 150 a day, there was still a backlog of files awaiting decryption.

'Tankado called me last month,' Strathmore said, interrupting Susan's thoughts.

Susan looked up. 'Tankado called *you?*'

He nodded. 'To warn me.'

'*Warn* you? He hates you.'

'He called to tell me he was perfecting an algorithm that wrote unbreakable codes. I didn't believe him.'

'But why would he tell you about it?' Susan demanded. 'Did he want you to buy it?'

'No. It was blackmail.'

Things suddenly began falling into place for Susan. 'Of course,' she said, amazed. 'He wanted you to clear his name.'

'No,' Strathmore frowned. 'Tankado wanted TRANSLTR.'

'TRANSLTR?'

'Yes. He ordered me to go public and tell the world we have TRANSLTR. He said if we admitted we can read public E-mail, he would destroy Digital Fortress.'

Susan looked doubtful.

Strathmore shrugged. 'Either way, it's too late now. He's posted a complimentary copy of Digital Fortress at his Internet site. Everyone in the world can download it.'

Susan went white. 'He *what!*'

'It's a publicity stunt. Nothing to worry about. The copy he posted is encrypted. People can download it, but nobody can open it. It's ingenious, really. The source code for Digital Fortress has been encrypted, locked shut.'

Susan looked amazed. 'Of course! So everybody can *have* a copy, but nobody can open it.'

'Exactly. Tankado's dangling a carrot.'

'Have you seen the algorithm?'

The commander looked puzzled. 'No, I told you it's encrypted.'

Susan looked equally puzzled. 'But we've got TRANSLTR; why not just decrypt it?' But when Susan saw Strathmore's face, she realized the rules had changed. 'Oh my God.' She gasped, suddenly understanding. 'Digital Fortress is encrypted with *itself?*'

Strathmore nodded. 'Bingo.'

Susan was amazed. The formula for Digital Fortress had been encrypted using Digital Fortress. Tankado had posted a priceless mathematical recipe, but the text of the recipe had been scrambled. And it had used *itself* to do the scrambling.

'It's Biggleman's Safe,' Susan stammered in awe.

Strathmore nodded. Biggleman's Safe was a hypothetical cryptography scenario in which a safe builder wrote blueprints for an unbreakable safe. He wanted to keep the blueprints a secret, so he built the safe and locked the blueprints inside. Tankado had done the same thing with Digital Fortress. He'd protected his blueprints by encrypting them with the formula outlined in his blueprints.

'And the file in TRANSLTR?' Susan asked.

'I downloaded it from Tankado's Internet site like everyone else. The NSA is now the proud owner of the Digital Fortress algorithm; we just can't open it.'

Susan marveled at Ensei Tankado's ingenuity. Without revealing his algorithm, he had proven to the NSA that it was unbreakable.

Strathmore handed her a newspaper clipping. It was a translated blurb from the *Nikkei Shimbun*, the Japanese equivalent of the *Wall Street Journal*, stating that the Japanese programmer Ensei Tankado had completed a mathematical formula he claimed could write unbreakable codes. The formula was called Digital Fortress and was available for review on the Internet. The programmer would be auctioning it off to the highest bidder. The column went on to say that although there was enormous interest in Japan, the few U.S. software companies who had heard about Digital Fortress deemed the claim preposterous, akin to turning lead to gold. The formula, they said, was a hoax and not to be taken seriously.

Susan looked up. 'An auction?'

Strathmore nodded. 'Right now every software company in Japan has downloaded an encrypted copy of Digital Fortress and is trying to crack it open. Every second they can't, the bidding price climbs.'

'That's absurd,' Susan shot back. 'All the new encrypted files are uncrackable unless you have TRANSLTR. Digital Fortress could be nothing more than a generic, public-domain algorithm, and none of these companies could break it.'

'But it's a brilliant marketing ploy,' Strathmore said. 'Think about it – all brands of bulletproof glass stop bullets, but if a company dares you to put a bullet through *theirs*, suddenly everybody's trying.'

'And the Japanese actually *believe* Digital Fortress is different? Better than everything else on the market?'

'Tankado may have been shunned, but everybody knows he's a genius. He's practically a cult icon among hackers. If Tankado says the algorithm's unbreakable, it's unbreakable.'

'But they're *all* unbreakable as far as the public knows!'

'Yes . . .' Strathmore mused. 'For the moment.'

'What's *that* supposed to mean?'

Strathmore sighed. 'Twenty years ago no one imagined we'd be breaking twelve-bit stream ciphers. But technology progressed. It always does. Software manufacturers assume at some point computers like TRANSLTR will exist. Technology is progressing exponentially, and eventually current public-key algorithms will lose their security. Better algorithms will be needed to stay ahead of tomorrow's computers.'

'And Digital Fortress is it?'

'Exactly. An algorithm that resists brute force will never become obsolete, no matter how powerful code-breaking computers get. It could become a world standard overnight.'

Susan pulled in a long breath. 'God help us,' she whispered. 'Can we make a bid?'

Strathmore shook his head. 'Tankado gave us our chance. He made that clear. It's too risky anyway; if we get caught, we're basically admitting that we're afraid of his algorithm. We'd be making a public confession not only that we have TRANSLTR but that Digital Fortress is immune.'

'What's the time frame?'

Strathmore frowned. 'Tankado planned to announce the highest bidder tomorrow at noon.'

Susan felt her stomach tighten. 'Then what?'

'The arrangement was that he would give the winner the pass-key.'

'The *pass-key?*'

'Part of the ploy. Everybody's already got the algorithm, so Tankado's auctioning off the pass-key that unlocks it.'

Susan groaned. 'Of course.' It was perfect. Clean and simple. Tankado had encrypted Digital Fortress, and he alone held the pass-key that unlocked it. She found it hard to fathom that somewhere out there – probably scrawled on a piece of paper in Tankado's pocket – there was a sixty-four-character pass-key that could end U.S. intelligence gathering forever.

Susan suddenly felt ill as she imagined the scenario.

Tankado would give his pass-key to the highest bidder, and that company would unlock the Digital Fortress file. Then it probably would embed the algorithm in a tamper-proof chip, and within five years every computer would come preloaded with a Digital Fortress chip. No commercial manufacturer had ever dreamed of creating an encryption chip because normal encryption algorithms eventually become obsolete. But Digital Fortress would never become obsolete; with a rotating cleartext function, no brute-force attack would ever find the right key. A new digital encryption standard. From now until forever. Every code unbreakable. Bankers, brokers, terrorists, spies. One world – one algorithm.

Anarchy.

'What are the options?' Susan probed. She was well aware that desperate times called for desperate measures, even at the NSA.

'We can't remove him, if that's what you're asking.'

It was exactly what Susan was asking. In her years with the NSA, Susan had heard rumors of its loose affiliations with the most skilled assassins in the world – hired hands brought in to do the intelligence community's dirty work.

Strathmore shook his head. 'Tankado's too smart to leave us an option like that.'

Susan felt oddly relieved. 'He's protected?'

'Not exactly.'

'In hiding?'

Strathmore shrugged. 'Tankado left Japan. He planned to check his bids by phone. But we know where he is.'

'And you don't plan to make a move?'

'No. He's got insurance. Tankado gave a copy of his

62

pass-key to an anonymous third party . . . in case anything happened.'

Of course, Susan marveled. *A guardian angel.* 'And I suppose if anything happens to Tankado, the mystery man sells the key?'

'Worse. Anyone hits Tankado, and his partner publishes.'

Susan looked confused. 'His partner *publishes* the key?'

Strathmore nodded. 'Posts it on the Internet, puts it in newspapers, on billboards. In effect, he *gives* it away.'

Susan's eyes widened. 'Free downloads?'

'Exactly. Tankado figured if he was dead, he wouldn't need the money – why not give the world a little farewell gift?'

There was a long silence. Susan breathed deeply as if to absorb the terrifying truth. *Ensei Tankado has created an unbreakable algorithm. He's holding us hostage.*

She suddenly stood. Her voice was determined. 'We must contact Tankado! There must be a way to convince him not to release! We can offer him triple the highest bid! We can clear his name! Anything!'

'Too late,' Strathmore said. He took a deep breath. 'Ensei Tankado was found dead this morning in Seville, Spain.'

CHAPTER 8

The twin-engine Learjet 60 touched down on the scorching runway. Outside the window, the barren landscape of Spain's lower Extremadura blurred and then slowed to a crawl.

'Mr Becker?' a voice crackled. 'We're here.'

Becker stood and stretched. After unlatching the overhead compartment, he remembered he had no luggage. There had been no time to pack. It didn't matter – he'd been promised the trip would be brief, in and out.

As the engines wound down, the plane eased out of the sun and into a deserted hangar opposite the main terminal. A moment later the pilot appeared and popped the hatch. Becker tossed back the last of his cranberry juice, put the glass on the wet bar, and scooped up his suit coat.

The pilot pulled a thick manila envelope from his flight suit. 'I was instructed to give you this.' He handed it to Becker. On the front, scrawled in blue pen, were the words:

KEEP THE CHANGE

Becker thumbed through the thick stack of reddish bills. 'What the . . . ?'

'Local currency,' the pilot offered flatly.

'I know what it is,' Becker stammered. 'But it's . . . it's too much. All I need is taxi fare.' Becker did the conversion in his head. 'What's in here is worth *thousands* of dollars!'

'I have my orders, sir.' The pilot turned and hoisted himself back into the cabin. The door slid shut behind him.

Becker stared up at the plane and then down at the money in his hand. After standing a moment in the empty hangar, he put the envelope in his breast pocket, shouldered his suit coat, and headed out across the runway. It was a strange beginning. Becker pushed it from his mind. With a little luck he'd be back in time to salvage some of his Stone Manor trip with Susan.

In and out, he told himself. *In and out.*

There was no way he could have known.

CHAPTER 9

Systems security technician Phil Chartrukian had only intended to be inside Crypto a minute – just long enough to grab some paperwork he'd forgotten the day before. But it was not to be.

After making his way across the Crypto floor and stepping into the Sys-Sec lab, he immediately knew something was not right. The computer terminal that perpetually monitored TRANSLTR's internal workings was unmanned and the monitor was switched off.

Chartrukian called out, 'Hello?'

There was no reply. The lab was spotless – as if no one had been there for hours.

Although Chartrukian was only twenty-three and relatively new to the Sys-Sec squad, he'd been trained well, and he knew the drill: There was *always* a Sys-Sec on duty in Crypto . . . especially on Saturdays when no cryptographers were around.

He immediately powered up the monitor and turned to the duty board on the wall. 'Who's on watch?' he demanded aloud, scanning the list of names. According to the schedule, a young rookie named Seidenberg was supposed to have started a double shift at midnight the night before. Chartrukian glanced around the empty lab and frowned. 'So where the hell is he?'

As he watched the monitor power up, Chartrukian wondered if Strathmore knew the Sys-Sec lab was unmanned. He had noticed on his way in that the curtains of Strathmore's workstation were closed, which meant the boss was in – not at all uncommon for a Saturday; Strathmore, despite requesting his cryptographers take Saturdays off, seemed to work 365 days a year.

There was one thing Chartrukian knew for certain – if Strathmore found out the Sys-Sec lab was unmanned, it would cost the absent rookie his job. Chartrukian eyed the phone, wondering if he should call the young techie and bail him out; there was an unspoken rule among Sys-Sec that they would watch each other's backs. In Crypto, Sys-Secs were second-class citizens, constantly at odds with the lords of the manor. It was no secret that the cryptographers ruled this multibillion-dollar roost; Sys-Secs were tolerated only because they kept the toys running smoothly.

Chartrukian made his decision. He grabbed the phone. But the receiver never reached his ear. He stopped short, his eyes transfixed on the monitor now coming into focus before him. As if in slow motion, he set down the phone and stared in open-mouthed wonder.

In eight months as a Sys-Sec, Phil Chartrukian had never seen TRANSLTR's Run-Monitor post anything other than a double zero in the *hours* field. Today was a first.

TIME ELAPSED: 15:17:21

'Fifteen hours and seventeen minutes?' he choked. 'Impossible!'

He rebooted the screen, praying it hadn't refreshed properly. But when the monitor came back to life, it looked the same.

Chartrukian felt a chill. Crypto's Sys-Secs had only one responsibility: Keep TRANSLTR 'clean' – virus free.

Chartrukian knew that a fifteen-hour run could only mean one thing – infection. An impure file had gotten inside TRANSLTR and was corrupting the programming. Instantly his training kicked in; it no longer mattered that the Sys-Sec lab had been unmanned or the monitors switched off. He focused on the matter at hand – TRANSLTR. He immediately called up a log of all the files that had entered TRANSLTR in the last forty-eight hours. He began scanning the list.

Did an infected file get through? he wondered. *Could the security filters have missed something?*

As a precaution, every file entering TRANSLTR had to pass through what was known as Gauntlet – a series of powerful circuit-level gateways, packet filters, and disinfectant programs that scanned inbound files for computer viruses and potentially dangerous subroutines. Files containing programming 'unknown' to Gauntlet were immediately rejected. They had to be checked by hand. Occasionally Gauntlet rejected entirely harmless files on the basis that they contained programming the filters had never seen before. In that case, the Sys-Secs did a scrupulous manual inspection, and only then, on confirmation that the file was clean, did they bypass Gauntlet's filters and send the file into TRANSLTR.

Computer viruses were as varied as bacterial viruses. Like their physiological counterparts, computer viruses had one goal – to attach themselves to a host system and replicate. In this case, the host was TRANSLTR.

Chartrukian was amazed the NSA hadn't had problems with viruses before. Gauntlet was a potent sentry, but still, the NSA was a bottom feeder, sucking in massive amounts of digital information from systems all over the world. Snooping data was a lot like having indiscriminate sex – protection or no protection, sooner or later you caught something.

Chartrukian finished examining the file list before him. He was now more puzzled than before. Every file checked out. Gauntlet had seen nothing out of the ordinary, which meant the file in TRANSLTR was totally clean.

'So what the hell's taking so long?' he demanded of the empty room. Chartrukian felt himself break a sweat. He wondered if he should go disturb Strathmore with the news.

'A virus probe,' Chartrukian said firmly, trying to calm himself down. 'I should run a virus probe.'

Chartrukian knew that a virus probe would be the first thing Strathmore would request anyway. Glancing out at the deserted Crypto floor, Chartrukian made his decision. He loaded the viral probe software and launched it. The run would take about fifteen minutes.

'Come back clean,' he whispered. 'Squeaky clean. Tell Daddy it's nothing.'

But Chartrukian sensed it was *not* 'nothing.' Instinct told him something very unusual was going on inside the great decoding beast.

CHAPTER 10

'Ensei Tankado is dead?' Susan felt a wave of nausea. 'You killed him? I thought you said—'

'We didn't touch him,' Strathmore assured her. 'He died of a heart attack. COMINT phoned early this morning. Their computer flagged Tankado's name in a Seville police log through Interpol.'

'Heart attack?' Susan looked doubtful. 'He was thirty years old.'

'Thirty-two,' Strathmore corrected. 'He had a congenital heart defect.'

'I'd never heard that.'

'Turned up in his NSA physical. Not something he bragged about.'

Susan was having trouble accepting the serendipity of the timing. 'A defective heart could kill him – just like that?' It seemed too convenient.

Strathmore shrugged. 'Weak heart . . . combine it with the heat of Spain. Throw in the stress of blackmailing the NSA . . .'

Susan was silent a moment. Even considering the conditions, she felt a pang of loss at the passing of such a brilliant fellow cryptographer. Strathmore's gravelly voice interrupted her thoughts.

'The only silver lining on this whole fiasco is that Tankado was traveling alone. Chances are good his partner doesn't know yet he's dead. The Spanish authorities said they'd contain the information for as long as possible. We only got the call because COMINT was on the ball.' Strathmore eyed Susan closely. 'I've got to find the partner before he finds out Tankado's dead. That's why I called you in. I need your help.'

Susan was confused. It seemed to her that Ensei Tankado's timely demise had solved their entire problem. 'Commander,' she argued, 'if the authorities are saying he died of a heart attack, we're off the hook; his partner will know the NSA is not responsible.'

'Not responsible?' Strathmore's eyes widened in disbelief. 'Somebody blackmails the NSA and turns up dead a few days later – and we're *not responsible?* I'd bet big money Tankado's mystery friend won't see it that way. Whatever happened, we look guilty as hell. It could easily have been poison, a rigged autopsy, any number of things.' Strathmore paused. 'What was your first reaction when I told you Tankado was dead?'

She frowned. 'I thought the NSA had killed him.'

'Exactly. If the NSA can put five Rhyolite satellites in geosynchronous orbit over the Mideast, I think it's safe to assume we have the resources to pay off a few Spanish policemen.' The commander had made his point.

Susan exhaled. *Ensei Tankado is dead. The NSA will be blamed.* 'Can we find his partner in time?'

'I think so. We've got a good lead. Tankado made numerous public announcements that he was working

71

with a partner. I think he hoped it would discourage software firms from doing him any harm or trying to steal his key. He threatened that if there was any foul play, his partner would publish the key, and all firms would suddenly find themselves in competition with free software.'

'Clever.' Susan nodded.

Strathmore went on. 'A few times, in public, Tankado referred to his partner by name. He called him North Dakota.'

'North Dakota? Obviously an alias of some sort.'

'Yes, but as a precaution I ran an Internet inquiry using North Dakota as a search string. I didn't think I'd find anything, but I turned up an E-mail account.' Strathmore paused. 'Of course I assumed it wasn't the North Dakota we were looking for, but I searched the account just to be sure. Imagine my shock when I found the account was full of E-mail from Ensei Tankado.' Strathmore raised his eyebrows. 'And the messages were full of references to Digital Fortress and Tankado's plans to blackmail the NSA.'

Susan gave Strathmore a skeptical look. She was amazed the commander was letting himself be played with so easily. 'Commander,' she argued, 'Tankado knows full well the NSA can snoop E-mail from the Internet; he would *never* use E-mail to send secret information. It's a trap. Ensei Tankado *gave* you North Dakota. He *knew* you'd run a search. Whatever information he's sending, he *wanted* you to find – it's a false trail.'

'Good instinct,' Strathmore fired back, 'except for a couple of things. I couldn't find anything under North Dakota, so I tweaked the search string. The account I found was under a variation – NDAKOTA.'

Susan shook her head. 'Running permutations is standard procedure. Tankado knew you'd try variations until you hit something. NDAKOTA's far too easy an alteration.'

'Perhaps,' Strathmore said, scribbling words on a piece of paper and handing it to Susan. 'But look at this.'

Susan read the paper. She suddenly understood the commander's thinking. On the paper was North Dakota's E-mail address.

NDAKOTA@ARA.ANON.ORG

It was the letters ARA in the address that had caught Susan's eye. ARA stood for American Remailers Anonymous, a well-known anonymous server.

Anonymous servers were popular among Internet users who wanted to keep their identities secret. For a fee, these companies protected an E-mailer's privacy by acting as a middleman for electronic mail. It was like having a numbered post office box – a user could send and receive mail without ever revealing his true address or name. The company received E-mail addressed to aliases and then forwarded it to the client's real account. The remailing company was bound by contract never to reveal the identity or location of its real users.

'It's not proof,' Strathmore said. 'But it's pretty suspicious.'

Susan nodded, suddenly more convinced. 'So you're saying Tankado didn't care if anybody searched for North Dakota because his identity and location are protected by ARA.'

'Exactly.'

Susan schemed for a moment. 'ARA services mainly U.S. accounts. You think North Dakota might be over here somewhere?'

Strathmore shrugged. 'Could be. With an American partner, Tankado could keep the two pass-keys separated geographically. Might be a smart move.'

Susan considered it. She doubted Tankado would have shared his pass-key with anyone except a very close friend, and as she recalled, Ensei Tankado didn't have many friends in the States.

'North Dakota,' she mused, her cryptological mind mulling over the possible meanings of the alias. 'What does his E-mail to Tankado sound like?'

'No idea. COMINT only caught Tankado's outbound. At this point all we have on North Dakota is an anonymous address.'

Susan thought a minute. 'Any chance it's a decoy?'

Strathmore raised an eyebrow. 'How so?'

'Tankado could be sending bogus E-mail to a dead account in hopes we'd snoop it. We'd think he's protected, and he'd never have to risk sharing his pass-key. He could be working alone.'

Strathmore chuckled, impressed. 'Tricky idea, except for one thing. He's not using any of his usual home or business Internet accounts. He's been dropping by Doshisha University and logging on to their mainframe. Apparently he's got an account there that he's managed to keep secret. It's a very well-hidden account, and I found it only by chance.' Strathmore paused. 'So . . . if Tankado wanted us to snoop his mail, why would he use a secret account?'

Susan contemplated the question. 'Maybe he used a secret account so you wouldn't suspect a ploy? Maybe

Tankado hid the account just deep enough that you'd stumble on to it and think you got lucky. It gives his E-mail credibility.'

Strathmore chuckled. 'You should have been a field agent. The idea's a good one. Unfortunately, every letter Tankado sends gets a response. Tankado writes, his partner responds.'

Susan frowned. 'Fair enough. So, you're saying North Dakota's for real.'

'Afraid so. And we've got to find him. And *quietly*. If he catches wind that we're on to him, it's all over.'

Susan now knew exactly why Strathmore had called her in. 'Let me guess,' she said. 'You want me to snoop ARA's secure database and find North Dakota's real identity?'

Strathmore gave her a tight smile. 'Ms Fletcher, you read my mind.'

When it came to discreet Internet searches, Susan Fletcher was the woman for the job. A year ago, a senior White House official had been receiving E-mail threats from someone with an anonymous E-mail address. The NSA had been asked to locate the individual. Although the NSA had the clout to demand the remailing company reveal the user's identity, it opted for a more subtle method – a 'tracer.'

Susan had created, in effect, a directional beacon disguised as a piece of E-mail. She could send it to the user's phony address, and the remailing company, performing the duty for which it had been contracted, would forward it to the user's real address. Once there, the program would record its Internet location and send word back to the NSA. Then the program would disintegrate without a trace. From that day on, as far as the NSA was concerned, anonymous remailers were nothing more than a minor annoyance.

'Can you find him?' Strathmore asked.

'Sure. Why did you wait so long to call me?'

'Actually' – he frowned – 'I hadn't planned on calling you at all. I didn't want anyone else in the loop. I tried to send a copy of your tracer myself, but you wrote the damn thing in one of those new hybrid languages; I couldn't get it to work. It kept returning nonsensical data. I finally had to bite the bullet and bring you in.'

Susan chuckled. Strathmore was a brilliant cryptographic programmer, but his repertoire was limited primarily to algorithmic work; the nuts and bolts of less lofty 'secular' programming often escaped him. What was more, Susan had written her tracer in a new, crossbreed programming language called LIMBO; it was understandable that Strathmore had encountered problems. 'I'll take care of it.' She smiled, turning to leave. 'I'll be at my terminal.'

'Any idea on a time frame?'

Susan paused. 'Well . . . it depends on how efficiently ARA forwards their mail. If he's here in the States and uses something like AOL or Compuserve, I'll snoop his credit card and get a billing address within the hour. If he's with a university or corporation, it'll take a little longer.' She smiled uneasily. 'After that, the rest is up to you.'

Susan knew that 'the rest' would be an NSA strike team, cutting power to the guy's house and crashing through his windows with stun guns. The team would probably think it was on a drug bust. Strathmore would undoubtedly stride through the rubble himself and locate the sixty-four-character pass-key. Then he would destroy it. Digital Fortress would languish forever on the Internet, locked for all eternity.

'Send the tracer carefully,' Strathmore urged. 'If North Dakota sees we're on to him, he'll panic, and I'll never get a team there before he disappears with the key.'

'Hit and run,' she assured. 'The moment this thing finds his account, it'll dissolve. He'll never know we were there.'

The commander nodded tiredly. 'Thanks.'

Susan gave him a soft smile. She was always amazed how even in the face of disaster Strathmore could muster a quiet calm. She was convinced it was this ability that had defined his career and lifted him to the upper echelons of power.

As Susan headed for the door, she took a long look down at TRANSLTR. The existence of an unbreakable algorithm was a concept she was still struggling to grasp. She prayed they'd find North Dakota in time.

'Make it quick,' Strathmore called, 'and you'll be in the Smoky Mountains by nightfall.'

Susan froze in her tracks. She knew she had never mentioned her trip to Strathmore. She wheeled. *Is the NSA tapping my phone?*

Strathmore smiled guiltily. 'David told me about your trip this morning. He said you'd be pretty ticked about postponing it.'

Susan was lost. 'You talked to David this *morning?*'

'Of course.' Strathmore seemed puzzled by Susan's reaction. 'I had to brief him.'

'Brief him?' she demanded. 'For *what?*'

'For his trip. I sent David to Spain.'

CHAPTER 11

Spain. *I sent David to Spain.* The commander's words stung.

'David's in Spain?' Susan was incredulous. 'You sent him to Spain?' Her tone turned angry. *'Why?'*

Strathmore looked dumbfounded. He was apparently not accustomed to being yelled at, even by his head cryptographer. He gave Susan a confused look. She was flexed like a mother tiger defending her cub.

'Susan,' he said. 'You spoke to him, didn't you? David *did* explain?'

She was too shocked to speak. *Spain? That's why David postponed our Stone Manor trip?*

'I sent a car for him this morning. He said he was going to call you before he left. I'm sorry. I thought—'

'Why would you send David to Spain?'

Strathmore paused and gave her an obvious look. 'To get the other pass-key.'

'What other pass-key?'

'Tankado's copy.'

Susan was lost. 'What are you talking about?'

Strathmore sighed. 'Tankado surely would have

had a copy of the pass-key on him when he died. I sure as hell didn't want it floating around the Seville morgue.'

'So you sent David Becker?' Susan was beyond shock. Nothing was making sense. 'David doesn't even work for you!'

Strathmore looked startled. No one ever spoke to the deputy director of the NSA that way. 'Susan,' he said, keeping his cool, 'that's the point. I needed—'

The tiger lashed out. 'You've got twenty thousand employees at your command! What gives you the right to send my fiancé?'

'I needed a civilian courier, someone totally removed from government. If I went through regular channels and someone caught wind—'

'And David Becker is the only civilian you know?'

'No! David Becker is *not* the only civilian I know! But at six this morning, things were happening quickly! David speaks the language, he's smart, I trust him, and I thought I'd do him a favor!'

'A favor?' Susan sputtered. 'Sending him to Spain is a favor?'

'Yes! I'm paying him ten thousand for one day's work. He'll pick up Tankado's belongings, and he'll fly home. That's a favor!'

Susan fell silent. She understood. It was all about money.

Her thoughts wheeled back five months to the night the president of Georgetown University had offered David a promotion to the language department chair. The president had warned him that his teaching hours would be cut back and that there would be increased paperwork, but there was also a substantial raise in salary. Susan had wanted to cry out *David, don't do it!*

You'll be miserable. We have plenty of money – who cares which one of us earns it? But it was not her place. In the end, she stood by his decision to accept. As they fell asleep that night, Susan tried to be happy for him, but something inside kept telling her it would be a disaster. She'd been right – but she'd never counted on being *so* right.

'You paid him ten thousand dollars?' she demanded. 'That's a dirty trick!'

Strathmore was fuming now. 'Trick? It wasn't any goddamn trick! I didn't even tell him about the money. I asked him as a personal favor. He agreed to go.'

'Of course he agreed! You're my boss! You're the deputy director of the NSA! He couldn't say no!'

'You're right,' Strathmore snapped. 'Which is why I called him. I didn't have the luxury of—'

'Does the director know you sent a civilian?'

'Susan,' Strathmore said, his patience obviously wearing thin, 'the director is not involved. He knows nothing about this.'

Susan stared at Strathmore in disbelief. It was as if she no longer knew the man she was talking to. He had sent her fiancé – a teacher – on an NSA mission and then failed to notify the director about the biggest crisis in the history of the organization.

'Leland Fontaine *hasn't* been notified?'

Strathmore had reached the end of his rope. He exploded. 'Susan, now listen here! I called you in here because I need an ally, not an inquiry! I've had one hell of a morning. I downloaded Tankado's file last night and sat here by the output printer for hours praying TRANSLTR could break it. At dawn I swallowed my pride and dialed the director – and let me tell you, *that* was a conversation I was *really* looking forward to. Good morning, sir. I'm sorry to wake you. Why am I calling? I just found out TRANSLTR is obsolete. It's because of an algorithm my entire top-dollar Crypto team couldn't come close to writing!' Strathmore slammed his fist on the desk.

Susan stood frozen. She didn't make a sound. In ten years, she had seen Strathmore lose his cool only a handful of times, and never once with her.

Ten seconds later neither one of them had spoken. Finally Strathmore sat back down, and Susan could hear his breathing slowing to normal. When he finally spoke, his voice was eerily calm and controlled.

'Unfortunately,' Strathmore said quietly, 'it turns out the director is in South America meeting with the President of Colombia. Because there's absolutely nothing he could do from down there, I had two options – request he cut his meeting short and return, or handle this myself.' There was a long silence. Strathmore finally looked up, and his tired eyes met Susan's. His expression softened immediately. 'Susan, I'm sorry. I'm exhausted. This is a nightmare come true. I know you're upset about David. I didn't mean for you to find out this way. I thought you knew.'

Susan felt a wave of guilt. 'I overreacted. I'm sorry. David is a good choice.'

Strathmore nodded absently. 'He'll be back tonight.'

Susan thought about everything the commander was going through – the pressure of overseeing TRANSLTR, the endless hours and meetings. It was rumored his wife of thirty years was leaving him. Then on top of it, there was Digital Fortress – the biggest intelligence threat in the history of the NSA, and the poor guy was flying solo. No wonder he looked about to crack.

'Considering the circumstances,' Susan said, 'I think you should probably call the director.'

Strathmore shook his head, a bead of sweat dripping on his desk. 'I'm not about to compromise the director's safety or risk a leak by contacting him about a major crisis he can do nothing about.'

Susan knew he was right. Even in moments like these, Strathmore was clear-headed. 'Have you considered calling the President?'

Strathmore nodded. 'Yes. I've decided against it.'

Susan had figured as much. Senior NSA officials had the right to handle verifiable intelligence emergencies without executive knowledge. The NSA was the only U.S. intelligence organization that enjoyed total immunity from federal accountability of any sort. Strathmore often availed himself of this right; he preferred to work his magic in isolation.

'Commander,' she argued, 'this is too big to be handled alone. You've got to let somebody else in on it.'

'Susan, the existence of Digital Fortress has major implications for the future of this organization. I have no intention of informing the President behind the director's back. We have a crisis, and I'm handling it.' He eyed her thoughtfully. 'I *am* the deputy director of operations.' A weary smile crept across his face. 'And besides, I'm not alone. I've got Susan Fletcher on my team.'

In that instant, Susan realized what she respected so much about Trevor Strathmore. For ten years, through thick and thin, he had always led the way for her. Steadfast. Unwavering. It was his dedication that amazed her – his unshakable allegiance to his principles, his country, and his ideals. Come what may, Commander Trevor Strathmore was a guiding light in a world of impossible decisions.

'You *are* on my team, aren't you?' he asked.

Susan smiled. 'Yes, sir, I am. One hundred percent.'

'Good. Now can we get back to work?'

CHAPTER 12

David Becker had been to funerals and seen dead bodies before, but there was something particularly unnerving about this one. It was not an immaculately groomed corpse resting in a silk-lined coffin. This body had been stripped naked and dumped unceremoniously on an aluminum table. The eyes had not yet found their vacant, lifeless gaze. Instead they were twisted upward toward the ceiling in an eerie freeze-frame of terror and regret.

'Dónde están sus efectos?' Becker asked in fluent Castillian Spanish. 'Where are his belongings?'

'Allí,' replied the yellow-toothed lieutenant. He pointed to a counter of clothing and other personal items.

'Es todo? Is that all?'

'Sí.'

Becker asked for a cardboard box. The lieutenant hurried off to find one.

It was Saturday evening, and the Seville morgue was technically closed. The young lieutenant had let Becker in under direct orders from the head of the Seville Guardia – it seemed the visiting American had powerful friends.

Becker eyed the pile of clothes. There was a passport, wallet, and glasses stuffed in one of the shoes. There was also a small duffel the Guardia had taken from the man's hotel. Becker's directions were clear: Touch nothing. Read nothing. Just bring it all back. Everything. Don't miss anything.

Becker surveyed the pile and frowned. *What could the NSA possibly want with this junk?*

The lieutenant returned with a small box, and Becker began putting the clothes inside.

The officer poked at the cadaver's leg. 'Quien es? Who is he?'

'No idea.'

'Looks Chinese.'

Japanese, Becker thought.

'Poor bastard. Heart attack, huh?'

Becker nodded absently. 'That's what they told me.'

The lieutenant sighed and shook his head sympathetically. 'The Seville sun can be cruel. Be careful out there tomorrow.'

'Thanks,' Becker said. 'But I'm headed home.'

The officer looked shocked. 'You just got here!'

'I know, but the guy paying my airfare is waiting for these items.'

The lieutenant looked offended in the way only a Spaniard can be offended. 'You mean you're not going to *experience* Seville?'

'I was here years ago. Beautiful city. I'd love to stay.'

'So you've seen La Giralda?'

Becker nodded. He'd never actually climbed the ancient Moorish tower, but he'd seen it.

'How about the Alcazar?'

Becker nodded again, remembering the night he'd

heard Paco de Lucia play guitar in the courtyard – flamenco under the stars in a fifteenth-century fortress. He wished he'd known Susan back then.

'And of course there's Christopher Columbus.' The officer beamed. 'He's buried in our cathedral.'

Becker looked up. 'Really? I thought Columbus was buried in the Dominican Republic.'

'Hell no! Who starts these rumors? Columbus's body is here in Spain! I thought you said you went to college.'

Becker shrugged. 'I must have missed that day.'

'The Spanish church is very proud to own his relics.'

The Spanish church. Becker knew there was only one church in Spain – the Roman Catholic church. Catholicism was bigger here than in Vatican City.

'We don't, of course, have his entire body,' the lieutenant added. 'Solo el escroto.'

Becker stopped packing and stared at the lieutenant. *Solo el escroto?* He fought off a grin. 'Just his scrotum?'

The officer nodded proudly. 'Yes. When the church obtains the remains of a great man, they saint him and spread the relics to different cathedrals so everyone can enjoy their splendor.'

'And you got the . . .' Becker stifled a laugh.

'Oye! It's a pretty important part!' the officer defended. 'It's not like we got a rib or a knuckle like those churches in Galicia! You should really stay and see it.'

Becker nodded politely. 'Maybe I'll drop in on my way out of town.'

'Mala suerte.' The officer sighed. 'Bad luck. The cathedral's closed till sunrise mass.'

'Another time then.' Becker smiled, hoisting the box. 'I should probably get going. My flight's waiting.' He made a final glance around the room.

'You want a ride to the airport?' the officer asked. 'I've got a Moto Guzzi out front.'

'No thanks. I'll catch a cab.' Becker had driven a motorcycle once in college and nearly killed himself on it. He had no intention of getting on one again, regardless of who was driving.

'Whatever you say,' the officer said, heading for the door. 'I'll get the lights.'

Becker tucked the box under his arm. *Have I got everything?* He took a last look at the body on the table. The figure was stark naked, faceup under fluorescent lights, clearly hiding nothing. Becker found his eyes drawn again to the strangely deformed hands. He gazed a minute, focusing more intently.

The officer killed the lights, and the room went dark.

'Hold on,' Becker said. 'Turn those back on.'

The lights flickered back on.

Becker set his box on the floor and walked over to the corpse. He leaned down and squinted at the man's left hand.

The officer followed Becker's gaze. 'Pretty ugly, huh?'

But the deformity was not what had caught Becker's eye. He'd seen something else. He turned to the officer. 'You're sure everything's in this box?'

The officer nodded. 'Yeah. That's it.'

Becker stood for a moment with his hands on his hips. Then he picked up the box, carried it back over to the counter, and dumped it out. Carefully, piece by piece, he shook out the clothing. Then he emptied the shoes and tapped them as if trying to remove a pebble. After going over everything a second time, he stepped back and frowned.

'Problem?' asked the lieutenant.

'Yeah,' Becker said. 'We're missing something.'

CHAPTER 13

Tokugen Numataka stood in his plush, penthouse office and gazed out at the Tokyo skyline. His employees and competitors knew him as *akuta same* – the deadly shark. For three decades he'd outguessed, outbid, and outadvertised all the Japanese competition; now he was on the brink of becoming a giant in the world market as well.

He was about to close the biggest deal of his life – a deal that would make his Numatech Corp. the Microsoft of the future. His blood was alive with the cool rush of adrenaline. Business was war – and war was exciting.

Although Tokugen Numataka had been suspicious when the call had come three days ago, he now knew the truth. He was blessed with *myouri* – good fortune. The gods had chosen him.

'I have a copy of the Digital Fortress pass-key,' the American accent had said. 'Would you like to buy it?'

Numataka had almost laughed aloud. He knew it was a ploy. Numatech Corp. had bid generously for Ensei Tankado's new algorithm, and now one of

Numatech's competitors was playing games, trying to find out the amount of the bid.

'You have the pass-key?' Numataka feigned interest.

'I do. My name is North Dakota.'

Numataka stifled a laugh. Everyone knew about North Dakota. Tankado had told the press about his secret partner. It had been a wise move on Tankado's part to have a partner; even in Japan, business practices had become dishonorable. Ensei Tankado was not safe. But one false move by an overeager firm, and the pass-key would be published; every software firm on the market would suffer.

Numataka took a long pull on his Umami cigar and played along with the caller's pathetic charade. 'So you're selling your pass-key? Interesting. How does Ensei Tankado feel about this?'

'I have no allegiance to Mr Tankado. Mr Tankado was foolish to trust me. The pass-key is worth hundreds of times what he is paying me to handle it for him.'

'I'm sorry,' Numataka said. 'Your pass-key alone is worth nothing to me. When Tankado finds out what you've done, he will simply publish his copy, and the market will be flooded.'

'You will receive both pass-keys,' the voice said. 'Mr Tankado's *and* mine.'

Numataka covered the receiver and laughed aloud. He couldn't help asking, 'How much are you asking for both keys?'

'Twenty million U.S. dollars.'

Twenty million was almost exactly what Numataka had bid. 'Twenty million?' He gasped in mock horror. 'That's outrageous!'

'I've seen the algorithm. I assure you it's well worth it.'

No shit, thought Numataka. *It's worth ten times that.* 'Unfortunately,' he said, tiring of the game, 'we both know Mr Tankado would never stand for this. Think of the legal repercussions.'

The caller paused ominously. 'What if Mr Tankado were no longer a factor?'

Numataka wanted to laugh, but he noted an odd determination in the voice. 'If Tankado were no longer a factor?' Numataka considered it. 'Then you and I would have a deal.'

'I'll be in touch,' the voice said. The line went dead.

CHAPTER 14

Becker gazed down at the cadaver. Even hours after death, the Asian's face radiated with a pinkish glow of a recent sunburn. The rest of him was a pale yellow – all except the small area of purplish bruising directly over his heart.

Probably from the CPR, Becker mused. *Too bad it didn't work.*

He went back to studying the cadaver's hands. They were like nothing Becker had ever seen. Each hand had only three digits, and they were twisted and askew. The disfigurement, however, was not what Becker was looking at.

'Well, I'll be.' The lieutenant grunted from across the room. 'He's Japanese, not Chinese.'

Becker looked up. The officer was thumbing through the dead man's passport. 'I'd rather you didn't look at that,' Becker requested. *Touch nothing. Read nothing.*

'Ensei Tankado . . . born January—'

'Please,' Becker said politely. 'Put it back.'

The officer stared at the passport a moment longer and then tossed it back on the pile. 'This guy's got a class-3 visa. He could have stayed here for years.'

Becker poked at the victim's hand with a pen. 'Maybe he lived here.'

'Nope. Date of entry was last week.'

'Maybe he was *moving* here,' Becker offered curtly.

'Yeah, maybe. Crummy first week. Sunstroke and a heart attack. Poor bastard.'

Becker ignored the officer and studied the hand. 'You're positive he wasn't wearing any jewelry when he died?'

The officer looked up, startled. 'Jewelry?'

'Yeah. Take a look at this.'

The officer crossed the room.

The skin on Tankado's left hand showed traces of sunburn, everywhere except a narrow band of flesh around the smallest finger.

Becker pointed to the strip of pale flesh. 'See how this isn't sunburned here? Looks like he was wearing a ring.'

The officer seemed surprised. 'A *ring?*' His voice sounded suddenly perplexed. He studied the corpse's finger. Then he flushed sheepishly. 'My God.' He chuckled. 'The story was *true?*'

Becker had a sudden sinking feeling. 'I beg your pardon?'

The officer shook his head in disbelief. 'I would have mentioned it before . . . but I thought the guy was nuts.'

Becker was not smiling. 'What guy?'

'The guy who phoned in the emergency. Some Canadian tourist. Kept talking about a ring. Babbling in the worst damn Spanish I ever heard.'

'He said Mr Tankado was wearing a *ring?*'

The officer nodded. He pulled out a Ducado ciga-rette, eyed the NO FUMAR sign, and lit up anyway. 'Guess I should have said something, but the guy sounded totally loco.'

Becker frowned. Strathmore's words echoed in his ears. *I want everything Ensei Tankado had with him. Everything. Leave nothing. Not even a tiny scrap of paper.*

'Where is the ring now?' Becker asked.

The officer took a puff. 'Long story.'

Something told Becker this was *not* good news. 'Tell me anyway.'

CHAPTER 15

Susan Fletcher sat at her computer terminal inside Node 3. Node 3 was the cryptographers' private, soundproofed chamber just off the main floor. A two-inch sheet of curved one-way glass gave the cryptographers a panorama of the Crypto floor while prohibiting anyone else from seeing inside.

At the back of the expansive Node 3 chamber, twelve terminals sat in a perfect circle. The annular arrangement was intended to encourage intellectual exchange between cryptographers, to remind them they were part of a larger team – something like a code-breaker's Knights of the Round Table. Ironically, secrets were frowned on inside Node 3.

Nicknamed the Playpen, Node 3 had none of the sterile feel of the rest of Crypto. It was designed to feel like home – plush carpets, high-tech sound system, fully stocked fridge, kitchenette, a Nerf basketball hoop. The NSA had a philosophy about Crypto: Don't drop a couple billion bucks into a code-breaking computer without enticing the best of the best to stick around and use it.

Susan slipped out of her Salvatore Ferragamo flats

and dug her stockinged toes into the thick pile carpet. Well-paid government employees were encouraged to refrain from lavish displays of personal wealth. It was usually no problem for Susan – she was perfectly happy with her modest duplex, Volvo sedan, and conservative wardrobe. But shoes were another matter. Even when Susan was in college, she'd budgeted for the best.

You can't jump for the stars if your feet hurt, her aunt had once told her. *And when you get where you're going, you darn well better look great!*

Susan allowed herself a luxurious stretch and then settled down to business. She pulled up her tracer and prepared to configure it. She glanced at the E-mail address Strathmore had given her.

NDAKOTA@ARA.ANON.ORG

The man calling himself North Dakota had an anonymous account, but Susan knew it would not remain anonymous for long. The tracer would pass through ARA, get forwarded to North Dakota, and then send information back containing the man's real Internet address.

If all went well, it would locate North Dakota soon, and Strathmore could confiscate the pass-key. That would leave only David. When he found Tankado's copy, both pass-keys could be destroyed; Tankado's little time bomb would be harmless, a deadly explosive without a detonator.

Susan double-checked the address on the sheet in front of her and entered the information in the correct datafield. She chuckled that Strathmore had encountered difficulty sending the tracer himself. Apparently he'd sent it twice, both times receiving Tankado's address back rather than North Dakota's. It was a simple mistake, Susan thought; Strathmore had probably interchanged the datafields, and the tracer had searched for the wrong account.

Susan finished configuring her tracer and queued it for release. Then she hit return. The computer beeped once.

TRACER SENT

Now came the waiting game.

Susan exhaled. She felt guilty for having been hard on the commander. If there was anyone qualified to handle this threat single-handed, it was Trevor Strathmore. He had an uncanny way of getting the best of all those who challenged him.

Six months ago, when the EFF broke a story that an NSA submarine was snooping underwater telephone cables, Strathmore calmly leaked a conflicting story that the submarine was actually illegally burying toxic waste. The EFF and the oceanic environmentalists spent so much time bickering over which version was true, the media eventually tired of the story and moved on.

Every move Strathmore made was meticulously planned. He depended heavily on his computer when devising and revising his plans. Like many NSA employees, Strathmore used NSA-developed software called BrainStorm – a risk-free way to carry out 'what-if' scenarios in the safety of a computer.

BrainStorm was an artificial intelligence experiment described by its developers as a Cause & Effect Simulator. It originally had been intended for use in political campaigns as a way to create real-time models of a given 'political environment.' Fed by enormous amounts of data, the program created a relationary web – a hypothesized model of interaction between political variables, including current prominent figures, their staffs, their personal ties to each other, hot issues, individuals' motivations weighted by variables like sex, ethnicity, money, and power. The user could then enter any hypothetical event and BrainStorm would predict the event's effect on 'the environment.'

Commander Strathmore worked religiously with BrainStorm – not for political purposes, but as a TFM device; Time-Line, Flowchart, & Mapping software was a powerful tool for outlining complex strategies and predicting weaknesses. Susan suspected there were schemes hidden in Strathmore's computer that someday would change the world.

Yes, Susan thought, *I was too hard on him.*

Her thoughts were jarred by the hiss of the Node 3 doors.

Strathmore burst in. 'Susan,' he said. 'David just called. There's been a setback.'

CHAPTER 16

'A ring?' Susan looked doubtful. 'Tankado's missing a ring?'

'Yes. We're lucky David caught it. It was a real heads-up play.'

'But you're after a pass-key, not jewelry.'

'I know,' Strathmore said, 'but I think they might be one and the same.'

Susan looked lost.

'It's a long story.'

She motioned to the tracer on her screen. 'I'm not going anywhere.'

Strathmore sighed heavily and began pacing. 'Apparently, there were witnesses to Tankado's death. According to the officer at the morgue, a Canadian tourist called the Guardia this morning in a panic – he said a Japanese man was having a heart attack in the park. When the officer arrived, he found Tankado dead and the Canadian there with him, so he radioed the paramedics. While the paramedics took Tankado's body to the morgue, the officer tried to get the Canadian to tell him what happened. All the old guy did was babble about

99

some ring Tankado had given away right before he died.'

Susan eyed him skeptically. 'Tankado *gave away* a ring?'

'Yeah. Apparently he forced it in this old guy's face – like he was begging him to take it. Sounds like the old guy got a close look at it.' Strathmore stopped pacing and turned. 'He said the ring was engraved – with some sort of lettering.'

'Lettering?'

'Yes, and according to him, it wasn't English.' Strathmore raised his eyebrows expectantly.

'Japanese?'

Strathmore shook his head. 'My first thought too. But get this – the Canadian complained that the letters didn't spell anything. Japanese characters could never be confused with our Roman lettering. He said the engraving looked like a cat had gotten loose on a type-writer.'

Susan laughed. 'Commander, you don't really think—'

Strathmore cut her off. 'Susan, it's crystal clear. Tankado engraved the Digital Fortress pass-key on his ring. Gold is durable. Whether he's sleeping, shower-ing, eating – the pass-key would always be with him, ready at a moment's notice for instant publication.'

Susan looked dubious. 'On his finger? In the open like that?'

'Why not? Spain isn't exactly the encryption capital of the world. Nobody would have any idea what the letters meant. Besides, if the key is a standard sixty-four-bit – even in broad daylight, nobody could possibly read and memorize all sixty-four characters.'

Susan looked perplexed. 'And Tankado gave this

ring to a total stranger moments before he died? Why?'

Strathmore's gaze narrowed. 'Why do you think?'

It took Susan only a moment before it clicked. Her eyes widened.

Strathmore nodded. 'Tankado was trying to get rid of it. He thought we'd killed him. He felt himself dying and logically assumed we were responsible. The timing was too coincidental. He figured we'd gotten to him, poison or something, a slow-acting cardiac arrestor. He knew the only way we'd dare kill him is if we'd found North Dakota.'

Susan felt a chill. 'Of course,' she whispered. 'Tankado thought that we neutralized his insurance policy so we could remove *him* too.'

It was all coming clear to Susan. The timing of the heart attack was so fortunate for the NSA that Tankado had assumed the NSA was responsible. His final instinct was revenge. Ensei gave away his ring as a last-ditch effort to publish the pass-key. Now, incredibly, some unsuspecting Canadian tourist held the key to the most powerful encryption algorithm in history.

Susan sucked in a deep breath and asked the inevitable question. 'So where is the Canadian now?'

Strathmore frowned. 'That's the problem.'

'The officer doesn't know where he is?'

'No. The Canadian's story was so absurd that the officer figured he was either in shock or senile. So he put the old guy on the back of his motorcycle to take him back to his hotel. But the Canadian didn't know enough to hang on; he fell off before they'd gone three feet – cracked his head and broke his wrist.'

'What!' Susan choked.

'The officer wanted to take him to a hospital, but the Canadian was furious – said he'd walk back to Canada before he'd get on the motorcycle again. So all the officer could do was walk him to a small public clinic near the park. He left him there to get checked out.'

Susan frowned. 'I assume there's no need to ask where David is headed.'

CHAPTER 17

David Becker stepped out onto the scorching tile concourse of Plaza de España. Before him, El Ayuntamiento – the ancient city council building – rose from the trees on a three-acre bed of blue and white azulejo tiles. Its Arabic spires and carved facade gave the impression it had been intended more as a palace than a public office. Despite its history of military coups, fires, and public hangings, most tourists visited because the local brochures plugged it as the English military headquarters in the film *Lawrence of Arabia*. It had been far cheaper for Columbia Pictures to film in Spain than in Egypt, and the Moorish influence on Seville's architecture was enough to convince moviegoers they were looking at Cairo.

Becker reset his Seiko for local time: 9:10 P.M. – still afternoon by local standards; a proper Spaniard never ate dinner before sunset, and the lazy Andalusian sun seldom surrendered the skies before ten.

Even in the early-evening heat, Becker found himself walking across the park at a brisk clip. Strathmore's tone had sounded a lot more urgent this time than it had that morning. His new orders left no room for misinterpretation: Find the Canadian, get the ring. Do whatever is necessary, just get that ring.

Becker wondered what could possibly be so important about a ring with lettering all over it. Strathmore hadn't offered, and Becker hadn't asked. *NSA,* he thought. *Never Say Anything.*

On the other side of Avenida Isabela Católica, the clinic was clearly visible – the universal symbol of a red cross in a white circle painted on the roof. The Guardia officer had dropped the Canadian off hours ago. Broken wrist, bumped head – no doubt the patient had been treated and discharged by now. Becker just hoped the clinic had discharge information – a local hotel or phone number where the man could be reached. With a little luck, Becker figured he could find the Canadian, get the ring, and be on his way home without any more complications.

Strathmore had told Becker, 'Use the ten thousand cash to buy the ring if you have to. I'll reimburse you.'

'That's not necessary,' Becker had replied. He'd intended to return the money anyway. He hadn't gone to Spain for money, he'd gone for Susan. Commander Trevor Strathmore was Susan's mentor and guardian. Susan owed him a lot; a one-day errand was the least Becker could do.

Unfortunately, things this morning hadn't gone quite as Becker had planned. He'd hoped to call Susan from the plane and explain everything. He considered having the pilot radio Strathmore so he could pass along a message but was hesitant to involve the deputy director in his romantic problems.

Three times Becker had tried to call Susan himself – first from a defunct cellular on board the jet, next from a pay phone at the airport, then again from the morgue. Susan was not in. David wondered where she could be. He'd gotten her answering machine but had not left a message; what he wanted to say was not a message for an answering machine.

As he approached the road, he spotted a phone booth near the park entrance. He jogged over, snatched up the receiver, and used his phone card to place the call. There was a long pause as the number connected. Finally it began to ring.

Come on. Be there.

After five rings the call connected.

'Hi. This is Susan Fletcher. Sorry I'm not in right now, but if you leave your name . . .'

Becker listened to the message. *Where is she?* By now Susan would be panicked. He wondered if maybe she'd gone to Stone Manor without him. There was a beep.

'Hi. It's David.' He paused, unsure what to say. One of the things he hated about answering machines was that if you stopped to think, they cut you off. 'Sorry I didn't call,' he blurted just in time. He wondered if he should tell her what was going on. He thought better of it. 'Call Commander Strathmore. He'll explain everything.' Becker's heart was pounding. *This is absurd*, he thought. 'I love you,' he added quickly and hung up.

Becker waited for some traffic to pass on Avenida Borbolla. He thought about how Susan undoubtedly would have assumed the worst; it was unlike him not to call when he'd promised to.

Becker stepped out onto the four-lane boulevard. 'In and out,' he whispered to himself. 'In and out.' He was too preoccupied to see the man in wire-rim glasses watching from across the street.

CHAPTER 18

Standing before the huge plate-glass window in his Tokyo skyrise, Numataka took a long pull on his cigar and smiled to himself. He could scarcely believe his good fortune. He had spoken to the American again, and if all was going according to the timetable, Ensei Tankado had been eliminated by now, and his copy of the pass-key had been confiscated.

It was ironic, Numataka thought, that he himself would end up with Ensei Tankado's pass-key. Tokugen Numataka had met Tankado once many years ago. The young programmer had come to Numatech Corp. fresh out of college, searching for a job. Numataka had denied him. There was no question that Tankado was brilliant, but at the time there were other considerations. Although Japan was changing, Numataka had been trained in the old school; he lived by the code of menboko – honor and face. Imperfection was not to be tolerated. If he hired a cripple, he would bring shame on his company. He had disposed of Tankado's résumé without a glance.

Numataka checked his watch again. The American, North Dakota, should have called by now. Numataka

106

felt a tinge of nervousness. He hoped nothing was wrong.

If the pass-keys were as good as promised, they would unlock the most sought-after product of the computer age – a totally invulnerable digital encryption algorithm. Numataka could embed the algorithm in tamper-proof, spray-sealed VSLI chips and mass market them to world computer manufacturers, governments, industries, and perhaps, even the darker markets . . . the black market of world terrorists.

Numataka smiled. It appeared, as usual, that he had found favor with the shichigosan – the seven deities of good luck. Numatech Corp. was about to control the only copy of Digital Fortress that would ever exist. Twenty million dollars was a lot of money – but considering the product, it was the steal of the century.

CHAPTER 19

'What if someone else is looking for the ring?' Susan asked, suddenly nervous. 'Could David be in danger?'

Strathmore shook his head. 'Nobody else knows the ring exists. That's why I sent David. I wanted to keep it that way. Curious spooks don't usually tail Spanish teachers.'

'He's a professor,' Susan corrected, immediately regretting the clarification. Every now and again Susan got the feeling David wasn't good enough for the commander, that he thought somehow she could do better than a schoolteacher.

'Commander,' she said, moving on, 'if you briefed David by car phone this morning, someone could have intercepted the—'

'One-in-a-million shot,' Strathmore interrupted, his tone reassuring. 'Any eavesdropper had to be in the immediate vicinity and know exactly what to listen for.' He put his hand on her shoulder. 'I would never have sent David if I thought it was dangerous.' He smiled. 'Trust me. Any sign of trouble, and I'll send in the pros.'

Strathmore's words were punctuated by the sudden

sound of someone pounding on the Node 3 glass. Susan and Strathmore turned.

Sys-Sec Phil Chartrukian had his face pressed against the pane and was pounding fiercely, straining to see through. Whatever he was excitedly mouthing was not audible through the soundproofed glass. He looked like he'd seen a ghost.

'What the hell is Chartrukian doing here?' Strathmore growled. 'He's not on duty today.'

'Looks like trouble,' Susan said. 'He probably saw the Run-Monitor.'

'Goddamn it!' the commander hissed. 'I specifically called the scheduled Sys-Sec last night and told him not to come in!'

Susan was not surprised. Canceling a Sys-Sec duty was irregular, but Strathmore undoubtedly had wanted privacy in the dome. The last thing he needed was some paranoid Sys-Sec blowing the lid off Digital Fortress.

'We better abort TRANSLTR,' Susan said. 'We can reset the Run-Monitor and tell Phil he was seeing things.'

Strathmore appeared to consider it, then shook his head. 'Not yet. TRANSLTR is fifteen hours into this attack. I want to run it a full twenty-four – just to be sure.'

This made sense to Susan. Digital Fortress was the first-ever use of a rotating cleartext function. Maybe Tankado had overlooked something; maybe TRANSLTR would break it after twenty-four hours. Somehow Susan doubted it.

'TRANSLTR keeps running,' Strathmore resolved. 'I need to know for sure this algorithm is untouchable.'

Chartrukian continued pounding on the pane.

'Here goes nothing.' Strathmore groaned. 'Back me up.'

The commander took a deep breath and then strode to the sliding glass doors. The pressure plate on the floor activated, and the doors hissed open.

Chartrukian practically fell into the room. 'Commander, sir. I . . . I'm sorry to bother you, but the Run-Monitor . . . I ran a virus probe and—'

'Phil, Phil, Phil,' the commander gushed pleasantly as he put a reassuring hand on Chartrukian's shoulder. 'Slow down. What seems to be the problem?'

From the easygoing tone in Strathmore's voice, nobody would ever have guessed his world was falling in around him. He stepped aside and ushered Chartrukian into the sacred walls of Node 3. The Sys-Sec stepped over the threshold hesitantly, like a well-trained dog that knew better.

From the puzzled look on Chartrukian's face, it was obvious he'd never seen the inside of this place. Whatever had been the source of his panic was momentarily forgotten. He surveyed the plush interior, the line of private terminals, the couches, the bookshelves, the soft lighting. When his gaze fell on the reigning queen of Crypto, Susan Fletcher, he quickly looked away. Susan intimidated the hell out of him. Her mind worked on a different plane. She was unsettlingly beautiful, and his words always seemed to get jumbled around her. Susan's unassuming air made it even worse.

'What seems to be the problem, Phil?' Strathmore said, opening the refrigerator. 'Drink?'

'No, ah – no, thank you, sir.' He seemed tongue-tied, not sure he was truly welcome. 'Sir . . . I think there's a problem with TRANSLTR.'

Strathmore closed the refrigerator and looked at Chartrukian casually. 'You mean the Run-Monitor?'

Chartrukian looked shocked. 'You mean you've *seen* it?'

'Sure. It's running at about sixteen hours, if I'm not mistaken.'

Chartrukian seemed puzzled. 'Yes, sir, sixteen hours. But that's not all, sir. I ran a virus probe, and it's turning up some pretty strange stuff.'

'Really?' Strathmore seemed unconcerned. 'What kind of stuff?'

Susan watched, impressed with the commander's performance.

Chartrukian stumbled on. 'TRANSLTR's processing something very advanced. The filters have never seen anything like it. I'm afraid TRANSLTR may have some sort of virus.'

'A virus?' Strathmore chuckled with just a hint of condescension. 'Phil, I appreciate your concern, I really do. But Ms Fletcher and I are running a new diagnostic, some very advanced stuff. I would have alerted you to it, but I wasn't aware you were on duty today.'

The Sys-Sec did his best to cover gracefully. 'I switched with the new guy. I took his weekend shift.'

Strathmore's eyes narrowed. 'That's odd. I spoke to him last night. I told him not to come in. He said nothing about switching shifts.'

Chartrukian felt a knot rise in his throat. There was a tense silence.

'Well.' Strathmore finally sighed. 'Sounds like an unfortunate mix-up.' He put a hand on the Sys-Sec's shoulder and led him toward the door. 'The good news is you don't have to stay. Ms Fletcher and I will be here all day. We'll hold the fort. You just enjoy your weekend.'

Chartrukian was hesitant. 'Commander, I really think we should check the—'

'Phil,' Strathmore repeated a little more sternly, 'TRANSLTR is fine. If your probe saw something strange, it's because *we* put it there. Now if you don't mind . . .' Strathmore trailed off, and the Sys-Sec understood. His time was up.

'A diagnostic, my ass!' Chartrukian muttered as he fumed back into the Sys-Sec lab. 'What kind of looping function keeps three million processors busy for sixteen hours?'

Chartrukian wondered if he should call the Sys-Sec supervisor. *Goddamn cryptographers,* he thought. *They just don't understand security!*

The oath Chartrukian had taken when he joined Sys-Sec began running through his head. He had sworn to use his expertise, training, and instinct to protect the NSA's multibillion-dollar investment.

'Instinct,' he said defiantly. *It doesn't take a psychic to know this isn't any goddamn diagnostic!*

Defiantly, Chartrukian strode over to the terminal and fired up TRANSLTR's complete array of system assessment software.

'Your baby's in trouble, Commander,' he grumbled. 'You don't trust instinct? I'll get you proof!'

CHAPTER 20

La Clínica de Salud Pública was actually a converted elementary school and didn't much resemble a hospital at all. It was a long, one-story brick building with huge windows and a rusted swing set out back. Becker headed up the crumbling steps.

Inside, it was dark and noisy. The waiting room was a line of folding metal chairs that ran the entire length of a long narrow corridor. A cardboard sign on a sawhorse read OFICINA with an arrow pointing down the hall.

Becker walked the dimly lit corridor. It was like some sort of eerie set conjured up for a Hollywood horror flick. The air smelled of urine. The lights at the far end were blown out, and the last forty or fifty feet revealed nothing but muted silhouettes. A bleeding woman . . . a young couple crying . . . a little girl praying . . . Becker reached the end of the darkened hall. The door to his left was slightly ajar, and he pushed it open. It was entirely empty except for an old, withered woman naked on a cot struggling with her bedpan.

Lovely. Becker groaned. He closed the door. *Where the hell is the office?*

Around a small dog-leg in the hall, Becker heard voices. He followed the sound and arrived at a translucent glass door that sounded as if a brawl were going on behind it. Reluctantly, Becker pushed the door open. The office. *Mayhem.* Just as he'd feared.

The line was about ten people deep, everyone pushing and shouting. Spain was not known for its efficiency, and Becker knew he could be there all night waiting for discharge info on the Canadian. There was only one secretary behind the desk, and she was fending off disgruntled patients. Becker stood in the doorway a moment and pondered his options. There was a better way.

'Con permiso!' an orderly shouted. A fast-rolling gurney sailed by.

Becker spun out of the way and called after the orderly 'Dónde está el teléfono?'

Without breaking stride, the man pointed to a set of double doors and disappeared around the corner. Becker walked over to the doors and pushed his way through.

The room before him was enormous – an old gymnasium. The floor was a pale green and seemed to swim in and out of focus under the hum of the fluorescent lights. On the wall, a basketball hoop hung limply from its backboard. Scattered across the floor were a few dozen patients on low cots. In the far corner, just beneath a burned-out scoreboard, was an old pay phone. Becker hoped it worked.

As he strode across the floor, he fumbled in his pocket for a coin. He found 75 pesetas in cinco-duros coins, change from the taxi – just enough for two local calls. He smiled politely to an exiting nurse and made his way to the phone. Scooping up the receiver, Becker dialed Directory Assistance. Thirty seconds later he had the number for the clinic's main office.

Regardless of the country, it seemed there was one universal truth when it came to offices: Nobody could stand the sound of an unanswered phone. It didn't matter how many customers were waiting to be helped, the secretary would always drop what she was doing to pick up the phone.

Becker punched the six-digit exchange. In a moment he'd have the clinic's office. There would undoubtedly be only one Canadian admitted today with a broken wrist and a concussion; his file would be easy to find. Becker knew the office would be hesitant to give out the man's name and discharge address to a total stranger, but he had a plan.

The phone began to ring. Becker guessed five rings was all it would take. It took nineteen.

'Clínica de Salud Pública,' barked the frantic secretary.

Becker spoke in Spanish with a thick Franco-American accent. 'This is David Becker. I'm with the Canadian Embassy. One of our citizens was treated by you today. I'd like his information such that the embassy can arrange to pay his fees.'

'Fine,' the woman said. 'I'll send it to the embassy on Monday.'

'Actually,' Becker pressed, 'it's important I get it immediately.'

'Impossible,' the woman snapped. 'We're very busy.'

Becker sounded as official as possible. 'It is an urgent matter. The man had a broken wrist and a head injury. He was treated sometime this morning. His file should be right on top.'

Becker thickened the accent in his Spanish – just clear enough to convey his needs, just confusing enough to be exasperating. People had a way of bending the rules when they were exasperated.

Instead of bending the rules, however, the woman cursed self-important North Americans and slammed down the phone.

Becker frowned and hung up. Strikeout. The thought of waiting hours in line didn't thrill him; the clock was ticking – the old Canadian could be anywhere by now. Maybe he had decided to go back to Canada. Maybe he would sell the ring. Becker didn't have hours to wait in line. With renewed determination, Becker snatched up the receiver and redialed. He pressed the phone to his ear and leaned back against the wall. It began to ring. Becker gazed out into the room. One ring . . . two rings . . . three—

A sudden surge of adrenaline coursed through his body.

Becker wheeled and slammed the receiver back down into its cradle. Then he turned and stared back into the room in stunned silence. There on a cot, directly in front of him, propped up on a pile of old pillows, lay an elderly man with a clean white cast on his right wrist.

CHAPTER 21

The American on Tokugen Numataka's private line sounded anxious.

'Mr Numataka – I only have a moment.'

'Fine. I trust you have both pass-keys.'

'There will be a small delay,' the American answered.

'Unacceptable,' Numataka hissed. 'You said I would have them by the end of today!'

'There is one loose end.'

'Is Tankado dead?'

'Yes,' the voice said. 'My man killed Mr Tankado, but he failed to get the pass-key. Tankado gave it away before he died. To a tourist.'

'Outrageous!' Numataka bellowed. 'Then how can you promise me exclusive—'

'Relax,' the American soothed. 'You will have exclusive rights. That is my guarantee. As soon as the missing pass-key is found, Digital Fortress will be yours.'

'But the pass-key could be copied!'

'Anyone who has seen the key will be eliminated.'

There was a long silence. Finally Numataka spoke. 'Where is the key now?'

'All you need to know is that it *will* be found.'

'How can you be so certain?'

'Because I am not the only one looking for it. American intelligence has caught wind of the missing key. For obvious reasons they would like to prevent the release of Digital Fortress. They have sent a man to locate the key. His name is David Becker.'

'How do you know this?'

'That is irrelevant.'

Numataka paused. 'And if Mr Becker locates the key?'

'My man will take it from him.'

'And after that?'

'You needn't be concerned,' the American said coldly. 'When Mr Becker finds the key, he will be properly rewarded.'

CHAPTER 22

David Becker strode over and stared down at the old man asleep on the cot. The man's right wrist was wrapped in a cast. He was between sixty and seventy years old. His snow-white hair was parted neatly to the side, and in the center of his forehead was a deep purple welt that spread down into his right eye.

A little bump? he thought, recalling the lieutenant's words. Becker checked the man's fingers. There was no gold ring anywhere. Becker reached down and touched the man's arm. 'Sir?' He shook him lightly. 'Excuse me . . . sir?'

The man didn't move.

Becker tried again, a little louder. 'Sir?'

The man stirred. 'Qu'est-ce . . . quelle heure est—' He slowly opened his eyes and focused on Becker. He scowled at having been disturbed. 'Qu'est-ce-que vous voulez?'

Yes, Becker thought, *a French Canadian!* Becker smiled down at him. 'Do you have a moment?'

Although Becker's French was perfect, he spoke in what he hoped would be the man's weaker language, English. Convincing a total stranger to hand over a gold ring might be a little tricky; Becker figured he could use any edge he could get.

There was a long silence as the man got his bearings. He surveyed his surroundings and lifted a long finger to smooth his limp white mustache. Finally he spoke. 'What do you want?' His English carried a thin, nasal accent.

'Sir,' Becker said, overpronouncing his words as if speaking to a deaf person, 'I need to ask you a few questions.'

The man glared up at him with a strange look on his face. 'Do you have some sort of problem?'

Becker frowned; the man's English was impeccable. He immediately lost the condescending tone. 'I'm sorry to bother you, sir, but were you by any chance at the Plaza de España today?'

The old man's eyes narrowed. 'Are you from the City Council?'

'No, actually I'm—'

'Bureau of Tourism?'

'No, I'm—'

'Look, I know why you're here!' The old man struggled to sit up. 'I'm not going to be intimidated! If I've said it once, I've said it a thousand times – Pierre Cloucharde writes the world the way he *lives* the world. Some of your corporate guidebooks might sweep this under the table for a free night on the town, but the *Montreal Times* is *not* for hire! I refuse!'

'I'm sorry, sir. I don't think you under—'

'Merde alors! I understand perfectly!' He wagged a bony finger at Becker, and his voice echoed through the gymnasium. 'You're not the first! They tried the same thing at the Moulin Rouge, Brown's Palace, and the Golfigno in Lagos! But *what* went to press? The truth! The worst Wellington I've ever eaten! The filthiest tub I've ever seen! And the rockiest beach I've ever walked! My readers expect no less!'

Patients on nearby cots began sitting up to see what was going on. Becker looked around nervously for a nurse. The last thing he needed was to get kicked out.

Cloucharde was raging. 'That miserable excuse for a police officer works for *your* city! He made me get on his motorcycle! Look at me!' He tried to lift his wrist. '*Now* who's going to write my column?'

'Sir, I—'

'I've never been so uncomfortable in my forty-three years of travel! Look at this place! You know, my column is syndicated in over—'

'Sir!' Becker held up both hands urgently signaling truce. 'I'm not interested in your column; I'm from the Canadian Consulate. I'm here to make sure you're okay!'

Suddenly there was a dead quiet in the gymnasium. The old man looked up from his bed and eyed the intruder suspiciously.

Becker ventured on in almost a whisper. 'I'm here to see if there's anything I can do to help.' *Like bring you a couple of Valium.*

After a long pause, the Canadian spoke. 'The consulate?' His tone softened considerably.

Becker nodded.

'So, you're *not* here about my column?'

'No, sir.'

It was as if a giant bubble had burst for Pierre Cloucharde. He settled slowly back down onto his mound of pillows. He looked heartbroken. 'I thought you were from the city . . . trying to get me to . . .' He faded off and then looked up. 'If it's not about my column, then why *are* you here?'

It was a good question, Becker thought, picturing the Smoky Mountains. 'Just an informal diplomatic courtesy,' he lied.

The man looked surprised. 'A diplomatic courtesy?'

'Yes, sir. As I'm sure a man of your stature is well aware, the Canadian government works hard to protect its countrymen from the indignities suffered in these, er – shall we say – less *refined* countries.'

Cloucharde's thin lips parted in a knowing smile. 'But of course . . . how pleasant.'

'You *are* a Canadian citizen, aren't you?'

'Yes, of course. How silly of me. Please forgive me. Someone in my position is often approached with . . . well . . . you understand.'

'Yes, Mr Cloucharde, I certainly do. The price one pays for celebrity.'

'Indeed.' Cloucharde let out a tragic sigh. He was an unwilling martyr tolerating the masses. 'Can you believe this hideous place?' He rolled his eyes at the bizarre surroundings. 'It's a mockery. And they've decided to keep me overnight.'

Becker looked around. 'I know. It's terrible. I'm sorry it took me so long to get here.'

Cloucharde looked confused. 'I wasn't even aware you were coming.'

Becker changed the subject. 'Looks like a nasty bump on your head. Does it hurt?'

'No, not really. I took a spill this morning – the price one pays for being a good Samaritan. The wrist is the thing that's hurting me. Stupid Guardia. I mean, really! Putting a man of *my* age on a motorcycle. It's reprehensible.'

'Is there anything I can get for you?'

Cloucharde thought a moment, enjoying the attention. 'Well, actually . . .' He stretched his neck and tilted his head left and right. 'I *could* use another pillow if it's not too much trouble.'

'Not at all.' Becker grabbed a pillow off a nearby cot and helped Cloucharde get comfortable.

The old man sighed contentedly. 'Much better . . . thank you.'

'Pas du tout,' Becker replied.

'Ah!' The man smiled warmly. 'So you *do* speak the language of the civilized world.'

'That's about the extent of it,' Becker said sheepishly.

'Not a problem,' Cloucharde declared proudly. 'My column is syndicated in the U.S.; my English is first rate.'

'So I've heard.' Becker smiled. He sat down on the edge of Cloucharde's cot. 'Now, if you don't mind my asking, Mr Cloucharde, why would a man such as yourself come to a place like *this*? There are far better hospitals in Seville.'

Cloucharde looked angry. 'That police officer . . . he bucked me off his motorcycle and then left me bleeding in the street like a stuck pig. I had to walk over here.'

'He didn't offer to take you to a better facility?'

'On that godawful bike of his? No thanks!'

'What exactly happened this morning?'

'I told it all to the lieutenant.'

'I've spoken to the officer and—'

'I hope you reprimanded him!' Cloucharde interrupted.

Becker nodded. 'In the severest terms. My office will be following up.'

'I should hope so.'

'Monsieur Cloucharde.' Becker smiled, pulling a pen out of his jacket pocket. 'I'd like to make a formal complaint to the city. Would you help? A man of your reputation would be a valuable witness.'

Cloucharde looked buoyed by the prospect of being quoted. He sat up. 'Why, yes . . . of course. It would be my pleasure.'

Becker took out a small note pad and looked up. 'Okay, let's start with this morning. Tell me about the accident.'

The old man sighed. 'It was sad really. The poor Asian fellow just collapsed. I tried to help him – but it was no use.'

'You gave him CPR?'

Cloucharde looked ashamed. 'I'm afraid I don't know how. I called an ambulance.'

Becker remembered the bluish bruises on Tankado's chest. 'Did the paramedics administer CPR?'

'Heavens, no!' Cloucharde laughed. 'No reason to whip a dead horse – the fellow was long gone by the time the ambulance got there. They checked his pulse and carted him off, leaving me with that horrific policeman.'

That's strange, Becker thought, wondering where the bruise had come from. He pushed it from his mind and got to the matter at hand. 'What about the ring?' he said as nonchalantly as possible.

Cloucharde looked surprised. 'The lieutenant told you about the ring?'

'Yes, he did.'

Cloucharde seemed amazed. 'Really? I didn't think he believed my story. He was so rude – as if he thought I were lying. But my story was accurate, of course. I pride myself on accuracy.'

'Where is the ring?' Becker pressed.

Cloucharde didn't seem to hear. He was glassy-eyed, staring into space. 'Strange piece really, all those letters – looked like no language I'd ever seen.'

'Japanese, maybe?' Becker offered.

'Definitely not.'

'So you got a good look at it?'

'Heavens, yes! When I knelt down to help, the man kept pushing his fingers in my face. He wanted to give me the ring. It was most bizarre, horrible really – his hands were quite dreadful.'

'And that's when you took the ring?'

Cloucharde went wide-eyed. 'That's what the officer told you! That *I* took the ring?'

Becker shifted uneasily.

Cloucharde exploded. 'I knew he wasn't listening! That's how rumors get started! I told him the Jap fellow gave away the ring – but not to *me*! There's no way I would take anything from a dying man! My heavens! The thought of it!'

Becker sensed trouble. 'So you don't have the ring?'

'Heavens, no!'

A dull ache crept through the pit of his stomach. 'Then who has it?'

Cloucharde glared at Becker indignantly. 'The German! The German has it!'

Becker felt like the floor had been pulled out from under him. 'German? What German?'

'The German in the park! I told the officer about him! I refused the ring but the fascist swine accepted it!'

Becker set down his pen and paper. The charade was over. This was trouble. 'So a *German* has the ring?'

'Indeed.'

125

'Where did he go?'

'No idea. I ran to call the police. When I got back, he was gone.'

'Do you know who he was?'

'Some tourist.'

'Are you sure?'

'My life is tourists,' Cloucharde snapped. 'I know one when I see one. He and his lady friend were out strolling the park.'

Becker was more and more confused every moment. 'Lady friend? There was somebody *with* the German?'

Cloucharde nodded. 'An escort. Gorgeous redhead. Mon dieu! Beautiful.'

'An escort?' Becker was stunned. 'As in . . . a prostitute?'

Cloucharde grimaced. 'Yes, if you must use the vulgar term.'

'But . . . the officer said nothing about—'

'Of course not! I never mentioned the escort.' Cloucharde dismissed Becker with a patronizing wave of his good hand. 'They aren't criminals – it's absurd that they're harassed like common thieves.'

Becker was still in a mild state of shock. 'Was there anyone else there?'

'No, just the three of us. It was hot.'

'And you're positive the woman was a prostitute?'

'Absolutely. No woman that beautiful would be with a man like that unless she were well paid! Mon dieu! He was fat, fat, *fat!* A loud-mouthed, over-weight, obnoxious German!' Cloucharde winced momentarily as he shifted his weight, but he ignored the pain and plowed on. 'This man was a beast – three hundred pounds at least. He locked on to that poor dear like she was about to run away – not that I'd blame her. I mean really! Hands all over her. Bragged that he had her all weekend for three hundred dollars! *He's* the one who should have dropped dead, not that poor Asian fellow.' Cloucharde came up for air, and Becker jumped in.

'Did you get his name?'

Cloucharde thought for a moment and then shook his head. 'No idea.' He winced in pain again and settled slowly back into his pillows.

Becker sighed. The ring had just evaporated before his eyes. Commander Strathmore was not going to be happy.

Cloucharde dabbed at his forehead. His burst of enthusiasm had taken its toll. He suddenly looked ill.

Becker tried another approach. 'Mr Cloucharde, I'd like to get a statement from the German and his escort as well. Do you have any idea where they're staying?'

Cloucharde closed his eyes, his strength fading. His breathing grew shallow.

'Anything at all?' Becker pressed. 'The escort's name?'

There was a long silence.

Cloucharde rubbed his right temple. He was suddenly looking pale. 'Well . . . ah . . . no. I don't believe . . .' His voice was shaky.

Becker leaned toward him. 'Are you all right?'

Cloucharde nodded lightly. 'Yes, fine . . . just a little . . . the excitement maybe . . .' He trailed off.

'Think, Mr Cloucharde,' Becker urged quietly. 'It's important.'

Cloucharde winced. 'I don't know . . . the woman . . . the man kept calling her . . .' He closed his eyes and groaned.

'What was her name?'

'I really don't recall . . .' Cloucharde was fading fast.

'Think,' Becker prodded. 'It's important that the consular file be as complete as possible. I'll need to support your story with statements from the other witnesses. Any information you can give me to help locate them . . .'

But Cloucharde was not listening. He was dabbing his forehead with the sheet. 'I'm sorry . . . perhaps tomorrow . . .' He looked nauseated.

'Mr Cloucharde, it's important you remember this *now*.' Becker suddenly realized he was speaking too loudly. People on nearby cots were still sitting up watching what was going on. On the far side of the room a nurse appeared through the double doors and strode briskly toward them.

'Anything at all,' Becker pressed urgently.

'The German called the woman—'

Becker lightly shook Cloucharde, trying to bring him back.

Cloucharde's eyes flickered momentarily. 'Her name . . .'

Stay with me, old fella . . .

'Dew . . .' Cloucharde's eyes closed again. The nurse was closing in. She looked furious.

'Dew?' Becker shook Cloucharde's arm.

The old man groaned. 'He called her . . .' Cloucharde was mumbling now, barely audible.

The nurse was less than ten feet away yelling at Becker in angry Spanish. Becker heard nothing. His eyes were fixed on the old man's lips. He shook Cloucharde one last time as the nurse bore down on him.

The nurse grabbed David Becker's shoulder. She

pulled him to his feet just as Cloucharde's lips parted. The single word leaving the old man's mouth was not actually spoken. It was softly sighed – like a distant sensual remembrance. 'Dewdrop . . .'

The scolding grasp yanked Becker away.

Dewdrop? Becker wondered. *What the hell kind of name is Dewdrop?* He spun away from the nurse and turned one last time to Cloucharde. 'Dewdrop? Are you *sure?*'

But Pierre Cloucharde was fast asleep.

CHAPTER 23

Susan sat alone in the plush surroundings of Node 3. She nursed a lemon mist herb tea and awaited the return of her tracer.

As senior cryptographer, Susan enjoyed the terminal with the best view. It was on the back side of the ring of computers and faced the Crypto floor. From this spot, Susan could oversee all of Node 3. She could also see, on the other side of the one-way glass, TRANSLTR standing dead-center of the Crypto floor.

Susan checked the clock. She had been waiting almost an hour. American Remailers Anonymous was apparently taking their time forwarding North Dakota's mail. She sighed heavily. Despite her efforts to forget her morning conversation with David, the words played over and over in her head. She knew she'd been hard on him. She prayed he was okay in Spain.

Her thoughts were jarred by the loud hiss of the glass doors. She looked up and groaned. Cryptographer Greg Hale stood in the opening.

Greg Hale was tall and muscular with thick blond hair and a deep cleft chin. He was loud, thick-fleshed, and perpetually overdressed. His fellow cryptographers had nicknamed him 'Halite' – after the mineral. Hale had always assumed it referred to some rare gem – paralleling his unrivaled intellect and rock-hard physique. Had his ego permitted him to consult an encyclopedia, he would have discovered it was nothing more than the salty residue left behind when oceans dried up.

Like all NSA cryptographers, Hale made a solid salary. However, he had a hard time keeping that fact to himself. He drove a white Lotus with a moon roof and a deafening subwoofer system. He was a gadget junkie, and his car was his showpiece; he'd installed a global positioning computer system, voice-activated door locks, a five-point radar jammer, and a cellular fax/phone so he'd never be out of touch with his message services. His vanity plate read MEGABYTE and was framed in violet neon.

Greg Hale had been rescued from a childhood of petty crime by the U.S. Marine Corps. It was there that he'd learned about computers. He was one of the best programmers the Marines had ever seen, well on his way to a distinguished military career. But two days before the completion of his third tour of duty, his future suddenly changed. Hale accidentally killed a fellow Marine in a drunken brawl. The Korean art of self-defense, Taekwondo, proved more deadly than defensive. He was promptly relieved of his duty.

After serving a brief prison term, Halite began looking for work in the private sector as a programmer. He was always up front about the incident in the Marines, and he courted prospective employers by offering a month's work without pay to prove his worth. He had

131

no shortage of takers, and once they found out what he could do with a computer, they never wanted to let him go.

As his computer expertise grew, Hale began making Internet connections all over the world. He was one of the new breed of cyberfreaks with E-mail friends in every nation, moving in and out of seedy electronic bulletin boards and European chat groups. He'd been fired by two different employers for using their business accounts to upload pornographic photos to some of his friends.

'What are *you* doing here?' Hale demanded, stopping in the doorway and staring at Susan. He'd obviously expected to have Node 3 to himself today.

Susan forced herself to stay cool. 'It's Saturday, Greg. I could ask you the same question.' But Susan knew what Hale was doing there. He was the consummate computer addict. Despite the Saturday rule, he often slipped into Crypto on weekends to use the NSA's unrivalled computing power to run new programs he was working on.

'Just wanted to re-tweak a few lines and check my E-mail,' Hale said. He eyed her curiously. 'What was it you said *you*'re doing here?'

'I didn't,' Susan replied.

Hale arched a surprised eyebrow. 'No reason to be coy. We have no secrets here in Node 3, remember? All for one and one for all.'

Susan sipped her lemon mist and ignored him. Hale shrugged and strode toward the Node 3 pantry. The pantry was always his first stop. As Hale crossed the room, he sighed heavily and made a point of ogling Susan's legs stretched out beneath her terminal.

132

Susan, without looking up, retracted her legs and kept working. Hale smirked.

Susan had gotten used to Hale hitting on her. His favorite line was something about interfacing to check the compatibility of their hardware. It turned Susan's stomach. She was too proud to complain to Strathmore about Hale; it was far easier just to ignore him.

Hale approached the Node 3 pantry and pulled open the lattice doors like a bull. He slid a Tupperware container of tofu out of the fridge and popped a few pieces of the gelatinous white substance in his mouth. Then he leaned on the stove and smoothed his gray Bellvienne slacks and well-starched shirt. 'You gonna be here long?'

'All night,' Susan said flatly.

'Hmm . . .' Halite cooed with his mouth full. 'A cozy Saturday in the playpen, just the two of us.'

'Just the *three* of us,' Susan interjected. 'Commander Strathmore's upstairs. You might want to disappear before he sees you.'

Hale shrugged. 'He doesn't seem to mind *you* here. He must really enjoy your company.'

Susan forced herself to keep silent.

Hale chuckled to himself and put away his tofu. Then he grabbed a quart of virgin olive oil and took a few swigs. He was a health fiend and claimed olive oil cleaned out his lower intestine. When he wasn't pushing carrot juice on the rest of the staff, he was preaching the virtues of high colonics.

Hale replaced the olive oil and went to down his computer directly opposite Susan. Even across the wide ring of terminals, Susan could smell his cologne. She crinkled her nose.

'Nice cologne, Greg. Use the entire bottle?'

Hale flicked on his terminal. 'Only for you, dear.'

As he sat there waiting for his terminal to warm up, Susan had a sudden unsettling thought. What if Hale accessed TRANSLTR's Run-Monitor? There was no logical reason why he would, but nonetheless Susan knew he would never fall for some half-baked story about a diagnostic that stumped TRANSLTR for sixteen hours. Hale would demand to know the truth. The truth was something Susan had no intention of telling him. She did not trust Greg Hale. He was not NSA material. Susan had been against hiring him in the first place, but the NSA had had no choice. Hale had been the product of damage control.

The Skipjack fiasco.

Four years ago, in an effort to create a single, public-key encryption standard, Congress charged the nation's best mathematicians, those at the NSA, to write a new superalgorithm. The plan was for Congress to pass legislation that made the new algorithm the nation's standard, thus alleviating the incompatibilities now suffered by corporations that used different algorithms.

Of course, asking the NSA to lend a hand in improving public-key encryption was somewhat akin to asking a condemned man to build his own coffin. TRANSLTR had not yet been conceived, and an encryption standard would only help to proliferate the use of code-writing and make the NSA's already difficult job that much harder.

The EFF understood this conflict of interest and lobbied vehemently that the NSA might create an algorithm of poor quality – something it could break. To appease these fears, Congress announced that when the NSA's algorithm was finished, the formula would be published for examination by the world's mathematicians to ensure its quality.

Reluctantly, the NSA's Crypto team, led by Commander Strathmore, created an algorithm they christened Skipjack. Skipjack was presented to Congress for their approval. Mathematicians from all over the world tested Skipjack and were unanimously impressed. They reported that it was a strong, untainted algorithm and would make a superb encryption standard. But three days before Congress was to vote their certain approval of Skipjack, a young programmer from Bell Laboratories, Greg Hale, shocked the world by announcing he'd found a back door hidden in the algorithm.

The back door consisted of a few lines of cunning programming that Commander Strathmore had inserted into the algorithm. It had been added in so shrewd a way that nobody, except Greg Hale, had seen it. Strathmore's covert addition, in effect, meant that any code written by Skipjack could be decrypted via a secret password known only to the NSA. Strathmore had come within inches of turning the nation's proposed encryption standard into the biggest intelligence coup the NSA had ever seen; the NSA would have held the master key to every code written in America.

The computer-savvy public was outraged. The EFF descended on the scandal like vultures, ripping Congress to shreds for their naïveté and proclaiming the NSA the biggest threat to the free world since Hitler. The encryption standard was dead.

It had come as little surprise when the NSA hired Greg Hale two days later. Strathmore felt it was better to have him on the inside working for the NSA than on the outside working against it.

Strathmore faced the Skipjack scandal head-on. He defended his actions vehemently to Congress. He argued that the public's craving for privacy would come back to haunt them. He insisted the public needed someone to watch over them; the public needed the NSA to break codes in order to keep the peace. Groups like the EFF felt differently. And they'd been fighting him ever since.

CHAPTER 24

David Becker stood in a phone booth across the street from La Clínica de Salud Pública; he'd just been ejected for harassing patient number 104, Monsieur Cloucharde.

Things were suddenly more complicated than he'd anticipated. His little favor to Strathmore – picking up some personal belongings – had turned into a scavenger hunt for some bizarre ring.

He'd just called Strathmore and told him about the German tourist. The news had not been received well. After demanding the specifics, Strathmore had fallen silent for a long time. 'David,' he had finally said very gravely, 'finding that ring is a matter of national security. I'm leaving it in your hands. Don't fail me.' The phone had gone dead.

David stood in the phone booth and sighed. He picked up the tattered Guía Telefónica and began scanning the yellow pages. 'Here goes nothing,' he muttered to himself.

There were only three listings for Escort Services in the directory, and he didn't have much to go on. All he knew was that the German's date had red hair, which conveniently was rare in Spain. The delirious Cloucharde had recalled the escort's name as Dewdrop. Becker cringed – Dewdrop? It sounded more like a cow than a beautiful girl. Not a good Catholic name at all; Cloucharde must have been mistaken.

Becker dialed the first number.

'Servicio Social de Sevilla,' a pleasant female voice answered.

Becker affected his Spanish with a thick German accent. 'Hola, hablas aleman?'

'No. But I speak English' came the reply.

Becker continued in broken English. 'Thank you. I wondering if you to help me?'

'How can we be of service?' The woman spoke slowly in an effort to aid her potential client. 'Perhaps you would like an escort?'

'Yes, please. Today my brother, Klaus, he has girl, very beautiful. Red hair. I want same. For tomorrow, please.'

'Your brother Klaus comes here?' The voice was suddenly effervescent, like they were old friends.

'Yes. He very fat. You remember him, no?'

'He was here today, you say?'

Becker could hear her checking the books. There would be no Klaus listed, but Becker figured clients seldom used their real names.

'Hmm, I'm sorry,' she apologized. 'I don't see him here. What was the girl's name your brother was with?'

'Had red hair,' Becker said, avoiding the question.

'Red hair?' she repeated. There was a pause. 'This is Servicio Social de Sevilla. Are you sure your brother comes here?'

'Sure, yes.'

'Señor, we have no redheads. We have only pure Andalusian beauties.'

'Red hair,' Becker repeated, feeling stupid.

'I'm sorry, we have no redheads at all, but if you—'

'Name is Dewdrop,' Becker blurted, feeling even stupider.

The ridiculous name apparently meant nothing to the woman. She apologized, suggested Becker was confusing her with another agency, and politely hung up.

Strike one.

Becker frowned and dialed the next number. It connected immediately.

'Buenas noches, Mujeres España. May I help you?'

Becker launched into his same spiel, a German tourist who was willing to pay top dollar for the red-haired girl who was out with his brother today.

This time the response was in polite German, but again no redheads. 'Keine Rotköpfe, I'm sorry.' The woman hung up.

Strike two.

Becker looked down at the phone book. There was only one number left. The end of the rope already.

He dialed.

'Escortes Belén,' a man answered in a very slick tone.

Again Becker told his story.

'Sí, sí, señor. My name is Señor Roldán. I would be pleased to help. We have two redheads. Lovely girls.'

Becker's heart leapt. 'Very beautiful?' he repeated in his German accent. 'Red hair?'

'Yes, what is your brother's name? I will tell you

who was his escort today. And we can send her to you tomorrow.'

'Klaus Schmidt.' Becker blurted a name recalled from an old textbook.

A long pause. 'Well, sir ... I don't see a Klaus Schmidt on our registry, but perhaps your brother chose to be discreet – perhaps a wife at home?' He laughed inappropriately.

'Yes, Klaus married. But he very fat. His wife no lie with him.' Becker rolled his eyes at himself reflected in the booth. *If Susan could hear me now,* he thought. 'I fat and lonely too. I want lie with her. Pay lots of money.'

Becker was giving an impressive performance, but he'd gone too far. Prostitution was illegal in Spain, and Señor Roldán was a careful man. He'd been burned before by Guardia officials posing as eager tourists. *I want lie with her.* Roldán knew it was a setup. If he said yes, he would be heavily fined and, as always, forced to provide one of his most talented escorts to the police commissioner free of charge for an entire weekend.

When Roldán spoke, his voice was not quite as friendly. 'Sir, this is Escortes Belén. May I ask who's calling?'

'Aah ... Sigmund Schmidt,' Becker invented weakly.

'Where did you get our number?'

'La Guía Telefónica – yellow pages.'

'Yes, sir, that's because we are an escort service.'

'Yes. I want escort.' Becker sensed something was wrong.

'Sir, Escortes Belén is a service providing escorts to businessmen for luncheons and dinners. This is why

140

we are listed in the phone book. What we do is legal. What you are looking for is a *prostitute.*' The word slid off his tongue like a vile disease.

'But my brother . . .'

'Sir, if your brother spent the day kissing a girl in the park, she was not one of ours. We have strict regulations about client–escort contact.'

'But . . .'

'You have us confused with someone else. We only have two redheads, Inmaculada and Rocío, and neither would allow a man to sleep with them for money. That is called prostitution, and it is illegal in Spain. Good night, sir.'

'But—'

CLICK.

Becker swore under his breath and dropped the phone back into its cradle. Strike three. He was certain Cloucharde had said the German had hired the girl for the entire weekend.

Becker stepped out of the phone booth at the intersection of Calle Salado and Avenida Asunción. Despite the traffic, the sweet scent of Seville oranges hung all around him. It was twilight – the most romantic hour. He thought of Susan. Strathmore's words invaded his mind: *Find the ring*. Becker flopped miserably on a bench and pondered his next move.

What move?

CHAPTER 25

Inside the Clínica de Salud Pública, visiting hours were over. The gymnasium lights had been turned out. Pierre Cloucharde was fast asleep. He did not see the figure hunched over him. The needle of a stolen syringe glinted in the dark. Then it disappeared into the IV tube just above Cloucharde's wrist. The hypodermic contained 30 cc of cleaning fluid stolen from a janitor's cart. With great force, a strong thumb rammed the plunger down and forced the bluish liquid into the old man's veins.

Cloucharde was awake only for a few seconds. He might have screamed in pain had a strong hand not been clamped across his mouth. He lay trapped on his cot, pinned beneath a seemingly immovable weight. He could feel the pocket of fire searing its way up his arm. There was an excruciating pain traveling through his armpit, his chest, and then, like a million shattering pieces of glass, it hit his brain. Cloucharde saw a brilliant flash of light . . . and then nothing.

The visitor released his grip and peered through the darkness at the name on the medical chart. Then he slipped silently out.

On the street, the man in wire-rim glasses reached to a tiny device attached to his belt. The rectangular pack was about the size of a credit card. It was a prototype of the new Monocle computer. Developed by the U.S. Navy to help technicians record battery voltages in cramped quarters on submarines, the miniature computer packed a cellular modem and the newest advances in microtechnology. Its visual monitor was a transparent liquid crystal display, mounted in the left lens of a pair of eyeglasses. The Monocle reflected a whole new age in personal computing; the user could now look *through* his data and still interact with the world around him.

The Monocle's real coup, though, was not its miniature display but rather its data entry system. A user entered information via tiny contacts fixed to his fingertips; touching the contacts together in sequence mimicked a shorthand similar to court stenography. The computer would then translate the shorthand into English.

The killer pressed a tiny switch, and his glasses flickered to life. His hands inconspicuously at his sides, he began touching different fingertips together in rapid succession. A message appeared before his eyes.

SUBJECT: P. CLOUCHARDE — TERMINATED

He smiled. Transmitting notification of kills was part of his assignment. But including victims' names . . . that, to the man in the wire-rim glasses, was elegance. His fingers flashed again, and his cellular modem activated.

MESSAGE SENT

CHAPTER 26

Sitting on the bench across from the public clinic, Becker wondered what he was supposed to do now. His calls to the escort agencies had turned up nothing. The commander, uneasy about communication over unsecured public phones, had asked David not to call again until he had the ring. Becker considered going to the local police for help – maybe they had a record of a red-headed hooker – but Strathmore had given strict orders about that too. *You are invisible. No one is to know this ring exists.*

Becker wondered if he was supposed to wander the drugged-out district of Triana in search of this mystery woman. Or maybe he was supposed to check all the restaurants for an obese German. Everything seemed like a waste of time.

Strathmore's words kept coming back: *It's a matter of national security . . . you must find that ring.*

A voice in the back of Becker's head told him he'd missed something – something crucial – but for the life of him, he couldn't think what it would be. *I'm a teacher, not a damned secret agent!* He was beginning to wonder why Strathmore hadn't sent a professional.

144

Becker stood up and walked aimlessly down Calle Delicias pondering his options. The cobblestone sidewalk blurred beneath his gaze. Night was falling fast. *Dewdrop.*

There was something about that absurd name that nagged at the back of his mind. *Dewdrop.* The slick voice of Señor Roldán at Escortes Belén was on endless loop in his head. *'We only have two redheads . . . Two redheads, Inmaculada and Rocío . . . Rocío . . . Rocío . . .'*

Becker stopped short. He suddenly knew. *And I call myself a language specialist?* He couldn't believe he'd missed it.

Rocío was one of the most popular girl's names in Spain. It carried all the right implications for a young Catholic girl – purity, virginity, natural beauty. The connotations of purity all stemmed from the name's literal meaning – *Drop of Dew!*

The old Canadian's voice rang in Becker's ears. *Dewdrop.* Rocío had translated her name to the only language she and her client had in common – English. Excited, Becker hurried off to find a phone.

Across the street, a man in wire-rim glasses followed just out of sight.

CHAPTER 27

On the Crypto floor, the shadows were growing long and faint. Overhead, the automatic lighting gradually increased to compensate. Susan was still at her terminal silently awaiting news from her tracer. It was taking longer than expected.

Her mind had been wandering – missing David and willing Greg Hale to go home. Although Hale hadn't budged, thankfully he'd been silent, engrossed in whatever he was doing at his terminal. Susan couldn't care less what Hale was doing, as long as he didn't access the Run-Monitor. He obviously hadn't – sixteen hours would have brought an audible yelp of disbelief.

Susan was sipping her third cup of tea when it finally happened – her terminal beeped once. Her pulse quickened. A flashing envelope icon appeared on her monitor announcing the arrival of E-mail. Susan shot a quick glance toward Hale. He was absorbed in his work. She held her breath and double-clicked the envelope.

'North Dakota,' she whispered to herself. 'Let's see who you are.'

When the E-mail opened, it was a single line. Susan read it. And then she read it again.

DINNER AT ALFREDO'S? 8 PM?

Across the room, Hale muffled a chuckle. Susan checked the message header.

FROM: GHALE@CRYPTO.NSA.GOV

Susan felt a surge of anger but fought it off. She deleted the message. 'Very mature, Greg.'

'They make a great carpaccio.' Hale smiled. 'What do you say? Afterward we could—'

'Forget it.'

'Snob.' Hale sighed and turned back to his terminal. That was strike eighty-nine with Susan Fletcher. The brilliant female cryptographer was a constant frustration to him. Hale had often fantasized about having sex with her – pinning her against TRANSLTR's curved hull and taking her right there against the warm black tile. But Susan would have nothing to do with him. In Hale's mind, what made things worse was that she was in love with some university teacher who slaved for hours on end for peanuts. It would be a pity for Susan to dilute her superior gene pool pro-creating with some geek – particularly when she could have Greg. *We'd have perfect children*, he thought.

'What are you working on?' Hale asked, trying a different approach.

Susan said nothing.

'Some team player *you* are. Sure I can't have a peek?' Hale stood and started moving around the circle of terminals toward her.

Susan sensed that Hale's curiosity had the potential to cause some serious problems today. She made a snap decision. 'It's a diagnostic,' she offered, falling back on the commander's lie.

Hale stopped in his tracks. 'Diagnostic?' He sounded doubtful. 'You're spending Saturday running a diagnostic instead of playing with the prof?'

'His name is David.'

'Whatever.'

Susan glared at him. 'Haven't you got anything better to do?'

'Are you trying to get rid of me?' Hale pouted.

'Actually, yes.'

'Gee, Sue, I'm hurt.'

Susan Fletcher's eyes narrowed. She hated being called Sue. She had nothing against the nickname, but Hale was the only one who'd ever used it.

'Why don't I help you?' Hale offered. He was suddenly circling toward her again. 'I'm great with diagnostics. Besides, I'm dying to see what diagnostic could make the mighty Susan Fletcher come to work on a Saturday.'

Susan felt a surge of adrenaline. She glanced down at the tracer on her screen. She knew she couldn't let Hale see it – he'd have too many questions. 'I've got it covered, Greg,' she said.

But Hale kept coming. As he circled toward her terminal, Susan knew she had to act fast. Hale was only a few yards away when she made her move. She stood to meet his towering frame, blocking his way. His cologne was overpowering.

She looked him straight in the eye. 'I said no.'

Hale cocked his head, apparently intrigued by her odd display of secrecy. He playfully stepped closer.

Greg Hale was not ready for what happened next.

With unwavering cool, Susan pressed a single index finger against his rock-hard chest, stopping his forward motion.

Hale halted and stepped back in shock. Apparently Susan Fletcher was serious; she had *never* touched him before, ever. It wasn't quite what Hale had had in mind for their first contact, but it was a start. He gave her a long puzzled look and slowly returned to his terminal. As he sat back down, one thing became perfectly clear: The lovely Susan Fletcher was working on something important, and it sure as hell wasn't any diagnostic.

CHAPTER 28

Señor Roldán was sitting behind his desk at Escortes Belén congratulating himself for deftly sidestepping the Guardia's newest pathetic attempt to trap him. Having an officer fake a German accent and request a girl for the night – it was entrapment; what would they think of next?

The phone on his desk buzzed loudly. Señor Roldán scooped up the receiver with a confident flair. 'Buenas noches, Escortes Belén.'

'Buenas noches,' a man's voice said in lightning-fast Spanish. He sounded nasal, like he had a slight cold. 'Is this a hotel?'

'No, sir. What number are you dialing?' Señor Roldán was not going to fall for any more tricks this evening.

'34-62-10,' the voice said.

Roldán frowned. The voice sounded vaguely familiar. He tried to place the accent – Burgos, maybe? 'You've dialed the correct number,' Roldán offered cautiously, 'but this is an escort service.'

There was a pause on the line. 'Oh ... I see. I'm sorry. Somebody wrote down this number; I thought it was a hotel. I'm visiting here, from Burgos. My apologies for disturbing you. Good nigh—'

'Espére! Wait!' Señor Roldán couldn't help himself; he was a salesman at heart. Was this a referral? A new client from up north? He wasn't going to let a little paranoia blow a potential sale.

'My friend,' Roldán gushed into the phone. 'I thought I recognized a bit of a Burgos accent on you. I myself am from Valencia. What brings you to Seville?'

'I sell jewelry. Majórica pearls.'

'Majóricas, reeaally! You must travel quite a bit.'

The voice coughed sickly. 'Well, yes, I do.'

'In Seville on business?' Roldán pressed. There was no way in hell this guy was Guardia; he was a customer with a capital C. 'Let me guess – a friend gave you our number? He told you to give us a call. Am I right?'

The voice was obviously embarrassed. 'Well, no, actually, it's nothing like that.'

'Don't be shy, señor. We are an escort service, nothing to be ashamed of. Lovely girls, dinner dates, that is all. Who gave you our number? Perhaps he is a regular. I can give you a special rate.'

The voice became flustered. 'Ah . . . nobody actually *gave* me this number. I found it with a passport. I'm trying to find the owner.'

Roldán's heart sank. This man was not a customer after all. 'You *found* the number, you say?'

'Yes, I found a man's passport in the park today. Your number was on a scrap of paper inside. I thought perhaps it was the man's hotel; I was hoping to return his passport to him. My mistake. I'll just drop it off at a police station on my way out of—'

'Perdón,' Roldán interrupted nervously. 'Might I

suggest a better idea?' Roldán prided himself on discretion, and visits to the Guardia had a way of making his customers ex-customers. 'Consider this,' he offered. 'Because the man with the passport had our number, he is most likely a client here. Perhaps I could save you a trip to the police.'

The voice hesitated. 'I don't know. I should probably just—'

'Do not be too hasty, my friend. I'm ashamed to admit that the police here in Seville are not always as efficient as the police up north. It could be *days* before this man's passport is returned to him. If you tell me his name, I could see that he gets his passport *immediately.*'

'Yes, well . . . I suppose there's no harm . . .' Some paper rustled, and the voice returned. 'It's a German name. I can't quite pronounce it . . . Gusta . . . Gustafson?'

Roldán didn't recognize the name, but he had clients from all over the world. They never left their real names. 'What does he look like – in his photo? Perhaps I will recognize him.'

'Well . . .' the voice said. 'His face is very, very fat.'

Roldán immediately knew. He remembered the obese face well. It was the man with Rocío. It was odd, he thought, to have two calls about the German in one night.

'Mr Gustafson?' Roldán forced a chuckle. 'Of course! I know him well. If you bring me his passport, I'll see he gets it.'

'I'm downtown without a car,' the voice interrupted. 'Maybe you could come to me?'

'Actually,' Roldán hedged, 'I can't leave the phone. But it's really not that far if you—'

'I'm sorry, it's late to be out wandering about. There's a Guardia precinct nearby. I'll drop it there, and when you see Mr Gustafson, you can tell him where it is.'

'No, wait!' Roldán cried. 'The police really needn't be involved. You said you're downtown, right? Do you know the Alfonso XIII Hotel? It's one of the city's finest.'

'Yes,' the voice said. 'I know the Alfonso XIII. It's nearby.'

'Wonderful! Mr Gustafson is a guest there tonight. He's probably there now.'

The voice hesitated. 'I see. Well, then . . . I suppose it would be no trouble.'

'Superb! He's having dinner with one of our escorts in the hotel restaurant.' Roldán knew they were probably in bed by now, but he needed to be careful not to offend the caller's refined sensibilities. 'Just leave the passport with the concierge, his name is Manuel. Tell him I sent you. Ask him to give it to Rocío. Rocío is Mr Gustafson's date for the evening. She will see that the passport is returned. You might slip your name and address inside – perhaps Mr Gustafson will send you a little thank you.'

'A fine idea. The Alfonso XIII. Very well, I'll take it over right now. Thank you for your help.'

David Becker hung up the phone. 'Alfonso XIII.' He chuckled. 'Just have to know how to ask.'

Moments later a silent figure followed Becker up Calle Delicias into the softly settling Andalusian night.

CHAPTER 29

Still unnerved from her encounter with Hale, Susan gazed out through the one-way glass of Node 3. The Crypto floor was empty. Hale was silent again, engrossed. She wished he would leave.

She wondered if she should call Strathmore; the commander could simply kick Hale out – after all, it *was* Saturday. Susan knew, however, that if Hale got kicked out, he would immediately become suspicious. Once dismissed, he probably would start calling other cryptographers asking what they thought was going on. Susan decided it was better just to let Hale be. He would leave on his own soon enough.

An unbreakable algorithm. She sighed, her thoughts returning to Digital Fortress. It amazed her that an algorithm like that could really be created – then again, the proof was right there in front of her; TRANSLTR appeared useless against it.

Susan thought of Strathmore, nobly bearing the weight of this ordeal on his shoulders, doing what was necessary, staying cool in the face of disaster.

Susan sometimes saw David in Strathmore. They had many of the same qualities – tenacity, dedication, intelligence. Sometimes Susan thought Strathmore would be lost without her; the purity of her love for cryptography seemed to be an emotional lifeline to Strathmore, lifting him from the sea of churning politics and reminding him of his early days as a code-breaker.

Susan relied on Strathmore too; he was her shelter in a world of power-hungry men, nurturing her career, protecting her, and, as he often joked, making all her dreams come true. There was some truth to that, she thought. As unintentional as it may have been, the commander was the one who'd made the call that brought David Becker to the NSA that fateful afternoon. Her mind reeled back to him, and her eyes fell instinctively to the pull-slide beside her keyboard. There was a small fax taped there.

The fax had been there for seven months. It was the only code Susan Fletcher had yet to break. It was from David. She read it for the five-hundredth time.

PLEASE ACCEPT THIS HUMBLE FAX
MY LOVE FOR YOU IS WITHOUT WAX

He'd sent it to her after a minor tiff. She'd begged him for months to tell her what it meant, but he had refused. *Without wax.* It was David's revenge. Susan had taught David a lot about code-breaking, and to keep him on his toes, she had taken to encoding all of her messages to him with some simple encryption scheme. Shopping lists, love notes – they were all encrypted. It was a game, and David had become quite a good cryptographer. Then he'd decided to return the favor. He'd started signing all his letters 'Without wax, David.' Susan had over two dozen notes from David. They were all signed the same way. *Without wax.*

Susan begged to know the hidden meaning, but David wasn't talking. Whenever she asked, he simply smiled and said, *'You're* the code-breaker.'

The NSA's head cryptographer had tried everything – substitutions, cipher boxes, even anagrams. She'd run the letters 'without wax' through her computer and asked for rearrangements of the letters into new phrases. All she'd gotten back was: TAXI HUT WOW. It appeared Ensei Tankado was not the only one who could write unbreakable codes.

Her thoughts were interrupted by the sound of the pneumatic doors hissing open. Strathmore strode in.

'Susan, any word yet?' Strathmore saw Greg Hale and stopped short. 'Well, good evening, Mr Hale.' He frowned, his eyes narrowing. 'On a Saturday, no less. To what do we owe the honor?'

Hale smiled innocently. 'Just making sure I pull my weight.'

'I see.' Strathmore grunted, apparently weighing his options. After a moment, it seemed he too decided not to rock Hale's boat. He turned coolly to Susan. 'Ms Fletcher, could I speak to you for a moment? *Outside?'*

Susan hesitated. 'Ah . . . yes, sir.' She shot an uneasy glance at her monitor and then across the room at Greg Hale. 'Just a minute.'

With a few quick keystrokes, she pulled up a program called ScreenLock. It was a privacy utility. Every terminal in Node 3 was equipped with it. Because the terminals stayed on around the clock, ScreenLock enabled cryptographers to leave their stations and know that nobody would tamper with their files.

Susan entered her five-character privacy code, and her screen went black. It would remain that way until she returned and typed the proper sequence.

Then she slipped on her shoes and followed the commander out.

'What the hell is *he* doing here?' Strathmore demanded as soon as he and Susan were outside Node 3.

'His usual,' Susan replied. 'Nothing.'

Strathmore looked concerned. 'Has he said anything about TRANSLTR?'

'No. But if he accesses the Run-Monitor and sees it registering seventeen hours, he'll have something to say all right.'

Strathmore considered it. 'There's no reason he'd access it.'

Susan eyed the commander. 'You want to send him home?'

'No. We'll let him be.' Strathmore glanced over at the Sys-Sec office. 'Has Chartrukian left yet?'

'I don't know. I haven't seen him.'

'Jesus.' Strathmore groaned. 'This is a circus.' He ran a hand across the beard stubble that had darkened his face over the past thirty-six hours. 'Any word yet on the tracer? I feel like I'm sitting on my hands up there.'

'Not yet. Any word from David?'

Strathmore shook his head. 'I asked him not to call me until he has the ring.'

Susan looked surprised. 'Why not? What if he needs help?'

Strathmore shrugged. 'I can't help him from here – he's on his own. Besides, I'd rather not talk on unsecured lines just in case someone's listening.'

Susan's eyes widened in concern. 'What's *that* supposed to mean?'

Strathmore immediately looked apologetic. He gave her a reassuring smile. 'David's fine. I'm just being careful.'

Thirty feet away from their conversation, hidden behind the one-way glass of Node 3, Greg Hale stood at Susan's terminal. Her screen was black. Hale glanced out at the commander and Susan. Then he reached for his wallet. He extracted a small index card and read it.

Double-checking that Strathmore and Susan were still talking, Hale carefully typed five keystrokes on Susan's keyboard. A second later her monitor sprang to life.

'Bingo.' He chuckled.

Stealing the Node 3 privacy codes had been simple. In Node 3, every terminal had an identical detachable keyboard. Hale had simply taken his keyboard home one night and installed a chip that kept a record of every keystroke made on it. Then he had come in early, swapped his modified keyboard for someone else's, and waited. At the end of the day, he switched back and viewed the data recorded by the chip. Even though there were millions of keystrokes to sort through, finding the access code was simple; the first thing a cryptographer did every morning was type the privacy code that unlocked his terminal. This, of course, made Hale's job effortless – the privacy code always appeared as the first five characters on the list.

It was ironic, Hale thought as he gazed at Susan's monitor. He'd stolen the privacy codes just for kicks.

He was happy now he'd done it; the program on Susan's screen looked significant.

Hale puzzled over it for a moment. It was written in LIMBO – not one of his specialties. Just by looking at it, though, Hale could tell one thing for certain – this was *not* a diagnostic. He could make sense of only two words. But they were enough.

TRACER SEARCHING . . .

'Tracer?' he said aloud. 'Searching for *what?*' Hale felt suddenly uneasy. He sat a moment studying Susan's screen. Then he made his decision.

Hale understood enough about the LIMBO programming language to know that it borrowed heavily from two other languages – C and Pascal – both of which he knew cold. Glancing up to check that Strathmore and Susan were still talking outside, Hale improvised. He entered a few modified Pascal commands and hit RETURN. The tracer's status window responded exactly as he had hoped.

TRACER ABORT?

He quickly typed: YES

ARE YOU SURE?

Again he typed: YES
After a moment the computer beeped.

TRACER ABORTED

Hale smiled. The terminal had just sent a message

telling Susan's tracer to self-destruct prematurely. Whatever she was looking for would have to wait.

Mindful to leave no evidence, Hale expertly navigated his way into her system activity log and deleted all the commands he'd just typed. Then he reentered Susan's privacy code.

The monitor went black.

When Susan Fletcher returned to Node 3, Greg Hale was seated quietly at his terminal.

CHAPTER 30

Alfonso XIII was a small four-star hotel set back from the Puerta de Jerez and surrounded by a thick wrought-iron fence and lilacs. David made his way up the marble stairs. As he reached for the door, it magically opened, and a bellhop ushered him inside.

'Baggage, señor? May I help you?'

'No, thanks. I need to see the concierge.'

The bellhop looked hurt, as if something in their two-second encounter had not been satisfactory. 'Por aquí, señor.' He led Becker into the lobby, pointed to the concierge, and hurried off.

The lobby was exquisite, small and elegantly appointed. Spain's Golden Age had long since passed, but for a while in the mid-1600s, this small nation had ruled the world. The room was a proud reminder of that era – suits of armor, military etchings, and a display case of gold ingots from the New World.

Hovering behind the counter marked CONSERJE was a trim, well-groomed man smiling so eagerly that it appeared he'd waited his entire life to be of assistance. 'En qué puedo servirle, señor? How may I serve you?'

He spoke with an affected lisp and ran his eyes up and down Becker's body.

Becker responded in Spanish. 'I need to speak to Manuel.'

The man's well-tanned face smiled even wider. 'Sí, sí, señor. I am Manuel. What is it you desire?'

'Señor Roldán at Escortes Belén told me you would—'

The concierge silenced Becker with a wave and glanced nervously around the lobby. 'Why don't you step over here?' He led Becker to the end of the counter. 'Now,' he continued, practically in a whisper. 'How may I help you?'

Becker began again, lowering his voice. 'I need to speak to one of his escorts whom I believe is dining here. Her name is Rocío.'

The concierge let out his breath as though overwhelmed. 'Aaah, Rocío – a beautiful creature.'

'I need to see her immediately.'

'But, señor, she is with a client.'

Becker nodded apologetically. 'It's important.' *A matter of national security.*

The concierge shook his head. 'Impossible. Perhaps if you left a—'

'It will only take a moment. Is she in the dining room?'

The concierge shook his head. 'Our dining room closed half an hour ago. I'm afraid Rocío and her guest have retired for the evening. If you'd like to leave me a message, I can give it to her in the morning.' He motioned to the bank of numbered message boxes behind him.

'If I could just call her room and—'

'I'm sorry,' the concierge said, his politeness

evaporating. 'The Alfonso XIII has strict policies regarding client privacy.'

Becker had no intention of waiting ten hours for a fat man and a prostitute to wander down for breakfast.

'I understand,' Becker said. 'Sorry to bother you.' He turned and walked back into the lobby. He strode directly to a cherry roll-top desk that had caught his eye on his way in. It held a generous supply of Alfonso XIII postcards and stationery as well as pens and envelopes. Becker sealed a blank piece of paper in an envelope and wrote one word on the envelope.

ROCÍO.

Then he went back to the concierge.

'I'm sorry to trouble you again,' Becker said approaching sheepishly. 'I'm being a bit of a fool, I know. I was hoping to tell Rocío personally how much I enjoyed our time together the other day. But I'm leaving town tonight. Perhaps I'll just leave her a note after all.' Becker laid the envelope on the counter.

The concierge looked down at the envelope and clucked sadly to himself. *Another lovesick heterosexual,* he thought. *What a waste.* He looked up and smiled. 'But of course, Mr . . . ?'

'Buisán,' Becker said. 'Miguel Buisán.'

'Of course. I'll be sure Rocío gets this in the morning.'

'Thank you.' Becker smiled and turned to go.

The concierge, after discreetly checking out Becker's backside, scooped up the envelope off the counter and turned to the bank of numbered slots on the wall behind him. Just as the man slipped the envelope into one of the slots, Becker spun with one final inquiry.

163

'Where might I call a taxi?'

The concierge turned from the wall of cubbyholes and answered. But Becker did not hear his response. The timing had been perfect. The concierge's hand was just emerging from a box marked Suite 301.

Becker thanked the concierge and slowly wandered off looking for the elevator.

In and out, he repeated to himself.

CHAPTER 31

Susan returned to Node 3. Her conversation with Strathmore had made her increasingly anxious about David's safety. Her imagination was running wild.

'So,' Hale spouted from his terminal. 'What did Strathmore want? A romantic evening alone with his head cryptographer?'

Susan ignored the comment and settled in at her terminal. She typed her privacy code and the screen came to life. The tracer program came into view; it still had not returned any information on North Dakota.

Damn, Susan thought. *What's taking so long?*

'You seem uptight,' Hale said innocently. 'Having trouble with your diagnostic?'

'Nothing serious,' she replied. But Susan wasn't so sure. The tracer was overdue. She wondered if maybe she'd made a mistake while writing it. She began scanning the long lines of LIMBO programming on her screen, searching for anything that could be holding things up.

Hale observed her smugly. 'Hey, I meant to ask you,' he ventured. 'What do you make of that unbreakable algorithm Ensei Tankado said he was writing?'

Susan's stomach did a flip. She looked up. 'Unbreakable algorithm?' She caught herself. 'Oh, yeah . . . I think I read something about that.'

'Pretty incredible claim.'

'Yeah,' Susan replied, wondering why Hale had suddenly brought it up. 'I don't buy it, though. Everyone knows an unbreakable algorithm is a mathematical impossibility.'

Hale smiled. 'Oh, yeah . . . the Bergofsky Principle.'

'And common sense,' she snapped.

'Who knows . . .' Hale sighed dramatically. 'There are more things in heaven and earth than are dreamt of in your philosophy.'

'I beg your pardon?'

'Shakespeare,' Hale offered. *'Hamlet.'*

'Read a lot while you were in jail?'

Hale chuckled. 'Seriously, Susan, did you ever think that maybe it *is* possible, that maybe Tankado really *did* write an unbreakable algorithm?'

This conversation was making Susan uneasy. 'Well, *we* couldn't do it.'

'Maybe Tankado's better than we are.'

'Maybe.' Susan shrugged, feigning disinterest.

'We corresponded for a while,' Hale offered casually. 'Tankado and me. Did you know that?'

Susan looked up, attempting to hide her shock. 'Really?'

'Yeah. After I uncovered the Skipjack algorithm, he wrote me – said we were brothers in the global fight for digital privacy.'

Susan could barely contain her disbelief. *Hale knows Tankado personally!* She did her best to look uninterested.

Hale went on. 'He congratulated me for proving

that Skipjack had a back door – called it a coup for privacy rights of civilians all over the world. You gotta admit, Susan, the back door in Skipjack was an underhanded play. Reading the world's E-mail? If you ask me, Strathmore *deserved* to get caught.'

'Greg,' Susan snapped, fighting her anger, 'that back door was so the NSA could decode E-mail that threatened this nation's security.'

'Oh, really?' Hale sighed innocently. 'And snooping the average citizen was just a lucky by-product?'

'We don't snoop average citizens, and you know it. The FBI can tap telephones, but that doesn't mean they listen to *every* call that's ever made.'

'If they had the manpower, they would.'

Susan ignored the remark. 'Governments should have the right to gather information that threatens the common good.'

'Jesus Christ' – Hale sighed – 'you sound like you've been brainwashed by Strathmore. You know damn well the FBI can't listen in whenever they want – they've got to get a warrant. A spiked encryption standard would mean the NSA could listen in to *anyone, anytime, anywhere*.'

'You're right – as we *should* be able to!' Susan's voice was suddenly harsh. 'If you hadn't uncovered the back door in Skipjack, we'd have access to *every* code we need to break, instead of just what TRANSLTR can handle.'

'If I hadn't found the back door,' Hale argued, 'someone else would have. I saved your asses by uncovering it when I did. Can you imagine the fallout if Skipjack had been in circulation when the news broke?'

'Either way,' Susan shot back, 'now we've got a

paranoid EFF who think we put back doors in *all* our algorithms.'

Hale asked smugly, 'Well, don't we?'

Susan eyed him coldly.

'Hey,' he said, backing off, 'the point is moot now anyway. You built TRANSLTR. You've got your instant information source. You can read *what* you want, *when* you want – no questions asked. You win.'

'Don't you mean *we* win? Last I heard, you worked for the NSA.'

'Not for long,' Hale chirped.

'Don't make promises.'

'I'm serious. Someday I'm getting out of here.'

'I'll be crushed.'

In that moment, Susan found herself wanting to curse Hale for everything that wasn't going right. She wanted to curse him for Digital Fortress, for her troubles with David, for the fact that she wasn't in the Smokies – but none of it was his fault. Hale's only fault was that he was obnoxious. Susan needed to be the bigger person. It was her responsibility as head cryptographer to keep the peace, to educate. Hale was young and naïve.

Susan looked over at him. It was frustrating, she thought, that Hale had the talent to be an asset in Crypto, but he still hadn't grasped the importance of what the NSA did.

'Greg,' Susan said, her voice quiet and controlled, 'I'm under a lot of pressure today. I just get upset when you talk about the NSA like we're some kind of high-tech peeping Tom. This organization was founded for one purpose – to protect the security of this nation. That may involve shaking a few trees and looking for the bad apples from time to time. I think most citizens would gladly sacrifice some privacy to know that the bad guys can't maneuver unchecked.'

Hale said nothing.

'Sooner or later,' Susan argued, 'the people of this nation need to put their trust somewhere. There's a lot of good out there – but there's also a lot of bad mixed in. Someone has to have access to all of it and separate the right from wrong. That's our job. That's our duty. Whether we like it or not, there is a frail gate separating democracy from anarchy. The NSA guards that gate.'

Hale nodded thoughtfully. 'Quis custodiet ipsos custodes?'

Susan looked puzzled.

'It's Latin,' Hale said. 'From *Satires* of Juvenal. It means "Who will guard the guards?" '

'I don't get it,' Susan said. '"Who will guard the guards?"'

'Yeah. If *we're* the guards of society, then who will watch *us* and make sure that *we're* not dangerous?'

Susan nodded, unsure how to respond.

Hale smiled. 'It's how Tankado signed all his letters to me. It was his favorite saying.'

CHAPTER 32

David Becker stood in the hallway outside suite 301. He knew that somewhere behind the ornately carved door was the ring. *A matter of national security.*

Becker could hear movement inside the room. Faint talking. He knocked. A deep German accent called out.

'Ja?'

Becker remained silent.

'Ja?'

The door opened a crack, and a rotund Germanic face gazed down at him.

Becker smiled politely. He did not know the man's name. 'Deutscher, ja?' he asked. 'German, right?'

The man nodded, uncertain.

Becker continued in perfect German. 'May I speak to you a moment?'

The man looked uneasy. 'Was wollen Sie? What do you want?'

Becker realized he should have rehearsed this before brazenly knocking on a stranger's door. He searched for the right words. 'You have something I need.'

These were apparently not the right words. The German's eyes narrowed.

'Ein ring,' Becker said. 'Du hast einen Ring. You have a ring.'

'Go away,' the German growled. He started to close the door. Without thinking, Becker slid his foot into the crack and jammed the door open. He immediately regretted the action.

The German's eyes went wide. 'Was tust du?' he demanded. 'What are you doing?'

Becker knew he was in over his head. He glanced nervously up and down the hall. He'd already been thrown out of the clinic; he had no intention of going two for two.

'Nimm deinen Fuß weg!' the German bellowed. 'Remove your foot!'

Becker scanned the man's pudgy fingers for a ring. Nothing. *I'm so close,* he thought. 'Ein Ring!' Becker repeated as the door slammed shut.

David Becker stood a long moment in the well-furnished hallway. A replica of a Salvador Dali hung nearby. 'Fitting,' Becker groaned. *Surrealism. I'm trapped in an absurd dream.* He'd woken up that morning in his own bed but had somehow ended up in Spain breaking into a stranger's hotel room on a quest for some magical ring.

Strathmore's stern voice pulled him back to reality: *You must find that ring.*

Becker took a deep breath and blocked out the words. He wanted to go home. He looked back to the door marked 301. His ticket home was just on the other side – a gold ring. All he had to do was get it.

He exhaled purposefully. Then he strode back to

suite 301 and knocked loudly on the door. It was time to play hardball.

The German yanked open the door and was about to protest, but Becker cut him off. He flashed his Maryland squash club ID and barked, 'Polizei!' Then Becker pushed his way into the room and threw on the lights.

Wheeling, the German squinted in shock. 'Was machst—'

'Silence!' Becker switched to English. 'Do you have a prostitute in this room?' Becker peered around the room. It was as plush as any hotel room he'd ever seen. Roses, champagne, a huge canopy bed. Rocío was nowhere to be seen. The bathroom door was closed.

'Prostituiert?' The German glanced uneasily at the closed bathroom door. He was larger than Becker had imagined. His hairy chest began right under his triple chin and sloped outward to his colossal gut. The drawstring of his white terry-cloth Alfonso XIII bathrobe barely reached around his waist.

Becker stared up at the giant with his most intimidating look. 'What is your name?'

A look of panic rippled across the German's corpulent face. 'Was willst du? What do you want?'

'I am with the tourist relations branch of the Spanish Guardia here in Seville. Do you have a prostitute in this room?'

The German glanced nervously at the bathroom door. He hesitated. 'Ja,' he finally admitted.

'Do you know this is illegal in Spain?'

'Nein,' the German lied. 'I did not know. I'll send her home right now.'

172

'I'm afraid it's too late for that,' Becker said with authority. He strolled casually into the room. 'I have a proposition for you.'

'Ein Vorschlag?' The German gasped. 'A proposition?'

'Yes. I can take you to headquarters right now . . .' Becker paused dramatically and cracked his knuckles.

'Or what?' the German asked, his eyes widening in fear.

'Or we make a deal.'

'What kind of deal?' The German had heard stories about the corruption in the Spanish Guardia Civil.

'You have something I want,' Becker said.

'Yes, of course!' the German effused, forcing a smile. He went immediately to the wallet on his dresser. 'How much?'

Becker let his jaw drop in mock indignation. 'Are you trying to bribe an officer of the law?' he bellowed.

'No! Of course not! I just thought . . .' The obese man quickly set down his wallet. 'I . . . I . . .' He was totally flustered. He collapsed on the corner of the bed and wrung his hands. The bed groaned under his weight. 'I'm sorry.'

Becker pulled a rose from the vase in the center of the room and casually smelled it before letting it fall to the floor. He spun suddenly. 'What can you tell me about the murder?'

The German went white. 'Mord? Murder?'

'Yes. The Asian man this morning? In the park? It was an assassination – Ermordung.' Becker loved the German word for assassination. Ermordung. It was so chilling.

'Ermordung? He . . . he was . . . ?'

'Yes.'

'But . . . but that's impossible,' the German choked. 'I was there. He had a heart attack. I saw it. No blood. No bullets.'

Becker shook his head condescendingly. 'Things are not always as they seem.'

The German went whiter still.

Becker gave an inward smile. The lie had served its purpose. The poor German was sweating profusely.

'Wh-wh-at do you want?' he stammered. 'I know nothing.'

Becker began pacing. 'The murdered man was wearing a gold ring. I need it.'

'I-I don't have it.'

Becker sighed patronizingly and motioned to the bathroom door. 'And Rocío? Dewdrop?'

The man went from white to purple. 'You know Dewdrop?' He wiped the sweat from his fleshy forehead and drenched his terry-cloth sleeve. He was about to speak when the bathroom door swung open.

Both men looked up.

Rocío Eva Granada stood in the doorway. A vision. Long flowing red hair, perfect Iberian skin, deep-brown eyes, a high smooth forehead. She wore a white terry-cloth robe that matched the German's. The tie was drawn snugly over her wide hips, and the neck fell loosely open to reveal her tanned cleavage. She stepped into the bedroom, the picture of confidence.

'May I help you?' she asked in throaty English.

Becker gazed across the room at the stunning woman before him and did not blink. 'I need the ring,' he said coldly.

'Who are you?' she demanded.

Becker switched to Spanish with a dead-on Andalusian accent. 'Guardia Civil.'

She laughed. 'Impossible,' she replied in Spanish.

Becker felt a knot rise in his throat. Rocío was clearly a little tougher than her client. 'Impossible?' he repeated, keeping his cool. 'Shall I take you downtown to prove it?'

Rocío smirked. 'I will not embarrass you by accepting your offer. Now, who are you?'

Becker stuck to his story. 'I am with the Seville Guardia.'

Rocío stepped menacingly toward him. 'I know every police officer on the force. They are my best clients.'

Becker felt her stare cutting right through him. He regrouped. 'I am with a special tourist task force. Give me the ring, or I'll have to take you down to the precinct and—'

'And what?' she demanded, raising her eyebrows in mock anticipation.

Becker fell silent. He was in over his head. The plan was backfiring. *Why isn't she buying this?*

Rocío came closer. 'I don't know who you are or what you want, but if you don't get out of this suite right now, I will call hotel security, and the *real* Guardia will arrest you for impersonating a police officer.'

Becker knew that Strathmore could have him out of jail in five minutes, but it had been made very clear to him that this matter was supposed to be handled discreetly. Getting arrested was not part of the plan.

Rocío had stopped a few feet in front of Becker and was glaring at him.

'Okay.' Becker sighed, accentuating the defeat in his voice. He let his Spanish accent slip. 'I am not with the Seville police. A U.S. government organization sent me to locate the ring. That's all I can reveal. I've been authorized to pay you for it.'

There was a long silence.

Rocío let his statement hang in the air a moment before parting her lips in a sly smile. 'Now that wasn't so hard, was it?' She sat down on a chair and crossed her legs. 'How much can you pay?'

Becker muffled his sigh of relief. He wasted no time getting down to business. 'I can pay you 750,000 pesetas. Five thousand American dollars.' It was half what he had on him but probably ten times what the ring was actually worth.

Rocío raised her eyebrows. 'That's a lot of money.'

'Yes it is. Do we have a deal?'

Rocío shook her head. 'I wish I could say yes.'

'A million pesetas?' Becker blurted. 'It's all I have.'

'My, my.' She smiled. 'You Americans don't bargain very well. You wouldn't last a day in our markets.'

'Cash, right now,' Becker said, reaching for the envelope in his jacket. *I just want to go home.*

Rocío shook her head. 'I can't.'

Becker bristled angrily. 'Why not?'

'I no longer have the ring,' she said apologetically. 'I've already sold it.'

CHAPTER 33

Tokugen Numataka stared out his window and paced like a caged animal. He had not yet heard from his contact, North Dakota. *Damn Americans! No sense of punctuality!*

He would have called North Dakota himself, but he didn't have a phone number for him. Numataka hated doing business this way – with someone else in control.

The thought had crossed Numataka's mind from the beginning that the calls from North Dakota could be a hoax – a Japanese competitor playing him for the fool. Now the old doubts were coming back. Numataka decided he needed more information.

He burst from his office and took a left down Numatech's main hallway. His employees bowed reverently as he stormed past. Numataka knew better than to believe they actually loved him – bowing was a courtesy Japanese employees offered even the most ruthless of bosses.

Numataka went directly to the company's main switchboard. All calls were handled by a single operator on a Corenco 2000, twelve-line switchboard terminal.

The woman was busy but stood and bowed as Numataka entered.

'Sit down,' he snapped.

She obeyed.

'I received a call at four forty-five on my personal line today. Can you tell me where it came from?' Numataka kicked himself for not having done this earlier.

The operator swallowed nervously. 'We don't have caller identification on this machine, sir. But I can contact the phone company. I'm sure they can help.'

Numataka had no doubt the phone company could help. In this digital age, privacy had become a thing of the past; there was a record of everything. Phone companies could tell you exactly who had called you and how long you'd spoken.

'Do it,' he commanded. 'Let me know what you find out.'

CHAPTER 34

Susan sat alone in Node 3, waiting for her tracer. Hale had decided to step outside and get some air – a decision for which she was grateful. Oddly, however, the solitude in Node 3 provided little asylum. Susan found herself struggling with the new connection between Tankado and Hale.

'Who will guard the guards?' she said to herself. *Quis custodiet ipsos custodes.* The words kept circling in her head. Susan forced them from her mind.

Her thoughts turned to David, hoping he was all right. She still found it hard to believe he was in Spain. The sooner they found the pass-keys and ended this, the better.

Susan had lost track of how long she'd been sitting there waiting for her tracer. Two hours? Three? She gazed out at the deserted Crypto floor and wished her terminal would beep. There was only silence. The late-summer sun had set. Overhead, the automatic fluorescents had kicked on. Susan sensed time was running out.

She looked down at her tracer and frowned. 'Come on,' she grumbled. 'You've had plenty of time.' She palmed her mouse and clicked her way into her tracer's status window. 'How long have you been running, anyway?'

Susan opened the tracer's status window – a digital clock much like the one on TRANSLTR; it displayed the hours and minutes her tracer had been running. Susan gazed at the monitor expecting to see a readout of hours and minutes. But she saw something else entirely. What she saw stopped the blood in her veins.

TRACER ABORTED

'Tracer aborted!' she choked aloud. 'Why?'

In a sudden panic, Susan scrolled wildly through the data, searching the programming for any commands that might have told the tracer to abort. But her search went in vain. It appeared her tracer had stopped all by itself. Susan knew this could mean only one thing – her tracer had developed a bug.

Susan considered 'bugs' the most maddening asset of computer programming. Because computers followed a scrupulously precise order of operations, the most minuscule programming errors often had crippling effects. Simple syntactical errors – such as a programmer mistakenly inserting a comma instead of a period – could bring entire systems to their knees. Susan had always thought the term 'bug' had an amusing origin:

It came from the world's first computer – the Mark 1 – a room-size maze of electromechanical circuits built in 1944 in a lab at Harvard University. The computer developed a glitch one day, and no one was able to locate the cause. After hours of searching, a lab assistant finally spotted the problem. It seemed a moth had landed on one of the computer's circuit boards and shorted it out. From that moment on, computer glitches were referred to as bugs.

'I don't have time for this,' Susan cursed.

Finding a bug in a program was a process that could take days. Thousands of lines of programming needed to be searched to find a tiny error – it was like inspecting an encyclopedia for a single typo.

Susan knew she had only one choice – to send her tracer again. She also knew the tracer was almost guaranteed to hit the same bug and abort all over again. Debugging the tracer would take time, time she and the commander didn't have.

But as Susan stared at her tracer, wondering what error she'd made, she realized something didn't make sense. She had used this exact same tracer last month with no problems at all. Why would it develop a glitch all of a sudden?

As she puzzled, a comment Strathmore made earlier echoed in her mind. *Susan, I tried to send the tracer myself, but the data it returned was nonsensical.*

Susan heard the words again. *The data it returned . . .*

She cocked her head. Was it possible? The data it returned?

If Strathmore had received data back from the tracer, then it obviously was working. His data was nonsensical, Susan assumed, because he had entered the wrong search strings – but nonetheless, the tracer was working.

Susan immediately realized that there was one other possible explanation for why her tracer aborted. Internal programming flaws were not the only reasons programs glitched; sometimes there were *external* forces – power surges, dust particles on circuit boards, faulty cabling. Because the hardware in Node 3 was so well tuned, she hadn't even considered it.

Susan stood and strode quickly across Node 3 to a large bookshelf of technical manuals. She grabbed a spiral binder marked SYS-OP and thumbed through. She found what she was looking for, carried the manual back to her terminal, and typed a few commands. Then she waited while the computer raced through a list of commands executed in the past three hours. She hoped the search would turn up some sort of external interrupt – an abort command generated by a faulty power supply or defective chip.

Moments later Susan's terminal beeped. Her pulse quickened. She held her breath and studied the screen.

ERROR CODE 22

Susan felt a surge of hope. It was good news. The fact that the inquiry had found an error code meant her tracer was fine. The trace had apparently aborted due to an external anomaly that was unlikely to repeat itself.

ERROR CODE 22. Susan racked her memory trying to remember what code 22 stood for. Hardware failures were so rare in Node 3 that she couldn't remember the numerical codings.

Susan flipped through the SYS-OP manual, scanning the list of error codes.

19: CORRUPT HARD PARTITION
20: DC SPIKE
21: MEDIA FAILURE

182

When she reached number 22, she stopped and stared a long moment. Baffled, she double-checked her monitor.

ERROR CODE 22

Susan frowned and returned to the SYS-OP manual. What she saw made no sense. The explanation simply read:

22: MANUAL ABORT

CHAPTER 35

Becker stared in shock at Rocío. 'You *sold* the ring?'

The woman nodded, her silky red hair falling around her shoulders.

Becker willed it not to be true. 'Pero . . . but . . .'

She shrugged and said in Spanish, 'A girl near the park.'

Becker felt his legs go weak. *This can't be!*

Rocío smiled coyly and motioned to the German. 'Él quería que lo guardará. He wanted to keep it, but I told him no. I've got Gitana blood in me, Gypsy blood; we Gitanas, in addition to having red hair, are very superstitious. A ring offered by a dying man is not a good sign.'

'Did you know the girl?' Becker interrogated.

Rocío arched her eyebrows. 'Vaya. You really want this ring, don't you?'

Becker nodded sternly. 'Who did you sell it to?'

The enormous German sat bewildered on the bed. His romantic evening was being ruined, and he apparently had no idea why. 'Was passiert?' he asked nervously. 'What's happening?'

Becker ignored him.

'I didn't actually sell it,' Rocío said. 'I tried to, but she was just a kid and had no money. I ended up giving it to her. Had I known about your generous offer, I would have saved it for you.'

'Why did you leave the park?' Becker demanded. 'Somebody had died. Why didn't you wait for the police? And give *them* the ring?'

'I solicit many things, Mr Becker, but *trouble* is not one of them. Besides, that old man seemed to have things under control.'

'The Canadian?'

'Yes, he called the ambulance. We decided to leave. I saw no reason to involve my date or myself with the police.'

Becker nodded absently. He was still trying to accept this cruel twist of fate. *She gave the damn thing away!*

'I tried to help the dying man,' Rocío explained. 'But he didn't seem to want it. He started with the ring – kept pushing it in our faces. He had these three crippled fingers sticking up. He kept pushing his hand at us – like we were supposed to take the ring. I didn't want to, but my friend here finally did. Then the guy died.'

'And you tried CPR?' Becker guessed.

'No. We didn't touch him. My friend got scared. He's big, but he's a wimp.' She smiled seductively at Becker. 'Don't worry – he can't speak a word of Spanish.'

Becker frowned. He was wondering again about the bruises on Tankado's chest. 'Did the paramedics give CPR?'

'I have no idea. As I told you, we left before they arrived.'

185

'You mean after you *stole* the ring.' Becker scowled.

Rocío glared at him. 'We did not steal the ring. The man was dying. His intentions were clear. We gave him his last wish.'

Becker softened. Rocío was right; he probably would have done the same damn thing. 'But then you gave the ring to some girl?'

'I told you. The ring made me nervous. The girl had lots of jewelry on. I thought she might like it.'

'And she didn't think it was strange? That you'd just *give* her a ring?'

'No. I told her I found it in the park. I thought she might offer to pay me for it, but she didn't. I didn't care. I just wanted to get rid of it.'

'When did you give it to her?'

Rocío shrugged. 'This afternoon. About an hour after I got it.'

Becker checked his watch: 11:48 P.M. The trail was eight hours old. *What the hell am I doing here? I'm supposed to be in the Smokys.* He sighed and asked the only question he could think of. 'What did the girl look like?'

'Era un punqui,' Rocío replied.

Becker looked up, puzzled. 'Un punqui?'

'Sí. Punqui.'

'A punk?'

'Yes, a punk,' she said in rough English, and then immediately switched back to Spanish. 'Mucha joyería. Lots of jewelry. A weird pendant in one ear. A skull, I think.'

'There are punk rockers in Seville?'

Rocío smiled. 'Todo bajo el sol. Everything under the sun.' It was the motto of Seville's Tourism Bureau.

'Did she give you her name?'

'No.'

'Did she say where she was going?'

'No. Her Spanish was poor.'

'She wasn't Spanish?' Becker asked.

'No. She was English, I think. She had wild hair – red, white, and blue.'

Becker winced at the bizarre image. 'Maybe she was American,' he offered.

'I don't think so,' Rocío said. 'She was wearing a T-shirt that looked like the British flag.'

Becker nodded dumbly. 'Okay. Red, white, and blue hair, a British flag T-shirt, a skull pendant in her ear. What else?'

'Nothing. Just your average punk.'

Average punk? Becker was from a world of collegiate sweatshirts and conservative haircuts – he couldn't even picture what the woman was talking about. 'Can you think of anything else at all?' he pressed.

Rocío thought a moment. 'No. That's it.'

Just then the bed creaked loudly. Rocío's client shifted his weight uncomfortably. Becker turned to him and spoke in fluent German. 'Noch etwas? Anything else? Anything to help me find the punk rocker with the ring?'

There was a long silence. It was as if the giant man had something he wanted to say, but he wasn't sure how to say it. His lower lip quivered momentarily, there was a pause, and then he spoke. The four words that came out were definitely English, but they were barely intelligible beneath his thick German accent. 'Fock off und die.'

Becker gaped in shock. 'I beg your pardon?'

'Fock off und die,' the man repeated, patting his left palm against his fleshy right forearm – a crude approximation of the Italian gesture for 'fuck you.'

Becker was too drained to be offended. *Fuck off and die? What happened to Das Wimp?* He turned back to Rocío and spoke in Spanish. 'Sounds like I've overstayed my welcome.'

'Don't worry about him.' She laughed. 'He's just a little frustrated. He'll get what's coming to him.' She tossed her hair and winked.

'Is there anything else?' Becker asked. 'Anything you can tell me that might help?'

Rocío shook her head. 'That's all. But you'll never find her. Seville is a big city – it can be very deceptive.'

'I'll do the best I can.' *It's a matter of national security . . .*

'If you have no luck,' Rocío said, eyeing the bulging envelope in Becker's pocket, 'please stop back. My friend will be sleeping, no doubt. Knock quietly. I'll find us an extra room. You'll see a side of Spain you'll never forget.' She pouted lusciously.

Becker forced a polite smile. 'I should be going.' He apologized to the German for interrupting his evening.

The giant smiled timidly. 'Keine Ursache.'

Becker headed out the door. *No problem? Whatever happened to 'Fuck off and die'?*

CHAPTER 36

'Manual abort?' Susan stared at her screen, mystified.

She knew she hadn't typed any manual abort command – at least not intentionally. She wondered if maybe she'd hit the wrong sequence of keys by mistake.

'Impossible,' she muttered. According to the headers, the abort command had been sent less than twenty minutes ago. Susan knew the only thing she'd typed in the last twenty minutes was her privacy code when she'd stepped out to talk to the commander. It was absurd to think the privacy code could have been misinterpreted as an abort command.

Knowing it was a waste of time, Susan pulled up her ScreenLock log and double-checked that her privacy code had been entered properly. Sure enough, it had.

'Then *where*,' she demanded angrily, 'where did it get a *manual* abort?'

Susan scowled and closed the ScreenLock window. Unexpectedly, however, in the split second as the window blipped away, something caught her eye. She reopened the window and studied the data. It made no sense. There was a proper 'locking' entry when she'd left Node 3, but the timing of the subsequent 'unlock' entry seemed strange. The two entries were less than one minute apart. Susan was certain she'd been outside with the commander for more than one minute.

Susan scrolled down the page. What she saw left her aghast. Registering three minutes later, a *second* set of lock-unlock entries appeared. According to the log, someone had unlocked her terminal while she was gone.

'Not possible!' she choked. The only candidate was Greg Hale, and Susan was quite certain she'd never given Hale her privacy code. Following good crypto-graphic procedure, Susan had chosen her code at random and never written it down; Hale's guessing the correct five-character alphanumeric was out of the question – it was thirty-six to the fifth power, over sixty million possibilities.

But the ScreenLock entries were as clear as day. Susan stared at them in wonder. Hale had somehow been on her terminal while she was gone. He had sent her tracer a manual abort command.

The questions of *how* quickly gave way to questions of *why?* Hale had no motive to break into her terminal. He didn't even know Susan was running a tracer. Even if he did know, Susan thought, why would he object to her tracking some guy named North Dakota?

The unanswered questions seemed to be multiply-ing in her head. 'First things first,' she said aloud. She would deal with Hale in a moment. Focusing on the matter at hand, Susan reloaded her tracer and hit the ENTER key. Her terminal beeped once.

Susan knew the tracer would take hours to return. She cursed Hale, wondering how in the world he'd gotten her privacy code, wondering what interest he had in her tracer.

Susan stood up and strode immediately for Hale's terminal. The screen was black, but she could tell it was not locked – the monitor was glowing faintly around the edges. Cryptographers seldom locked their terminals except when they left Node 3 for the night. Instead, they simply dimmed the brightness on their monitors – a universal, honor-code indication that no one should disturb the terminal.

Susan reached for Hale's terminal. 'Screw the honor code,' she said. 'What the hell are you up to?'

Throwing a quick glance out at the deserted Crypto floor, Susan turned up Hale's brightness controls. The monitor came into focus, but the screen was entirely empty. Susan frowned at the blank screen. Uncertain how to proceed, she called up a search engine and typed:

SEARCH FOR: 'TRACER'

It was a long shot, but if there were any references to Susan's tracer in Hale's computer, this search would find them. It might shed some light on why Hale had manually aborted her program. Seconds later the screen refreshed.

NO MATCHES FOUND

Susan sat a moment, unsure what she was even looking for. She tried again.

191

The monitor refreshed and provided a handful of innocuous references – no hint that Hale had any copies of Susan's privacy code on his computer.

Susan sighed loudly. *So what programs has he been using today?* She went to Hale's 'recent applications' menu to find the last program he had used. It was his E-mail server. Susan searched his hard drive and eventually found his E-mail folder hidden discreetly inside some other directories. She opened the folder, and additional folders appeared; it seemed Hale had numerous E-mail identities and accounts. One of them, Susan noticed with little surprise, was an anonymous account. She opened the folder, clicked one of the old, inbound messages, and read it.

She instantly stopped breathing. The message read:

TO: NDAKOTA@ARA.ANON.ORG
FROM: ET@DOSHISHA.EDU
GREAT PROGRESS! DIGITAL FORTRESS IS ALMOST DONE.
THIS THING WILL SET THE NSA BACK DECADES!

As if in a dream, Susan read the message over and over. Then, trembling, she opened another.

TO: NDAKOTA@ARA.ANON.ORG
FROM: ET@DOSHISHA.EDU
ROTATING CLEARTEXT WORKS! MUTATION STRINGS ARE THE TRICK!

It was unthinkable, and yet there it was. E-mail from Ensei Tankado. He had been writing to Greg Hale. They were working together. Susan went numb as the impossible truth stared up at her from the terminal.

Greg Hale is NDAKOTA?

Susan's eyes locked on the screen. Her mind searched desperately for some other explanation, but there was none. It was proof – sudden and inescapable: Tankado had used mutation strings to create a rotating cleartext function, and Hale had conspired with him to bring down the NSA.

'It's . . .' Susan stammered. 'It's . . . not possible.'

As if to disagree, Hale's voice echoed from the past: *Tankado wrote me a few times . . . Strathmore took a gamble hiring me . . . I'm getting out of here someday.*

Still, Susan could not accept what she was seeing. True, Greg Hale was obnoxious and arrogant – but he wasn't a traitor. He knew what Digital Fortress would do to the NSA; there was no way he was involved in a plot to release it!

And yet, Susan realized, there was nothing to stop him – nothing except honor and decency. She thought of the Skipjack algorithm. Greg Hale had ruined the NSA's plans once before. What would prevent him from trying again?

'But Tankado . . .' Susan puzzled. *Why would someone as paranoid as Tankado trust someone as unreliable as Hale?*

She knew that none of it mattered now. All that mattered was getting to Strathmore. By some ironic stroke of fate, Tankado's partner was right there under their noses. She wondered if Hale knew yet that Ensei Tankado was dead.

She quickly began closing Hale's E-mail files in order to leave the terminal exactly as she had found it. Hale could suspect nothing – not yet. The Digital

Fortress pass-key, she realized in amazement, was probably hidden somewhere inside that very computer.

But as Susan closed the last of the files, a shadow passed outside the Node 3 window. Her gaze shot up, and she saw Greg Hale approaching. Her adrenaline surged. He was almost to the doors.

'Damn!' she cursed, eyeing the distance back to her seat. She knew she'd never make it. Hale was almost there.

She wheeled desperately, searching Node 3 for options. The doors behind her clicked. Then they engaged. Susan felt instinct take over. Digging her shoes into the carpet, she accelerated in long, reaching strides toward the pantry. As the doors hissed open, Susan slid to a stop in front of the refrigerator and yanked open the door. A glass pitcher on top tipped precariously and then rocked to a stop.

'Hungry?' Hale asked, entering Node 3 and walking toward her. His voice was calm and flirtatious. 'Want to share some tofu?'

Susan exhaled and turned to face him. 'No thanks,' she offered. 'I think I'll just—' But the words got caught in her throat. She went white.

Hale eyed her oddly. 'What's wrong?'

Susan bit her lip and locked eyes with him. 'Nothing,' she managed. But it was a lie. Across the room, Hale's terminal glowed brightly. She'd forgotten to dim it.

CHAPTER 37

Downstairs at the Alfonso XIII, Becker wandered tiredly over to the bar. A dwarf-like bartender laid a napkin in front of him. 'Qué bebe usted? What are you drinking?'

'Nothing, thanks,' Becker replied. 'I need to know if there are any clubs in town for punk rockers?'

The bartender eyed him strangely. 'Clubs? For punks?'

'Yeah. Is there anyplace in town where they all hang out?'

'No lo sé, señor. I don't know. But certainly not here!' He smiled. 'How about a drink?'

Becker felt like shaking the guy. Nothing was going quite the way he'd planned.

'Quiere Vd. algo?' The bartender repeated. 'Fino? Jerez?'

Faint strains of classical music were being piped in overhead. *Brandenburg Concertos,* Becker thought. *Number four.* He and Susan had seen the Academy of St Martin in the Fields play the Brandenburgs at the university last year. He suddenly wished she were with him now. The breeze from an overhead air-conditioning

195

vent reminded Becker what it was like outside. He pictured himself walking the sweaty, drugged-out streets of Triana looking for some punk in a British flag T-shirt. He thought of Susan again. 'Zumo de arándano,' he heard himself say. 'Cranberry juice.'

The bartender looked baffled. 'Solo?' Cranberry juice was a popular drink in Spain, but drinking it alone was unheard of.

'Sí,' Becker said. 'Solo.'

'Echo un poco de Smirnoff?' The bartender pressed. 'A splash of vodka?'

'No, gracias.'

'Gratis?' he coaxed. 'On the house?'

Through the pounding in his head, Becker pictured the filthy streets of Triana, the stifling heat, and the long night ahead of him. *What the hell.* He nodded. 'Sí, échame un poco de vodka.'

The bartender seemed much relieved and hustled off to make the drink.

Becker glanced around the ornate bar and wondered if he was dreaming. Anything would make more sense than the truth. *I'm a university teacher,* he thought, *on a secret mission.*

The bartender returned with a flourish and presented Becker's beverage. 'A su gusto, señor. Cranberry with a splash of vodka.'

Becker thanked him. He took a sip and gagged. *That's a splash?*

CHAPTER 38

Hale stopped halfway to the Node 3 pantry and stared at Susan. 'What's wrong, Sue? You look terrible.'

Susan fought her rising fear. Ten feet away, Hale's monitor glowed brightly. 'I'm . . . I'm okay,' she managed, her heart pounding.

Hale eyed her with a puzzled look on his face. 'You want some water?'

Susan could not answer. She cursed herself. *How could I forget to dim his damn monitor?* Susan knew the moment Hale suspected her of searching his terminal, he'd suspect she knew his real identity, North Dakota. She feared Hale would do anything to keep that information inside Node 3.

Susan wondered if she should make a dash for the door. But she never got the chance. Suddenly there was a pounding at the glass wall. Both Hale and Susan jumped. It was Chartrukian. He was banging his sweaty fists against the glass again. He looked like he'd seen Armageddon.

Hale scowled at the crazed Sys-Sec outside the window, then turned back to Susan. 'I'll be right back. Get yourself a drink. You look pale.' Hale turned and went outside.

Susan steadied herself and moved quickly to Hale's terminal. She reached down and adjusted the brightness controls. The monitor went black.

Her head was pounding. She turned and eyed the conversation now taking place on the Crypto floor. Apparently, Chartrukian had not gone home, after all. The young Sys-Sec was now in a panic, spilling his guts to Greg Hale. Susan knew it didn't matter – Hale knew everything there was to know.

I've got to get to Strathmore, she thought. *And fast.*

CHAPTER 39

Room 301. Rocío Eva Granada stood naked in front of the bathroom mirror. This was the moment she'd been dreading all day. The German was on the bed waiting for her. He was the biggest man she'd ever been with.

Reluctantly, she took an ice cube from the water bucket and rubbed it across her nipples. They quickly hardened. This was her gift – to make men feel wanted. It's what kept them coming back. She ran her hands across her supple, well-tanned body and hoped it would survive another four or five more years until she had enough to retire. Señor Roldán took most of her pay, but without him she knew she'd be with the rest of the hookers picking up drunks in Triana. These men at least had money. They never beat her, and they were easy to satisfy. She slipped into her lingerie, took a deep breath, and opened the bathroom door.

As Rocío stepped into the room, the German's eyes bulged. She was wearing a black negligee. Her chestnut skin radiated in the soft light, and her nipples stood at attention beneath the lacy fabric.

'Komm doch hierher,' he said eagerly, shedding his robe and rolling onto his back.

Rocío forced a smile and approached the bed. She gazed down at the enormous German. She chuckled in relief. The organ between his legs was tiny.

He grabbed at her and impatiently ripped off her negligee. His fat fingers groped at every inch of her body. She fell on top of him and moaned and writhed in false ecstasy. As he rolled her over and climbed on top of her, she thought she would be crushed. She gasped and choked against his puttylike neck. She prayed he would be quick.

'Sí! Sí!' she gasped in between thrusts. She dug her fingernails into his backside to encourage him.

Random thoughts cascaded through her mind – faces of the countless men she'd satisfied, ceilings she'd stared at for hours in the dark, dreams of having children . . .

Suddenly, without warning, the German's body arched, stiffened, and almost immediately collapsed on top of her. *That's all?* she thought, surprised and relieved.

She tried to slide out from under him. 'Darling,' she whispered huskily. 'Let me get on top.' But the man did not move.

She reached up and pushed at his massive shoulders. 'Darling, I . . . I can't breathe!' She began feeling faint. She felt her ribs cracking. 'Despiértate!' Her fingers instinctively started pulling at his matted hair. *Wake up!*

It was then that she felt the warm sticky liquid. It was matted in his hair – flowing onto her cheeks, into her mouth. It was salty. She twisted wildly beneath him. Above her, a strange shaft of light illuminated the German's contorted face. The bullet hole in his temple was gushing blood all over her. She tried to scream, but there was no air left in her lungs. He was crushing her. Delirious, she clawed toward the shaft of light coming from the doorway. She saw a hand. A gun with a silencer. A flash of light. And then nothing.

CHAPTER 40

Outside Node 3, Chartrukian looked desperate. He was trying to convince Hale that TRANSLTR was in trouble. Susan raced by them with only one thought in mind – to find Strathmore.

The panicked Sys-Sec grabbed Susan's arm as she passed. 'Ms Fletcher! We have a virus! I'm positive! You have to—'

Susan shook herself free and glared ferociously. 'I thought the commander told you to go home.'

'But the Run-Monitor! It's registering eighteen—'

'Commander Strathmore told you to go home!'

'FUCK STRATHMORE!' Chartrukian screamed, the words resounding throughout the dome.

A deep voice boomed from above. 'Mr Chartrukian?'

The three Crypto employees froze.

High above them, Strathmore stood at the railing outside his office.

For a moment, the only sound inside the dome was the uneven hum of the generators below. Susan tried desperately to catch Strathmore's eye. *Commander! Hale is North Dakota!*

But Strathmore was fixated on the young Sys-Sec. He descended the stairs without so much as a blink, keeping his eyes trained on Chartrukian the whole way down. He made his way across the Crypto floor and stopped six inches in front of the trembling technician. '*What* did you say?'

'Sir,' Chartrukian choked, 'TRANSLTR's in trouble.'

'Commander?' Susan interjected. 'If I could—'

Strathmore waved her off. His eyes never left the Sys-Sec.

Phil blurted, 'We have an infected file, sir. I'm sure of it!'

Strathmore's complexion turned a deep red. 'Mr Chartrukian, we've been through this. There is *no* file infecting TRANSLTR!'

'Yes, there is!' he cried. 'And if it makes its way to the main databank—'

'Where the hell is this infected file?' Strathmore bellowed. 'Show it to me!'

Chartrukian hesitated. 'I can't.'

'Of course you can't! It doesn't exist!'

Susan said, 'Commander, I must—'

Again Strathmore silenced her with an angry wave.

Susan eyed Hale nervously. He seemed smug and detached. *It makes perfect sense*, she thought. *Hale wouldn't be worried about a virus; he knows what's really going on inside TRANSLTR.*

Chartrukian was insistent. 'The infected file *exists*, sir. But Gauntlet never picked it up.'

'If Gauntlet never picked it up,' Strathmore fumed, 'then how the hell do you know it exists?'

Chartrukian suddenly sounded more confident. 'Mutation strings, sir. I ran a full analysis, and the probe turned up mutation strings!'

Susan now understood why the Sys-Sec was so concerned. *Mutation strings*, she mused. She knew mutation strings were programming sequences that corrupted data in extremely complex ways. They were very common in computer viruses, particularly viruses that altered large blocks of data. Of course, Susan also knew from Tankado's E-mail that the mutation strings Chartrukian had seen were harmless – simply part of Digital Fortress.

The Sys-Sec went on. 'When I first saw the strings, sir, I thought Gauntlet's filters had failed. But then I ran some tests and found out . . .' He paused, looking suddenly uneasy. 'I found out that somebody manually *bypassed* Gauntlet.'

The statement met with a sudden hush. Strathmore's face turned an even deeper shade of crimson. There was no doubt whom Chartrukian was accusing; Strathmore's terminal was the only one in Crypto with clearance to bypass Gauntlet's filters.

When Strathmore spoke, his voice was like ice. 'Mr Chartrukian, not that it is any concern of yours, but *I* bypassed Gauntlet.' He went on, his temper hovering near the boiling point. 'As I told you earlier, I'm running a very advanced diagnostic. The mutation strings you see in TRANSLTR are part of that diagnostic; they are there because *I* put them there. Gauntlet refused to let me load the file, so I bypassed its filters.' Strathmore's eyes narrowed sharply at Chartrukian. 'Now, will there be anything else before you go?'

In a flash, it all clicked for Susan. When Strathmore had downloaded the encrypted Digital Fortress algorithm from the Internet and tried to run it through TRANSLTR, the mutation strings had tripped

Gauntlet's filters. Desperate to know whether Digital Fortress was breakable, Strathmore decided to bypass the filters.

Normally, bypassing Gauntlet was unthinkable. In this situation, however, there was no danger in sending Digital Fortress directly into TRANSLTR; the commander knew exactly what the file was and where it came from.

'With all due respect, sir,' Chartrukian pressed, 'I've never heard of a diagnostic that employs mutation—'

'Commander,' Susan interjected, not able to wait another moment. 'I really need to—'

This time her words were cut short by the sharp ring of Strathmore's cellular phone. The commander snatched up the receiver. 'What is it!' he barked. Then he fell silent and listened to the caller.

Susan forgot about Hale for an instant. She prayed the caller was David. *Tell me he's okay,* she thought. *Tell me he found the ring!* But Strathmore caught her eye and he gave her a frown. It was not David.

Susan felt her breath grow short. All she wanted to know was that the man she loved was safe. Strathmore, Susan knew, was impatient for other reasons; if David took much longer, the commander would have to send backup – NSA field agents. It was a gamble he had hoped to avoid.

'Commander?' Chartrukian urged. 'I really think we should check—'

'Hold on,' Strathmore said, apologizing to his caller. He covered his mouthpiece and leveled a fiery stare at his young Sys-Sec. 'Mr Chartrukian,' he growled, 'this discussion is over. You are to leave Crypto. *Now.* That's an order.'

Chartrukian stood stunned. 'But, sir, mutation str—'

'NOW!' Strathmore bellowed.

Chartrukian stared a moment, speechless. Then he stormed off toward the Sys-Sec lab.

Strathmore turned and eyed Hale with a puzzled look. Susan understood the commander's mystification. Hale had been quiet – too quiet. Hale knew very well there was no such thing as a diagnostic that used mutation strings, much less one that could keep TRANSLTR busy eighteen hours. And yet Hale hadn't said a word. He appeared indifferent to the entire commotion. Strathmore was obviously wondering *why*. Susan had the answer.

'Commander,' she said insistently, 'if I could just speak—'

'In a minute,' he interjected, still eyeing Hale quizzically. 'I need to take this call.' With that, Strathmore turned on his heel and headed for his office.

Susan opened her mouth, but the words stalled on the tip of her tongue. *Hale is North Dakota!* She stood rigid, unable to breathe. She felt Hale staring at her. Susan turned. Hale stepped aside and swung his arm graciously toward the Node 3 door. 'After you, Sue.'

CHAPTER 41

In a linen closet on the third floor of the Alfonso XIII, a maid lay unconscious on the floor. The man with wire-rim glasses was replacing a hotel master key in her pocket. He had not sensed her scream when he struck her, but he had no way of knowing for sure – he had been deaf since he was twelve.

He reached to the battery pack on his belt with a certain kind of reverence; a gift from a client, the machine had given him new life. He could now receive his contracts anywhere in the world. All communications arrived instantaneously and untraceably.

He was eager as he touched the switch. His glasses flickered to life. Once again his fingers carved into the empty air and began clicking together. As always, he had recorded the names of his victims – a simple matter of searching a wallet or purse. The contacts on his fingers connected, and the letters appeared in the lens of his glasses like ghosts in the air.

SUBJECT: ROCIO EVA GRANADA – TERMINATED
SUBJECT: HANS HUBER – TERMINATED

Three stories below David Becker paid his tab and wandered across the lobby, his half-finished drink in hand. He headed toward the hotel's open terrace for some fresh air. *In and out,* he mused. Things hadn't panned out quite as he expected. He had a decision to make. Should he just give up and go back to the airport? *A matter of national security.* He swore under his breath. So why the hell had they sent a schoolteacher?

Becker moved out of sight of the bartender and dumped the remaining drink in a potted jasmine. The vodka had made him light-headed. *Cheapest drunk in history,* Susan often called him. After refilling the heavy crystal glass from a water fountain, Becker took a long swallow.

He stretched a few times trying to shake off the light haze that had settled over him. Then he set down his glass and walked across the lobby.

As he passed the elevator, the doors slid open. There was a man inside. All Becker saw were thick wire-rim glasses. The man raised a handkerchief to blow his nose. Becker smiled politely and moved on . . . out into the stifling Sevillian night.

CHAPTER 42

Inside Node 3, Susan caught herself pacing frantically. She wished she'd exposed Hale when she'd had the chance.

Hale sat at his terminal. 'Stress is a killer, Sue. Something you want to get off your chest?'

Susan forced herself to sit. She had thought Strathmore would be off the phone by now and return to speak to her, but he was nowhere to be seen. Susan tried to keep calm. She gazed at her computer screen. The tracer was still running – for the second time. It was immaterial now. Susan knew whose address it would return: GHALE@crypto.nsa.gov.

Susan gazed up toward Strathmore's workstation and knew she couldn't wait any longer. It was time to interrupt the commander's phone call. She stood and headed for the door.

Hale seemed suddenly uneasy, apparently noticing Susan's odd behavior. He strode quickly across the room and beat her to the door. He folded his arms and blocked her exit.

'Tell me what's going on,' he demanded. 'There's something going on here today. What is it?'

'Let me out,' Susan said as evenly as possible, feeling a sudden twinge of danger.

'Come on,' Hale pressed. 'Strathmore practically fired Chartrukian for doing his job. What's going on inside TRANSLTR? We don't have any diagnostics that run eighteen hours. That's bullshit, and you know it. Tell me what's going on.'

Susan's eyes narrowed. *You know damn well what's going on!* 'Back off, Greg,' she demanded. 'I need to use the bathroom.'

Hale smirked. He waited a long moment and then stepped aside. 'Sorry, Sue. Just flirting.'

Susan pushed by him and left Node 3. As she passed the glass wall, she sensed Hale's eyes boring into her from the other side.

Reluctantly, she circled toward the bathrooms. She would have to make a detour before visiting the Commander. Greg Hale could suspect nothing.

CHAPTER 43

A jaunty forty-five, Chad Brinkerhoff was well-pressed, well-groomed, and well-informed. His summer-weight suit, like his tan skin, showed not a wrinkle or hint of wear. His hair was thick, sandy blond, and – most importantly – all his own. His eyes were a brilliant blue – subtly enhanced by the miracle of tinted contact lenses.

He surveyed the wood-paneled office around him and knew he had risen as far as he would rise in the NSA. He was on the ninth floor – Mahogany Row. Office 9A197. The Directorial Suite.

It was a Saturday night, and Mahogany Row was all but deserted, its executives long gone – off enjoying whatever pastimes influential men enjoyed in their leisure. Although Brinkerhoff had always dreamed of a 'real' post with the agency, he had somehow ended up as a 'personal aide' – the official cul de sac of the political rat race. The fact that he worked side by side with the single most powerful man in American intelligence was little consolation. Brinkerhoff had graduated with honors from Andover and Williams, and yet here he was, middle-aged, with no real power

– no real stake. He spent his days arranging someone else's calendar.

There were definite benefits to being the director's personal aide – Brinkerhoff had a plush office in the directorial suite, full access to all the NSA departments, and a certain level of distinction that came from the company he kept. He ran errands for the highest echelons of power. Deep down Brinkerhoff knew he was born to be a PA – smart enough to take notes, handsome enough to give press conferences, and lazy enough to be content with it.

The sticky-sweet chime of his mantel clock accented the end of another day of his pathetic existence. *Shit,* he thought. *Five o'clock on a Saturday. What the hell am I doing here?*

'Chad?' A woman appeared in his doorway.

Brinkerhoff looked up. It was Midge Milken, Fontaine's internal security analyst. She was sixty, slightly heavy, and, much to the puzzlement of Brinkerhoff, quite appealing. A consummate flirt and an ex-wife three times over, Midge prowled the six-room directorial suite with a saucy authority. She was sharp, intuitive, worked ungodly hours, and was rumored to know more about the NSA's inner workings than God himself.

Damn, Brinkerhoff thought, eyeing her in her gray cashmere dress. *Either I'm getting older, or she's looking younger.*

'Weekly reports.' She smiled, waving a fanfold of paper. 'You need to check the figures.'

Brinkerhoff eyed her body. 'Figures look good from here.'

'Really, Chad,' she laughed. 'I'm old enough to be your mother.'

Don't remind me, he thought.

Midge strode in and sidled up to his desk. 'I'm on my way out, but the director wants these compiled by the time he gets back from South America. That's Monday, bright and early.' She dropped the printouts in front of him.

'What am I, an accountant?'

'No, hon, you're a cruise director. Thought you knew that.'

'So what am I doing crunching numbers?'

She ruffled his hair. 'You wanted more responsibility. Here it is.'

He looked up at her sadly. 'Midge . . . I have no life.'

She tapped her finger on the paper. '*This* is your life, Chad Brinkerhoff.' She looked down at him and softened. 'Anything I can get you before I go?'

He eyed her pleadingly and rolled his aching neck. 'My shoulders are tight.'

Midge didn't bite. 'Take an aspirin.'

He pouted. 'No back rub?'

She shook her head. '*Cosmopolitan* says two-thirds of backrubs end in sex.'

Brinkerhoff looked indignant. '*Ours* never do!'

'Precisely.' She winked. 'That's the problem.'

'Midge—'

'Night, Chad.' She headed for the door.

'You're leaving?'

'You know I'd stay,' Midge said, pausing in the doorway, 'but I do have *some* pride. I just can't see playing second fiddle – particularly to a teenager.'

'My wife's *not* a teenager,' Brinkerhoff defended. 'She just acts like one.'

Midge gave him a surprised look. 'I wasn't talking about your wife.' She batted her eyes innocently. 'I was talking about *Carmen*.' She spoke the name with a thick Puerto Rican accent.

Brinkerhoff's voice cracked slightly. 'Who?'

'Carmen? In food services?'

Brinkerhoff felt himself flush. Carmen Huerta was a twenty-seven-year-old pastry chef who worked in the NSA commissary. Brinkerhoff had enjoyed a number of presumably secret after-hours flings with her in the stockroom.

She gave him a wicked wink. 'Remember, Chad . . . Big Brother knows all.'

Big Brother? Brinkerhoff gulped in disbelief. *Big Brother watches the STOCKROOMS too?*

Big Brother, or 'Brother' as Midge often called it, was a Centrex 333 that sat in a small closetlike space off the suite's central room. Brother was Midge's whole world. It received data from 148 closed circuit video cameras, 399 electronic doors, 377 phone taps, and 212 free-standing bugs in the NSA complex.

The directors of the NSA had learned the hard way that 26,000 employees were not only a great asset but a great liability. Every major security breach in the NSA's history had come from within. It was Midge's job as internal security analyst, to watch everything that went on within the walls of the NSA . . . including, apparently, the commissary stockroom.

Brinkerhoff stood to defend himself, but Midge was already on her way out.

'Hands *above* the desk,' she called over her shoulder. 'No funny stuff after I go. The walls have eyes.'

Brinkerhoff sat and listened to the sound of her heels fading down the corridor. At least he knew Midge would never tell. She was not without her weaknesses. Midge had indulged in a few indiscretions of her own – mostly wandering back rubs with Brinkerhoff.

His thoughts turned back to Carmen. He pictured her lissome body, those dark thighs, that AM radio she played full blast – hot San Juan salsa. He smiled. *Maybe I'll drop by for a snack when I'm done.*

He opened the first printout.

CRYPTO – PRODUCTION / EXPENDITURE

His mood immediately lightened. Midge had given him a freebie; the Crypto report was always a piece of cake. Technically he was supposed to compile the whole thing, but the only figure the director ever asked for was the MCD – the mean cost per decryption. The MCD represented the estimated amount it cost TRANSLTR to break a single code. As long as the figure was below $1,000 per code, Fontaine didn't flinch. *A grand a pop.* Brinkerhoff chuckled. *Our tax dollars at work.*

As he began plowing through the document and checking the daily MCDs, images of Carmen Huerta smearing herself with honey and confectioner's sugar began playing in his head. Thirty seconds later he was almost done. The Crypto data was perfect – as always.

But just before moving on to the next report, something caught his eye. At the bottom of the sheet, the last MCD was off. The figure was so large that it had carried over into the next column and made a mess of the page. Brinkerhoff stared at the figure in shock.

999,999,999? He gasped. *A billion dollars?* The images of Carmen vanished. A *billion*-dollar code?

Brinkerhoff sat there a minute, paralyzed. Then in a burst of panic, he raced out into the hallway. 'Midge! Come back!'

CHAPTER 44

Phil Chartrukian stood fuming in the Sys-Sec lab. Strathmore's words echoed in his head: *Leave now! That's an order!* He kicked the trash can and swore in the empty lab.

'Diagnostic, my ass! Since when does the deputy director bypass Gauntlet's filters!?'

The Sys-Secs were well paid to protect the computer systems at the NSA, and Chartrukian had learned that there were only two job requirements: be utterly brilliant and exhaustively paranoid.

Hell, he cursed, *this isn't paranoia! The fucking Run-Monitor's reading eighteen hours!*

It was a virus. Chartrukian could feel it. There was little doubt in his mind what was going on: Strathmore had made a mistake by bypassing Gauntlet's filters, and now he was trying to cover it up with some half-baked story about a diagnostic.

Chartrukian wouldn't have been quite so edgy had TRANSLTR been the only concern. But it wasn't. Despite its appearance, the great decoding beast was by no means an island. Although the cryptographers believed Gauntlet was constructed for the sole purpose of protecting their code-breaking masterpiece, the Sys-Secs understood the truth. The Gauntlet filters served a much higher god. The NSA's main databank.

The history behind the databank's construction had always fascinated Chartrukian. Despite the efforts of the Department of Defense to keep the Internet to themselves in the late 1970s, it was too useful a tool not to attract the public sector. Eventually universities pried their way in. Shortly after that came the commercial servers. The floodgates opened, and the public poured in. By the early 90s, the government's once-secure 'Internet' was a congested wasteland of public E-mail and cyberporn.

Following a number of unpublicized, yet highly damaging computer infiltrations at the Office of Naval Intelligence, it became increasingly clear that government secrets were no longer safe on computers connected to the burgeoning Internet. The President, in conjunction with the Department of Defense, passed a classified decree that would fund a new, totally secure government network to replace the tainted Internet and function as a link between U.S. intelligence agencies. To prevent further computer pilfering of government secrets, all sensitive data was relocated to one highly secure location – the newly constructed NSA databank – the Fort Knox of U.S. intelligence data.

Literally millions of the country's most classified photos, tapes, documents, and videos were digitized and transferred to the immense storage facility and then the hard copies were destroyed. The databank was protected by a triple-layer power relay and a tiered digital backup system. It was also 214 feet underground to shield it from magnetic fields and possible explosions. Activities within the control room were designated *Top Secret Umbra* ... the country's highest level of security.

The secrets of the country had never been safer. This impregnable databank now housed blueprints for advanced weaponry, witness protection lists, aliases of field agents, detailed analyses and proposals for covert operations. The list was endless. There would be no more black-bag jobs damaging U.S. intelligence.

Of course, the officers of the NSA realized that stored data had value only if it was accessible. The real coup of the databank was not getting the classified data off the streets, it was making it accessible only to the correct people. All stored information had a security rating and, depending on the level of secrecy, was accessible to government officials on a compartmentalized basis. A submarine commander could dial in and check the NSA's most recent satellite photos of Russian ports, but he would not have access to the plans for an antidrug mission in South America. CIA analysts could access histories of known assassins but could not access launch codes reserved for the President.

Sys-Secs, of course, had no clearance for the information in the databank, but they were responsible for its safety. Like all large databanks – from insurance companies to universities – the NSA facility was constantly under attack by computer hackers trying to sneak a peek at the secrets waiting inside. But the NSA security programmers were the best in the world. No one had ever come close to infiltrating the NSA databank – and the NSA had no reason to think anybody ever would.

*

Inside the Sys-Sec lab, Chartrukian broke into a sweat trying to decide whether to leave. Trouble in TRANSLTR meant trouble in the databank too. Strathmore's lack of concern was bewildering.

Everyone knew that TRANSLTR and the NSA main databank were inextricably linked. Each new code, once broken, was fired from Crypto through 450 yards of fiber-optic cable to the NSA databank for safe keeping. The sacred storage facility had limited points of entry – and TRANSLTR was one of them. Gauntlet was supposed to be the impregnable threshold guardian. And Strathmore had bypassed it.

Chartrukian could hear his own heart pounding. *TRANSLTR's been stuck eighteen hours!* The thought of a computer virus entering TRANSLTR and then running wild in the basement of the NSA proved too much. 'I've got to report this,' he blurted aloud.

In a situation like this, Chartrukian knew there was only one person to call: the NSA's senior Sys-Sec officer, the short-fused, 400-pound computer guru who had built Gauntlet. His nickname was Jabba. He was a demigod at the NSA – roaming the halls, putting out virtual fires, and cursing the feeblemindedness of the inept and the ignorant. Chartrukian knew that as soon as Jabba heard Strathmore had bypassed Gauntlet's filters, all hell would break loose. *Too bad*, he thought, *I've got a job to do*. He grabbed the phone and dialed Jabba's twenty-four-hour cellular.

CHAPTER 45

David Becker wandered aimlessly down Avenida del Cid and tried to collect his thoughts. Muted shadows played on the cobblestones beneath his feet. The vodka was still with him. Nothing about his life seemed in focus at the moment. His mind drifted back to Susan, wondering if she'd gotten his phone message yet.

Up ahead, a Seville Transit Bus screeched to a halt in front of a bus stop. Becker looked up. The bus's doors cranked open, but no one disembarked. The diesel engine roared back to life, but just as the bus was pulling out, three teenagers appeared out of a bar up the street and ran after it, yelling and waving. The engines wound down again, and the kids hurried to catch up.

Thirty yards behind them, Becker stared in utter incredulity. His vision was suddenly focused, but he knew what he was seeing was impossible. It was a one-in-a-million chance.

I'm hallucinating.

But as the bus doors opened, the kids crowded around to board. Becker saw it again. This time he was certain. Clearly illuminated in the haze of the corner streetlight, he'd seen her.

The passengers climbed on, and the bus's engines revved up again. Becker suddenly found himself at a full sprint, the bizarre image fixed in his mind – black lipstick, wild eye shadow, and that hair . . . spiked straight up in three distinctive spires. Red, white, and blue.

As the bus started to move, Becker dashed up the street into a wake of carbon monoxide.

'Espera!' he called, running behind the bus.

Becker's cordovan loafers skimmed the pavement. His usual squash agility was not with him, though; he felt off balance. His brain was having trouble keeping track of his feet. He cursed the bartender and his jet lag.

The bus was one of Seville's older diesels, and fortunately for Becker, first gear was a long, arduous climb. Becker felt the gap closing. He knew he had to reach the bus before it downshifted.

The twin tailpipes choked out a cloud of thick smoke as the driver prepared to drop the bus into second gear. Becker strained for more speed. As he surged even with the rear bumper, Becker moved right, racing up beside the bus. He could see the rear doors – and as on all Seville buses, it was propped wide open: cheap air-conditioning.

Becker fixed his sights on the opening and ignored the burning sensation in his legs. The tires were beside him, shoulder-high, humming at a higher and higher pitch every second. He surged toward the door, missing the handle and almost losing his balance. He pushed harder. Underneath the bus, the clutch clicked as the driver prepared to change gears.

He's shifting! I won't make it!

But as the engine cogs disengaged to align the larger gears, the bus let up ever so slightly. Becker lunged. The engine reengaged just as his fingertips curled around the door handle. Becker's shoulder almost ripped from its socket as the engine dug in, catapulting him up onto the landing.

David Becker lay collapsed just inside the vehicle's doorway. The pavement raced by only inches away. He was now sober. His legs and shoulder ached. Wavering, he stood, steadied himself, and climbed into the darkened bus. In the crowd of silhouettes, only a few seats away, were the three distinctive spikes of hair.

Red, white, and blue! I made it!

Becker's mind filled with images of the ring, the waiting Learjet 60, and at the end of it all, Susan.

As Becker came even with the girl's seat wondering what to say to her, the bus passed beneath a streetlight. The punk's face was momentarily illuminated.

Becker stared in horror. The makeup on her face was smeared across a thick stubble. She was not a girl at all, but a young man. He wore a silver stud in his upper lip, a black leather jacket, and no shirt.

'What the fuck do *you* want?' the hoarse voice asked. His accent was New York.

With the disoriented nausea of a slow-motion free fall, Becker gazed at the busload of passengers staring back at him. They were all punks. At least half of them had red, white, and blue hair.

'Siéntate!' the driver yelled.

Becker was too dazed to hear.

'*Siéntate!*' The driver screamed. '*Sit down!*'

Becker turned vaguely to the angry face in the rearview mirror. But he had waited too long.

Annoyed, the driver slammed down hard on the brakes. Becker felt his weight shift. He reached for a seat back but missed. For an instant, David Becker was airborne. Then he landed hard on the gritty floor.

On Avenida del Cid, a figure stepped from the shadows. He adjusted his wire-rim glasses and peered after the departing bus. David Becker had escaped, but it would not be for long. Of all the buses in Seville, Mr Becker had just boarded the infamous number 27.

Bus 27 had only one destination.

CHAPTER 46

Phil Chartrukian slammed down his receiver. Jabba's line was busy; Jabba spurned call-waiting as an intrusive gimmick that was introduced by AT&T to increase profits by connecting every call; the simple phrase 'I'm on the other line, I'll call you back' made phone companies millions annually. Jabba's refusal of call-waiting was his own brand of silent objection to the NSA's requirement that he carry an emergency cellular at all times.

Chartrukian turned and looked out at the deserted Crypto floor. The hum of the generators below sounded louder every minute. He sensed that time was running out. He knew he was supposed to leave, but from out of the rumble beneath Crypto, the Sys-Sec mantra began playing in his head: *Act first, explain later.*

In the high-stakes world of computer security, minutes often meant the difference between saving a system or losing it. There was seldom time to justify a defensive procedure before taking it. Sys-Secs were paid for their technical expertise . . . and their instinct.

Act first, explain later. Chartrukian knew what he

had to do. He also knew that when the dust settled, he would be either an NSA hero or in the unemployment line.

The great decoding computer had a virus – of that, the Sys-Sec was certain. There was one responsible course of action. Shut it down.

Chartrukian knew there were only two ways to shut down TRANSLTR. One was the commander's private terminal, which was locked in his office – out of the question. The other was the manual kill-switch located on one of the sublevels beneath the Crypto floor.

Chartrukian swallowed hard. He hated the sublevels. He'd only been there once, during training. It was like something out of an alien world with its long mazes of catwalks, freon ducts, and a dizzy 136-foot drop to the rumbling power supplies below . . .

It was the last place he felt like going, and Strathmore was the last person he felt like crossing, but duty was duty. *They'll thank me tomorrow*, he thought, wondering if he was right.

Taking a deep breath, Chartrukian opened the senior Sys-Sec's metal locker. On a shelf of disassembled computer parts, hidden behind a media concentrator and LAN tester, was a Stanford alumni mug. Without touching the rim, he reached inside and lifted out a single Medeco key.

'It's amazing,' he grumbled, 'what System-Security officers *don't* know about security.'

CHAPTER 47

'A billion-dollar code?' Midge snickered, accompanying Brinkerhoff back up the hallway. 'That's a good one.'

'I swear it,' he said.

She eyed him askance. 'This better not be some ploy to get me out of this dress.'

'Midge, I would never—' he said self-righteously.

'I know, Chad. Don't remind me.'

Thirty seconds later, Midge was sitting in Brinkerhoff's chair and studying the Crypto report.

'See?' he said, leaning over her and pointing to the figure in question. 'This MCD? A billion dollars!'

Midge chuckled. 'It *does* appear to be a touch on the high side, doesn't it?'

'Yeah.' He groaned. 'Just a touch.'

'Looks like a divide-by-zero.'

'A who?'

'A divide-by-zero,' she said, scanning the rest of the data. 'The MCD's calculated as a fraction – total expense divided by number of decryptions.'

'Of course.' Brinkerhoff nodded blankly and tried not to peer down the front of her dress.

'When the denominator's zero,' Midge explained, 'the quotient goes to infinity. Computers hate infinity, so they type all nines.' She pointed to a different column. 'See this?'

'Yeah.' Brinkerhoff refocused on the paper.

'It's today's raw production data. Take a look at the number of decryptions.'

Brinkerhoff dutifully followed her finger down the column.

$$\text{NUMBER OF DECRYPTIONS} = 0$$

Midge tapped on the figure. 'It's just as I suspected. Divide-by-zero.'

Brinkerhoff arched his eyebrows. 'So everything's okay?'

She shrugged. 'Just means we haven't broken any codes today. TRANSLTR must be taking a break.'

'A break?' Brinkerhoff looked doubtful. He'd been with the director long enough to know that 'breaks' were not part of his preferred modus operandi – particularly with respect to TRANSLTR. Fontaine had paid $2 billion for the code-breaking behemoth, and he wanted his money's worth. Every second TRANSLTR sat idle was money down the toilet.

'Ah . . . Midge?' Brinkerhoff said. 'TRANSLTR doesn't take any breaks. It runs day and night. You know that.'

She shrugged. 'Maybe Strathmore didn't feel like hanging out last night to prepare the weekend run. He probably knew Fontaine was away and ducked out early to go fishing.'

'Come on, Midge.' Brinkerhoff gave her a disgusted look. 'Give the guy a break.'

It was no secret Midge Milken didn't like Trevor Strathmore. Strathmore had attempted a cunning maneuver rewriting Skipjack, but he'd been caught. Despite Strathmore's bold intentions, the NSA had paid dearly. The EFF had gained strength, Fontaine had lost credibility with Congress, and worst of all, the agency had lost a lot of its anonymity. There were suddenly housewives in Minnesota complaining to America Online and Prodigy that the NSA might be reading their E-mail – like the NSA gave a damn about a secret recipe for candied yams.

Strathmore's blunder had cost the NSA, and Midge felt responsible – not that she could have anticipated the commander's stunt, but the bottom line was that an unauthorized action had taken place behind Director Fontaine's back, a back Midge was paid to cover. Fontaine's hands-off attitude made him susceptible; and it made Midge nervous. But the director had learned long ago to stand back and let smart people do their jobs; that's exactly how he handled Trevor Strathmore.

'Midge, you know damn well Strathmore's not slacking,' Brinkerhoff argued. 'He runs TRANSLTR like a fiend.'

Midge nodded. Deep down, she knew that accusing Strathmore of shirking was absurd. The commander was as dedicated as they came – dedicated to a fault. He bore the evils of the world as his own personal cross. The NSA's Skipjack plan had been Strathmore's brainchild – a bold attempt to change the world. Unfortunately, like so many divine quests, this crusade ended in crucifixion.

'Okay,' she admitted, 'so I'm being a little harsh.'

'A little?' Brinkerhoff's eyes narrowed. 'Strathmore's

228

got a backlog of files a mile long. He's not about to let TRANSLTR sit idle for a whole weekend.'

'Okay, okay.' Midge sighed. 'My mistake.' She furrowed her brow and puzzled why TRANSLTR hadn't broken any codes all day. 'Let me double-check something,' she said, and began flipping through the report. She located what she was looking for and scanned the figures. After a moment she nodded. 'You're right, Chad. TRANSLTR's been running full force. Raw consumables are even a little on the high side; we're at over half a million kilowatt-hours since midnight last night.'

'So where does that leave us?'

Midge was puzzled. 'I'm not sure. It's odd.'

'You want to rerun the data?'

She gave him a disapproving stare. There were two things one never questioned about Midge Milken. One of them was her data. Brinkerhoff waited while Midge studied the figures.

'Huh,' she finally grunted. 'Yesterday's stats look fine: 237 codes broken. MCD, $874. Average time per code, a little over six minutes. Raw consumables, average. Last code entering TRANSLTR—' She stopped.

'What is it?'

'That's funny,' she said. 'Last file on yesterday's queue log ran at 11:37 P.M.'

'So?'

'So, TRANSLTR breaks codes every six minutes or so. The last file of the day usually runs closer to midnight. It sure doesn't look like—' Midge suddenly stopped short and gasped.

Brinkerhoff jumped. 'What!'

Midge was staring at the readout in disbelief. 'This file? The one that entered TRANSLTR last night?'

'Yeah?'

'It hasn't broken yet. Its queue time was 23:37:08 – but it lists *no* decrypt time.' Midge fumbled with the sheets. 'Yesterday *or* today!'

Brinkerhoff shrugged. 'Maybe those guys are running a tough diagnostic.'

Midge shook her head. *'Eighteen hours tough?'* She paused. 'Not likely. Besides, the queue data says it's an outside file. We should call Strathmore.'

'At home?' Brinkerhoff swallowed. 'On a Saturday night?'

'No,' Midge said. 'If I know Strathmore, he's on top of this. I'll bet good money he's here. Just a hunch.' Midge's hunches were the other thing one never questioned. 'Come on,' she said, standing up. 'Let's see if I'm right.'

Brinkerhoff followed Midge to her office, where she sat down and began to work Big Brother's keypads like a virtuoso pipe organist.

Brinkerhoff gazed up at the array of closed-caption video monitors on her wall, their screens all freeze frames of the NSA seal. 'You're gonna snoop Crypto?' he asked nervously.

'Nope,' Midge replied. 'Wish I could, but Crypto's a sealed deal. It's got no video. No sound. No nothing. Strathmore's orders. All I've got is approach stats and basic TRANSLTR stuff. We're lucky we've even got *that*. Strathmore wanted total isolation, but Fontaine insisted on the basics.'

Brinkerhoff looked puzzled. 'Crypto hasn't got video?'

'Why?' she asked, without turning from her monitor. 'You and Carmen looking for a little more privacy?'

Brinkerhoff grumbled something inaudible.

Midge typed some more keys. 'I'm pulling Strathmore's elevator log.' She studied her monitor a moment and then rapped her knuckle on the desk. 'He's here,' she said matter-of-factly. 'He's in Crypto right now. Look at this. Talk about long hours – he went in yesterday morning bright and early, and his elevator hasn't budged since. I'm showing no magno-card use for him on the main door. So he's definitely in there.'

Brinkerhoff breathed a slight sigh of relief. 'So, if Strathmore's in there, everything's okay, right?'

Midge thought a moment. 'Maybe,' she finally decided.

'Maybe?'

'We should call him and double-check.'

Brinkerhoff groaned. 'Midge, he's the deputy direc-tor. I'm sure he has everything under control. Let's not second-guess—'

'Oh, come on, Chad – don't be such a child. We're just doing our job. We've got a snag in the stats, and we're following up. Besides,' she added, 'I'd like to remind Strathmore that Big Brother's watching. Make him think twice before planning any more of his hare-brained stunts to save the world.' Midge picked up the phone and began dialing.

Brinkerhoff looked uneasy. 'You really think you should bother him?'

'I'm not bothering him,' Midge said, tossing him the receiver. '*You* are.'

CHAPTER 48

'What?' Midge sputtered in disbelief. 'Strathmore claims our data is wrong?'

Brinkerhoff nodded and hung up the phone.

'Strathmore *denied* that TRANSLTR's been stuck on one file for eighteen hours?'

'He was quite pleasant about the whole thing.' Brinkerhoff beamed, pleased with himself for surviving the phone call. 'He assured me TRANSLTR was working fine. Said it was breaking codes every six minutes even as we speak. Thanked me for checking up on him.'

'He's lying,' Midge snapped. 'I've been running these Crypto stats for two years. The data is never wrong.'

'First time for everything,' he said casually.

She shot him a disapproving look. 'I run all data *twice.*'

'Well . . . you know what they say about computers. When they screw up, at least they're consistent about it.'

Midge spun and faced him. 'This isn't funny, Chad! The DDO just told a blatant lie to the director's office. I want to know why!'

Brinkerhoff suddenly wished he hadn't called her back in. Strathmore's phone call had set her off. Ever since Skipjack, whenever Midge had a sense that something suspicious was going on, she made an eerie transition from flirt to fiend. There was no stopping her until she sorted it out.

'Midge, it *is* possible our data is off,' Brinkerhoff said firmly. 'I mean, think about it – a file that ties up TRANSLTR for eighteen hours? It's unheard of. Go home. It's late.'

She gave him a haughty look and tossed the report on the counter. 'I trust the data. Instinct says it's right.'

Brinkerhoff frowned. Not even the director questioned Midge Milken's instincts anymore – she had an uncanny habit of always being right.

'Something's up,' she declared. 'And I intend to find out what it is.'

CHAPTER 49

Becker dragged himself off the floor of the bus and collapsed in an empty seat.

'Nice move, dipshit.' The kid with the three spikes sneered. Becker squinted in the stark lighting. It was the kid he'd chased onto the bus. He glumly surveyed the sea of red, white, and blue coiffures.

'What's with the hair?' Becker moaned, motioning to the others. 'It's all . . .'

'Red, white, and blue?' the kid offered.

Becker nodded, trying not to stare at the infected perforation in the kid's upper lip.

'Judas Taboo,' the kid said matter-of-factly.

Becker looked bewildered.

The punk spat in the aisle, obviously disgusted with Becker's ignorance. 'Judas Taboo? Greatest punk since Sid Vicious? Blew his head off here a year ago today. It's his anniversary.'

Becker nodded vaguely, obviously missing the connection.

'Taboo did his hair this way the day he signed off.' The kid spat again. 'Every fan worth his weight in piss has got red, white, and blue hair today.'

For a long moment, Becker said nothing. Slowly, as if he had been shot with a tranquilizer, he turned and faced front. Becker surveyed the group on the bus. Every last one was a punk. Most were staring at him.

Every fan has red, white, and blue hair today.

Becker reached up and pulled the driver-alert cord on the wall. It was time to get off. He pulled again. Nothing happened. He pulled a third time, more frantically. Nothing.

'They disconnect 'em on bus 27.' The kid spat again. 'So we don't fuck with 'em.'

Becker turned. 'You mean, I can't get off?'

The kid laughed. 'Not till the end of the line.'

Five minutes later, the bus was barreling along an unlit Spanish country road. Becker turned to the kid behind him. 'Is this thing ever going to stop?'

The kid nodded. 'Few more miles.'

'Where are we going?'

He broke into a sudden wide grin. 'You mean you don't know?'

Becker shrugged.

The kid started laughing hysterically. 'Oh, shit. You're gonna love it.'

CHAPTER 50

Only yards from TRANSLTR's hull, Phil Chartrukian stood over a patch of white lettering on the Crypto floor.

CRYPTO SUBLEVELS
AUTHORIZED PERSONNEL ONLY

He knew he was definitely *not* authorized personnel. He shot a quick glance up at Strathmore's office. The curtains were still pulled. Chartrukian had seen Susan Fletcher go into the bathrooms, so he knew she wasn't a problem. The only other question was Hale. He glanced toward Node 3, wondering if the cryptographer were watching.

'Fuck it,' he grumbled.

Below his feet the outline of a recessed trapdoor was barely visible in the floor. Chartrukian palmed the key he'd just taken from the Sys-Sec lab.

He knelt down, inserted the key in the floor, and turned. The bolt beneath clicked. Then he unscrewed the large external butterfly latch and freed the door. Checking once again over his shoulder, he squatted down and pulled. The panel was small, only three feet by three feet, but it was heavy. When it finally opened, the Sys-Sec stumbled back.

A blast of hot air hit him in the face. It carried with it the sharp bite of freon gas. Billows of steam swirled out of the opening, illuminated by the red utility lighting below. The distant hum of the generators became a rumble. Chartrukian stood up and peered into the opening. It looked more like the gateway to hell than a service entrance for a computer. A narrow ladder led to a platform under the floor. Beyond that, there were stairs, but all he could see was swirling red mist.

Greg Hale stood behind the one-way glass of Node 3. He watched as Phil Chartrukian eased himself down the ladder toward the sublevels. From where Hale was standing, the Sys-Sec's head appeared to have been severed from his body and left out on the Crypto floor. Then, slowly, it sank into the swirling mist.

'Gutsy move,' Hale muttered. He knew where Chartrukian was headed. An emergency manual abort of TRANSLTR was a logical action if he thought the computer had a virus. Unfortunately, it was also a sure way to have Crypto crawling with Sys-Secs in about ten minutes. Emergency actions raised alert flags at the main switchboard. A Sys-Sec investigation of Crypto was something Hale could not afford. Hale left Node 3 and headed for the trapdoor. Chartrukian had to be stopped.

CHAPTER 51

Jabba resembled a giant tadpole. Like the cinematic creature for whom he was nicknamed, the man was a hairless spheroid. As resident guardian angel of all NSA computer systems, Jabba marched from department to department, tweaking, soldering, and reaffirming his credo that prevention was the best medicine. No NSA computer had ever been infected under Jabba's reign; he intended to keep it that way.

Jabba's home base was a raised workstation overlooking the NSA's underground, ultra-secret databank. It was there that a virus would do the most damage and there that he spent the majority of his time. At the moment, however, Jabba was taking a break and enjoying pepperoni calzones in the NSA's all-night commissary. He was about to dig into his third when his cellular phone rang.

'Go,' he said, coughing as he swallowed a mouthful.

'Jabba,' a woman's voice cooed. 'It's Midge.'

'Data Queen!' the huge man gushed. He'd always had a soft spot for Midge Milken. She was sharp, and

238

she was also the only woman Jabba had ever met who flirted with him. 'How the hell are you?'

'No complaints.'

Jabba wiped his mouth. 'You on site?'

'Yup.'

'Care to join me for a calzone?'

'Love to, Jabba, but I'm watching these hips.'

'Really?' He snickered. 'Mind if I join you?'

'You're bad.'

'You have no idea. . . .'

'Glad I caught you in,' she said. 'I need some advice.'

He took a long swallow of Dr Pepper. 'Shoot.'

'It might be nothing,' Midge said, 'but my Crypto stats turned up something odd. I was hoping you could shed some light.'

'What ya got?' He took another sip.

'I've got a report saying TRANSLTR's been running the same file for eighteen hours and hasn't cracked it.'

Jabba sprayed Dr Pepper all over his calzone. 'You *what?*'

'Any ideas?'

He dabbed at his calzone with a napkin. 'What report is this?'

'Production report. Basic cost analysis stuff.' Midge quickly explained what she and Brinkerhoff had found.

'Have you called Strathmore?'

'Yes. He said everything's fine in Crypto. Said TRANSLTR's running full speed ahead. Said our data's wrong.'

Jabba furrowed his bulbous forehead. 'So what's the problem? Your report glitched.' Midge did not respond. Jabba caught her drift. He frowned. 'You don't think your report glitched?'

'Correct.'

'So you think Strathmore's lying?'

'It's not that,' Midge said diplomatically, knowing she was on fragile ground. 'It's just that my stats have never been wrong in the past. I thought I'd get a second opinion.'

'Well,' Jabba said, 'I hate to be the one to break it to you, but your data's fried.'

'You think so?'

'I'd bet my job on it.' Jabba took a big bite of soggy calzone and spoke with his mouth full. 'Longest a file has ever lasted inside TRANSLTR is three hours. That includes diagnostics, boundary probes, everything. Only thing that could lock it down for eighteen hours would have to be viral. Nothing else could do it.'

'Viral?'

'Yeah, some kind of redundant cycle. Something that got into the processors, created a loop, and basically gummed up the works.'

'Well,' she ventured, 'Strathmore's been in Crypto for about thirty-six hours straight. Any chance he's fighting a virus?'

Jabba laughed. 'Strathmore's been in there for thirty-six hours? Poor bastard. His wife probably said he can't come home. I hear she's bagging his ass.'

Midge thought a moment. She'd heard that too. She wondered if maybe she was being paranoid.

'Midge.' Jabba wheezed and took another long drink. 'If Strathmore's toy had a virus, he would have called me. Strathmore's sharp, but he doesn't know shit about viruses. TRANSLTR's all he's got. First sign of trouble, he would have pressed the panic button –

and around here, that means *me.*' Jabba sucked in a long strand of mozzarella. 'Besides, there's no way in hell TRANSLTR has a virus. Gauntlet's the best set of package filters I've ever written. Nothing gets through.'

After a long silence, Midge sighed. 'Any other thoughts?'

'Yup. Your data's fried.'

'You already said that.'

'Exactly.'

She frowned. 'You haven't caught wind of anything? Anything at all?'

Jabba laughed harshly. 'Midge . . . listen up. Skipjack sucked. Strathmore blew it. But move on – it's over.' There was a long silence on the line, and Jabba realized he'd gone too far. 'Sorry, Midge. I know you took heat over that whole mess. Strathmore was wrong. I know how you feel about him.'

'This has nothing to do with Skipjack,' she said firmly.

Yeah, sure, Jabba thought. 'Listen, Midge, I don't have feelings for Strathmore one way or another. I mean, the guy's a cryptographer. They're basically all self-centered assholes. They need their data yesterday. Every damn file is the one that could save the world.'

'So what are you saying?'

Jabba sighed. 'I'm saying Strathmore's a psycho like the rest of them. But I'm also saying he loves TRANSLTR more than his own goddamn wife. If there were a problem, he would have called me.'

Midge was quiet a long time. Finally she let out a reluctant sigh. 'So you're saying my data's fried?'

Jabba chuckled. 'Is there an echo in here?'

She laughed.

'Look, Midge. Drop me a work order. I'll be up on Monday to double-check your machine. In the meantime, get the hell out of here. It's Saturday night. Go get yourself laid or something.'

She sighed. 'I'm trying, Jabba. Believe me, I'm trying.'

CHAPTER 52

Club Embrujo – 'Warlock' in English – was situated in the suburbs at the end of the number 27 bus line. Looking more like a fortification than a dance club, it was surrounded on all sides by high stucco walls into which were embedded shards of shattered beer bottles – a crude security system preventing anyone from entering illegally without leaving behind a good portion of flesh.

During the ride, Becker had resolved himself to the fact that he'd failed. It was time to call Strathmore with the bad news – the search was hopeless. He had done the best he could; now it was time to go home.

But now, gazing out at the mob of patrons pushing their way through the club's entrance, Becker was not so sure his conscience would allow him to give up the search. He was staring at the biggest crowd of punks he'd ever seen; there were coiffures of red, white, and blue everywhere.

Becker sighed, weighing his options. He scanned the crowd and shrugged. *Where else would she be on a Saturday night?* Cursing his good fortune, Becker climbed off the bus.

The access to Club Embrujo was a narrow stone corridor. As Becker entered he immediately felt himself caught up in the inward surge of eager patrons.

'Outta my way, faggot!' A human pincushion pawed past him, giving Becker an elbow in the side.

'Nice tie.' Someone gave Becker's necktie a hard yank.

'Wanna fuck?' A teenage girl stared up at him looking like something out of *Dawn of the Dead.*

The darkness of the corridor spilled out into a huge cement chamber that reeked of alcohol and body odor. The scene was surreal – a deep mountain grotto in which hundreds of bodies moved as one. They surged up and down, hands pressed firmly to their sides, heads bobbing like lifeless bulbs on top of rigid spines. Crazed souls took running dives off a stage and landed on a sea of human limbs. Bodies were passed back and forth like human beach balls. Overhead, the pulsating strobes gave the whole thing the look of an old, silent movie.

On the far wall, speakers the size of minivans shook so deeply that not even the most dedicated dancers could get closer than thirty feet from the pounding woofers.

Becker plugged his ears and searched the crowd. Everywhere he looked was another red, white, and blue head. The bodies were packed so closely together that he couldn't see what they were wearing. He saw no hint of a British flag anywhere. It was obvious he'd never be able to enter the crowd without getting trampled. Someone nearby started vomiting.

Lovely. Becker groaned. He moved off down a spray-painted hallway.

The hall turned into a narrow mirrored tunnel,

which opened to an outdoor patio scattered with tables and chairs. The patio was crowded with punk rockers, but to Becker it was like the gateway to Shangri-La – the summer sky opened up above him and the music faded away.

Ignoring the curious stares, Becker walked out into the crowd. He loosened his tie and collapsed into a chair at the nearest unoccupied table. It seemed like a lifetime since Strathmore's early-morning call.

After clearing the empty beer bottles from his table, Becker laid his head in his hands. *Just for a few minutes,* he thought.

Five miles away, the man in wire-rim glasses sat in the back of a Fiat taxi as it raced headlong down a country road.

'Embrujo,' he grunted, reminding the driver of their destination.

The driver nodded, eyeing his curious new fare in the rearview mirror. 'Embrujo,' he grumbled to himself. 'Weirder crowd every night.'

CHAPTER 53

Tokugen Numataka lay naked on the massage table in his penthouse office. His personal masseuse worked out the kinks in his neck. She ground her palms into the fleshy pockets surrounding his shoulder blades, slowly working her way down to the towel covering his backside. Her hands slipped lower . . . beneath his towel. Numataka barely noticed. His mind was elsewhere. He had been waiting for his private line to ring. It had not.

There was a knock at the door.

'Enter,' Numataka grunted.

The masseuse quickly pulled her hands from beneath the towel.

The switchboard operator entered and bowed. 'Honored chairman?'

'Speak.'

The operator bowed a second time. 'I spoke to the phone exchange. The call originated from country code 1 – the United States.'

Numataka nodded. This was good news. *The call came from the States.* He smiled. *It was genuine.*

'Where in the U.S.?' he demanded.

'They're working on it, sir.'

'Very well. Tell me when you have more.'

The operator bowed again and left.

Numataka felt his muscles relax. Country code 1. Good news indeed.

CHAPTER 54

Susan Fletcher paced impatiently in the Crypto bathroom and counted slowly to fifty. Her head was throbbing. *Just a little longer,* she told herself. *Hale is North Dakota!*

Susan wondered what Hale's plans were. Would he announce the pass-key? Would he be greedy and try to sell the algorithm? Susan couldn't bear to wait any longer. It was time. She had to get to Strathmore.

Cautiously she cracked the door and peered out at the reflective wall on the far side of Crypto. There was no way to know if Hale was still watching. She'd have to move quickly to Strathmore's office. Not too quickly, of course – she could not let Hale suspect she was on to him. She reached for the door and was about to pull it open when she heard something. Voices. Men's voices.

The voices were coming through the ventilation shaft near the floor. She released the door and moved toward the vent. The words were muffled by the dull hum of the generators below. The conversation sounded like it was coming up from the sublevel cat-walks. One voice was shrill, angry. It sounded like Phil Chartrukian.

'You don't believe me?'

The sound of more arguing rose.

'We have a virus!'

Then the sound of harsh yelling.

'We need to call Jabba!'

Then there were sounds of a struggle.

'Let me go!'

The noise that followed was barely human. It was a long wailing cry of horror, like a tortured animal about to die. Susan froze beside the vent. The noise ended as abruptly as it had begun. Then there was a silence.

An instant later, as if choreographed for some cheap horror matinee, the lights in the bathroom slowly dimmed. Then they flickered and went out. Susan Fletcher found herself standing in total blackness.

CHAPTER 55

'You're in my seat, asshole.'

Becker lifted his head off his arms. *Doesn't anyone speak Spanish in this damn country?*

Glaring down at him was a short, pimple-faced teenager with a shaved head. Half of his scalp was red and half was purple. He looked like an Easter egg. 'I said you're in my seat, asshole.'

'I heard you the first time,' Becker said, standing up. He was in no mood for a fight. It was time to go.

'Where'd you put my bottles?' the kid snarled. There was a safety pin in his nose.

Becker pointed to the beer bottles he'd set on the ground. 'They were empty.'

'They were *my* fuckin' empties!'

'My apologies,' Becker said, and turned to go.

The punk blocked his way. 'Pick 'em up!'

Becker blinked, not amused. 'You're kidding, right?' He was a full foot taller and outweighed the kid by about fifty pounds.

'Do I fuckin' *look* like I'm kidding?'

Becker said nothing.

'Pick 'em up!' The kid's voice cracked.

Becker attempted to step around him, but the teenager blocked his way. 'I said, fuckin' pick 'em up!'

Stoned punks at nearby tables began turning to watch the excitement.

'You don't want to do this, kid,' Becker said quietly.

'I'm warning you!' The kid seethed. 'This is my table! I come here every night. Now *pick 'em up!*'

Becker's patience ran out. Wasn't he supposed to be in the Smokys with Susan? What was he doing in Spain arguing with a psychotic adolescent?

Without warning, Becker caught the kid under the armpits, lifted him up, and slammed his rear end down on the table. 'Look, you runny-nosed little runt. You're going to back off right now, or I'm going to rip that safety pin out of your nose and pin your mouth shut.'

The kid's face went pale.

Becker held him a moment, then he released his grip. Without taking his eyes off the frightened kid, Becker stooped down, picked up the bottles, and returned them to the table. 'What do you say?' he asked.

The kid was speechless.

'You're welcome,' Becker snapped. *This kid's a walking billboard for birth control.*

'Go to hell!' the kid yelled, now aware of his peers laughing at him. 'Ass-wipe!'

Becker didn't move. Something the kid had said suddenly registered. *I come here every night.* Becker wondered if maybe the kid could help him. 'I'm sorry,' Becker said, 'I didn't catch your name.'

'Two-Tone,' he hissed, as if he were giving a death sentence.

'Two-Tone?' Becker mused. 'Let me guess . . . because of your hair?'

251

'No shit, Sherlock.'

'Catchy name. Make that up yourself?'

'Damn straight,' he said proudly. 'I'm gonna *patent* it.'

Becker scowled. 'You mean *trademark it?'*

The kid looked confused.

'You'd need a trademark for a name,' Becker said. 'Not a patent.'

'Whatever!' the punk screamed in frustration.

The motley assortment of drunken and drugged-out kids at the nearby tables were now in hysterics. Two-Tone stood up and sneered at Becker. 'What the fuck do you want from me?'

Becker thought a moment. *I want you to wash your hair, clean up your language, and get a job.* Becker figured it was too much to ask on a first meeting. 'I need some information,' he said.

'Fuck you.'

'I'm looking for someone.'

'I ain't seen him.'

'Haven't seen him,' Becker corrected as he flagged a passing waitress. He bought two Aguila beers and handed one to Two-Tone. The boy looked shocked. He took a swig of beer and eyed Becker warily.

'You hitting on me, mister?'

Becker smiled. 'I'm looking for a girl.'

Two-Tone let out a shrill laugh. 'You sure as hell ain't gonna get any action dressed like that!'

Becker frowned. 'I'm not looking for action. I just need to talk to her. Maybe you could help me find her.'

Two-Tone set down his beer. 'You a cop?'

Becker shook his head.

The kid's eyes narrowed. 'You look like a cop.'

'Kid, I'm from Maryland. If I were a cop, I'd be a little out of my jurisdiction, don't you think?'

The question seemed to stump him.

'My name's David Becker.' Becker smiled and offered his hand across the table.

The punk recoiled in disgust. 'Back off, fag boy.'

Becker retracted the hand.

The kid sneered. 'I'll help you, but it'll cost you.'

Becker played along. 'How much?'

'A hundred bucks.'

Becker frowned. 'I've only got pesetas.'

'Whatever! Make it a hundred *pesetas*.'

Foreign currency exchange was obviously not one of Two-Tone's fortes; a hundred pesetas was about eighty-seven cents. 'Deal,' Becker said, rapping his bottle on the table.

The kid smiled for the first time. 'Deal.'

'Okay,' Becker continued in his hushed tone. 'I figure the girl I'm looking for might hang out here. She's got red, white, and blue hair.'

Two-Tone snorted. 'It's Judas Taboo's anniversary. Everybody's got—'

'She's also wearing a British flag T-shirt and has a skull pendant in one ear.'

A faint look of recognition crossed Two-Tone's face. Becker saw it and felt a surge of hope. But a moment later Two-Tone's expression turned stern. He slammed his bottle down and grabbed Becker's shirt.

'She's Eduardo's, you asshole! I'd watch it! You touch her, and he'll kill you!'

CHAPTER 56

Midge Milken prowled angrily into the conference room across from her office. In addition to the thirty-two-foot mahogany table with the NSA seal inlaid in black cherry and walnut, the conference room contained three Marion Pike watercolors, a Boston fern, a marble wet bar, and of course, the requisite Sparkletts water cooler. Midge helped herself to a glass of water, hoping it might calm her nerves.

As she sipped at the liquid, she gazed across at the window. The moonlight was filtering through the open venetian blind and playing on the grain of the table. She'd always thought this would make a nicer director's office than Fontaine's current location on the front of the building. Rather than looking out over the NSA parking lot, the conference room looked out over an impressive array of NSA outbuildings – including the Crypto dome, a high-tech island floating separate from the main building on three wooded acres. Purposefully situated behind the natural cover of a grove of maples, Crypto was difficult to see from most windows in the NSA complex, but the view from the directorial suite was perfect. To Midge the conference room seemed the perfect vantage point for a king to survey his domain. She had suggested once that Fontaine move his office, but the director had simply replied, 'Not on the rear.' Fontaine was not a man to be found on the back end of anything.

Midge pulled apart the blinds. She stared out at the hills. Sighing ruefully, she let her eyes fall toward the spot where Crypto stood. Midge had always felt comforted by the sight of the Crypto dome – a glowing beacon regardless of the hour. But tonight, as she gazed out, there was no comfort. Instead she found herself staring into a void. As she pressed her face to the glass, she was gripped by a wild, girlish panic. Below her there was nothing but blackness. Crypto had disappeared!

CHAPTER 57

The Crypto bathrooms had no windows, and the darkness surrounding Susan Fletcher was absolute. She stood dead still for a moment trying to get her bearings, acutely aware of the growing sense of panic gripping her body. The horrible cry from the ventilation shaft seemed to hang all around her. Despite her effort to fight off a rising sense of dread, fear swept across her flesh and took control.

In a flurry of involuntary motion, Susan found herself groping wildly across stall doors and sinks. Disoriented, she spun through the blackness with her hands out in front of her and tried to picture the room. She knocked over a garbage can and found herself against a tiled wall. Following the wall with her hand, she scrambled toward the exit and fumbled for the door handle. She pulled it open and stumbled out onto the Crypto floor.

There she froze for a second time.

The Crypto floor looked nothing like it had just moments ago. TRANSLTR was a gray silhouette against the faint twilight coming in through the dome. All of the overhead lighting was dead. Not even the electronic keypads on the doors were glowing.

As Susan's eyes became accustomed to the dark, she saw that the only light in Crypto was coming through the open trapdoor – a faint red glow from the utility lighting below. She moved toward it. There was the faint smell of ozone in the air.

When she made it to the trapdoor, she peered into the hole. The freon vents were still belching swirling mist through the redness, and from the higher-pitched drone of the generators, Susan knew Crypto was running on backup power. Through the mist she could make out Strathmore standing on the platform below. He was leaning over the railing and staring into the depths of TRANSLTR's rumbling shaft.

'Commander!'

There was no response.

Susan eased onto the ladder. The hot air from below rushed in under her skirt. The rungs were slippery with condensation. She set herself down on the grated landing.

'Commander?'

Strathmore did not turn. He continued staring down with a blank look of shock, as if in a trance. Susan followed his gaze over the banister. For a moment she could see nothing except wisps of steam. Then suddenly she saw it. A figure. Six stories below. It appeared briefly in the billows of steam. There it was again. A tangled mass of twisted limbs. Lying ninety feet below them, Phil Chartrukian was sprawled across the sharp iron fins of the main generator. His body was darkened and burned. His fall had shorted out Crypto's main power supply.

But the most chilling image of all was not of Chartrukian but of someone else, another body, halfway down the long staircase, crouched, hiding in the shadows. The muscular frame was unmistakable. It was Greg Hale.

CHAPTER 58

The punk screamed at Becker, 'Megan belongs to my friend Eduardo! You stay away from her!'

'Where is she?' Becker's heart was racing out of control.

'Fuck you!'

'It's an emergency!' Becker snapped. He grabbed the kid's sleeve. 'She's got a ring that belongs to me. I'll pay her for it! A lot!'

Two-Tone stopped dead and burst into hysterics. 'You mean that ugly, gold piece of shit is yours?'

Becker's eyes widened. 'You've seen it?'

Two-Tone nodded coyly.

'Where is it?' Becker demanded.

'No clue.' Two-Tone chuckled. 'Megan was up here trying to hock it.'

'She was trying to *sell* it?'

'Don't worry, man, she didn't have any luck. You've got shitty taste in jewelry.'

'Are you sure nobody bought it?'

'Are you shitting me? For four hundred bucks? I told her I'd give her fifty, but she wanted more. She was trying to buy a plane ticket – standby.'

Becker felt the blood drain from his face. 'Where to?'

'Fuckin' Connecticut,' Two-tone snapped. 'Eddie's bummin'.'

'Connecticut?'

'Shit, yeah. Going back to Mommy and Daddy's mansion in the burbs. Hated her Spanish homestay family. Three Spic brothers always hitting on her. No fucking hot water.'

Becker felt a knot rise in his throat. 'When is she leaving?'

Two-Tone looked up. 'When?' He laughed. 'She's long gone by now. Went to the airport hours ago. Best spot to hock the ring – rich tourists and shit. Once she got the cash, she was flying out.'

A dull nausea swept through Becker's gut. *This is some kind of sick joke, isn't it?* He stood a long moment. 'What's her last name?'

Two-Tone pondered the question and shrugged.

'What flight was she taking?'

'She said something about the Roach Coach.'

'Roach Coach?'

'Yeah. Weekend red-eye – Seville, Madrid, La Guardia. That's what they call it. College kids take it 'cause it's cheap. Guess they sit in back and smoke roaches.'

Great. Becker groaned, running a hand through his hair. 'What time did it leave?'

'Two A.M. sharp, every Saturday night. She's somewhere over the Atlantic by now.'

Becker checked his watch. It read 1:45 A.M. He turned to Two-Tone, confused. 'You said it's a two A.M. flight?'

The punk nodded, laughing. 'Looks like you're fucked, ol' man.'

259

Becker pointed angrily to his watch. 'But it's only quarter to two!'

Two-Tone eyed the watch, apparently puzzled. 'Well, I'll be damned.' He laughed. 'I'm usually not this buzzed till four A.M.!'

'What's the fastest way to the airport?' Becker snapped.

'Taxi stand out front.'

Becker grabbed a 1,000-peseta note from his pocket and stuffed it in Two-Tone's hand.

'Hey, man, thanks!' the punk called after him. 'If you see Megan, tell her I said hi!' But Becker was already gone.

Two-Tone sighed and staggered back toward the dance floor. He was too drunk to notice the man in wire-rim glasses following him.

Outside, Becker scanned the parking lot for a taxi. There was none. He ran over to a stocky bouncer. 'Taxi!'

The bouncer shook his head. 'Demasiado temprano. Too early.'

Too early? Becker swore. *It's two o'clock in the morning!*

'Pídame uno! Call me one!'

The man pulled out a walkie-talkie. He said a few words and then signed off. 'Veinte minutos,' he offered.

'Twenty minutes?!' Becker demanded. 'Y el autobus?'

The bouncer shrugged. 'Forty-five minutos.'

Becker threw up his hands. *Perfect!*

The sound of a small engine turned Becker's head. It sounded like a chainsaw. A big kid and his chain-clad date pulled into the parking lot on an old Vespa 250 motorcycle. The girl's skirt had blown high on her thighs. She didn't seem to notice. Becker dashed over. *I can't believe I'm doing this,* he thought. *I hate motorcycles.* He yelled to the driver. 'I'll pay you ten thousand pesetas to take me to the airport!'

The kid ignored him and killed the engine.

'Twenty thousand!' Becker blurted. 'I need to get to the airport!'

The kid looked up. 'Scusi?' He was Italian.

'Aeropórto! Per favore. Sulla Vespa! Venti mille pesete!'

The Italian eyed his crummy, little bike and laughed. 'Venti mille pesete? La Vespa?'

'Cinquanta mille! Fifty thousand!' Becker offered. It was about four hundred dollars.

The Italian laughed doubtfully. 'Dov'é la plata? Where's the cash?'

Becker pulled five 10,000-peseta notes from his pocket and held them out. The Italian looked at the money and then at his girlfriend. The girl grabbed the cash and stuffed it in her blouse.

'Grazie!' the Italian beamed. He tossed Becker the keys to his Vespa. Then he grabbed his girlfriend's hand, and they ran off laughing into the building.

'Aspetta!' Becker yelled. 'Wait! I wanted a *ride!*'

CHAPTER 59

Susan reached for Commander Strathmore's hand as he helped her up the ladder onto the Crypto floor. The image of Phil Chartrukian lying broken on the generators was burned into her mind. The thought of Hale hiding in the bowels of Crypto had left her dizzy. The truth was inescapable – Hale had pushed Chartrukian.

Susan stumbled past the shadow of TRANSLTR back toward Crypto's main exit – the door she'd come through hours earlier. Her frantic punching on the unlit keypad did nothing to move the huge portal. She was trapped; Crypto was a prison. The dome sat like a satellite, 109 yards away from the main NSA structure, accessible only through the main portal. Since Crypto made its own power, the switchboard probably didn't even know they were in trouble.

'The main power's out,' Strathmore said, arriving behind her. 'We're on aux.'

The backup power supply in Crypto was designed so that TRANSLTR and its cooling systems took precedence over all other systems, including lights and doorways. That way an untimely power outage would not interrupt TRANSLTR during an important run. It also meant TRANSLTR would never run without its freon cooling system; in an uncooled enclosure, the heat generated by three million processors would rise to treacherous levels – perhaps even igniting the silicon chips and resulting in a fiery meltdown. It was an image no one dared consider.

Susan fought to get her bearings. Her thoughts were consumed by the single image of the Sys-Sec on the generators. She stabbed at the keypad again. Still no response. 'Abort the run!' she demanded. Telling TRANSLTR to stop searching for the Digital Fortress pass-key would shut down its circuits and free up enough backup power to get the doors working again.

'Easy, Susan,' Strathmore said, putting a steadying hand on her shoulder.

The commander's reassuring touch lifted Susan from her daze. She suddenly remembered why she had been going to get him. She wheeled, 'Commander! Greg Hale is North Dakota!'

There was a seemingly endless beat of silence in the dark. Finally Strathmore replied. His voice sounded more confused than shocked. 'What are you talking about?'

'Hale . . .' Susan whispered. 'He's North Dakota.'

There was more silence as Strathmore pondered Susan's words. 'The tracer?' He seemed confused. 'It fingered Hale?'

'The tracer isn't back yet. Hale aborted it!'

Susan went on to explain how Hale had stopped her tracer and how she'd found E-mail from Tankado in Hale's account. Another long moment of silence followed. Strathmore shook his head in disbelief.

'There's no way *Greg Hale* is Tankado's insurance! It's absurd! Tankado would never trust Hale.'

'Commander,' she said, 'Hale sank us once before – Skipjack. Tankado trusted him.'

Strathmore could not seem to find words.

'Abort TRANSLTR,' Susan begged him. 'We've got North Dakota. Call building security. Let's get out of here.'

Strathmore held up his hand requesting a moment to think.

Susan looked nervously in the direction of the trap-door. The opening was just out of sight behind TRANSLTR, but the reddish glow spilled out over the black tile like fire on ice. *Come on, call Security, Commander! Abort TRANSLTR! Get us out of here!*

Suddenly Strathmore sprang to action. 'Follow me,' he said. He strode toward the trapdoor.

'Commander! Hale is dangerous! He—'

But Strathmore disappeared into the dark. Susan hurried to follow his silhouette. The commander circled around TRANSLTR and arrived over the opening in the floor. He peered into the swirling, steaming pit. Silently he looked around the darkened Crypto floor. Then he bent down and heaved the heavy trapdoor. It swung in a low arc. When he let go, it slammed shut with a deadening thud. Crypto was once again a silent, blackened cave. It appeared North Dakota was trapped.

Strathmore knelt down. He turned the heavy butterfly lock. It spun into place. The sublevels were sealed.

Neither he nor Susan heard the faint steps in the direction of Node 3.

CHAPTER 60

Two-Tone headed through the mirrored corridor that led from the outside patio to the dance floor. As he turned to check his safety pin in the reflection, he sensed a figure looming up behind him. He spun, but it was too late. A pair of rocklike arms pinned his body face-first against the glass.

The punk tried to twist around. 'Eduardo? Hey, man, is that you?' Two-Tone felt a hand brush over his wallet before the figure leaned firmly into his back. 'Eddie!' the punk cried. 'Quit fooling around! Some guy was lookin' for Megan.'

The figure held him firmly.

'Hey, Eddie, man, cut it out!' But when Two-Tone looked up into the mirror, he saw the figure pinning him was not his friend at all.

The face was pockmarked and scarred. Two lifeless eyes stared out like coal from behind wire-rim glasses. The man leaned forward, placing his mouth against Two-Tone's ear. A strange, voice choked, '*Adónde fué? Where'd he go?*' The words sounded somehow misshapen.

The punk froze, paralyzed with fear.

'*Adónde fué?*' the voice repeated. 'El Americano.'

'The . . . the airport. Aeropuerto,' Two-Tone stammered.

'Aeropuerto?' the man repeated, his dark eyes watching Two-Tone's lips in the mirror.

The punk nodded.

'Tenía el anillo? Did he have the ring?'

Terrified, Two-Tone shook his head. 'No.'

'Viste el anillo? Did you see the ring?'

Two-Tone paused. What was the right answer?

'Viste el anillo?' the muffled voice demanded.

Two-Tone nodded affirmatively, hoping honesty would pay. It did not. Seconds later he slid to the floor, his neck broken.

CHAPTER 61

Jabba lay on his back lodged halfway inside a dismantled mainframe computer. There was a penlight in his mouth, a soldering iron in his hand, and a large schematic blueprint propped on his belly. He had just finished attaching a new set of attenuators to a faulty motherboard when his cellular phone sprang to life.

'Shit,' he swore, groping for the receiver through a pile of cables. 'Jabba here.'

'Jabba, it's Midge.'

He brightened. 'Twice in one night? People are gonna start talking.'

'Crypto's got problems.' Her voice was tense.

Jabba frowned. 'We been through this already. Remember?'

'It's a *power* problem.'

'I'm not an electrician. Call Engineering.'

'The dome's dark.'

'You're seeing things. Go home.' He turned back to his schematic.

'*Pitch black!*' she yelled.

Jabba sighed and set down his penlight. 'Midge, first of all, we've got aux power in there. It would never be *pitch* black. Second, Strathmore's got a slightly better view of Crypto than I do right now. Why don't you call *him?'*

'Because this has to do with *him*. He's hiding something.'

Jabba rolled his eyes. 'Midge, sweetie, I'm up to my armpits in serial cable here. If you need a date, I'll cut loose. Otherwise, call Engineering.'

'Jabba, this is *serious*. I can *feel* it.'

She can feel it? It was official, Jabba thought, Midge was in one of her *moods*. 'If Strathmore's not worried, I'*m* not worried.'

'Crypto's pitch black, dammit!'

'So maybe Strathmore's stargazing.'

'Jabba! I'm not kidding around here!'

'Okay, okay,' he grumbled, propping himself up on an elbow. 'Maybe a generator shorted out. As soon as I'm done here, I'll stop by Crypto and—'

'What about aux power!' Midge demanded. 'If a generator blew, why is there no aux power?'

'I don't know. Maybe Strathmore's got TRANSLTR running and aux power is tapped out.'

'So why doesn't he abort? Maybe it's a virus. You said something earlier about a virus.'

'Damn it, Midge!' Jabba exploded. 'I told you, there's *no* virus in Crypto! Stop being so damned *paranoid!'*

There was a long silence on the line.

'Aw, shit, Midge,' Jabba apologized. 'Let me explain.' His voice was tight. 'First of all, we've got Gauntlet – no virus could possibly get through. Second, if there's a power failure, it's *hardware*-related – viruses don't kill *power*, they attack software and data. Whatever's going on in Crypto, it's *not* a virus.'

Silence.

'Midge? You there?'

Midge's response was icy. 'Jabba, I have a job to do. I don't expect to be yelled at for doing it. When I call to ask why a multibillion-dollar facility is in the dark, I expect a professional response.'

'Yes, ma'am.'

'A simple yes or no will suffice. Is it possible the problem in Crypto is virus-related?'

'Midge . . . I told you—'

'Yes or no. Could TRANSLTR have a virus?'

Jabba sighed. 'No, Midge. It's totally impossible.'

'Thank you.'

He forced a chuckle and tried to lighten the mood. 'Unless you think Strathmore wrote one himself and bypassed my filters.'

There was a stunned silence. When Midge spoke, her voice had an eerie edge. 'Strathmore can *bypass* Gauntlet?'

Jabba sighed. 'It was a *joke*, Midge.' But he knew it was too late.

CHAPTER 62

The Commander and Susan stood beside the closed trapdoor and debated what to do next.

'We've got Phil Chartrukian dead down there,' Strathmore argued. 'If we call for help, Crypto will turn into a circus.'

'So what do you propose we do?' Susan demanded, wanting only to leave.

Strathmore thought a moment. 'Don't ask me how it happened,' he said, glancing down at the locked trapdoor, 'but it looks like we've inadvertently located and neutralized North Dakota.' He shook his head in disbelief. 'Damn lucky break if you ask me.' He still seemed stunned by the idea that Hale was involved in Tankado's plan. 'My guess is that Hale's got the passkey hidden in his terminal somewhere – maybe he's got a copy at home. Either way, he's trapped.'

'So why not call building security and let them cart him away?'

'Not yet,' Strathmore said. 'If the Sys-Secs uncover stats of this endless TRANSLTR run, we've got a whole new set of problems. I want all traces of Digital Fortress deleted before we open the doors.'

Susan nodded reluctantly. It was a good plan. When Security finally pulled Hale from the sublevels and charged him with Chartrukian's death, he probably would threaten to tell the world about Digital Fortress. But the proof would be erased – Strathmore could play dumb. *An endless run? An unbreakable algorithm? But that's absurd! Hasn't Hale heard of the Bergofsky Principle?*

'Here's what we need to do.' Strathmore coolly outlined his plan. 'We erase all of Hale's correspondence with Tankado. We erase all records of my bypassing Gauntlet, all of Chartrukian's Sys-Sec analysis, the Run-Monitor records, everything. Digital Fortress disappears. It was never here. We bury Hale's key and pray to God David finds Tankado's copy.'

David, Susan thought. She forced him from her mind. She needed to stay focused on the matter at hand.

'I'll handle the Sys-Sec lab,' Strathmore said. 'Run-Monitor stats, mutation activity stats, the works. You handle Node 3. Delete all of Hale's E-mail. Any records of correspondence with Tankado, anything that mentions Digital Fortress.'

'Okay,' Susan replied, focusing. 'I'll erase Hale's whole drive. Reformat everything.'

'No!' Strathmore's response was stern. 'Don't do that. Hale most likely has a copy of the pass-key in there. I want it.'

Susan gaped in shock. 'You want the pass-key? I thought the whole point was to *destroy* the pass-keys!'

'It is. But I want a copy. I want to crack open this damn file and have a look at Tankado's program.'

Susan shared Strathmore's curiosity, but instinct told her unlocking the Digital Fortress algorithm was

271

not wise, regardless of how interesting it would be. Right now, the deadly program was locked safely in its encrypted vault – totally harmless. As soon as he decrypted it. . . . 'Commander, wouldn't we be better off just to—'

'I want the key,' he replied.

Susan had to admit, ever since hearing about Digital Fortress, she'd felt a certain academic curiosity to know how Tankado had managed to write it. Its mere existence contradicted the most fundamental rules of cryptography. Susan eyed the commander. 'You'll delete the algorithm immediately after we see it?'

'Without a trace.'

Susan frowned. She knew that finding Hale's key would not happen instantly. Locating a random pass-key on one of the Node 3 hard drives was somewhat like trying to find a single sock in a bedroom the size of Texas. Computer searches only worked when you knew what you were looking for; this pass-key was random. Fortunately, however, because Crypto dealt with so much random material, Susan and some others had developed a complex process known as a nonconformity search. The search essentially asked the computer to study every string of characters on its hard drive, compare each string against an enormous dictionary, and flag any strings that seemed nonsensical or random. It was tricky work to refine the parameters continually, but it was possible.

Susan knew she was the logical choice to find the pass-key. She sighed, hoping she wouldn't regret it. 'If all goes well, it will take me about half an hour.'

'Then let's get to work,' Strathmore said, putting a hand on her shoulder and leading her through the darkness toward Node 3.

Above them, a star-filled sky had stretched itself across the dome. Susan wondered if David could see the same stars from Seville.

As they approached the heavy glass doors of Node 3, Strathmore swore under his breath. The Node 3 keypad was unlit, and the doors were dead.

'Damn it,' he said. 'No power. I forgot.'

Strathmore studied the sliding doors. He placed his palms flat against the glass. Then he leaned sideways trying to slide them open. His hands were sweaty and slipped. He wiped them on his pants and tried again. This time the doors slid open a tiny crack.

Susan, sensing progress, got in behind Strathmore and they both pushed together. The doors slid open about an inch. They held it a moment, but the pressure was too great. The doors sprang shut again.

'Hold on,' Susan said, repositioning herself in front of Strathmore. 'Okay, now try.'

They heaved. Again the door opened only about an inch. A faint ray of blue light appeared from inside Node 3; the terminals were still on; they were considered critical to TRANSLTR and were receiving aux power.

Susan dug the toe of her Ferragamo into the floor and pushed harder. The door started to move. Strathmore moved to get a better angle. Centering his palms on the left slider, he pushed straight back. Susan pushed the right slider in the opposite direction. Slowly, arduously, the doors began to separate. They were now almost a foot apart.

'Don't let go,' Strathmore said, panting as they pushed harder. 'Just a little farther.'

Susan repositioned herself with her shoulder in the crack. She pushed again, this time with a better angle. The doors fought back against her.

Before Strathmore could stop her, Susan squeezed her slender body into the opening. Strathmore protested, but she was intent. She wanted out of Crypto, and she knew Strathmore well enough to know she wasn't going anywhere until Hale's pass-key was found.

She centered herself in the opening and pushed with all her strength. The doors seemed to push back. Suddenly Susan lost her grip. The doors sprang toward her. Strathmore fought to hold them off, but it was too much. Just as the doors slammed shut, Susan squeezed through and collapsed on the other side.

The commander fought to reopen the door a tiny sliver. He put his face to the narrow crack. 'Jesus, Susan – are you okay?'

Susan stood up and brushed herself off. 'Fine.'

She looked around. Node 3 was deserted, lit only by the computer monitors. The bluish shadows gave the place a ghostly ambiance. She turned to Strathmore in the crack of the door. His face looked pallid and sickly in the blue light.

'Susan,' he said. 'Give me twenty minutes to delete the files in Sys-Sec. When all traces are gone, I'll go up to my terminal and abort TRANSLTR.'

'You *better*,' Susan said, eyeing the heavy glass doors. She knew that until TRANSLTR stopped hoarding aux power, she was a prisoner in Node 3.

Strathmore let go of the doors, and they snapped shut. Susan watched through the glass as the commander disappeared into the Crypto darkness.

CHAPTER 63

Becker's newly purchased Vespa motorcycle struggled up the entry road to Aeropuerto de Sevilla. His knuckles had been white the whole way. His watch read just after 2:00 A.M. local time.

As he approached the main terminal, he rode up on the sidewalk and jumped off the bike while it was still moving. It clattered to the pavement and sputtered to a stop. Becker dashed on rubbery legs through the revolving door. *Never again,* he swore to himself.

The terminal was sterile and starkly lit. Except for a janitor buffing the floor, the place was deserted. Across the concourse, a ticket agent was closing down the Iberia Airlines counter. Becker took it as a bad sign.

He ran over. 'El vuelo a los Estados Unidos?'

The attractive Andalusian woman behind the counter looked up and smiled apologetically. 'Acaba de salir. You just missed it.' Her words hung in the air for a long moment.

I missed it. Becker's shoulders slumped. 'Was there standby room on the flight?'

'Plenty,' the woman smiled. 'Almost empty. But tomorrow's eight A.M. also has—'

'I need to know if a friend of mine made that flight. She was flying standby.'

The woman frowned. 'I'm sorry, sir. There were several standby passengers tonight, but our privacy clause states—'

'It's very important,' Becker urged. 'I just need to know if she made the flight. That's all.'

The woman gave a sympathetic nod. 'Lovers' quarrel?'

Becker thought a moment. Then he gave her a sheepish grin. 'It's *that* obvious?'

She gave him a wink. 'What's her name?'

'Megan,' he replied sadly.

The agent smiled. 'Does your lady friend have a last name?'

Becker exhaled slowly. *Yes, but I don't know it!* 'Actually, it's kind of a complicated situation. You said the plane was almost empty. Maybe you could—'

'Without a last name I really can't . . .'

'Actually,' Becker interrupted, having another idea. 'Have you been on all night?'

The woman nodded. 'Seven to seven.'

'Then maybe you saw her. She's a young girl. Maybe fifteen or sixteen? Her hair was—' Before the words left his mouth, Becker realized his mistake.

The agent's eyes narrowed. 'Your lover is fifteen years old?'

'No!' Becker gasped. 'I mean . . .' *Shit.* 'If you could just help me, it's very important.'

'I'm sorry,' the woman said coldly.

'It's not the way it sounds. If you could just—'

'Good night, sir.' The woman yanked the metal grate down over the counter and disappeared into a back room.

Becker groaned and stared skyward. *Smooth*, David. Very smooth. He scanned the open concourse. Nothing. *She must have sold the ring and made the flight.* He headed for the custodian. 'Has visto a una niña?' he called over the sound of the tile buffer. 'Have you seen a girl?'

The old man reached down and killed the machine. 'Eh?'

'Una niña?' Becker repeated. 'Pelo rojo, azul, y blanco. Red white and blue hair.'

The custodian laughed. 'Qué fea. Sounds ugly.' He shook his head and went back to work.

David Becker stood in the middle of the deserted airport concourse and wondered what to do next. The evening had been a comedy of errors. Strathmore's words pounded in his head: Don't call until you have the ring. A profound exhaustion settled over him. If Megan had sold the ring and made the flight, there was no telling who had the ring now.

Becker closed his eyes and tried to focus. *What's my next move?* He decided to consider it in a moment. First, he needed to make a long-overdue trip to a rest room.

CHAPTER 64

Susan stood alone in the dimly lit silence of Node 3. The task at hand was simple: Access Hale's terminal, locate his key, and then delete all of his communication with Tankado. There could be no hint of Digital Fortress anywhere.

Susan's initial fears of saving the key and unlocking Digital Fortress were nagging at her again. She felt uneasy tempting fate; they'd been lucky so far. North Dakota had miraculously appeared right under their noses and been trapped. The only remaining question was David; he had to find the other pass-key. Susan hoped he was making progress.

As she made her way deeper into Node 3, Susan tried to clear her mind. It was odd that she felt uneasy in such a familiar space. Everything in Node 3 seemed foreign in the dark. But there was something else. Susan felt a momentary hesitation and glanced back at the inoperable doors. There was no escape. *Twenty minutes*, she thought.

As she turned toward Hale's terminal, she noticed a strange, musky odor – it was definitely not a Node 3 smell. She wondered if maybe the deionizer was malfunctioning. The smell was vaguely familiar, and with it came an unsettling chill. She pictured Hale locked below in his enormous steaming cell. *Did he set something on fire?* She looked up at the vents and sniffed. But the odor seemed to be coming from nearby.

Susan glanced toward the latticed doors of the kitchenette. And in an instant she recognized the smell. It was *cologne . . . and sweat.*

She recoiled instinctively, not prepared for what she saw. From behind the lattice slats of the kitchenette, two eyes stared out at her. It only took an instant for the horrifying truth to hit her. Greg Hale was not locked on the sublevels – he was in Node 3! He'd slipped upstairs before Strathmore closed the trap-door. He'd been strong enough to open the doors all by himself.

Susan had once heard that raw terror was paralyz-ing – she now knew that was a myth. In the same instant her brain grasped what was happening, she was in motion – stumbling backward through the dark with a single thought in mind: escape.

The crash behind her was instantaneous. Hale had been sitting silently on the stove and extended his legs like two battering rams. The doors exploded off their hinges. Hale launched himself into the room and thundered after her with powerful strides.

Susan knocked over a lamp behind her, attempting to trip Hale as he moved toward her. She sensed him vault it effortlessly. Hale was gaining quickly.

When his right arm circled her waist from behind, it felt like she'd hit a steel bar. She gasped in pain as the wind went out of her. His biceps flexed against her rib cage.

Susan resisted and began twisting wildly. Somehow

her elbow struck cartilage. Hale released his grip, his hands clutching his nose. He fell to his knees, hands cupped over his face.

'Son of a—' He screamed in pain.

Susan dashed onto the door's pressure plates saying a fruitless prayer that Strathmore would in that instant restore power and the doors would spring open. Instead, she found herself pounding against the glass.

Hale lumbered toward her, his nose covered with blood. In an instant, his hands were around her again – one of them clamped firmly on her left breast and the other on her midsection. He yanked her away from the door.

She screamed, her hand outstretched in a futile attempt to stop him.

He pulled her backward, his belt buckle digging into her spine. Susan couldn't believe his strength. He dragged her back across the carpet, and her shoes came off. In one fluid motion, Hale lifted her and dumped her on the floor next to his terminal.

Susan was suddenly on her back, her skirt bunched high on her hips. The top button of her blouse had released, and her chest was heaving in the bluish light. She stared up in terror as Hale straddled her, pinning her down. She couldn't decipher the look in his eyes. It looked like fear. Or was it anger? His eyes bore into her body. She felt a new wave of panic.

Hale sat firmly on her midsection, staring down at her with an icy glare. Everything Susan had ever learned about self-defense was suddenly racing through her mind. She tried to fight, but her body did not respond. She was numb. She closed her eyes.

Oh, please, God. No!

CHAPTER 65

Brinkerhoff paced Midge's office. 'Nobody bypasses Gauntlet. It's impossible!'

'Wrong,' she fired back. 'I just talked to Jabba. He said he installed a bypass switch last year.'

The PA looked doubtful. 'I never heard that.'

'Nobody did. It was hush-hush.'

'Midge,' Brinkerhoff argued, 'Jabba's compulsive about security! He would never put in a switch to bypass—'

'Strathmore made him do it,' she interrupted.

Brinkerhoff could almost hear her mind clicking.

'Remember last year,' she asked, 'when Strathmore was working on that anti-Semitic terrorist ring in California?'

Brinkerhoff nodded. It had been one of Strathmore's major coups last year. Using TRANSLTR to decrypt an intercepted code, he had uncovered a plot to bomb a Hebrew school in Los Angeles. He decrypted the terrorists' message only twelve minutes before the bomb went off, and using some fast phone work, he saved three hundred schoolchildren.

'Get this,' Midge said, lowering her voice unnecessarily.

'Jabba said Strathmore intercepted that terrorist code *six hours* before that bomb went off.'

Brinkerhoff's jaw dropped. 'But . . . then why did he wait—'

'Because he couldn't get TRANSLTR to decrypt the file. He tried, but Gauntlet kept rejecting it. It was encrypted with some new public key algorithm that the filters hadn't seen yet. It took Jabba almost six hours to adjust them.'

Brinkerhoff looked stunned.

'Strathmore was furious. He made Jabba install a bypass switch in Gauntlet in case it ever happened again.'

'Jesus.' Brinkerhoff whistled. 'I had no idea.' Then his eyes narrowed. 'So what's your point?'

'I think Strathmore used the switch today . . . to process a file that Gauntlet rejected.'

'So? That's what the switch is for, right?'

Midge shook her head. 'Not if the file in question is a virus.'

Brinkerhoff jumped. 'A virus? Who said anything about a virus!'

'It's the only explanation,' she said. 'Jabba said a virus is the only thing that could keep TRANSLTR running this long, so—'

'Wait a minute!' Brinkerhoff flashed her the time-out sign. 'Strathmore said everything's fine!'

'He's lying.'

Brinkerhoff was lost. 'You're saying Strathmore *intentionally* let a virus into TRANSLTR?'

'No,' she snapped. 'I don't think he *knew* it was a virus. I think he was tricked.'

Brinkerhoff was speechless. Midge Milken was definitely losing it.

'It explains a lot,' she insisted. 'It explains what he's been doing in there all night.'

'Planting viruses in his own computer?'

'No,' she said, annoyed. 'Trying to cover up his mistake! And now he can't abort TRANSLTR and get aux power back because the virus has the processors locked down!'

Brinkerhoff rolled his eyes. Midge had gone nuts in the past, but never like this. He tried to calm her. 'Jabba doesn't seem to be too worried.'

'Jabba's a fool,' she hissed.

Brinkerhoff looked surprised. Nobody had ever called Jabba a fool – a pig maybe, but never a fool. 'You're trusting feminine intuition over Jabba's advanced degrees in anti-invasive programming?'

She eyed him harshly.

Brinkerhoff held up his hands in surrender. 'Never mind. I take it back.' He didn't need to be reminded of Midge's uncanny ability to sense disaster. 'Midge,' he begged. 'I know you hate Strathmore, but—'

'This has nothing to do with Strathmore!' Midge was in overdrive. 'The first thing we need to do is confirm Strathmore bypassed Gauntlet. Then we call the director.'

'Great.' Brinkerhoff moaned. 'I'll call Strathmore and ask him to send us a signed statement.'

'No,' she replied, ignoring his sarcasm. 'Strathmore's lied to us once already today.' She glanced up, her eyes probing his. 'Do you have keys to Fontaine's office?'

'Of course. I'm his PA.'

'I need them.'

Brinkerhoff stared in disbelief. 'Midge, there's no way in hell I'm letting you into Fontaine's office.'

'You have to!' she demanded. Midge turned and

started typing on Big Brother's keyboard. 'I'm requesting a TRANSLTR queue list. If Strathmore manually bypassed Gauntlet, it'll show up on the printout.'

'What does that have to do with Fontaine's office?'

She spun and glared at him. 'The queue list only prints to Fontaine's printer. You know that!'

'That's because it's *classified*, Midge!'

'This is an emergency. I need to see that list.'

Brinkerhoff put his hands on her shoulders. 'Midge, please settle down. You know I can't—'

She huffed loudly and spun back to her keyboard. 'I'm printing a queue list. I'm going to walk in, pick it up, and walk out. Now give me the key.'

'Midge . . .'

She finished typing and spun back to him. 'Chad, the report prints in thirty seconds. Here's the deal. You give me the key. If Strathmore bypassed, we call Security. If I'm wrong, I leave, and you can go smear marmalade all over Carmen Huerta.' She gave him a malicious glare and held out her hands for the keys. 'I'm waiting.'

Brinkerhoff groaned, regretting that he had called her back to check the Crypto report. He eyed her outstretched hand. 'You're talking about classified information inside the director's private quarters. Do you have any idea what would happen if we got caught?'

'The director is in South America.'

'I'm sorry. I just can't.' Brinkerhoff crossed his arms and walked out.

Midge stared after him, her gray eyes smoldering. 'Oh, yes you can,' she whispered. Then she turned back to Big Brother and called up the video archives.

*

Midge'll get over it, Brinkerhoff told himself as he settled in at his desk and started going over the rest of his reports. He couldn't be expected to hand out the director's keys whenever Midge got paranoid.

He had just begun checking the COMSEC breakdowns when his thoughts were interrupted by the sound of voices coming from the other room. He set down his work and walked to his doorway.

The main suite was dark – all except a dim shaft of grayish light from Midge's half-open door. He listened. The voices continued. They sounded excited. 'Midge?'

No response.

He strode through the darkness to her workspace. The voices were vaguely familiar. He pushed the door open. The room was empty. Midge's chair was empty. The sound was coming from overhead. Brinkerhoff looked up at the video monitors and instantly felt ill. The same image was playing on each one of the twelve screens – a kind of perversely choreographed ballet. Brinkerhoff steadied himself on the back of Midge's chair and watched in horror.

'Chad?' The voice was behind him.

He spun and squinted into the darkness. Midge was standing kitty-corner across the main suite's reception area in front of the director's double doors. Her palm was outstretched. 'The key, Chad.'

Brinkerhoff flushed. He turned back to the monitors. He tried to block out the images overhead, but it was no use. He was everywhere, groaning with pleasure and eagerly fondling Carmen Huerta's small, honey-covered breasts.

285

CHAPTER 66

Becker crossed the concourse toward the rest room doors only to find the door marked CABALLEROS blocked by an orange pylon and a cleaning cart filled with detergent and mops. He eyed the other door. DAMAS. He strode over and rapped loudly.

'Hola?' he called, pushing the ladies' room door open an inch. 'Con permiso?'

Silence.

He went in.

The rest room was typical, Spanish institutional – perfectly square, white tile, one incandescent bulb overhead. As usual, there was one stall and one urinal. Whether the urinals were ever used in the women's bathrooms was immaterial – adding them saved the contractors the expense of having to build the extra stall.

Becker peered into the rest room in disgust. It was filthy. The sink was clogged with murky brown water. Dirty paper towels were strewn everywhere. The floor was soaked. The old electric handblower on the wall was smeared with greenish fingerprints.

Becker stepped in front of the mirror and sighed.

The eyes that usually stared back with fierce clarity were not so clear tonight. *How long have I been running around over here?* he wondered. The math escaped him. Out of professorial habit, he shimmied his necktie's Windsor knot up on his collar. Then he turned to the urinal behind him.

As he stood there, he found himself wondering if Susan was home yet. *Where could she have gone? To Stone Manor without me?*

'Hey!' a female voice behind him said angrily.

Becker jumped. 'I-I'm . . .' he stammered, hurrying to zip up. 'I'm sorry . . . I . . .'

Becker turned to face the girl who had just entered. She was a young sophisticate, right off the pages of *Seventeen* magazine. She wore conservative plaid pants and a white sleeveless blouse. In her hand was a red L.L. Bean duffel. Her blond hair was perfectly blow-dried.

'I'm sorry.' Becker fumbled, buckling his belt. 'The men's room was . . . anyway . . . I'm leaving.'

'Fuckin' weirdo!'

Becker did a double-take. The profanity seemed inappropriate coming from her lips – like sewage flowing from a polished decanter. But as Becker studied her, he saw that she was not as polished as he'd first thought. Her eyes were puffy and bloodshot, and her left forearm was swollen. Underneath the reddish irritation on her arm, the flesh was blue.

Jesus, Becker thought. *Intravenous drugs. Who would have guessed?*

'Get out!' she yelled. 'Just get out!'

Becker momentarily forgot all about the ring, the NSA, all of it. His heart went out to the young girl. Her parents had probably sent her over here with

some prep school study program and a VISA card –
and she'd ended up all alone in a bathroom in the
middle of the night doing drugs.

'Are you okay?' he asked, backing toward the door.

'I'm fine.' Her voice was haughty. 'You can leave
now!'

Becker turned to go. He shot her forearm a last sad
glance. *There's nothing you can do, David. Leave it alone.*

'Now!' she hollered.

Becker nodded. As he left he gave her a sad smile.
'Be careful.'

CHAPTER 67

'Susan?' Hale panted, his face in hers.

He was sitting, one leg on either side of her, his full weight on her midsection. His tailbone ground painfully into her pubis through the thin fabric of her skirt. His nose was dripping blood all over her. She tasted vomit in the back of her throat. His hands were at her chest.

She felt nothing. *Is he touching me?* It took a moment for Susan to realize Hale was buttoning her top button and covering her up.

'Susan.' Hale gasped, breathless. 'You've got to get me out of here.'

Susan was in a daze. Nothing made sense.

'Susan, you've got to help me! Strathmore killed Chartrukian! I saw it!'

It took a moment for the words to register. *Strathmore killed Chartrukian?* Hale obviously had no idea Susan had seen him downstairs.

'Strathmore knows I saw him!' Hale spat. 'He'll kill me too!'

Had Susan not been breathless with fear, she would have laughed in his face. She recognized the divide-and-conquer mentality of an ex-Marine. Invent lies – pit your enemies against each other.

'It's true!' he yelled. 'We've got to call for help! I think we're both in danger!'

She did not believe a word he said.

Hale's muscular legs were cramping, and he rolled up on his haunches to shift his weight slightly. He opened his mouth to speak, but he never got the chance.

As Hale's body rose, Susan felt the circulation surge back into her legs. Before she knew what had happened, a reflex instinct jerked her left leg back hard into Hale's crotch. She felt her kneecap crush the soft sac of tissue between his legs.

Hale whimpered in agony and instantly went limp. He rolled onto his side, clutching himself. Susan twisted out from under his dead weight. She staggered toward the door, knowing she'd never be strong enough to get out.

Making a split-second decision, Susan positioned herself behind the long maple meeting table and dug her feet into the carpet. Mercifully the table had casters. She strode with all her might toward the arched glass wall, pushing the table before her. The casters were good, and the table rolled well. Halfway across Node 3, she was at a full sprint.

Five feet from the glass wall, Susan heaved and let go. She leapt to one side and covered her eyes. After a sickening crack, the wall exploded in a shower of glass. The sounds of Crypto rushed into Node 3 for the first time since its construction.

Susan looked up. Through the jagged hole, she could see the table. It was still rolling. It spun wide circles out across the Crypto floor and eventually dis-appeared into the darkness.

Susan rammed her mangled Ferragamo back on her feet, shot a last glance at the still-writhing Greg Hale, and dashed across the sea of broken glass out onto the Crypto floor.

CHAPTER 68

'Now wasn't that easy?' Midge said with a sneer as Brinkerhoff handed over the key to Fontaine's office.

Brinkerhoff looked beaten.

'I'll erase it before I go,' Midge promised. 'Unless you and your wife want it for your private collection.'

'Just get the damned printout,' he snapped. 'And then get out!'

'Sí, señor,' Midge cackled in a thick Puerto Rican accent. She winked and headed across the suite to Fontaine's double doors.

Leland Fontaine's private office looked nothing like the rest of the directorial suite. There were no paintings, no overstuffed chairs, no ficus plants, no antique clocks. His space was streamlined for efficiency. His glass-topped desk and black leather chair sat directly in front of his enormous picture window. Three file cabinets stood in the corner next to a small table with a French press coffeepot. The moon had risen high over Fort Meade, and the soft light filtering through the window accentuated the starkness of the director's furnishings.

What the hell am I doing? Brinkerhoff wondered.

Midge strode to the printer and scooped up the queue list. She squinted in the darkness. 'I can't read the data,' she complained. 'Turn on the lights.'

'You're reading it *outside*. Now come on.'

But Midge was apparently having too much fun. She toyed with Brinkerhoff, walking to the window and angling the readout for a better view.

'Midge . . .'

She kept reading.

Brinkerhoff shifted anxiously in the doorway. 'Midge . . . come on. These are the director's private quarters.'

'It's here somewhere,' she muttered, studying the printout. 'Strathmore bypassed Gauntlet, I know it.' She moved closer to the window.

Brinkerhoff began to sweat. Midge kept reading.

After a few moments, she gasped. 'I knew it! Strathmore did it! He really did! The idiot!' She held up the paper and shook it. 'He bypassed Gauntlet! Have a look!'

Brinkerhoff stared dumbfounded a moment and then raced across the director's office. He crowded in next to Midge in front of the window. She pointed to the end of the readout.

Brinkerhoff read in disbelief. 'What the . . . ?'

The printout contained a list of the last thirty-six files that had entered TRANSLTR. After each file was a four-digit Gauntlet clearance code. However, the last file on the sheet had no clearance code – it simply read: MANUAL BYPASS.

Jesus, Brinkerhoff thought. *Midge strikes again.*

'The idiot!' Midge sputtered, seething. 'Look at this! Gauntlet rejected the file twice! Mutation strings! And he *still* bypassed! What the hell was he thinking?'

Brinkerhoff felt weak-kneed. He wondered why Midge was always right. Neither of them noticed the reflection that had appeared in the window beside them. A massive figure was standing in Fontaine's open doorway.

'Jeez,' Brinkerhoff choked. 'You think we have a virus?'

Midge sighed. 'Nothing else it could be.'

'Could be none of your damn business!' the deep voice boomed from behind them.

Midge knocked her head against the window. Brinkerhoff tipped over the director's chair and wheeled toward the voice. He immediately knew the silhouette.

'Director!' Brinkerhoff gasped. He strode over and extended his hand. 'Welcome home, sir.'

The huge man ignored it.

'I-I thought,' Brinkerhoff stammered, retracting his hand, 'I thought you were in South America.'

Leland Fontaine glared down at his aide with eyes like bullets. 'Yes . . . and now I'm back.'

CHAPTER 69

'Hey, mister!'

Becker had been walking across the concourse toward a bank of pay phones. He stopped and turned. Coming up behind him was the girl he'd just surprised in the bathroom. She waved for him to wait. 'Mister, wait!'

Now what? Becker groaned. *She wants to press invasion-of-privacy charges?*

The girl dragged her duffel toward him. When she arrived, she was now wearing a huge smile. 'Sorry to yell at you back there. You just kind of startled me.'

'No problem,' Becker assured, somewhat puzzled. 'I was in the wrong place.'

'This will sound crazy,' she said, batting her blood-shot eyes. 'But you wouldn't happen to have some money you can lend me, would you?'

Becker stared at her in disbelief. 'Money for what?' he demanded. *I'm not funding your drug habit if that's what you're asking.*

'I'm trying to get back home,' the blonde said. 'Can you help?'

'Miss your flight?'

She nodded. 'Lost my ticket. They wouldn't let me

295

get on. Airlines can be such assholes. I don't have the cash to buy another.'

'Where are your parents?' Becker asked.

'States.'

'Can you reach them?'

'Nope. Already tried. I think they're weekending on somebody's yacht.'

Becker scanned the girl's expensive clothing. 'You don't have a credit card?'

'Yeah, but my dad canceled it. He thinks I'm on drugs.'

'*Are* you on drugs?' Becker asked, deadpan, eyeing her swollen forearm.

The girl glared, indignant. 'Of course not!' She gave Becker an innocent huff, and he suddenly got the feeling he was being played.

'Come on,' she said. 'You look like a rich guy. Can't you spot me some cash to get home? I could send it to you later.'

Becker figured any cash he gave this girl would end up in the hands of some drug dealer in Triana. 'First of all,' he said, 'I'm not a rich guy – I'm a teacher. But I'll tell you what I'll do . . .' *I'll call your bluff, that's what I'll do.* 'Why don't I *charge* the ticket for you?'

The blonde stared at him in utter shock. 'You'd do that?' she stammered, eyes wide with hope. 'You'd buy me a ticket home? Oh, God, thank you!'

Becker was speechless. He had apparently misjudged the moment.

The girl threw her arms around him. 'It's been a shitty summer,' she choked, almost bursting into tears. 'Oh, thank you! I've got to get out of here!'

Becker returned her embrace halfheartedly. The girl let go of him, and he eyed her forearm again.

She followed his gaze to the bluish rash. 'Gross, huh?'

Becker nodded. 'I thought you said you weren't on drugs.'

The girl laughed. 'It's Magic Marker! I took off half my skin trying to scrub it off. The ink smeared.'

Becker looked closer. In the fluorescent light, he could see, blurred beneath the reddish swelling on her arm, the faint outline of writing – words scrawled on flesh.

'But . . . but your *eyes,*' Becker said, feeling dumb. 'They're all red.'

She laughed. 'I was crying. I told you, I missed my flight.'

Becker looked back at the words on her arm.

She frowned, embarrassed. 'Oops, you can still kind of read it, can't you?'

Becker leaned closer. He could read it all right. The message was crystal clear. As he read the four faint words, the last twelve hours flashed before his eyes.

David Becker found himself back in the Alfonso XIII hotel room. The obese German was touching his own forearm and speaking broken English: Fock off und die.

'You okay?' the girl asked, eyeing the dazed Becker.

Becker did not look up from her arm. He was dizzy. The four words smeared across the girl's flesh carried a very simple message: FUCK OFF AND DIE.

The blonde looked down at it, embarrassed. 'This friend of mine wrote it . . . pretty stupid, huh?'

Becker couldn't speak. *Fock off und die.* He couldn't believe it. The German hadn't been insulting him, he'd been trying to help. Becker lifted his gaze to the girl's face. In the fluorescent light of the concourse, he could see faint traces of red and blue in the girl's blond hair.

'Y-you . . .' Becker stammered, staring at her unpierced ears. 'You wouldn't happen to wear earrings, would you?'

The girl eyed him strangely. She fished a tiny object from her pocket and held it out. Becker gazed at the skull pendant dangling in her hand.

'A clip-on?' he stammered.

'Hell, yes,' the girl replied. 'I'm scared shitless of needles.'

CHAPTER 70

David Becker stood in the deserted concourse and felt his legs go weak. He eyed the girl before him and knew his search was over. She had washed her hair and changed clothes – maybe in hopes of having better luck selling the ring – but she'd never boarded for New York.

Becker fought to keep his cool. His wild journey was about to end. He scanned her fingers. They were bare. He gazed down at her duffel. *It's in there,* he thought. *It's got to be!*

He smiled, barely containing his excitement. 'This is going to sound crazy,' he said, 'but I think you've got something I need.'

'Oh?' Megan seemed suddenly uncertain.

Becker reached for his wallet. 'Of course I'd be happy to pay you.' He looked down and started sorting through the cash in his billfold.

As Megan watched him count out his money, she drew a startled gasp, apparently misunderstanding his intentions. She shot a frightened glance toward the revolving door . . . measuring the distance. It was fifty yards.

'I can give you enough to buy your ticket home if—'

'Don't say it,' Megan blurted, offering a forced smile. 'I think I know exactly what you need.' She bent down and started rifling through her duffel.

Becker felt a surge of hope. *She's got it!* he told himself. *She's got the ring!* He didn't know how the hell she knew what it was he wanted, but he was too tired to care. Every muscle in his body relaxed. He pictured himself handing the ring to the beaming deputy director of the NSA. Then he and Susan would lie in the big canopy bed at Stone Manor and make up for lost time.

The girl finally found what she was looking for – her PepperGard – the environmentally safe alternative to Mace, made from a potent blend of cayenne and chili peppers. In one swift motion, she swung around and fired a direct stream into Becker's eyes. She grabbed her duffel and dashed for the door. When she looked back, David Becker was on the floor, holding his face, writhing in agony.

CHAPTER 71

Tokugen Numataka lit his fourth cigar and kept pacing. He snatched up his phone and buzzed the main switchboard.

'Any word yet on that phone number?' he demanded before the operator could speak.

'Nothing yet, sir. It's taking a bit longer than expected – it came from a cellular.'

A cellular, Numataka mused. *Figures.* Fortunately for the Japanese economy, the Americans had an insatiable appetite for electronic gadgets.

'The boosting station,' the operator added, 'is in the 202 area code. But we have no number yet.'

'202? Where's that?' *Where in the vast American expanse is this mysterious North Dakota hiding?*

'Somewhere near Washington, D.C., sir.'

Numataka arched his eyebrows. 'Call me as soon as you have a number.'

CHAPTER 72

Susan Fletcher stumbled across the darkened Crypto floor toward Strathmore's catwalk. The commander's office was as far from Hale as Susan could get inside the locked complex.

When Susan reached the top of the catwalk stairs, she found the commander's door hanging loosely, the electronic lock rendered ineffective by the power outage. She barged in.

'Commander?' The only light inside was the glow of Strathmore's computer monitors. 'Commander!' she called once again. *'Commander!'*

Susan suddenly remembered that the commander was in the Sys-Sec lab. She turned circles in his empty office, the panic of her ordeal with Hale still in her blood. She had to get out of Crypto. Digital Fortress or no Digital Fortress, it was time to act – time to abort the TRANSLTR run and escape. She eyed Strathmore's glowing monitors, then dashed to his desk. She fumbled with his keypad. *Abort TRANSLTR!* The task was simple now that she was on an authorized terminal. Susan called up the proper command window and typed:

Her finger hovered momentarily over the ENTER key.

'Susan!' a voice barked from the doorway. Susan wheeled scared, fearing it was Hale. But it was not, it was Strathmore. He stood, pale and eerie in the electronic glow, his chest heaving. 'What the hell's going on!'

'Com . . . mander!' Susan gasped. 'Hale's in Node 3! He just attacked me!'

'What? Impossible! Hale's locked down in—'

'No, he's not! He's loose! We need security in here now! I'm aborting TRANSLTR!' Susan reached for the keypad.

'DON'T TOUCH THAT!' Strathmore lunged for the terminal and pulled Susan's hands away.

Susan recoiled, stunned. She stared at the commander and for the second time that day did not recognize him. Susan felt suddenly alone.

Strathmore saw the blood on Susan's shirt and immediately regretted his outburst. 'Jesus, Susan. Are you okay?'

She didn't respond.

He wished he hadn't jumped on her unnecessarily. His nerves were frayed. He was juggling too much. There were things on his mind – things Susan Fletcher did not know about – things he had not told her and prayed he'd never have to.

'I'm sorry,' he said softly. 'Tell me what happened.'

She turned away. 'It doesn't matter. The blood's not mine. Just get me out of here.'

'Are you hurt?' Strathmore put a hand on her shoulder. Susan recoiled. He dropped his hand and looked away. When he looked back at Susan's face, she seemed to be staring over his shoulder at something on the wall.

There, in the darkness, a small keypad glowed full force. Strathmore followed her gaze and frowned. He'd hoped Susan wouldn't notice the glowing control panel. The illuminated keypad controlled his private elevator. Strathmore and his high-powered guests used it to come and go from Crypto without advertising the fact to the rest of the staff. The personal lift dropped down fifty feet below the Crypto dome and then moved laterally 109 yards through a reinforced underground tunnel to the sublevels of the main NSA complex. The elevator connecting Crypto to the NSA was powered from the main complex; it was on-line despite Crypto's power outage.

Strathmore had known all along it was on-line, but even as Susan had been pounding on the main exit downstairs, he hadn't mentioned it. He could not afford to let Susan out – not yet. He wondered how much he'd have to tell her to make her want to stay.

Susan pushed past Strathmore and raced to the back wall. She jabbed furiously at the illuminated buttons.

'Please,' she begged. But the door did not open.

'Susan,' Strathmore said quietly. 'The lift takes a password.'

'A password?' she repeated angrily. She glared at the controls. Below the main keypad was a second keypad – a smaller one, with tiny buttons. Each button was marked with a letter of the alphabet. Susan wheeled to him. 'What is the password!' she demanded.

Strathmore thought a moment and sighed heavily. 'Susan, have a seat.'

Susan looked as if she could hardly believe her ears.

'Have a seat,' the commander repeated, his voice firm.

'Let me out!' Susan shot an uneasy glance toward the commander's open office door.

Strathmore eyed the panicked Susan Fletcher. Calmly he moved to his office door. He stepped out onto the landing and peered into the darkness. Hale was nowhere to be seen. The commander stepped back inside and pulled the door shut. Then he propped a chair in front to keep it closed, went to his desk, and removed something from a drawer. In the pale glow of the monitors Susan saw what he was holding. Her face went pale. It was a gun.

Strathmore pulled two chairs into the middle of the room. He rotated them to face the closed office door. Then he sat. He lifted the glittering Beretta semi-automatic and aimed steadily at the slightly open door. After a moment he laid the gun back in his lap.

He spoke solemnly. 'Susan, we're safe here. We need to talk. If Greg Hale comes through that door . . .' He let it hang.

Susan was speechless.

Strathmore gazed at her in the dim light of his office. He patted the seat beside him. 'Susan, sit. I have something to tell you.' She did not move. 'When I'm done,' he said, 'I'll give you the password to the elevator. You can decide whether to leave or not.'

There was a long silence. In a daze, Susan moved across the office and sat next to Strathmore.

'Susan,' he began, 'I haven't been entirely honest with you.'

CHAPTER 73

David Becker felt as if his face had been doused in turpentine and ignited. He rolled over on the floor and squinted through bleary tunnel vision at the girl halfway to the revolving doors. She was running in short, terrified bursts, dragging her duffel behind her across the tile. Becker tried to pull himself to his feet, but he could not. He was blinded by red-hot fire. *She can't get away!*

He tried to call out, but there was no air in his lungs, only a sickening pain. 'No!' He coughed. The sound barely left his lips.

Becker knew the second she went through the door, she would disappear forever. He tried to call out again, but his throat was searing.

The girl had almost reached the revolving door. Becker staggered to his feet, gasping for breath. He stumbled after her. The girl dashed into the first compartment of the revolving door, dragging her duffel behind her. Twenty yards back, Becker was staggering blindly toward the door.

'Wait!' He gasped. *'Wait!'*

The girl pushed furiously on the inside of the door.

The door began to rotate, but then it jammed. She wheeled in terror and saw her duffel snagged in the opening. She knelt and pulled furiously to free it.

Becker fixed his bleary vision on the fabric protruding through the door. As he dove, the red corner of nylon protruding from the crack was all he could see. He flew toward it, arms outstretched.

As David Becker fell toward the door, his hands only inches away, the fabric slipped into the crack and disappeared. His fingers clutched empty air as the door lurched into motion. The girl and the duffel tumbled into the street outside.

'Megan!' Becker wailed as he hit the floor. White-hot needles shot through the back of his eye sockets. His vision tunneled to nothing, and a new wave of nausea rolled in. His own voice echoed in the blackness. *Megan!*

David Becker wasn't sure how long he'd been lying there before he became aware of the hum of fluorescent bulbs overhead. Everything else was still. Through the silence came a voice. Someone was calling. He tried to lift his head off the floor. The world was cockeyed, watery. *Again the voice.* He squinted down the concourse and saw a figure twenty yards away.

'Mister?'

Becker recognized the voice. It was the girl. She was standing at another entrance farther down the concourse, clutching her duffel to her chest. She looked more frightened now than she had before.

'Mister?' she asked, her voice trembling. 'I never told you my name. How come you know my name?'

CHAPTER 74

Director Leland Fontaine was a mountain of a man, sixty-three years old, with a close-cropped military haircut and a rigid demeanor. His jet-black eyes were like coal when he was irritated, which was almost always. He'd risen through the ranks of the NSA through hard work, good planning, and the well-earned respect of his predecessors. He was the first African American director of the National Security Agency, but nobody ever mentioned the distinction; Fontaine's politics were decidedly color-blind, and his staff wisely followed suit.

Fontaine had kept Midge and Brinkerhoff standing as he went through the silent ritual of making himself a mug of Guatemalan java. Then he'd settled at his desk, left them standing, and questioned them like schoolchildren in the principal's office.

Midge did the talking – explaining the unusual series of events that led them to violate the sanctity of Fontaine's office.

'A virus?' the director asked coldly. 'You two think we've got a virus?'

Brinkerhoff winced.

'Yes, sir,' Midge snapped.

'Because Strathmore bypassed Gauntlet?' Fontaine eyed the printout in front of him.

'Yes,' she said. 'And there's a file that hasn't broken in over twenty hours!'

Fontaine frowned. 'Or so your data says.'

Midge was about to protest, but she held her tongue. Instead she went for the throat. 'There's a blackout in Crypto.'

Fontaine looked up, apparently surprised.

Midge confirmed with a curt nod. 'All power's down. Jabba thought maybe—'

'You called Jabba?'

'Yes, sir, I—'

'Jabba?' Fontaine stood up, furious. 'Why the hell didn't you call Strathmore?'

'We did!' Midge defended. 'He said everything was fine.'

Fontaine stood, his chest heaving. 'Then we have no reason to doubt him.' There was closure in his voice. He took a sip of coffee. 'Now if you'll excuse me, I have work to do.'

Midge's jaw dropped. 'I beg your pardon?'

Brinkerhoff was already headed for the door, but Midge was cemented in place.

'I said good night, Ms Milken,' Fontaine repeated. 'You are excused.'

'But – but sir,' she stammered, 'I . . . I have to protest. I think—'

'*You* protest?' the director demanded. He set down his coffee. '*I* protest! I protest to your presence in my office. I protest to your insinuations that the deputy director of this agency is lying. I protest—'

'We have a virus, sir! My instincts tell me—'

309

'Well, your instincts are wrong, Ms. Milken! For once, they're wrong!'

Midge stood fast. 'But, sir! Commander Strathmore bypassed Gauntlet!'

Fontaine strode toward her, barely controlling his anger. 'That is *his* prerogative! I pay you to watch analysts and service employees – not spy on the deputy director! If it weren't for him we'd still be breaking codes with pencil and paper! Now leave me!' He turned to Brinkerhoff, who stood in the doorway colorless and trembling. 'Both of you.'

'With all due respect, sir,' Midge said. 'I'd like to recommend we send a Sys-Sec team to Crypto just to ensure—'

'We will do no such thing!'

After a tense beat, Midge nodded. 'Very well. Good night.' She turned and left. As she passed, Brinkerhoff could see in her eyes that she had no intention of letting this rest – not until her intuition was satisfied.

Brinkerhoff gazed across the room at his boss, massive and seething behind his desk. This was not the director he knew. The director he knew was a stickler for detail, for neatly tied packages. He always encouraged his staff to examine and clarify any inconsistencies in daily procedure, no matter how minute. And yet here he was, asking them to turn their backs on a very bizarre series of coincidences.

The director was obviously hiding something, but Brinkerhoff was paid to assist, not to question. Fontaine had proven over and over that he had everyone's best interests at heart; if assisting him now meant turning a blind eye, then so be it. Unfortunately, Midge was paid to question, and Brinkerhoff feared she was headed for Crypto to do just that.

Time to get out the résumés, Brinkerhoff thought as he turned to the door.

'Chad!' Fontaine barked, from behind him. Fontaine had seen the look in Midge's eyes when she left. 'Don't let her out of this suite.'

Brinkerhoff nodded and hustled after Midge.

Fontaine sighed and put his head in his hands. His sable eyes were heavy. It had been a long, unexpected trip home. The past month had been one of great anticipation for Leland Fontaine. There were things happening right now at the NSA that would change history, and ironically, Director Fontaine had found out about them only by chance.

Three months ago, Fontaine had gotten news that Commander Strathmore's wife was leaving him. He'd also heard reports that Strathmore was working absurd hours and seemed about to crack under the pressure. Despite differences of opinion with Strathmore on many issues, Fontaine had always held his deputy director in the highest esteem; Strathmore was a brilliant man, maybe the best the NSA had. At the same time, ever since the Skipjack fiasco, Strathmore had been under tremendous stress. It made Fontaine uneasy; the commander held a lot of keys around the NSA – and Fontaine had an agency to protect.

Fontaine needed someone to keep tabs on the wavering Strathmore and make sure he was 100 percent – but it was not that simple. Strathmore was a proud and powerful man; Fontaine needed a way to check up on the commander without undermining his confidence or authority.

Fontaine decided, out of respect for Strathmore, to

do the job himself. He had an invisible tap installed on Commander Strathmore's Crypto account – his E-mail, his interoffice correspondence, his brainstorms, all of it. If Strathmore was going to crack, the director would see warning signs in his work. But instead of signs of a breakdown, Fontaine uncovered the groundwork for one of the most incredible intelligence schemes he'd ever encountered. It was no wonder Strathmore was busting his ass; if he could pull this plan off, it would make up for the Skipjack fiasco a hundred times over.

Fontaine had concluded Strathmore was fine, working at 110 percent – as sly, smart, and patriotic as ever. The best thing the director could do would be to stand clear and watch the commander work his magic. Strathmore had devised a plan . . . a plan Fontaine had no intention of interrupting.

CHAPTER 75

Strathmore fingered the Beretta in his lap. Even with the rage boiling in his blood, he was programmed to think clearly. The fact that Greg Hale had dared lay a finger on Susan Fletcher sickened him, but the fact that it was his own fault made him even sicker; Susan going into Node 3 had been his idea. Strathmore knew enough to compartmentalize his emotion – it could in no way affect his handling of Digital Fortress. He was the deputy director of the National Security Agency. And today his job was more critical than it had ever been.

Strathmore slowed his breathing. 'Susan.' His voice was efficient and unclouded. 'Did you delete Hale's E-mail?'

'No,' she said, confused.

'Do you have the pass-key?'

She shook her head.

Strathmore frowned, chewing his lip. His mind was racing. He had a dilemma. He could easily enter his elevator password, and Susan would be gone. But he needed her there. He needed her help to find Hale's pass-key. Strathmore hadn't told her yet, but finding that pass-key was far more than a matter of academic interest – it was an absolute necessity. Strathmore suspected he could run Susan's nonconformity search and find the pass-key himself, but he'd already encountered problems running her tracer. He was not about to risk it again.

'Susan.' He sighed resolutely. 'I'd like you to help me find Hale's pass-key.'

'What!' Susan stood up, her eyes wild.

Strathmore fought off the urge to stand along with her. He knew a lot about negotiating – the position of power was always seated. He hoped she would follow suit. She did not.

'Susan, sit down.'

She ignored him.

'Sit down.' It was an order.

Susan remained standing. 'Commander, if you've still got some burning desire to check out Tankado's algorithm, you can do it alone. I want out.'

Strathmore hung his head and took a deep breath. It was clear she would need an explanation. *She deserves one,* he thought. Strathmore made his decision – Susan Fletcher would hear it all. He prayed he wasn't making a mistake.

'Susan,' he began, 'it wasn't supposed to come to this.' He ran his hand across his scalp. 'There are some things I haven't told you. Sometimes a man in my position . . .' The commander wavered as if making a painful confession. 'Sometimes a man in my position is forced to lie to the people he loves. Today was one of those days.' He eyed her sadly. 'What I'm about to tell you, I never planned to have to say . . . to you . . . or to anyone.'

Susan felt a chill. The commander had a deadly

serious look on his face. There was obviously some aspect of his agenda to which she was not privy. Susan sat down.

There was a long pause as Strathmore stared at the ceiling, gathering his thoughts. 'Susan,' he finally said, his voice frail. 'I have no family.' He returned his gaze to her. 'I have no marriage to speak of. My life has been my love for this country. My life has been my work here at the NSA.'

Susan listened in silence.

'As you may have guessed,' he continued, 'I planned to retire soon. But I wanted to retire with pride. I wanted to retire knowing that I'd truly made a difference.'

'But you *have* made a difference,' Susan heard herself say. 'You built TRANSLTR.'

Strathmore didn't seem to hear. 'Over the past few years, our work here at the NSA has gotten harder and harder. We've faced enemies I never imagined would challenge us. I'm talking about our own citizens. The lawyers, the civil rights fanatics, the EFF – they've all played a part, but it's more than that. It's the *people*. They've lost faith. They've become paranoid. They suddenly see *us* as the enemy. People like you and me, people who truly have the nation's best interests at heart, we find ourselves having to fight for our right to serve our country. We're no longer peacekeepers. We're eavesdroppers, peeping Toms, violators of people's rights.' Strathmore heaved a sigh. 'Unfortunately, there are naive people in the world, people who can't imagine the horrors they'd face if we didn't intervene. I truly believe it's up to us to save them from their own ignorance.'

Susan waited for his point.

The commander stared wearily at the floor and then looked up. 'Susan, hear me out,' he said, smiling tenderly at her. 'You'll want to stop me, but hear me out. I've been decrypting Tankado's E-mail for about two months now. As you can imagine, I was shocked when I first read his messages to North Dakota about an unbreakable algorithm called Digital Fortress. I didn't believe it was possible. But every time I intercepted a new message, Tankado sounded more and more convincing. When I read that he'd used mutation strings to write a rotating key-code, I realized he was light-years ahead of us; it was an approach no one here had ever tried.'

'Why *would* we?' Susan asked. 'It barely makes sense.'

Strathmore stood up and started pacing, keeping one eye on the door. 'A few weeks ago, when I heard about the Digital Fortress auction, I finally accepted the fact that Tankado was serious. I knew if he sold his algorithm to a Japanese software company, we were sunk, so I tried to think of any way I could stop him. I considered having him killed, but with all the publicity surrounding the algorithm and all his recent claims about TRANSLTR, we would be prime suspects. That's when it dawned on me.' He turned to Susan. 'I realized that Digital Fortress should *not* be stopped.'

Susan stared at him, apparently lost.

Strathmore went on. 'I suddenly saw Digital Fortress as the opportunity of a lifetime. It hit me that with a few changes, Digital Fortress could work *for* us instead of against us.'

Susan had never heard anything so absurd. Digital Fortress was an unbreakable algorithm; it would destroy them.

'If,' Strathmore continued, 'if I could just make a small modification in the algorithm . . . before it was released . . .' He gave her a cunning glint of the eye.

It took only an instant.

Strathmore saw the amazement register in Susan's eyes. He excitedly explained his plan. 'If I could get the pass-key, I could unlock our copy of Digital Fortress and insert a modification.'

'A back door,' Susan said, forgetting the commander had ever lied to her. She felt a surge of anticipation. 'Just like Skipjack.'

Strathmore nodded. 'Then we could replace Tankado's give-away file on the Internet with our *altered* version. Because Digital Fortress is a Japanese algorithm, no one will ever suspect the NSA had any part in it. All we have to do is make the switch.'

Susan realized the plan was beyond ingenious. It was pure . . . Strathmore. He planned to facilitate the release of an algorithm the NSA could break!

'Full access,' Strathmore said. 'Digital Fortress will become the encryption standard overnight.'

'Overnight?' Susan said. 'How do you figure *that?* Even if Digital Fortress becomes available everywhere for free, most computer users will stick with their old algorithms for convenience. Why would they switch to Digital Fortress?'

Strathmore smiled. 'Simple. We have a security leak. The whole world finds out about TRANSLTR.'

Susan's jaw dropped.

'Quite simply, Susan, we let the truth hit the street. We tell the world that the NSA has a computer that can break every algorithm except Digital Fortress.'

Susan was amazed. 'So everyone jumps ship to Digital Fortress . . . not knowing we can break it!'

Strathmore nodded. 'Exactly.' There was a long silence. 'I'm sorry I lied to you. Trying to rewrite Digital Fortress is a pretty big play, I didn't want you involved.'

'I . . . understand,' she replied slowly, still reeling from the brilliance of it all. 'You're not a bad liar.'

Strathmore chuckled. 'Years of practice. Lying was the only way to keep you out of the loop.'

Susan nodded. 'And how big a loop is it?'

'You're looking at it.'

Susan smiled for the first time in an hour. 'I was afraid you'd say that.'

He shrugged. 'Once Digital Fortress is in place, I'll brief the director.'

Susan was impressed. Strathmore's plan was a global intelligence coup the magnitude of which had never before been imagined. And he'd attempted it single-handedly. It looked like he might pull it off too. The pass-key was downstairs. Tankado was dead. Tankado's partner had been located.

Susan paused.

Tankado is dead. That seemed very convenient. She thought of all the lies that Strathmore had told her and felt a sudden chill. She looked uneasily at the commander. 'Did you kill Ensei Tankado?'

Strathmore looked surprised. He shook his head. 'Of course not. There was no need to kill Tankado. In fact, I'd prefer he were alive. His death could cast suspicion on Digital Fortress. I wanted this switch to go as smoothly and inconspicuously as possible. The original plan was to make the switch and let Tankado sell his key.'

Susan had to admit it made sense. Tankado would have no reason to suspect the algorithm on the

Internet was not the original. Nobody had access to it except himself and North Dakota. Unless Tankado went back and studied the programming after it was released, he'd never know about the back door. He'd slaved over Digital Fortress for long enough that he'd probably never want to see the programming again.

Susan let it all soak in. She suddenly understood the commander's need for privacy in Crypto. The task at hand was time-consuming and delicate – writing a concealed back door in a complex algorithm and making an undetected Internet switch. Concealment was of paramount importance. The simple suggestion that Digital Fortress was tainted could ruin the commander's plan.

Only now did she fully grasp why he had decided to let TRANSLTR keep running. *If Digital Fortress is going to be the NSA's new baby, Strathmore wanted to be sure it was unbreakable!*

'Still want out?' he asked.

Susan looked up. Somehow sitting there in the dark with the great Trevor Strathmore, her fears were swept away. Rewriting Digital Fortress was a chance to make history – a chance to do incredible good – and Strathmore could use her help. Susan forced a reluctant smile. 'What's our next move?'

Strathmore beamed. He reached over and put a hand on her shoulder. 'Thanks.' He smiled and then got down to business. 'We'll go downstairs together.' He held up his Beretta. 'You'll search Hale's terminal. I'll cover you.'

Susan bristled at the thought of going downstairs. 'Can't we wait for David to call with Tankado's copy?'

Strathmore shook his head. 'The sooner we make the switch, the better. We have no guarantees that

319

David will even find the other copy. If by some fluke the ring falls into the wrong hands over there, I'd prefer we'd already made the algorithm switch. That way, whoever ends up with the key will download *our* version of the algorithm.' Strathmore fingered his gun and stood. 'We need to go for Hale's key.'

Susan fell silent. The commander had a point. They needed Hale's pass-key. And they needed it now.

When Susan stood, her legs were jittery. She wished she'd hit Hale harder. She eyed Strathmore's weapon and suddenly felt queasy. 'You'd actually shoot Greg Hale?'

'No.' Strathmore frowned, striding to the door. 'But let's hope *he* doesn't know that.'

CHAPTER 76

Outside the Seville airport terminal, a taxi sat idle, the meter running. The passenger in the wire-rim glasses gazed through the plate-glass windows of the well-lit terminal. He knew he'd arrived in time.

He could see a blond girl. She was helping David Becker to a chair. Becker was apparently in pain. *He does not yet know pain,* the passenger thought. The girl pulled a small object from her pocket and held it out. Becker held it up and studied it in the light. Then he slipped it on his finger. He pulled a stack of bills from his pocket and paid the girl. They talked a few minutes longer, and then the girl hugged him. She waved, shouldered her duffel, and headed off across the concourse.

At last, the man in the taxi thought. *At last.*

CHAPTER 77

Strathmore stepped out of his office onto the landing with his gun leveled. Susan trailed close behind, wondering if Hale was still in Node 3.

The light from Strathmore's monitor behind them threw eerie shadows of their bodies out across the grated platform. Susan inched closer to the commander.

As they moved away from the door, the light faded, and they were plunged into darkness. The only light on the Crypto floor came from the stars above and the faint haze from behind the shattered Node 3 window.

Strathmore inched forward, looking for the place where the narrow staircase began. Switching the Beretta to his left hand, he groped for the banister with his right. He figured he was probably just as bad a shot with his left, and he needed his right for support. Falling down this particular set of stairs could cripple someone for life, and Strathmore's dreams for his retirement did not involve a wheelchair.

Susan, blinded by the blackness of the Crypto dome, descended with a hand on Strathmore's shoulder. Even at the distance of two feet, she could not see

322

the commander's outline. As she stepped onto each metal tread, she shuffled her toes forward looking for the edge.

Susan began having second thoughts about risking a visit to Node 3 to get Hale's pass-key. The commander insisted Hale wouldn't have the guts to touch them, but Susan wasn't so sure. Hale was desperate. He had two options: Escape Crypto or go to jail.

A voice kept telling Susan they should wait for David's call and use *his* pass-key, but she knew there was no guarantee he would even find it. She wondered what was taking David so long. Susan swallowed her apprehension and kept going.

Strathmore descended silently. There was no need to alert Hale they were coming. As they neared the bottom, Strathmore slowed, feeling for the final step. When he found it, the heel of his loafer clicked on hard black tile. Susan felt his shoulder tense. They'd entered the danger zone. Hale could be anywhere.

In the distance, now hidden behind TRANSLTR, was their destination – Node 3. Susan prayed Hale was still there, lying on the floor, whimpering in pain like the dog he was.

Strathmore let go of the railing and switched the gun back to his right hand. Without a word, he moved out into the darkness. Susan held tight to his shoulder. If she lost him, the only way she'd find him again was to speak. Hale might hear them. As they moved away from the safety of the stairs, Susan recalled late-night games of tag as a kid – she'd left home base, she was in the open. She was vulnerable.

TRANSLTR was the only island in the vast black sea. Every few steps Strathmore stopped, gun poised, and listened. The only sound was the faint hum from below. Susan wanted to pull him back, back to safety, back to home base. There seemed to be faces in the dark all around her.

Halfway to TRANSLTR, the silence of Crypto was broken. Somewhere in the darkness, seemingly right on top of them, a high-pitched beeping pierced the night. Strathmore spun, and Susan lost him. Fearful, Susan shot her arm out, groping for him. But the commander was gone. The space where his shoulder had been was now just empty air. She staggered forward into the emptiness.

The beeping noise continued. It was nearby. Susan wheeled in the darkness. There was a rustle of clothing, and suddenly the beeping stopped. Susan froze. An instant later, as if from one of her worst childhood nightmares, a vision appeared. A face materialized directly in front of her. It was ghostly and green. It was the face of a demon, sharp shadows jutting upward across deformed features. She jumped back. She turned to run, but it grabbed her arm.

'Don't move!' it commanded.

For an instant, she thought she saw Hale in those two burning eyes. But the voice was not Hale's. And the touch was too soft. It was Strathmore. He was lit from beneath by a glowing object that he'd just pulled from his pocket. Her body sagged with relief. She felt herself start breathing again. The object in Strathmore's hand had some sort of electronic LED that was giving off a greenish glow.

'Damn,' Strathmore cursed under his breath. 'My new pager.' He stared in disgust at the SkyPager in his palm. He'd forgotten to engage the silent-ring feature. Ironically, he'd gone to a local electronics store to buy the device. He'd paid cash to keep it anonymous;

nobody knew better than Strathmore how closely the NSA watched their own – and the digital messages sent and received from this pager were something Strathmore definitely needed to keep private.

Susan looked around uneasily. If Hale hadn't known they were coming, he knew now.

Strathmore pressed a few buttons and read the incoming message. He groaned quietly. It was more bad news from Spain – not from David Becker, but from the *other* party Strathmore had sent to Seville.

Three thousand miles away, a mobile surveillance van sped along the darkened Seville streets. It had been commissioned by the NSA under 'Umbra' secrecy from a military base in Rota. The two men inside were tense. It was not the first time they'd received emergency orders from Fort Meade, but the orders didn't usually come from so high up.

The agent at the wheel called over his shoulder. 'Any sign of our man?'

The eyes of his partner never left the feed from the wide-angle video monitor on the roof. 'No. Keep driving.'

CHAPTER 78

Underneath the twisting mass of cables, Jabba was sweating. He was still on his back with a penlight clenched in his teeth. He'd gotten used to working late on weekends; the less hectic NSA hours were often the only times he could perform hardware maintenance. As he maneuvered the red-hot soldering iron through the maze of wires above him, he moved with exceptional care; singeing any of the dangling sheaths would be disaster.

Just another few inches, he thought. The job was taking far longer than he'd imagined.

Just as he brought the tip of the iron against the final thread of raw solder, his cellular phone rang sharply. Jabba started, his arm twitched, and a large glob of sizzling, liquefied lead fell on his arm.

'*Shit!*' He dropped the iron and practically swallowed his penlight. 'Shit! Shit! Shit!'

He scrubbed furiously at the drop of cooling solder. It rolled off, leaving an impressive welt. The chip he was trying to solder in place fell out and hit him in the head.

'Goddamn it!'

Jabba's phone summoned him again. He ignored it.

'Midge,' he cursed under his breath. *Damn you! Crypto's fine!* The phone rang on. Jabba went back to work reseating the new chip. A minute later the chip was in place, but his phone was still ringing. *For Christ's sake, Midge! Give it up!*

The phone rang another fifteen seconds and finally stopped. Jabba breathed a sigh of relief.

Sixty seconds later the intercom overhead crackled. 'Would the chief Sys-Sec please contact the main switchboard for a message?'

Jabba rolled his eyes in disbelief. *She just doesn't give up, does she?* He ignored the page.

CHAPTER 79

Strathmore replaced his SkyPager in his pocket and peered through the darkness toward Node 3.

He reached for Susan's hand. 'Come on.'

But their fingers never touched.

There was a long guttural cry from out of the darkness. A thundering figure loomed – a Mack truck bearing down with no headlights. An instant later, there was a collision and Strathmore was skidding across the floor.

It was Hale. The pager had given them away.

Susan heard the Beretta fall. For a moment she was planted in place, unsure where to run, what to do. Her instincts told her to escape, but she didn't have the elevator code. Her heart told her to help Strathmore, but how? As she spun in desperation, she expected to hear the sounds of a life-and-death struggle on the floor, but there was nothing. Everything was suddenly silent – as if Hale had hit the commander and then disappeared back into the night.

Susan waited, straining her eyes into the darkness, hoping Strathmore wasn't hurt. After what seemed like an eternity, she whispered, 'Commander?'

Even as she said it, she realized her mistake. An instant later Hale's odor welled up behind her. She turned too late. Without warning, she was twisting, gasping for air. She found herself crushed in a familiar headlock, her face against Hale's chest.

'My balls are killing me,' Hale panted in her ear.

Susan's knees buckled. The stars in the dome began to spin above her.

CHAPTER 80

Hale clamped down on Susan's neck and yelled into the darkness. 'Commander, I've got your sweetheart. I want out!'

His demands were met with silence.

Hale's grip tightened. 'I'll break her neck!'

A gun cocked directly behind them. Strathmore's voice was calm and even. 'Let her go.'

Susan winced in pain. 'Commander!'

Hale spun Susan's body toward the sound. 'You shoot and you'll hit your precious Susan. You ready to take that chance?'

Strathmore's voice moved closer. 'Let her go.'

'No way. You'll kill me.'

'I'm not going to kill anyone.'

'Oh, yeah? Tell that to Chartrukian!'

Strathmore moved closer. 'Chartrukian's dead.'

'No shit. You killed him. I saw it!'

'Give it up, Greg,' Strathmore said calmly.

Hale clutched at Susan and whispered in her ear, 'Strathmore pushed Chartrukian – I swear it!'

'She's not going to fall for your divide-and-conquer technique,' Strathmore said, moving closer. 'Let her go.'

Hale hissed into the darkness, 'Chartrukian was just a *kid*, for Christ's sake! Why'd you do it? To protect your little secret?'

Strathmore stayed cool. 'And what little secret is that?'

'You know damn-fucking-well what secret that is! Digital Fortress!'

'My, my,' Strathmore muttered condescendingly, his voice like an iceberg. 'So you *do* know about Digital Fortress. I was starting to think you'd deny *that* too.'

'Fuck you.'

'A witty defense.'

'You're a fool,' Hale spat. 'For your information, TRANSLTR is overheating.'

'Really?' Strathmore chuckled. 'Let me guess – I should open the doors and call in the Sys-Secs?'

'Exactly,' Hale fired back. 'You'd be an idiot not to.'

This time Strathmore laughed out loud. 'That's your big play? TRANSLTR's overheating, so open the doors and let us out?'

'It's true, dammit! I've been down to the sublevels! The aux power isn't pulling enough freon!'

'Thanks for the tip,' Strathmore said. 'But TRANSLTR's got automatic shutdown; if it's overheating, Digital Fortress will quit all by itself.'

Hale sneered. 'You're insane. What the fuck do I care if TRANSLTR blows? The damn machine should be outlawed anyway.'

Strathmore sighed. 'Child psychology only works on children, Greg. Let her go.'

'So you can shoot me?'

'I won't shoot you. I just want the pass-key.'

'What pass-key?'

Strathmore sighed again. 'The one Tankado sent you.'

'I have no idea what you're talking about.'

'Liar!' Susan managed. 'I saw Tankado's mail in your account!'

Hale went rigid. He spun Susan around. 'You went in my account?'

'And *you* aborted my tracer,' she snapped.

Hale felt his blood pressure skyrocket. He thought he'd covered his tracks; he had no idea Susan knew what he'd done. It was no wonder she wasn't buying a word he said. Hale felt the walls start to close in. He knew he could never talk his way out of that one – not in time. He whispered to her in desperation, 'Susan . . . Strathmore killed Chartrukian!'

'Let her go,' the commander said evenly. 'She doesn't believe you.'

'Why *should* she?' Hale fired back. 'You lying bastard! You've got her brainwashed! You only tell her what suits your needs! Does she know what you *really* plan to do with Digital Fortress?'

'And what's that?' Strathmore taunted.

Hale knew what he was about to say would either be his ticket to freedom or his death warrant. He took a deep breath and went for broke. 'You plan to write a back door in Digital Fortress.'

The words met with a bewildered silence from the darkness. Hale knew he had hit a bull's-eye.

Apparently Strathmore's unflappable cool was being put to the test. 'Who told you that?' he demanded, his voice rough around the edges.

'I read it,' Hale said smugly, trying to capitalize on the change of momentum. 'In one of your brain-storms.'

'Impossible. I *never* print my brainstorms.'

'I know. I read it directly off your account.'

Strathmore seemed doubtful. 'You got into my office?'

'No. I snooped you from Node 3.' Hale forced a self-assured chuckle. He knew he'd need all the negotiating skills he'd learned in the Marines to get out of Crypto alive.

Strathmore edged closer, the Beretta leveled in the darkness. 'How do you know about my back door?'

'I told you, I snooped your account.'

'Impossible.'

Hale forced a cocky sneer. 'One of the problems of hiring the best, Commander – sometimes they're better than you.'

'Young man,' Strathmore seethed, 'I don't know where you get your information, but you're in way over your head. You will let Ms Fletcher go right now or I'll call in Security and have you thrown in jail for life.'

'You won't do it,' Hale stated matter-of-factly. 'Calling Security ruins your plans. I'll tell them everything.' Hale paused. 'But let me out clean, and I'll never say a word about Digital Fortress.'

'No deal,' Strathmore fired back. 'I want the pass-key.'

'I don't have any fucking pass-key!'

'Enough lies!' Strathmore bellowed. 'Where is it?'

Hale clamped down on Susan's neck. 'Let me out, or she dies!'

Trevor Strathmore had done enough high-stakes bargaining in his life to know that Hale was in a very dangerous state of mind. The young crypto-grapher had backed himself into a corner, and a cornered opponent was always the most dangerous kind – desperate and unpredictable. Strathmore knew his next move was a critical one. Susan's life depended on it – and so did the future of Digital Fortress.

Strathmore knew the first thing he had to do was release the tension of the situation. After a long moment, he sighed reluctantly. 'Okay, Greg. You win. What do you want me to do?'

Silence. Hale seemed momentarily unsure how to handle the commander's cooperative tone. He let up a bit on Susan's neck.

'W-well . . .' he stammered, his voice wavering sud-denly. 'First thing you do is give me your gun. You're both coming with me.'

'Hostages?' Strathmore laughed coldly. 'Greg, you'll have to do better than that. There are about a dozen armed guards between here and the parking lot.'

'I'm not a fool,' Hale snapped. 'I'm taking your ele-vator. Susan comes with me! *You* stay!'

'I hate to tell you this,' Strathmore replied, 'but there's no power to the elevator.'

'Bullshit!' Hale snapped. 'The lift runs on power from the main building! I've seen the schematics!'

'We tried it already,' Susan choked, trying to help. 'It's dead.'

'You're both so full of shit, it's incredible.' Hale tightened his grip. 'If the elevator's dead, I'll abort TRANSLTR and restore power.'

'The elevator takes a password,' Susan managed feistily.

334

'Big deal.' Hale laughed. 'I'm sure the commander will share. Won't you, Commander?'

'No chance,' Strathmore hissed.

Hale boiled over. 'Now you listen to me, old man – here's the deal! You let Susan and me out through your elevator, we drive a few hours, and then I let her go.'

Strathmore felt the stakes rising. He'd gotten Susan into this, and he needed to get her out. His voice stayed steady as a rock. 'What about my plans for Digital Fortress?'

Hale laughed. 'You can write your back door – I won't say a word.' Then his voice turned ominous. 'But the day I think you're tracking me, I go to the press with the whole story. I tell them Digital Fortress is tainted, and I sink this whole fucking organization!'

Strathmore considered Hale's offer. It was clean and simple. Susan lived, and Digital Fortress got its back door. As long as Strathmore didn't chase Hale, the back door stayed a secret. Strathmore knew Hale couldn't keep his mouth shut for long. But still . . . the knowledge of Digital Fortress was Hale's only insurance – maybe he'd be smart. Whatever happened, Strathmore knew Hale could be removed later if necessary.

'Make up your mind, old man!' Hale taunted. 'Are we leaving or not?' Hale's arms tightened around Susan like a vise.

Strathmore knew that if he picked up the phone right now and called Security, Susan would live. He'd bet his life on it. He could see the scenario clearly. The call would take Hale completely by surprise. He would panic, and in the end, faced with a small army, Hale would be unable to act. After a brief standoff, he would give in. *But if I call Security,* Strathmore thought, *my plan is ruined.*

Hale clamped down again. Susan cried out in pain.

'What's it gonna be?' Hale yelled. 'Do I kill her?'

Strathmore considered his options. If he let Hale take Susan out of Crypto, there were no guarantees. Hale might drive for a while, park in the woods. He'd have a gun. . . . Strathmore's stomach turned. There was no telling what would happen before Hale set Susan free . . . *if* he set her free. *I've got to call Security,* Strathmore decided. *What else can I do?* He pictured Hale in court, spilling his guts about Digital Fortress. *My plan will be ruined. There must be some other way.*

'Decide!' Hale yelled, dragging Susan toward the staircase.

Strathmore wasn't listening. If saving Susan meant his plans were ruined, then so be it – nothing was worth losing her. Susan Fletcher was a price Trevor Strathmore refused to pay.

Hale had Susan's arm twisted behind her back and her neck bent to one side. 'This is your last chance, old man! Give me the gun!'

Strathmore's mind continued to race, searching for another option. *There are always other options!* Finally he spoke – quietly, almost sadly. 'No, Greg, I'm sorry. I just can't let you go.'

Hale choked in apparent shock. 'What!'

'I'm calling Security.'

Susan gasped. 'Commander! No!'

Hale tightened his grip. 'You call Security, and she dies!'

Strathmore pulled the cellular off his belt and flicked it on. 'Greg, you're bluffing.'

'You'll never do it!' Hale yelled. 'I'll talk! I'll ruin your plan! You're only hours away from your dream! Controlling all the data in the world! No more TRANSLTR. No more limits – just free information. It's a chance of a lifetime! You won't let it slip by!'

Strathmore's voice was like steel. 'Watch me.'

'But – but what about Susan?' Hale stammered. 'You make that call, and she dies!'

Strathmore held firm. 'That's a chance I'm ready to take.'

'Bullshit! You've got a bigger hard-on for her than you do for Digital Fortress! I know you! You won't risk it!'

Susan began to make an angry rebuttal, but Strathmore beat her to it. 'Young man! You *don't* know me! I take risks for a living. If you're looking to play hardball, let's play!' He started punching keys on his phone. 'You misjudged me, son! Nobody threatens the lives of my employees and walks out!' He raised the phone and barked into the receiver, 'Switchboard! Get me Security!'

Hale began to torque Susan's neck. 'I-I'll kill her. I swear it!'

'You'll do no such thing!' Strathmore proclaimed. 'Killing Susan will just make things wor—' He broke off and rammed the phone against his mouth. 'Security! This is Commander Trevor Strathmore. We've got a hostage situation in Crypto! Get some men in here! Yes, *now*, goddamn it! We also have a generator failure. I want power routed from all available external sources. I want all systems on-line in five minutes! Greg Hale killed one of my junior Sys-Secs. He's holding my senior cryptographer hostage. You're cleared to use tear gas on all of us if necessary! If Mr

Hale doesn't cooperate, have snipers shoot him dead. I'll take full responsibility. Do it now!'

Hale stood motionless – apparently limp in disbelief. His grip on Susan eased.

Strathmore snapped his phone shut and shoved it back onto his belt. 'Your move, Greg.'

CHAPTER 81

Becker stood bleary-eyed beside the telephone booth on the terminal concourse. Despite his burning face and a vague nausea, his spirits were soaring. It was over. Truly over. He was on his way home. The ring on his finger was the grail he'd been seeking. He held his hand up in the light and squinted at the gold band. He couldn't focus well enough to read, but the inscription didn't appear to be in English. The first symbol was either a Q, an O, or a zero, his eyes hurt too much to tell. Becker studied the first few characters. They made no sense. *This was a matter of national security?*

Becker stepped into the phone booth and dialed Strathmore. Before he had finished the international prefix, he got a recording. 'Todos los circuitos están ocupados,' the voice said. 'Please hang up and try your call later.' Becker frowned and hung up. He'd forgotten: Getting an international connection from Spain was like roulette, all a matter of timing and luck. He'd have to try again in a few minutes.

Becker fought to ignore the waning sting of the pepper in his eyes. Megan had told him rubbing his eyes would only make them worse; he couldn't imagine. Impatient, he tried the phone again. Still no circuits. Becker couldn't wait any longer – his eyes were on fire; he had to flush them with water. Strathmore would have to wait a minute or two. Half blind, Becker made his way toward the bathrooms.

The blurry image of the cleaning cart was still in front of the men's room, so Becker turned again toward the door marked DAMAS. He thought he heard sounds inside. He knocked. 'Hola?'

Silence.

Probably Megan, he thought. She had five hours to kill before her flight and had said she was going to scrub her arm till it was clean.

'Megan?' he called. He knocked again. There was no reply. Becker pushed the door open. 'Hello?' He went in. The bathroom appeared empty. He shrugged and walked to the sink.

The sink was still filthy, but the water was cold. Becker felt his pores tighten as he splashed the water in his eyes. The pain began to ease, and the fog gradually lifted. Becker eyed himself in the mirror. He looked like he'd been crying for days.

He dried his face on the sleeve of his jacket, and then it suddenly occurred to him. In all the excitement, he'd forgotten where he was. He was at the airport! Somewhere out there on the tarmac, in one of the Seville airport's three private hangars, there was a Learjet 60 waiting to take him home. The pilot had stated very clearly, *I have orders to stay here until you return.*

It was hard to believe, Becker thought, that after all this, he had ended up right back where he'd started. *What am I waiting for?* he laughed. *I'm sure the pilot can radio a message to Strathmore!*

Chuckling to himself, Becker glanced in the mirror and straightened his tie. He was about to go when the reflection of something behind him caught his eye. He turned. It appeared to be one end of Megan's duffel, protruding from under a partially open stall door.

'Megan?' he called. There was no reply. *'Megan?'*

Becker walked over. He rapped loudly on the side of the stall. No answer. He gently pushed the door. It swung open.

Becker fought back a cry of horror. Megan was on the toilet, her eyes rolled skyward. Dead center of her forehead, a bullet hole oozed bloody liquid down her face.

'Oh, Jesus!' Becker cried in shock.

'Está muerta,' a barely human voice croaked behind him. 'She's dead.'

It was like a dream. Becker turned.

'Señor Becker?' the eerie voice asked.

Dazed, Becker studied the man stepping into the rest room. He looked oddly familiar.

'Soy Hulohot,' the killer said. 'I am Hulohot.' The misshapen words seemed to emerge from the depths of his stomach. Hulohot held out his hand. 'El anillo. The ring.'

Becker stared blankly.

The man reached in his pocket and produced a gun. He raised the weapon and trained it on Becker's head. 'El anillo.'

In an instant of clarity, Becker felt a sensation he had never known. As if cued by some subconscious survival instinct, every muscle in his body tensed simultaneously. He flew through the air as the shot spat out. Becker crashed down on top of Megan. A bullet exploded against the wall behind him.

'Mierda!' Hulohot seethed. Somehow, at the last possible instant, David Becker had dived out of the way. The assassin advanced.

Becker pulled himself off the lifeless teenager. There were approaching footsteps. Breathing. The cock of a weapon.

'Adiós,' the man whispered as he lunged like a panther, swinging his weapon into the stall.

The gun went off. There was a flash of red. But it was not blood. It was something else. An object had materialized as if out of nowhere, sailing out of the stall and hitting the killer in the chest, causing his gun to fire a split second early. It was Megan's duffel.

Becker exploded from the stall. He buried his shoulder in the man's chest and drove him back into the sink. There was a bone-crushing crash. A mirror shattered. The gun fell free. The two men collapsed to the floor. Becker tore himself away and dashed for the exit. Hulohot scrambled for his weapon, spun, and fired. The bullet ripped into the slamming bathroom door.

The empty expanse of the airport concourse loomed before Becker like an uncrossable desert. His legs surged beneath him faster than he'd ever known they could move.

As he skidded into the revolving door, a shot rang out behind him. The glass panel in front of him exploded in a shower of glass. Becker pushed his shoulder into the frame and the door rotated forward. A moment later he stumbled onto the pavement outside.

A taxi stood waiting.

'Déjame entrar!' Becker screamed, pounding on the locked door. 'Let me in!' The driver refused; his fare

342

with the wire-rim glasses had asked him to wait. Becker turned and saw Hulohot streaking across he concourse, gun in hand. Becker eyed his little Vespa on the sidewalk. *I'm dead.*

Hulohot blasted through the revolving doors just in time to see Becker trying in vain to kickstart his Vespa. Hulohot smiled and raised his weapon.

The choke! Becker fumbled with the levers under the gas tank. He jumped on the starter again. It coughed and died.

'El anillo. The ring.' The voice was close.

Becker looked up. He saw the barrel of a gun. The chamber was rotating. He rammed his foot on the starter once again.

Hulohot's shot just missed Becker's head as the little bike sprang to life and lurched forward. Becker hung on for his life as the motorcycle bounced down a grassy embankment and wobbled around the corner of the building onto the runway.

Enraged, Hulohot raced toward his waiting taxi. Seconds later, the driver lay stunned on the curb watching his taxi peel out in a cloud of dust.

CHAPTER 82

As the implications of the commander's phone call to Security began to settle on the dazed Greg Hale, he found himself weakened by a wave of panic. *Security is coming!* Susan began to slip away. Hale recovered, clutching at her midsection, pulling her back.

'Let me go!' she cried, her voice echoing through the dome.

Hale's mind was in overdrive. The commander's call had taken him totally by surprise. *Strathmore phoned Security! He's sacrificing his plans for Digital Fortress!*

Not in a million years had Hale imagined the commander would let Digital Fortress slip by. This back door was the chance of a lifetime.

As the panic rushed in, Hale's mind seemed to play tricks on him. He saw the barrel of Strathmore's Beretta everywhere he looked. He began to spin, holding Susan close, trying to deny the commander a shot. Driven by fear, Hale dragged Susan blindly toward the stairs. In five minutes the lights would come on, the doors would open, and a SWAT team would pour in.

'You're hurting me!' Susan choked. She gasped for

breath as she stumbled through Hale's desperate pirouettes.

Hale considered letting her go and making a mad dash for Strathmore's elevator, but it was suicide. He had no password. Besides, once outside the NSA without a hostage, Hale knew he was as good as dead. Not even his Lotus could outrun a fleet of NSA helicopters. *Susan is the only thing that will keep Strathmore from blowing me off the road!*

'Susan,' Hale blurted, dragging her toward the stairs. 'Come with me! I swear I won't hurt you!'

As Susan fought him, Hale realized he had new problems. Even if he somehow managed to get Strathmore's elevator open and take Susan with him, she would undoubtedly fight him all the way out of the building. Hale knew full well that Strathmore's elevator made only one stop: 'the Underground Highway,' a restricted labyrinth of underground access tunnels through which NSA powerbrokers moved in secrecy. Hale had no intention of ending up lost in the basement corridors of the NSA with a struggling hostage. It was a death trap. Even if he got out, he realized, he had no gun. How would he get Susan across the parking lot? How would he drive?

It was the voice of one of Hale's Marine, military-strategy professors that gave him his answer:

Force a hand, the voice warned, *and it will fight you. But convince a mind to think as you want it to think, and you have an ally.*

'Susan,' Hale heard himself saying, 'Strathmore's a killer! You're in danger here!'

Susan didn't seem to hear. Hale knew it was an absurd angle anyway; Strathmore would never hurt Susan, and she knew it.

Hale strained his eyes into the darkness, wondering where the commander was hidden. Strathmore had fallen silent suddenly, which made Hale even more panicky. He sensed his time was up. Security would arrive at any moment.

With a surge of strength, Hale wrapped his arms around Susan's waist and pulled her hard up the stairs. She hooked her heels on the first step and pulled back. It was no use, Hale overpowered her.

Carefully, Hale backed up the stairs with Susan in tow. Pushing her up might have been easier, but the landing at the top was illuminated from Strathmore's computer monitors. If Susan went first, Strathmore would have a clear shot at Hale's back. Pulling Susan behind him, Hale had a human shield between himself and the Crypto floor.

About a third of the way up, Hale sensed movement at the bottom of the stairs. *Strathmore's making his move!* 'Don't try it, Commander,' he hissed. 'You'll only get her killed.'

Hale waited. But there was only silence. He listened closely. Nothing. The bottom of the stairs was still. Was he imagining things? It didn't matter. Strathmore would never risk a shot with Susan in the way.

But as Hale backed up the stairs dragging Susan behind him, something unexpected happened. There was a faint thud on the landing behind him. Hale stopped, adrenaline surging. Had Strathmore slipped upstairs? Instinct told him Strathmore was at the *bottom* of the stairs. But then, suddenly, it happened again – louder this time. A distinct step on the upper landing!

In terror, Hale realized his mistake. *Strathmore's on the landing behind me! He has a clear shot of my back!* In

346

desperation, he spun Susan back to his uphill side and started retreating backwards down the steps.

As he reached the bottom step, he stared wildly up at the landing and yelled, 'Back off, Commander! Back off, or I'll break her—'

The butt of a Beretta came slicing through the air at the foot of the stairs and crashed down into Hale's skull.

As Susan tore free of the slumping Hale, she wheeled in confusion. Strathmore grabbed her and reeled her in, cradling her shaking body. 'Shhh,' he soothed. 'It's me. You're okay.'

Susan was trembling. 'Com . . . mander,' she gasped, disoriented. 'I thought . . . I thought you were upstairs . . . I heard . . .'

'Easy now,' he whispered. 'You heard me toss my loafers up onto the landing.'

Susan found herself laughing and crying at the same time. The commander had just saved her life. Standing there in the darkness, Susan felt an overwhelming sense of relief. It was not, however, without guilt; Security was coming. She had foolishly let Hale grab her, and he had used her against Strathmore. Susan knew the commander had paid a huge price to save her. 'I'm sorry,' she said.

'What for?'

'Your plans for Digital Fortress . . . they're ruined.'

Strathmore shook his head. 'Not at all.'

'But . . . but what about Security? They'll be here any minute. We won't have time to—'

'Security's not coming, Susan. We've got all the time in the world.'

Susan was lost. *Not coming?* 'But you phoned . . .'

Strathmore chuckled. 'Oldest trick in the book. I faked the call.'

CHAPTER 83

Becker's Vespa was no doubt the smallest vehicle ever to tear down the Seville runway. Its top speed, a whining 50 mph, sounded more like a chainsaw than a motorcycle and was unfortunately well below the necessary power to become airborne.

In his side mirror, Becker saw the taxi swing out onto the darkened runway about four hundred yards back. It immediately started gaining. Becker faced front. In the distance, the contour of the airplane hangars stood framed against the night sky about a half mile out. Becker wondered if the taxi would overtake him in that distance. He knew Susan could do the math in two seconds and calculate his odds. Becker suddenly felt fear like he had never known.

He lowered his head and twisted the throttle as far as it would go. The Vespa was definitely topped out. Becker guessed the taxi behind him was doing almost ninety, twice his speed. He set his sights on the three structures looming in the distance. *The middle one. That's where the Learjet is.* A shot rang out.

The bullet buried itself in the runway yards behind him. Becker looked back. The assassin was hanging out the window taking aim. Becker swerved and his side mirror exploded in a shower of glass. He could feel the impact of the bullet all the way up the handlebars. He lay his body flat on the bike. *God help me, I'm not going to make it!*

The tarmac in front of Becker's Vespa was growing brighter now. The taxi was closing, the headlights throwing ghostly shadows down the runway. A shot fired. The bullet ricocheted off the hull of the bike.

Becker struggled to keep from going into a swerve. *I've got to make the hangar!* He wondered if the Learjet pilot could see them coming. *Does he have a weapon? Will he open the cabin doors in time?* But as Becker approached the lit expanse of the open hangars, he realized the question was moot. The Learjet was nowhere to be seen. He squinted through blurred vision and prayed he was hallucinating. He was not. The hangar was bare. *Oh my God! Where's the plane!*

As the two vehicles rocketed into the empty hangar, Becker desperately searched for an escape. There was none. The building's rear wall, an expansive sheet of corrugated metal, had no doors or windows. The taxi roared up beside him, and Becker looked left to see Hulohot raising his gun.

Reflex took over. Becker slammed down on his brakes. He barely slowed. The hangar floor was slick with oil. The Vespa went into a headlong skid.

Beside him there was a deafening squeal as the taxi's brakes locked and the balding tires hydroplaned on the slippery surface. The car spun around in a cloud of smoke and burning rubber only inches to the left of Becker's skidding Vespa.

Now side by side, the two vehicles skimmed out of control on a collision course with the rear of the hangar. Becker desperately pumped his brakes, but there was no traction; it was like driving on ice. In front of him, the metal wall loomed. It was coming fast. As the taxi spiraled wildly beside him, Becker faced the wall and braced for the impact.

There was an earsplitting crash of steel and corrugated metal. But there was no pain. Becker found himself suddenly in the open air, still on his Vespa, bouncing across a grassy field. It was as if the hangar's back wall had vanished before him. The taxi was still beside him, careening across the field. An enormous sheet of corrugated metal from the hangar's back wall billowed off the taxi's hood and sailed over Becker's head.

Heart racing, Becker gunned the Vespa and took off into the night.

CHAPTER 84

Jabba let out a contented sigh as he finished the last of his solder points. He switched off the iron, put down his penlight, and lay a moment in the darkness of the mainframe computer. He was beat. His neck hurt. Internal work was always cramped, especially for a man of his size.

And they just keep building them smaller, he mused.

As he closed his eyes for a well-deserved moment of relaxation, someone outside began pulling on his boots.

'Jabba! Get out here!' a woman's voice yelled.

Midge found me. He groaned.

'Jabba! Get out here!'

Reluctantly he slithered out. 'For the love of God, Midge! I told you—' But it was not Midge. Jabba looked up, surprised. 'Soshi?'

Soshi Kuta was a ninety-pound live wire. She was Jabba's right-hand assistant, a razor-sharp Sys-Sec techie from MIT. She often worked late with Jabba and was the one member of his staff who seemed unintimidated by him. She glared at him and demanded, 'Why the hell didn't you answer your phone? Or my page?'

'*Your* page,' Jabba repeated. 'I thought it was—'

'Never mind. There's something strange going on in the main databank.'

Jabba checked his watch. 'Strange?' Now he was growing concerned. 'Can you be any more specific?'

Two minutes later Jabba was dashing down the hall toward the databank.

CHAPTER 85

Greg Hale lay curled on the Node 3 floor. Strathmore and Susan had just dragged him across Crypto and bound his hands and feet with twelve-gauge printer cable from the Node 3 laser-printers.

Susan couldn't get over the artful maneuver the commander had just executed. *He faked the call!* Somehow Strathmore had captured Hale, saved Susan, and bought himself the time needed to rewrite Digital Fortress.

Susan eyed the bound cryptographer uneasily. Hale was breathing heavily. Strathmore sat on the couch with the Beretta propped awkwardly in his lap. Susan returned her attention to Hale's terminal and continued her random-string search.

Her fourth string search ran its course and came up empty. 'Still no luck.' She sighed. 'We may need to wait for David to find Tankado's copy.'

Strathmore gave her a disapproving look. 'If David fails, and Tankado's key falls into the wrong hands . . .'

Strathmore didn't need to finish. Susan understood. Until the Digital Fortress file on the Internet had been replaced with Strathmore's modified version, Tankado's pass-key was dangerous.

'After we make the switch,' Strathmore added, 'I don't care how many pass-keys are floating around; the more the merrier.' He motioned for her to continue searching. 'But until then, we're playing beat-the-clock.'

Susan opened her mouth to acknowledge, but her words were drowned out by a sudden deafening blare. The silence of Crypto was shattered by a warning horn from the sublevels. Susan and Strathmore exchanged startled looks.

'What's *that?*' Susan yelled, timing her question between the intermittent bursts.

'TRANSLTR!' Strathmore called back, looking troubled. 'It's too hot! Maybe Hale was right about the aux power not pulling enough freon.'

'What about the auto-abort?'

Strathmore thought a moment, then yelled, 'Something must have shorted.' A yellow siren light spun above the Crypto floor and swept a pulsating glare across his face.

'You better abort!' Susan called.

Strathmore nodded. There was no telling what would happen if three million silicon processors overheated and decided to ignite. Strathmore needed to get upstairs to his terminal and abort the Digital Fortress run – particularly before anyone outside of Crypto noticed the trouble and decided to send in the cavalry.

Strathmore shot a glance at the still-unconscious Hale. He laid the Beretta on a table near Susan and yelled over the sirens, 'Be right back!' As he disappeared through the hole in the Node 3 wall,

354

Strathmore called over his shoulder, 'And find me that pass-key!'

Susan eyed the results of her unproductive pass-key search and hoped Strathmore would hurry up and abort. The noise and lights in Crypto felt like a missile launch.

On the floor, Hale began to stir. With each blast of the horn, he winced. Susan surprised herself by grabbing the Beretta. Hale opened his eyes to Susan Fletcher standing over him with the gun leveled at his crotch.

'Where's the pass-key?' Susan demanded.

Hale was having trouble getting his bearings. 'Wh-what happened?'

'You blew it, that's what happened. Now, where's the pass-key?'

Hale tried to move his arms but realized he was tied. His face became taut with panic. 'Let me go!'

'I need the pass-key,' Susan repeated.

'I don't have it! Let me go!' Hale tried to get up. He could barely roll over.

Susan yelled between blasts of the horn. 'You're North Dakota, and Ensei Tankado gave you a copy of his key. I need it now!'

'You're crazy!' Hale gasped. 'I'm not North Dakota!' He struggled unsuccessfully to free himself.

Susan charged angrily, 'Don't lie to me. Why the hell is all of North Dakota's mail in *your* account?'

'I told you before!' Hale pleaded as the horns blared on. 'I snooped Strathmore! That E-mail in my account was mail I copied out of *Strathmore's* account – E-mail COMINT stole from Tankado!'

'Bull! You could never snoop the commander's account!'

'You don't understand!' Hale yelled. 'There was *already* a tap on Strathmore's account!' Hale delivered his words in short bursts between the sirens. 'Someone else put the tap there. I think it was Director Fontaine! I just piggybacked! You've got to believe me! That's how I found out about his plan to rewrite Digital Fortress! I've been reading Strathmore's brainstorms!'

BrainStorms? Susan paused. Strathmore had undoubtedly outlined his plans for Digital Fortress using his BrainStorm software. If anyone had snooped the commander's account, all the information would have been available . . .

'Rewriting Digital Fortress is *sick!*' Hale cried. 'You know damn well what it implies – *total* NSA access!' The sirens blasted, drowning him out, but Hale was possessed. 'You think we're ready for that responsibility? You think *anyone* is? It's fucking shortsighted! You say our government has the people's best interests at heart? Great! But what happens when some future government *doesn't* have our best interests at heart! This technology is *forever!*'

Susan could barely hear him; the noise in Crypto was deafening.

Hale struggled to get free. He looked Susan in the eye and kept yelling. 'How the hell do civilians defend themselves against a police state when the guy at the top has access to *all* their lines of communication? How do they plan a revolt?'

Susan had heard this argument many times. The future-governments argument was a stock EFF complaint.

'Strathmore *had* to be stopped!' Hale screamed as the sirens blasted. 'I swore *I'd* do it. That's what I've been doing here all day – watching his account, waiting for him to make his move so I could record the switch in progress. I needed proof – evidence that he'd written in a back door. That's why I copied all his E-mail into my account. It was evidence that he'd been watching Digital Fortress. I planned to go to the press with the information.'

Susan's heart skipped. Had she heard correctly? Suddenly this did sound like Greg Hale. *Was it possible?* If Hale had known about Strathmore's plan to release a tainted version of Digital Fortress, he could wait until the whole world was using it and then drop his bombshell – complete with proof!

Susan imagined the headlines: CRYPTOGRAPHER GREG HALE UNVEILS SECRET U.S. PLAN TO CONTROL GLOBAL INFORMATION!

Was it Skipjack all over again? Uncovering an NSA back door a second time would make Greg Hale famous beyond his wildest dreams. It would also sink the NSA. She suddenly found herself wondering if maybe Hale was telling the truth. *No!* she decided. *Of course not!*

Hale continued to plead. 'I aborted your tracer because I thought you were looking for *me!* I thought you suspected Strathmore was being snooped! I didn't want you to find the leak and trace it back to me!'

It was plausible but unlikely. 'Then why'd you kill Chartrukian?' Susan snapped.

'I didn't!' Hale screamed over the noise. 'Strathmore was the one who pushed him! I saw the whole thing from downstairs! Chartrukian was about to call the Sys-Secs and ruin Strathmore's plans for the back door!'

Hale's good, Susan thought. *He's got an angle for everything.*

'Let me go!' Hale begged. 'I didn't do anything!'

'Didn't *do* anything?' Susan shouted, wondering what was taking Strathmore so long. 'You and Tankado were holding the NSA hostage. At least until you double-crossed him. Tell me,' she pressed, 'did Tankado really die of a heart attack, or did you have one of your buddies take him out?'

'You're so blind!' Hale yelled. 'Can't you see I'm not involved? Untie me! Before Security gets here!'

'Security's not coming,' she snapped flatly.

Hale turned white. 'What?'

'Strathmore faked the phone call.'

Hale's eyes went wide. He seemed momentarily paralyzed. Then he began writhing fiercely. 'Strathmore'll kill me! I know he will! I know too much!'

'Easy, Greg.'

The sirens blared as Hale yelled out, 'But I'm innocent!'

'You're lying! And I have proof!' Susan strode around the ring of terminals. 'Remember that tracer you aborted?' she asked, arriving at her own terminal. 'I sent it again! Shall we see if it's back yet?'

Sure enough, on Susan's screen, a blinking icon alerted her that her tracer had returned. She palmed her mouse and opened the message. *This data will seal Hale's fate*, she thought. *Hale is North Dakota*. The data-box opened. *Hale is—*

Susan stopped. The tracer materialized, and Susan stood in stunned silence. There had to be some mistake; the tracer had fingered someone else – a most unlikely person.

Susan steadied herself on the terminal and reread the databox before her. It was the same information Strathmore said *he'd* received when *he* ran the tracer! Susan had figured Strathmore had made a mistake, but she knew she'd configured the tracer perfectly.

And yet the information on the screen was unthinkable:

NDAKOTA = ET@DOSHISHA.EDU

'ET?' Susan demanded, her head swimming. 'Ensei Tankado is North Dakota?'

It was inconceivable. If the data was correct, Tankado and his partner were the *same* person. Susan's thoughts were suddenly disconnected. She wished the blaring horn would stop. *Why doesn't Strathmore turn that damn thing off?*

Hale twisted on the floor, straining to see Susan. 'What does it say? Tell me!'

Susan blocked out Hale and the chaos around her. *Ensei Tankado is North Dakota. . . .*

She reshuffled the pieces trying to make them fit. If Tankado was North Dakota, then he was sending E-mail to *himself* . . .which meant North Dakota didn't exist. Tankado's partner was a hoax.

North Dakota is a ghost, she said to herself. *Smoke and mirrors.*

The ploy was a brilliant one. Apparently Strathmore had been watching only one side of a tennis match. Since the ball kept coming back, he assumed there was someone on the other side of the net. But Tankado had been playing against a wall. He had been proclaiming the virtues of Digital Fortress in E-mail he'd sent to himself. He had written letters, sent them to an anonymous remailer, and a few hours later, the remailer had sent them right back to him.

Now, Susan realized, it was all so obvious. Tankado had *wanted* the commander to snoop him . . . he'd *wanted* him to read the E-mail. Ensei Tankado had created an imaginary insurance policy without ever having to trust another soul with his pass-key. Of course, to make the whole farce seem authentic, Tankado had used a secret account . . . just secret enough to allay any suspicions that the whole thing was a setup. Tankado was his own partner. North Dakota did not exist. Ensei Tankado was a one-man show.

A one-man show.

A terrifying thought gripped Susan. *Tankado could have used his fake correspondence to convince Strathmore of just about anything.*

She remembered her first reaction when Strathmore told her about the unbreakable algorithm. She'd sworn it was impossible. The unsettling potential of the situation settled hard in Susan's stomach. What proof did they actually have that Tankado had *really* created Digital Fortress? Only a lot of hype in his E-mail. And of course . . . TRANSLTR. The computer had been locked in an endless loop for almost twenty hours. Susan knew, however, that there were other programs that could keep TRANSLTR busy that long, programs far easier to create than an unbreakable algorithm.

Viruses.

The chill swept across her body.

But how could a virus get into TRANSLTR?

Like a voice from the grave, Phil Chartrukian gave the answer. *Strathmore bypassed Gauntlet!*

In a sickening revelation, Susan grasped the truth. Strathmore had downloaded Tankado's Digital Fortress file and tried to send it into TRANSLTR to break it. But Gauntlet had rejected the file because it contained dangerous mutation strings. Normally Strathmore would have been concerned, but he had seen Tankado's E-mail – *Mutation strings are the trick!* Convinced Digital Fortress was safe to load, Strathmore bypassed Gauntlet's filters and sent the file into TRANSLTR.

Susan could barely speak. 'There *is* no Digital Fortress,' she choked as the sirens blared on. Slowly, weakly, she leaned against her terminal. Tankado had gone fishing for fools . . . and the NSA had taken the bait.

Then, from upstairs, came a long cry of anguish. It was Strathmore.

CHAPTER 86

Trevor Strathmore was hunched at his desk when Susan arrived breathless at his door. His head was down, his sweaty head glistening in the light of his monitor. The horns on the sublevels blared.

Susan raced over to his desk. 'Commander?'

Strathmore didn't move.

'Commander! We've got to shut down TRANSLTR! We've got a—'

'He got us,' Strathmore said without looking up. 'Tankado fooled us all . . .'

She could tell by the tone of his voice he understood. All of Tankado's hype about the unbreakable algorithm . . . auctioning off the pass-key – it was all an act, a charade. Tankado had tricked the NSA into snooping his mail, tricked them into believing he had a partner, and tricked them into downloading a very dangerous file.

'The mutation strings—' Strathmore faltered.

'I know.'

The commander looked up slowly. 'The file I downloaded off the Internet . . . it was a . . .'

Susan tried to stay calm. All the pieces in the game

had shifted. There had never been any unbreakable algorithm – never any Digital Fortress. The file Tankado had posted on the Internet was an encrypted virus, probably sealed with some generic, mass-market encryption algorithm, strong enough to keep everyone out of harm's way – everyone except the NSA. TRANSLTR had cracked the protective seal and released the virus.

'The mutation strings,' the commander croaked. 'Tankado said they were just part of the algorithm.' Strathmore collapsed back onto his desk.

Susan understood the commander's pain. He had been completely taken in. Tankado had never intended to let any computer company buy his algorithm. There *was* no algorithm. The whole thing was a charade. Digital Fortress was a ghost, a farce, a piece of bait created to tempt the NSA. Every move Strathmore had made, Tankado had been behind the scenes, pulling the strings.

'I bypassed Gauntlet.' The commander groaned.

'You didn't know.'

Strathmore pounded his fist on his desk. 'I *should* have known! His screen name, for Christ's sake! NDAKOTA! Look at it!'

'What do you mean?'

'He's laughing at us! It's a goddamn anagram!'

Susan puzzled a moment. *NDAKOTA is an anagram?* She pictured the letters and began reshuffling them in her mind. *Ndakota . . . Kado-tan . . . Oktadan . . . Tandoka . . .* Her knees went weak. Strathmore was right. It was as plain as day. How could they have missed it? North Dakota wasn't a reference to the U.S. state at all – it was Tankado rubbing salt in the wound! He'd even sent the NSA a warning, a blatant clue that he himself was NDAKOTA. The letters spelled TANKADO. But the best code-breakers in the world had missed it, just as he had planned.

'Tankado was mocking us,' Strathmore said.

'You've got to abort TRANSLTR,' Susan declared.

Strathmore stared blankly at the wall.

'Commander. Shut it down! God only knows what's going on in there!'

'I tried,' Strathmore whispered, sounding as faint as she'd ever heard him.

'What do you mean you *tried?*'

Strathmore rotated his screen toward her. His monitor had dimmed to a strange shade of maroon. At the bottom, the dialogue box showed numerous attempts to shut down TRANSLTR. They were all followed by the same response:

> SORRY. UNABLE TO ABORT.
> SORRY. UNABLE TO ABORT.
> SORRY. UNABLE TO ABORT.

Susan felt a chill. *Unable to abort? But why?* She feared she already knew the answer. *So this is Tankado's revenge? Destroying TRANSLTR!* For years Ensei Tankado had wanted the world to know about TRANSLTR, but no one had believed him. So he'd decided to destroy the great beast himself. He'd fought to the death for what he believed – the individual's right to privacy.

Downstairs the sirens blared.

'We've got to kill all power,' Susan demanded. 'Now!'

Susan knew that if they hurried, they could save the great parallel processing machine. Every computer in

364

the world – from Radio Shack PCs to NASA's satellite control systems – had a built-in fail-safe for situations like this. It wasn't a glamorous fix, but it always worked. It was known as 'pulling the plug.'

By shutting off the remaining power in Crypto, they could force TRANSLTR to shut down. They could remove the virus later. It would be a simple matter of reformatting TRANSLTR's hard drives. Reformatting would completely erase the computer's memory – data, programming, virus, *everything*. In most cases, reformatting resulted in the loss of thousands of files, sometimes years of work. But TRANSLTR was different – it could be reformatted with virtually no loss at all. Parallel processing machines were designed to think, not to remember. Nothing was actually stored inside TRANSLTR. Once it broke a code, it sent the results to the NSA's main databank in order to—

Susan froze. In a stark instant of realization, she brought her hand to her mouth and muffled a scream. 'The main databank!'

Strathmore stared into the darkness, his voice disembodied. He'd apparently already made this realization. 'Yes, Susan. The main databank. . . .'

Susan nodded blankly. *Tankado used TRANSLTR to put a virus in our main databank.*

Strathmore motioned sickly to his monitor. Susan returned her gaze to the screen in front of her and looked beneath the dialogue box. Across the bottom of the screen were the words:

TELL THE WORLD ABOUT TRANSLTR
ONLY THE TRUTH WILL SAVE YOU NOW . . .

Susan felt cold. The nation's most classified information was stored at the NSA: military communication protocols, SIGINT confirmation codes, identities of foreign spies, blueprints for advanced weaponry, digitized documents, trade agreements – the list was unending.

'Tankado wouldn't dare!' she declared. 'Corrupting a country's classified records?' Susan couldn't believe even Ensei Tankado would dare attack the NSA databank. She stared at his message.

ONLY THE TRUTH WILL SAVE YOU NOW

'The truth?' she asked. 'The truth about what?'

Strathmore was breathing heavily. 'TRANSLTR,' he croaked. 'The truth about TRANSLTR.'

Susan nodded. It made perfect sense. Tankado was forcing the NSA to tell the world about TRANSLTR. It was blackmail after all. He was giving the NSA a choice – either tell the world about TRANSLTR or lose your databank. She stared in awe at the text before her. At the bottom of the screen, a single line blinked menacingly.

ENTER PASS-KEY

Staring at the pulsating words, Susan understood – the virus, the pass-key, Tankado's ring, the ingenious blackmail plot. The pass-key had nothing to do with unlocking an algorithm; it was an *antidote*. The pass-key stopped the virus. Susan had read a lot about viruses like this – deadly programs that included a built-in cure, a secret key that could be used to deactivate them. *Tankado never planned to destroy the NSA*

databank – he just wanted us go public with TRANSLTR!
Then he would give us the pass-key, so we could stop the
virus!

It was now clear to Susan that Tankado's plan had gone terribly wrong. He had not planned on dying. He'd planned on sitting in a Spanish bar and listening to the CNN press conference about America's top-secret code-breaking computer. Then he'd planned on calling Strathmore, reading the pass-key off the ring, and saving the databank in the nick of time. After a good laugh, he'd disappear into oblivion, an EFF hero.

Susan pounded her fist on the desk. 'We need that ring! It's the *only* pass-key!' She now understood – there *was* no North Dakota, no second pass-key. Even if the NSA went public with TRANSLTR, Tankado was no longer around to save the day.

Strathmore was silent.

The situation was more serious than Susan had ever imagined. The most shocking thing of all was that Tankado had allowed it to go this far. He had obviously known what would happen if the NSA didn't get the ring – and yet, in his final seconds of life, he'd given the ring away. He had deliberately tried to keep it from them. Then again, Susan realized, what could she *expect* Tankado to do – save the ring for them, when he thought the NSA had killed him?

Still, Susan couldn't believe that Tankado would have allowed this to happen. He was a pacifist. He didn't want to wreak destruction; all he wanted was to set the record straight. This was about TRANSLTR. This was about everyone's right to keep a secret. This was about letting the world know that the NSA was listening. Deleting the NSA's databank was an act of aggression Susan could not imagine Ensei Tankado committing.

The sirens pulled her back to reality. Susan eyed the debilitated commander and knew what he was thinking. Not only were his plans for a back door in Digital Fortress shot, but his carelessness had put the NSA on the brink of what could turn out to be the worst security disaster in U.S. history.

'Commander, this is *not* your fault!' she insisted over the blare of the horns. 'If Tankado hadn't died, we'd have bargaining power – we'd have options!'

But Commander Strathmore heard nothing. His life was over. He'd spent thirty years serving his country. This was supposed to be his moment of glory, his pièce de résistance – a back door in the world encryption standard. But instead, he had sent a virus into the main databank of the National Security Agency. There was no way to stop it – not without killing power and erasing every last one of the billions of bytes of irretrievable data. Only the ring could save them, and if David hadn't found the ring by now . . .

'I need to shut down TRANSLTR!' Susan took control. 'I'm going down to the sublevels to throw the circuit breaker.'

Strathmore turned slowly to face her. He was a broken man. 'I'll do it,' he croaked. He stood up, stumbling as he tried to slide out from behind his desk.

Susan sat him back down. 'No,' she barked. '*I'm* going.' Her tone left no room for debate.

Strathmore put his face in his hands. 'Okay. Bottom floor. Beside the freon pumps.'

Susan spun and headed for the door. Halfway there, she turned and looked back. 'Commander,' she yelled.

'This is *not* over. We're not beaten yet. If David finds the ring in time, we can save the databank!'

Strathmore said nothing.

'Call the databank!' Susan ordered. 'Warn them about the virus! You're the deputy director of the NSA. You're a survivor!'

In slow motion, Strathmore looked up. Like a man making the decision of a lifetime, he gave her a tragic nod.

Determined, Susan tore into the darkness.

CHAPTER 87

The Vespa lurched into the slow lane of the Carretera de Huelva. It was almost dawn, but there was plenty of traffic – young Sevillians returning from their all-night beach verbenas. A van of teenagers laid on its horn and flew by. Becker's motorcycle felt like a toy out there on the freeway.

A quarter of a mile back, a demolished taxi swerved out onto the freeway in a shower of sparks. As it accelerated, it sideswiped a Peugeot 504 and sent it careening onto the grassy median.

Becker passed a freeway marker: SEVILLA CENTRO – 2 KM. If he could just reach the cover of downtown, he knew he might have a chance. His speedometer read 60 kilometers per hour. *Two minutes to the exit.* He knew he didn't have that long. Somewhere behind him, the taxi was gaining. Becker gazed out at the nearing lights of downtown Seville and prayed he would reach them alive.

He was only halfway to the exit when the sound of scraping metal loomed up behind him. He hunched on his bike, wrenching the throttle as far as it would go. There was a muffled gunshot, and a bullet sailed by. Becker cut left, weaving back and forth across the lanes in hopes of buying more time. It was no use. The exit ramp was still three hundred yards when the taxi roared to within a few car lengths behind him. Becker knew that in a matter of seconds he would be either shot or run down. He scanned ahead for any possible escape, but the highway was bounded on both sides by steep gravel slopes. Another shot rang out. Becker made his decision.

In a scream of rubber and sparks, he leaned violently to his right and swerved off the road. The bike's tires hit the bottom of the embankment. Becker strained to keep his balance as the Vespa threw up a cloud of gravel and began fish-tailing its way up the slope. The wheels spun wildly, clawing at the loose earth. The little engine whimpered pathetically as it tried to dig in. Becker urged it on, hoping it wouldn't stall. He didn't dare look behind him, certain at any moment the taxi would be skidding to a stop, bullets flying.

The bullets never came.

Becker's bike broke over the crest of the hill, and he saw it – the centro. The downtown lights spread out before him like a star-filled sky. He gunned his way through some underbrush and out over the curb. His Vespa suddenly felt faster. The Avenue Luis Montoto seemed to race beneath his tires. The soccer stadium zipped past on the left. He was in the clear.

It was then that Becker heard the familiar screech of metal on concrete. He looked up. A hundred yards ahead of him, the taxi came roaring up the exit ramp. It skidded out onto Luis Montoto and accelerated directly toward him.

Becker knew he should have felt a surge of panic.

But he did not. He knew exactly where he was going. He swerved left on Menendez Pelayo and opened the throttle. The bike lurched across a small park and into the cobblestoned corridor of Mateus Gago – the narrow one-way street that led to the portal of Barrio Santa Cruz.

Just a little farther, he thought.

The taxi followed, thundering closer. It trailed Becker through the gateway of Santa Cruz, ripping off its side mirror on the narrow archway. Becker knew he had won. Santa Cruz was the oldest section of Seville. It had no roads between the buildings, only mazes of narrow walkways built in Roman times. They were only wide enough for pedestrians and the occasional moped. Becker had once been lost for hours in the narrow caverns.

As Becker accelerated down the final stretch of Mateus Gago, Seville's eleventh-century Gothic cathedral rose like a mountain before him. Directly beside it, the Giralda tower shot 419 feet skyward into the breaking dawn. This was Santa Cruz, home to the second largest cathedral in the world as well as Seville's oldest, most pious Catholic families.

Becker sped across the stone square. There was a single shot, but it was too late. Becker and his motorcycle disappeared down a tiny passageway – Callita de la Virgen.

CHAPTER 88

The headlight of Becker's Vespa threw stark shadows on the walls of the narrow passageways. He struggled with the gear shift and roared between the white-washed buildings, giving the inhabitants of Santa Cruz an early wake-up call this Sunday morning.

It had been less than thirty minutes since Becker's escape from the airport. He'd been on the run ever since, his mind grappling with endless questions: *Who's trying to kill me? What's so special about this ring? Where is the NSA jet?* He thought of Megan dead in the stall, and the nausea crept back.

Becker had hoped to cut directly across the barrio and exit on the other side, but Santa Cruz was a bewildering labyrinth of alleyways. It was peppered with false starts and dead ends. Becker quickly became disoriented. He looked up for the tower of the Giralda to get his bearings, but the surrounding walls were so high he could see nothing except a thin slit of breaking dawn above him.

Becker wondered where the man in wire-rim glasses was; he knew better than to think the assailant had given up. The killer probably was after him on foot. Becker struggled to maneuver his Vespa around tight corners. The sputtering of the engine echoed up and down the alleys. Becker knew he was an easy target in the silence of Santa Cruz. At this point, all he had in his favor was speed. *Got to get to the other side!*

After a long series of turns and straightaways, Becker skidded into a three-way intersection marked Esquina de los Reyes. He knew he was in trouble – he had been there already. As he stood straddling the idling bike, trying to decide which way to turn, the engine sputtered to a stop. The gas gauge read VACIO. As if on cue, a shadow appeared down an alley on his left.

The human mind is the fastest computer in existence. In the next fraction of a second, Becker's mind registered the shape of the man's glasses, searched his memory for a match, found one, registered danger, and requested a decision. He got one. He dropped the useless bike and took off at a full sprint.

Unfortunately for Becker, Hulohot was now on solid ground rather than in a lurching taxi. He calmly raised his weapon and fired.

The bullet caught Becker in the side just as he stumbled around the corner out of range. He took five or six strides before the sensation began to register. At first it felt like a muscle pull, just above the hip. Then it turned to a warm tingling. When Becker saw the blood, he knew. There was no pain, no pain anywhere, just a headlong race through the winding maze of Santa Cruz.

Hulohot dashed after his quarry. He had been tempted to hit Becker in the head, but he was a professional; he played the odds. Becker was a moving target, and aiming at his midsection provided the greatest margin of error both vertically and horizontally. The odds had paid off. Becker had shifted at the last instant, and rather than missing his head, Hulohot had caught a piece of his side. Although he knew the bullet had barely grazed Becker and would do no lasting damage, the shot had served its purpose. Contact had been made. The prey had been touched by death. It was a whole new game.

Becker raced forward blindly. Turning. Winding. Staying out of the straightaways. The footsteps behind him seemed relentless. Becker's mind was blank. Blank to everything – where he was, who was chasing him – all that was left was instinct, self preservation, no pain, only fear, and raw energy.

A shot exploded against the azulejo tile behind him. Shards of glass sprayed across the back of his neck. He stumbled left, into another alley. He heard himself call for help, but except for the sound of footsteps and strained breathing, the morning air remained deathly still.

Becker's side was burning now. He feared he was leaving a crimson trail on the whitewashed walks. He searched everywhere for an open door, an open gate, any escape from the suffocating canyons. Nothing. The walkway narrowed.

'Socorro!' Becker's voice was barely audible. 'Help!'

The walls grew closer on each side. The walkway curved. Becker searched for an intersection, a tributary, any way out. The passageway narrowed. Locked doors. Narrowing. Locked gates. The footsteps were closing. He was in a straightaway, and suddenly the alley began to slope upward. Steeper. Becker felt his legs straining. He was slowing.

And then he was there.

Like a freeway that had run out of funding, the alley just stopped. There was a high wall, a wooden bench, and nothing else. No escape. Becker looked up three stories to the top of the building and then spun and started back down the long alley, but he had only taken a few steps before he stopped short.

At the foot of the inclined straightaway, a figure appeared. The man moved toward Becker with a measured determination. In his hand, a gun glinted in the early morning sun.

Becker felt a sudden lucidity as he backed up toward the wall. The pain in his side suddenly registered. He touched the spot and looked down. There was blood smeared across his fingers and across Ensei Tankado's golden ring. He felt dizzy. He stared at the engraved band, puzzled. He'd forgotten he was wearing it. He'd forgotten why he had come to Seville. He looked up at the figure approaching. He looked down at the ring. Was this why Megan had died? Was this why *he* would die?

The shadow advanced up the inclined passageway. Becker saw walls on all sides – a dead end behind him. A few gated entryways between them, but it was too late to call for help.

Becker pressed his back against the dead end. Suddenly he could feel every piece of grit beneath the soles of his shoes, every bump in the stucco wall behind him. His mind was reeling backward, his childhood, his parents . . . Susan.

Oh, God . . . Susan.

For the first time since he was a kid, Becker prayed.

He did not pray for deliverance from death; he did not believe in miracles. Instead he prayed that the woman he left behind would find strength, that she would know without a doubt that she had been loved. He closed his eyes. The memories came like a torrent. They were not memories of department meetings, university business, and the things that made up 90 percent of his life; they were memories of her. Simple memories: teaching her to use chopsticks, sailing on Cape Cod. *I love you,* he thought. *Know that . . . forever.*

It was as if every defense, every facade, every insecure exaggeration of his life had been stripped away. He was standing naked – flesh and bones before God. *I am a man,* he thought. And in a moment of irony he thought, *A man without wax.* He stood, eyes closed, as the man in wire-rim glasses drew nearer. Somewhere nearby, a bell began to toll. Becker waited in darkness, for the sound that would end his life.

CHAPTER 89

The morning sun was just breaking over the Seville rooftops and shining down into the canyons below. The bells atop the Giralda cried out for sunrise mass. This was the moment inhabitants had all been waiting for. Everywhere in the ancient barrio, gates opened and families poured into the alleyways. Like lifeblood through the veins of old Santa Cruz, they coursed toward the heart of their pueblo, toward the core of their history, toward their God, their shrine, their cathedral.

Somewhere in Becker's mind, a bell was tolling. *Am I dead?* Almost reluctantly, he opened his eyes and squinted into the first rays of sunlight. He knew exactly where he was. He leveled his gaze and searched the alley for his assailant. But the man in wire-rims was not there. Instead, there were others. Spanish families, in their finest clothes, stepping from their gated portals into the alleyways, talking, laughing.

At the bottom of the alley, hidden from Becker's view, Hulohot cursed in frustration. At first there had been only a single couple separating him from his quarry. Hulohot had been certain they would leave. But the sound of the bells kept reverberating down the alley, drawing others from their homes. A second couple, with children. They greeted each other. Talking, laughing, kissing three times on the cheek. Another group appeared, and Hulohot could no longer see his prey. Now, in a boiling rage, he raced into the quickly growing crowd. He had to get to David Becker!

The killer fought his way toward the end of the alley. He found himself momentarily lost in a sea of bodies – coats and ties, black dresses, lace mantles over hunched women. They all seemed oblivious to Hulohot's presence; they strolled casually, all in black, shuffling, moving as one, blocking his way. Hulohot dug his way through the crowd and dashed up the alley into the dead end, his weapon raised. Then he let out a muted, inhuman scream. David Becker was gone.

Becker stumbled and sidestepped his way through the crowd. *Follow the crowd,* he thought. *They know the way out.* He cut right at the intersection and the alley widened. Everywhere gates were opening and people were pouring out. The pealing of the bells grew louder.

Becker's side was still burning, but he sensed the bleeding had stopped. He raced on. Somewhere behind him, closing fast, was a man with a gun.

Becker ducked in and out of the groups of church-goers and tried to keep his head down. It was not much farther. He could sense it. The crowd had thickened. The alley had widened. They were no longer in a little tributary, this was the main river. As he rounded a bend, Becker suddenly saw it, rising before them – the cathedral and Giralda tower.

The bells were deafening, the reverberations trapped in the high-walled plaza. The crowds converged, everyone in black, pushing across the square toward the gaping doors of the Seville Cathedral. Becker tried to break away toward Mateus Gago, but he was trapped. He was shoulder to shoulder, heel to toe with the shoving throngs. The Spaniards had always had a different idea of closeness than the rest of the world. Becker was wedged between two heavy-set women, both with their eyes closed, letting the crowd carry them. They mumbled prayers to themselves and clutched rosary beads in their fingers.

As the crowd closed on the enormous stone structure, Becker tried to cut left again, but the current was stronger now. The anticipation, the pushing and shoving, the blind, mumbled prayers. He turned into the crowd, trying to fight backward against the eager throngs. It was impossible, like swimming upstream in a mile-deep river. He turned. The cathedral doors loomed before him – like the opening to some dark carnival ride he wished he hadn't taken. David Becker suddenly realized he was going to church.

CHAPTER 90

The Crypto sirens were blaring. Strathmore had no idea how long Susan had been gone. He sat alone in the shadows, the drone of TRANSLTR calling to him. *You're a survivor . . . you're a survivor. . . .*

Yes, he thought. *I'm a survivor – but survival is nothing without honor. I'd rather die than live in the shadow of disgrace.*

And disgrace was what was waiting for him. He had kept information from the director. He had sent a virus into the nation's most secure computer. There was no doubt he would be hung out to dry. His intentions had been patriotic, but nothing had gone as he'd planned. There had been death and treachery. There would be trials, accusations, public outrage. He had served his country with honor and integrity for so many years, he couldn't allow it to end this way.

I'm a survivor, he thought.

You're a liar, his own thoughts replied.

It was true. He *was* a liar. There were people he hadn't been honest with. Susan Fletcher was one of them. There were so many things he hadn't told her – things he was now desperately ashamed of. For years

381

she'd been his illusion, his living fantasy. He dreamed of her at night; he cried out for her in his sleep. He couldn't help it. She was as brilliant and as beautiful as any woman he could imagine. His wife had tried to be patient, but when she finally met Susan, she immediately lost hope. Bev Strathmore never blamed her husband for his feelings. She tried to endure the pain as long as possible, but recently it had become too much. She'd told him their marriage was ending; another woman's shadow was no place to spend the rest of her life.

Gradually the sirens lifted Strathmore from his daze. His analytical powers searched for any way out. His mind reluctantly confirmed what his heart had suspected. There was only one true escape, only one solution.

Strathmore gazed down at the keyboard and began typing. He didn't bother to turn the monitor so he could see it. His fingers pecked out the words slowly and decisively.

Dearest friends, I am taking my life today . . .

This way, no one would ever wonder. There would be no questions. There would be no accusations. He would spell out for the world what had happened. Many had died . . . but there was still one life to take.

CHAPTER 91

In a cathedral, it is always night. The warmth of the day turns to damp coolness. The traffic is silenced behind thick granite walls. No number of candelabra can illuminate the vast darkness overhead. Shadows fall everywhere. There's only the stained glass, high above, filtering the ugliness of the outside world into rays of muted reds and blues.

The Seville Cathedral, like all great cathedrals of Europe, is laid out in the shape of a cross. The sanctuary and altar are located just above the midpoint and open downward onto the main sanctuary. Wooden pews fill the vertical axis, a staggering 113 yards from the altar to the base of the cross. To the left and right of the altar, the transept of the cross houses confessionals, sacred tombs, and additional seating.

Becker found himself wedged in the middle of a long pew about halfway back. Overhead, in the dizzying empty space, a silver censer the size of a refrigerator swung enormous arcs on a frayed rope, leaving a trail of frankincense. The bells of the Giralda kept ringing, sending low rumbling shock waves through the stone. Becker lowered his gaze to the gilded wall behind the altar. He had a lot to be thankful for. He was breathing. He was alive. It was a miracle.

As the priest prepared to give the opening prayer, Becker checked his side. There was a red stain on his shirt, but the bleeding had stopped. The wound was small, more of a laceration than a puncture. Becker tucked his shirt back in and craned his neck. Behind him, the doors were cranking shut. He knew if he'd been followed, he was now trapped. The Seville Cathedral had a single functional entrance, a design popularized in the days when churches were used as fortresses, a safe haven against Moorish invasion. With a single entrance, there was only one door to barricade. Now the single entrance had another function – it ensured all tourists entering the cathedral had purchased a ticket.

The twenty-two-foot-high gilded doors slammed with a decisive crash. Becker was sealed in the house of God. He closed his eyes and slid low in his pew. He was the only one in the building not dressed in black. Somewhere voices began to chant.

Toward the back of the church, a figure moved slowly up the side aisle, keeping to the shadows. He had slipped in just before the doors closed. He smiled to himself. The hunt was getting interesting. *Becker is here . . . I can feel it.* He moved methodically, one row at a time. Overhead the frankincense decanter swung its long, lazy arcs. *A fine place to die,* Hulohot thought. *I hope I do as well.*

Becker knelt on the cold cathedral floor and ducked his head out of sight. The man seated next to him glared down – it was most irregular behavior in the house of God.

'Enfermo,' Becker apologized. 'Sick.'

Becker knew he had to stay low. He had glimpsed a familiar silhouette moving up the side aisle. *It's him! He's here!*

Despite being in the middle of an enormous congregation, Becker feared he was an easy target – his khaki blazer was like a roadside flare in the crowd of black. He considered removing it, but the white oxford shirt underneath was no better. Instead he huddled lower.

The man beside him frowned. 'Turista.' He grunted. Then he whispered, half sarcastically, 'Llamo un médico? Shall I call a doctor?'

Becker looked up at the old man's mole-ridden face. 'No, gracias. Estoy bien.'

The man gave him an angry look. 'Pues siéntate! Then sit down!' There were scattered shushes around them, and the old man bit his tongue and faced front.

Becker closed his eyes and huddled lower, wondering how long the service would last. Becker, raised Protestant, had always had the impression Catholics were long-winded. He prayed it was true – as soon as the service ended, he would be forced to stand and let the others out. In khaki he was dead.

Becker knew he had no choice at the moment. He simply knelt there on the cold stone floor of the great cathedral. Eventually, the old man lost interest. The congregation was standing now, singing a hymn. Becker stayed down. His legs were starting to cramp. There was no room to stretch them. *Patience,* he thought. *Patience.* He closed his eyes and took a deep breath.

It felt like only minutes later that Becker felt some-one kicking him. He looked up. The mole-faced man was standing to his right, waiting impatiently to leave the pew.

Becker panicked. *He wants to leave already? I'll have to stand up!* Becker motioned for the man to step over him. The man could barely control his anger. He grabbed the tails of his black blazer, pulled them down in a huff, and leaned back to reveal the entire row of people waiting to leave. Becker looked left and saw that the woman who had been seated there was gone. The length of pew to his left was empty all the way to the center aisle.

The service can't be over! It's impossible! We just got here!

But when Becker saw the altar boy at the end of the row and the two single-file lines moving up the center aisle toward the altar, he knew what was happening.

Communion. He groaned. *The damn Spaniards do it first!*

CHAPTER 92

Susan climbed down the ladder into the sublevels. Thick steam was now boiling up around TRANSLTR's hull. The catwalks were wet with condensation. She almost fell, her flats providing very little traction. She wondered how much longer TRANSLTR would survive. The sirens continued their intermittent warning. The emergency lights spun in two-second intervals. Three stories below, the aux generators shook in a taxed whine. Susan knew somewhere at the bottom in the foggy dimness there was a circuit breaker. She sensed time was running out.

Upstairs, Strathmore held the Beretta in his hand. He reread his note and laid it on the floor of the room where he was standing. What he was about to do was a cowardly act, there was no doubt. *I'm a survivor,* he thought. He thought of the virus in the NSA databank, he thought of David Becker in Spain, he thought of his plans for a back door. He had told so many lies. He was guilty of so much. He knew this was the only way to avoid accountability . . . the only way to avoid the shame. Carefully he aimed the gun. Then he closed his eyes and pulled the trigger.

Susan had only descended six flights when she heard the muffled shot. It was far off, barely audible over the generators. She had never heard a gunshot except on television, but she had no doubt what it was.

She stopped short, the sound resounding in her ears. In a wave of horror, she feared the worst. She pictured the commander's dreams – the back door in Digital Fortress, the incredible coup it would have been. She pictured the virus in the databank, his failing marriage, that eerie nod he had given her. Her footing faltered. She spun on the landing, grappling for the banister. *Commander! No!*

Susan was momentarily frozen, her mind blank. The echo of the gunshot seemed to drown out the chaos around her. Her mind told her to keep on going, but her legs refused. *Commander!* An instant later she found herself stumbling back up the stairs, entirely forgetting the danger around her.

She ran blindly, slipping on the slick metal. Above her the humidity fell like rain. When she reached the ladder and began climbing, she felt herself lifted from below by a tremendous surge of steam that practically jettisoned her through the trapdoor. She rolled onto the Crypto floor and felt the cool air wash over her. Her white blouse clung to her body, soaked through.

It was dark. Susan paused, trying to get her bearings. The sound of the gunshot was on endless loop in her head. Hot steam billowed up through the trapdoor like gases from a volcano about to explode.

Susan cursed herself for leaving the Beretta with Strathmore. She *had* left it with him, hadn't she? *Or was it in Node 3?* As her eyes adjusted to the dark, she glanced toward the gaping hole in the Node 3 wall.

The glow from the monitors was faint, but in the distance she could see Hale lying motionless on the floor where she'd left him. There was no sign of Strathmore. Terrified of what she'd find, she turned toward the commander's office.

But as she began to move, something registered as strange. She backpedaled a few steps and peered into Node 3 again. In the soft light she could see Hale's arm. It was not at his side. He was no longer tied like a mummy. His arm was up over his head. He was sprawled backward on the floor. Had he gotten free? There was no movement. Hale was deathly still.

Susan gazed up at Strathmore's workstation perched high on the wall. 'Commander?'

Silence.

Tentatively she moved toward Node 3. There was an object in Hale's hand. It glimmered in the light of the monitors. Susan moved closer . . . closer. Suddenly she could see what Hale was holding. It was the Beretta.

Susan gasped. Following the arch of Hale's arm, her eyes moved to his face. What she saw was grotesque. Half of Greg Hale's head was soaked in blood. The dark stain had spread out across the carpet.

Oh my God! Susan staggered backward. It wasn't the commander's shot she'd heard, it was *Hale's!*

As if in a trance, Susan moved toward the body. Apparently, Hale had managed to free himself. The printer cables were piled on the floor beside him. *I must have left the gun on the couch,* she thought. The blood flowing through the hole in his skull looked black in the bluish light.

On the floor beside Hale was a piece of paper. Susan went over unsteadily, and picked it up. It was a letter.

Dearest friends, I am taking my life today in penance for the following sins . . .

In utter disbelief, Susan stared at the suicide note in her hand. She read slowly. It was surreal – so unlike Hale – a laundry list of crimes. He was admitting to everything – figuring out that NDAKOTA was a hoax, hiring a mercenary to kill Ensei Tankado and take the ring, pushing Phil Chartrukian, planning to sell Digital Fortress.

Susan reached the final line. She was not prepared for what she read. The letter's final words delivered a numbing blow.

Above all, I'm truly sorry about David Becker. Forgive me, I was blinded by ambition.

As Susan stood trembling over Hale's body, the sound of running footsteps approached behind her. In slow motion, she turned.

Strathmore appeared in the broken window, pale and out of breath. He stared down at Hale's body in apparent shock.

'Oh my God!' he said. 'What happened?'

CHAPTER 93

Communion.

Hulohot spotted Becker immediately. The khaki blazer was impossible to miss, particularly with the small bloodstain on one side. The jacket was moving up the center aisle in a sea of black. *He must not know I'm here.* Hulohot smiled. *He's a dead man.*

He fanned the tiny metal contacts on his fingertips, eager to tell his American contact the good news. *Soon,* he thought, *very soon.*

Like a predator moving downwind, Hulohot moved to the back of the church. Then he began his approach – straight up the center aisle. Hulohot was in no mood to track Becker through the crowds leaving the church. His quarry was trapped, a fortunate turn of events. Hulohot just needed a way to eliminate him quietly. His silencer, the best money could buy, emitted no more than a tiny spitting cough. That would be fine.

As Hulohot closed on the khaki blazer, he was unaware of the quiet murmurs coming from those he was passing. The congregation could understand this man's excitement to receive the blessing of God, but nevertheless, there were strict rules of protocol – two lines, single file.

Hulohot kept moving. He was closing quickly. He thumbed the revolver in his jacket pocket. The moment had arrived. David Becker had been exceptionally fortunate so far; there was no need to tempt fortune any further.

The khaki blazer was only ten people ahead, facing front, head down. Hulohot rehearsed the kill in his mind. The image was clear – cutting in behind Becker, keeping the gun low and out of sight, firing two shots into Becker's back, Becker slumping, Hulohot catching him and helping him into a pew like a concerned friend. Then Hulohot would move quickly to the back of the church as if going for help. In the confusion, he would disappear before anyone knew what had happened.

Five people. Four. Three.

Hulohot fingered the gun in his pocket, keeping it low. He would fire from hip level upward into Becker's spine. That way the bullet would hit either the spine or a lung before finding the heart. Even if the bullet missed the heart, Becker would die. A punctured lung was fatal, maybe not in more medically advanced parts of the world, but in *Spain*, it was fatal.

Two people ... one. And then Hulohot was there. Like a dancer performing a well-rehearsed move, he turned to his right. He laid his hand on the shoulder of the khaki blazer, aimed the gun, and ... fired. Two muffled spats.

Instantly the body was rigid. Then it was falling. Hulohot caught his victim under the armpits. In a single motion, he swung the body into a pew before any bloodstains spread across his back. Nearby, people turned. Hulohot paid no heed – he would be gone in an instant.

He groped the man's lifeless fingers for the ring. Nothing. He felt again. The fingers were bare. Hulohot spun the man around angrily. The horror was instantaneous. The face was not David Becker's.

Rafael de la Maza, a banker from the suburbs of Seville, had died almost instantly. He was still clutching the 50,000 pesetas the strange American had paid him for a cheap black blazer.

CHAPTER 94

Midge Milken stood fuming at the water cooler near the entrance to the conference room. *What the hell is Fontaine doing?* She crumpled her paper cup and threw it forcefully into the trash can. *There's something happening in Crypto! I can feel it!* Midge knew there was only one way to prove herself right. She'd go check out Crypto herself – track down Jabba if need be. She spun on her heel and headed for the door.

Brinkerhoff appeared out of nowhere, blocking her way. 'Where are you headed?'

'Home!' Midge lied.

Brinkerhoff refused to let her pass.

Midge glared. 'Fontaine told you not to let me out, didn't he?'

Brinkerhoff looked away.

'Chad, I'm telling you, there's something happening in Crypto – something big. I don't know why Fontaine's playing dumb, but TRANSLTR's in trouble. Something is not right down there tonight!'

'Midge,' he soothed, walking past her toward the curtained conference room windows, 'let's let the director handle it.'

Midge's gaze sharpened. 'Do you have any idea what happens to TRANSLTR if the cooling system fails?'

Brinkerhoff shrugged and approached the window. 'Power's probably back on-line by now anyway.' He pulled apart the curtains and looked.

'Still dark?' Midge asked.

But Brinkerhoff did not reply. He was spellbound. The scene below in the Crypto dome was unimaginable. The entire glass cupola was filled with spinning lights, flashing strobes, and swirling steam. Brinkerhoff stood transfixed, teetering light-headed against the glass. Then, in a frenzy of panic, he raced out. 'Director! *Director!*'

CHAPTER 95

The blood of Christ . . . the cup of salvation . . .

People gathered around the slumped body in the pew. Overhead, the frankincense swung its peaceful arcs. Hulohot wheeled wildly in the center aisle and scanned the church. *He's got to be here!* He spun back toward the altar.

Thirty rows ahead, holy communion was proceeding uninterrupted. Padre Gustaphes Herrera, the head chalice bearer, glanced curiously at the quiet commotion in one of the center pews; he was not concerned. Sometimes some of the older folks were overcome by the Holy Spirit and passed out. A little air usually did the trick.

Meanwhile, Hulohot was searching frantically. Becker was nowhere in sight. A hundred or so people were kneeling at the long altar receiving communion. Hulohot wondered if Becker was one of them. He scanned their backs. He was prepared to shoot from fifty yards away and make a dash for it.

El cuerpo de Jesus, el pan del cielo.

The young priest serving Becker communion gave

him a disapproving stare. He could understand the stranger's eagerness to receive communion, but it was no excuse to cut in line.

Becker bowed his head and chewed the wafer as best he could. He sensed something was happening behind him, some sort of disturbance. He thought of the man from whom he'd bought the jacket and hoped he had listened to his warning and not taken Becker's in exchange. He started to turn and look, but he feared the wire-rim glasses would be staring back. He crouched in hopes his black jacket was covering the back of his khaki pants. It was not.

The chalice was coming quickly from his right. People were already swallowing their wine, crossing themselves, and standing to leave. *Slow down!* Becker was in no hurry to leave the altar. But with two thousand people waiting for communion and only eight priests serving, it was considered bad form to linger over a sip of wine.

The chalice was just to the right of Becker when Hulohot spotted the mismatched khaki pants. 'Estás ya muerto,' he hissed softly. 'You're already dead.' Hulohot moved up the center aisle. The time for subtlety had passed. Two shots in the back, and he would grab the ring and run. The biggest taxi stand in Seville was half a block away on Mateus Gago. He reached for his weapon.

Adiós, Señor Becker . . .

La sangre de Cristo, la copa de la salvación.

The thick scent of red wine filled Becker's nostrils as Padre Herrera lowered the hand-polished, silver chalice. *Little early for drinking,* Becker thought as he leaned forward. But as the silver goblet dropped past eye level, there was a blur of movement. A figure, coming fast, his shape warped in the reflection of the cup.

Becker saw a flash of metal, a weapon being drawn. Instantly, unconsciously, like a runner from a starting block at the sound of a gun, Becker was vaulting forward. The priest fell back in horror as the chalice sailed through the air, and red wine rained down on white marble. Priests and altar boys went scattering as Becker dove over the communion rail. A silencer coughed out a single shot. Becker landed hard, and the shot exploded in the marble floor beside him. An instant later he was tumbling down three granite stairs into the valle, a narrow passageway through which the clergy entered, allowing them to rise onto the altar as if by divine grace.

At the bottom of the steps, he stumbled and dove. Becker felt himself sliding out of control across the slick polished stone. A dagger of pain shot through his gut as he landed on his side. A moment later he was stumbling through a curtained entryway and down a set of wooden stairs.

Pain. Becker was running through a dressing room. It was dark. There were screams from the altar. Loud footsteps in pursuit. Becker burst through a set of double doors and stumbled into some sort of study. It was dark, furnished with rich Oriental rugs and polished mahogany. On the far wall was a life-size crucifix. Becker staggered to a stop. Dead end. He was at the tip of the cross. He could hear Hulohot closing fast. Becker stared at the crucifix and cursed his bad luck.

'*Goddamn it!*' he screamed.

There was the sudden sound of breaking glass to Becker's left. He wheeled. A man in red robes gasped and turned to eye Becker in horror. Like a cat caught with a canary, the holy man wiped his mouth and tried to hide the broken bottle of holy communion wine at his feet.

'*Salida!*' Becker demanded. 'Salida! Let me out!'

Cardinal Guerra reacted on instinct. A demon had entered his sacred chambers screaming for deliverance from the house of God. Guerra would grant him that wish – immediately. The demon had entered at a most inopportune moment.

Pale, the cardinal pointed to a curtain on the wall to his left. Hidden behind the curtain was a door. He'd installed it three years ago. It led directly to the courtyard outside. The cardinal had grown tired of exiting the church through the front door like a common sinner.

CHAPTER 96

Susan was wet and shivering, huddled on the Node 3 couch. Strathmore draped his suit coat over her shoulders. Hale's body lay a few yards away. The sirens blared. Like ice thawing on a frozen pond, TRANSLTR's hull let out a sharp crack.

'I'm going down to kill power,' Strathmore said, laying a reassuring hand on her shoulder. 'I'll be right back.'

Susan stared absently after the commander as he dashed across the Crypto floor. He was no longer the catatonic man she'd seen ten minutes before. Commander Trevor Strathmore was back – logical, controlled, doing whatever was necessary to get the job done.

The final words of Hale's suicide note ran through her mind like a train out of control: *Above all, I'm truly sorry about David Becker. Forgive me, I was blinded by ambition.*

Susan Fletcher's nightmare had just been confirmed. David was in danger . . . or worse. Maybe it was already too late. *I'm truly sorry about David Becker.*

She stared at the note. Hale hadn't even signed it – he'd just typed his name at the bottom: *Greg Hale.* He'd poured out his guts, pressed PRINT, and then shot himself – just like that. Hale had sworn he'd never go back to prison; he'd kept his vow – he'd chosen death instead.

'David . . .' She sobbed. *David!*

At that moment, ten feet below the Crypto floor, Commander Strathmore stepped off the ladder onto the first landing. It had been a day of fiascos. What had started out as a patriotic mission had swerved wildly out of control. The commander had been forced to make impossible decisions, commit horrific acts – acts he'd never imagined himself capable of.

It was a solution! It was the only *damn solution!*

There was duty to think of: country and honor. Strathmore knew there was still time. He could shut down TRANSLTR. He could use the ring to save the country's most valuable databank. *Yes,* he thought, *there was still time.*

Strathmore looked out over the disaster around him. The overhead sprinklers were on. TRANSLTR was groaning. The sirens blared. The spinning lights looked like helicopters closing in through dense fog. With every step, all he could see was Greg Hale – the young cryptographer gazing up, his eyes pleading, and then, the shot. Hale's death was for country . . . for honor. The NSA could not afford another scandal. Strathmore needed a scapegoat. Besides, Greg Hale was a disaster waiting to happen.

Strathmore's thoughts were jarred free by the sound of his cellular. It was barely audible over the sirens and hissing fumes. He snatched it off his belt without breaking stride.

'Speak.'

'Where's my pass-key?' a familiar voice demanded.

'Who is this?' Strathmore yelled over the din.

'It's Numataka!' the angry voice bellowed back. 'You promised me a pass-key!'

Strathmore kept moving.

'I want Digital Fortress!' Numataka hissed.

'There *is* no Digital Fortress!' Strathmore shot back.

'What?'

'There is no unbreakable algorithm!'

'Of course there is! I've seen it on the Internet! My people have been trying to unlock it for days!'

'It's an encrypted virus, you fool – and you're damn lucky you can't open it!'

'But—'

'The deal is off!' Strathmore yelled. 'I'm not North Dakota. There *is* no North Dakota! Forget I ever mentioned it!' He clamped the cellular shut, turned off the ringer, and rammed it back on his belt. There would be no more interruptions.

Twelve thousand miles away, Tokugen Numataka stood stunned at his plate-glass window. His Umami cigar hung limply in his mouth. The deal of his lifetime had just disintegrated before his eyes.

Strathmore kept descending. *The deal is off.* Numatech Corp. would never get the unbreakable algorithm . . . and the NSA would never get its back door.

Strathmore's dream had been a long time in the planning – he'd chosen Numatech carefully. Numatech was wealthy, a likely winner of the pass-key auction.

No one would think twice if it ended up with the key. Conveniently there was no company less likely to be suspected of consorting with the U.S. government. Tokugen Numataka was old-world Japan – death before dishonor. He hated Americans. He hated their food, he hated their customs, and most of all, he hated their grip on the world's software market.

Strathmore's vision had been bold – a world encryption standard with a back door for the NSA. He'd longed to share his dream with Susan, to carry it out with her by his side, but he knew he could not. Even though Ensei Tankado's death would save thousands of lives in the future, Susan would never have agreed; she was a pacifist. *I'm a pacifist too,* thought Strathmore, *I just don't have the luxury of acting like one.*

There had never been any doubt in the commander's mind who would kill Tankado. Tankado was in Spain – and Spain meant Hulohot. The forty-two-year-old Portuguese mercenary was one of the commander's favorite pros. He'd been working for the NSA for years. Born and raised in Lisbon, Hulohot had done work for the NSA all over Europe. Never once had his kills been traced back to Fort Meade. The only catch was that Hulohot was deaf; telephone communication was impossible. Recently Strathmore had arranged for Hulohot to receive the NSA's newest toy, the Monocle computer. Strathmore bought himself a SkyPager and programmed it to the same frequency. From that moment on, his communication with Hulohot was not only instantaneous but also entirely untraceable.

The first message Strathmore had sent Hulohot left

little room for misunderstanding. They had already discussed it. Kill Ensei Tankado. Obtain pass-key.

Strathmore never asked how Hulohot worked his magic, but somehow he had done it again. Ensei Tankado was dead, and the authorities were convinced it was a heart attack. A textbook kill – except for one thing. Hulohot had misjudged the location. Apparently Tankado dying in a public place was a necessary part of the illusion. But unexpectedly, the public had appeared too soon. Hulohot was forced into hiding before he could search the body for the pass-key. When the dust settled, Tankado's body was in the hands of Seville's coroner.

Strathmore was furious. Hulohot had blown a mission for the first time ever – and he'd picked an inauspicious time to do it. Getting Tankado's pass-key was critical, but Strathmore knew that sending a deaf assassin into the Seville morgue was a suicide mission. He had pondered his other options. A second scheme began to materialize. Strathmore suddenly saw a chance to win on two fronts – a chance to realize two dreams instead of just one. At six-thirty that morning, he had called David Becker.

CHAPTER 97

Fontaine burst into the conference room at a full sprint. Brinkerhoff and Midge were close at his heels.

'Look!' Midge choked, motioning frantically to the window.

Fontaine looked out the window at the strobes in the Crypto dome. His eyes went wide. This was definitely *not* part of the plan.

Brinkerhoff sputtered. 'It's a goddamn disco down there!'

Fontaine stared out, trying to make sense of it. In the few years TRANSLTR had been operational, it had never done this. *It's overheating,* he thought. He wondered why the hell Strathmore hadn't shut it down. It took Fontaine only an instant to make up his mind.

He snatched an interoffice phone off the conference table and punched the extension for Crypto. The receiver began beeping as if the extension were out of order.

Fontaine slammed down the receiver. 'Damn it!' He immediately picked up again and dialed Strathmore's private cellular line. This time the line began to ring.

Six rings went by.

Brinkerhoff and Midge watched as Fontaine paced the length of his phone cable like a tiger on a chain. After a full minute, Fontaine was crimson with rage.

He slammed down the receiver again. 'Unbelievable!' he bellowed. 'Crypto's about to blow, and Strathmore won't answer his goddamn phone!'

CHAPTER 98

Hulohot burst out of Cardinal Guerra's chambers into the blinding morning sun. He shielded his eyes and cursed. He was standing outside the cathedral in a small patio, bordered by a high stone wall, the west face of the Giralda tower, and two wrought-iron fences. The gate was open. Outside the gate was the square. It was empty. The walls of Santa Cruz were in the distance. There was no way Becker could have made it so far so quickly. Hulohot turned and scanned the patio. *He's in here. He must be!*

The patio, Jardin de los Naranjos, was famous in Seville for its twenty blossoming orange trees. The trees were renowned in Seville as the birthplace of English marmalade. An eighteenth-century English trader had purchased three dozen bushels of oranges from the Seville church and taken them back to London only to find the fruit inedibly bitter. He tried to make jam from the rinds and ended up having to add pounds of sugar just to make it palatable. Orange marmalade had been born.

Hulohot moved forward through the grove, gun leveled. The trees were old, and the foliage had moved high on their trunks. Their lowest branches were unreachable, and the thin bases provided no cover. Hulohot quickly saw the patio was empty. He looked straight up. The Giralda.

The entrance to the Giralda's spiral staircase was cordoned off by a rope and small wooden sign. The rope hung motionless. Hulohot's eyes climbed the 419-foot tower and immediately knew it was a ridiculous thought. There was no way Becker would have been that stupid. The single staircase wound straight up to a square stone cubicle. There were narrow slits in the wall for viewing, but there was no way out.

David Becker climbed the last of the steep stairs and staggered breathless into a tiny stone cubicle. There were high walls all around him and narrow slits in the perimeter. No exit.

Fate had done Becker no favors this morning. As he'd dashed from the cathedral into the open courtyard, his jacket had caught on the door. The fabric had stopped him midstride and swung him hard left before tearing. Becker was suddenly stumbling off balance into the blinding sun. When he'd looked up, he was heading straight for a staircase. He'd jumped over the rope and dashed up. By the time he realized where it led, it was too late.

Now he stood in the confined cell and caught his breath. His side burned. Narrow slats of morning sun streamed through the openings in the wall. He looked out. The man in the wire-rim glasses was far below, his back to Becker, staring out at the plaza. Becker shifted his body in front of the crack for a better view. *Cross the plaza*, he willed him.

*

The shadow of the Giralda lay across the square like a giant felled sequoia. Hulohot stared the length of it. At the far end, three slits of light cut through the tower's viewing apertures and fell in crisp rectangles on the cobblestone below. One of those rectangles had just been blotted out by the shadow of a man. Without so much as a glance toward the top of the tower, Hulohot spun and dashed toward the Giralda stairs.

CHAPTER 99

Fontaine pounded his fist into his hand. He paced the conference room and stared out at the spinning Crypto lights. 'Abort! Goddamn it! Abort!'

Midge appeared in the doorway waving a fresh readout. 'Director! Strathmore *can't* abort!'

'What!' Brinkerhoff and Fontaine gasped in unison.

'He tried, sir!' Midge held up the report. 'Four times already! TRANSLTR's locked in some sort of endless loop.'

Fontaine spun and stared back out the window. 'Jesus Christ!'

The conference room phone rang sharply. The director threw up his arms. 'It's got to be Strathmore! About goddamn time!'

Brinkerhoff scooped up the phone. 'Director's office.'

Fontaine held out his hand for the receiver.

Brinkerhoff looked uneasy and turned to Midge. 'It's Jabba. He wants *you*.'

The director swung his gaze over to Midge, who was already crossing the room. She activated the speaker phone. 'Go ahead, Jabba.'

Jabba's metallic voice boomed into the room. 'Midge, I'm in the main databank. We're showing some strange stuff down here. I was wondering if—'

'Dammit, Jabba!' Midge came unglued. 'That's what I've been trying to tell you!'

'It could be nothing,' Jabba hedged, 'but—'

'Stop saying that! It's *not* nothing! Whatever's going on down there, take it seriously, *very* seriously. My data isn't fried – never has been, never will.' She started to hang up and then added, 'Oh, and Jabba? Just so there aren't any surprises . . . Strathmore bypassed Gauntlet.'

CHAPTER 100

Hulohot took the Giralda stairs three at a time. The only light in the spiral passage was from small open-air windows every 180 degrees. *He's trapped! David Becker will die!* Hulohot circled upward, gun drawn. He kept to the outside wall in case Becker decided to attack from above. The iron candle poles on each landing would make good weapons if Becker decided to use one. But by staying wide, Hulohot would be able to spot him in time. Hulohot's gun had a range significantly longer than a five-foot candle pole.

Hulohot moved quickly but carefully. The stairs were steep; tourists had died here. This was not America – no safety signs, no handrails, no insurance disclaimers. This was Spain. If you were stupid enough to fall, it was your own damn fault, regardless of who built the stairs.

Hulohot paused at one of the shoulder-high openings and glanced out. He was on the north face and, from the looks of things, about halfway up.

The opening to the viewing platform was visible around the corner. The staircase to the top was empty. David Becker had not challenged him. Hulohot realized maybe Becker had not seen him enter the tower. That meant the element of surprise was on Hulohot's side as well – not that he'd need it. Hulohot held all the cards. Even the layout of the tower was in his favor; the staircase met the viewing platform in the southwest corner – Hulohot would have a clear line of fire to every point of the cell with no possibility that Becker could get behind him. And to top things off, Hulohot would be moving out of the dark into the light. *A killing box*, he mused.

Hulohot measured the distance to the doorway. Seven steps. He practiced the kill in his mind. If he stayed right as he approached the opening, he would be able to see the leftmost corner of the platform before he reached it. If Becker was there, Hulohot would fire. If not, he would shift inside and enter moving east, facing the right corner, the only place remaining that Becker could be. He smiled.

SUBJECT: DAVID BECKER – TERMINATED

The time had come. He checked his weapon.

With a violent surge, Hulohot dashed up. The platform swung into view. The left corner was empty. As rehearsed, Hulohot shifted inside and burst through the opening facing right. He fired into the corner. The bullet ricocheted back off the bare wall and barely missed him. Hulohot wheeled wildly and let out a muted scream. There was no one there. David Becker had vanished.

Three flights below, suspended 325 feet over the Jardin de los Naranjos, David Becker hung on the outside of the Giralda like a man doing chin-ups on a

413

window ledge. As Hulohot had been racing up the staircase, Becker had descended three flights and lowered himself out one of the openings. He'd dropped out of sight just in time. The killer had run right by him. He'd been in too much of a hurry to notice the white knuckles grasping the window ledge.

Hanging outside the window, Becker thanked God that his daily squash routine involved twenty minutes on the Nautilus machine to develop his biceps for a harder overhead serve. Unfortunately, despite his strong arms, Becker was now having trouble pulling himself back in. His shoulders burned. His side felt as if it were tearing open. The rough-cut stone ledge provided little grip, grating into his fingertips like broken glass.

Becker knew it was only a matter of seconds before his assailant would come running down from above. From the higher ground, the killer would undoubtedly see Becker's fingers on the ledge.

Becker closed his eyes and pulled. He knew he would need a miracle to escape death. His fingers were losing their leverage. He glanced down, past his dangling legs. The drop was the length of a football field to the orange trees below. Unsurvivable. The pain in his side was getting worse. Footsteps now thundered above him, loud leaping footsteps rushing down the stairs. Becker closed his eyes. It was now or never. He gritted his teeth and pulled.

The stone tore against the skin on his wrists as he yanked himself upward. The footsteps were coming fast. Becker grappled at the inside of the opening, trying to secure his hold. He kicked his feet. His body felt like lead, as if someone had a rope tied to his legs and were pulling him down. He fought it. He surged up onto his elbows. He was in plain view now, his head half through the window like a man in a guillotine. He wriggled his legs, kicking himself into the opening. He was halfway through. His torso now hung into the stairwell. The footsteps were close. Becker grabbed the sides of the opening and in a single motion launched his body through. He hit the staircase hard.

Hulohot sensed Becker's body hit the floor just below him. He leapt forward, gun leveled. A window spun into view. *This is it!* Hulohot moved to the outside wall and aimed down the staircase. Becker's legs dashed out of sight just around the curve. Hulohot fired in frustration. The bullet ricocheted down the stairwell.

As Hulohot dashed down the stairs after his prey, he kept to the outside wall for the widest angle view. As the staircase revolved into view before him, it seemed Becker was always 180 degrees ahead of him, just out of sight. Becker had taken the inside track, cutting off the angle and leaping four or five stairs at a time. Hulohot stayed with him. It would take only a single shot. Hulohot was gaining. He knew that even if Becker made the bottom, there was nowhere to run; Hulohot could shoot him in the back as he crossed the open patio. The desperate race spiraled downward.

Hulohot moved inside to the faster track. He sensed he was gaining. He could see Becker's shadow every time they passed an opening. Down. Down. Spiraling. It seemed that Becker was always just around the corner. Hulohot kept one eye on his shadow and one eye on the stairs.

Suddenly it appeared to Hulohot that Becker's

shadow had stumbled. It made an erratic lurch left and then seemed to spin in midair and sail back toward the center of the stairwell. Hulohot leapt forward. *I've got him!*

On the stairs in front of Hulohot, there was a flash of steel. It jabbed into the air from around the corner. It thrust forward like a fencer's foil at ankle level. Hulohot tried to shift left, but it was too late. The object was between his ankles. His back foot came forward, caught it hard, and the post slammed across his shin. Hulohot's arms went out for support but found only empty air. He was abruptly airborne, turning on his side. As Hulohot sailed downward, he passed over David Becker, prone on his stomach, arms outstretched. The candle pole in his hands was now caught up in Hulohot's legs as he spun downward.

Hulohot crashed into the outside wall before he hit the staircase. When he finally found the floor, he was tumbling. His gun clattered to the floor. Hulohot's body kept going, head over heels. He spiraled five complete 360-degree rotations before he rolled to a stop. Twelve more steps, and he would have tumbled out onto the patio.

CHAPTER 101

David Becker had never held a gun, but he was holding one now. Hulohot's body was twisted and mangled in the darkness of the Giralda staircase. Becker pressed the barrel of the gun against his assailant's temple and carefully knelt down. One twitch and Becker would fire. But there was no twitch. Hulohot was dead.

Becker dropped the gun and collapsed on the stairs. For the first time in ages he felt tears well up. He fought them. He knew there would be time for emotion later; now it was time to go home. Becker tried to stand, but he was too tired to move. He sat a long while, exhausted, on the stone staircase.

Absently, he studied the twisted body before him. The killer's eyes began to glaze over, gazing out at nothing in particular. Somehow, his glasses were still intact. They were odd glasses, Becker thought, with a wire protruding from behind the earpiece and leading to a pack of some sort on his belt. Becker was too exhausted to be curious.

As he sat alone in the staircase and collected his thoughts, Becker shifted his gaze to the ring on his finger. His vision had cleared somewhat, and he could finally read the inscription. As he had suspected, it was not English. He stared at the engraving a long moment and then frowned. *This is worth killing for?*

The morning sun was blinding when Becker finally stepped out of the Giralda onto the patio. The pain in his side had subsided, and his vision was returning to normal. He stood a moment, in a daze, enjoying the fragrance of the orange blossoms. Then he began moving slowly across the patio.

As Becker strode away from the tower, a van skidded to a stop nearby. Two men jumped out. They were young and dressed in military fatigues. They advanced on Becker with the stiff precision of well-tuned machines.

'David Becker?' one demanded.

Becker stopped short, amazed they knew his name. 'Who . . . who are you?'

'Come with us, please. Right away.'

There was something unreal about the encounter – something that made Becker's nerve endings start to tingle again. He found himself backing away from them.

The shorter man gave Becker an icy stare. 'This way, Mr Becker. *Right now.*'

Becker turned to run. But he only took one step. One of the men drew a weapon. There was a shot.

A searing lance of pain erupted in Becker's chest. It rocketed to his skull. His fingers went stiff, and Becker fell. An instant later, there was nothing but blackness.

CHAPTER 102

Strathmore reached the TRANSLTR floor and stepped off the catwalk into an inch of water. The giant computer shuddered beside him. Huge droplets of water fell like rain through the swirling mist. The warning horns sounded like thunder.

The commander looked across at the failed main generators. Phil Chartrukian was there, his charred remains splayed across a set of coolant fins. The scene looked like some sort of perverse Halloween display.

Although Strathmore regretted the man's death, there was no doubt it had been 'a warranted casualty.' Phil Chartrukian had left Strathmore no choice. When the Sys-Sec came racing up from the depths, screaming about a virus, Strathmore met him on the landing and tried to talk sense to him. But Chartrukian was beyond reason. *We've got a virus! I'm calling Jabba!* When he tried to push past, the commander blocked his way. The landing was narrow. They struggled. The railing was low. It was ironic, Strathmore thought, that Chartrukian had been right about the virus all along.

The man's plunge had been chilling – a momentary

howl of terror and then silence. But it was not half as chilling as the next thing Commander Strathmore saw. Greg Hale was staring up at him from the shadows below, a look of utter horror on his face. It was then that Strathmore knew Greg Hale would die.

TRANSLTR crackled, and Strathmore turned his attention back to the task at hand. Kill power. The circuit breaker was on the other side of the freon pumps to the left of the body. Strathmore could see it clearly. All he had to do was pull a lever and the remaining power in Crypto would die. Then, after a few seconds, he could restart the main generators; all doorways and functions would come back on-line; the freon would start flowing again, and TRANSLTR would be safe.

But as Strathmore slogged toward the breaker, he realized there was one final obstacle: Chartrukian's body was still on the main generator's cooling fins. Killing and then restarting the main generator would only cause another power failure. The body had to be moved.

Strathmore eyed the grotesque remains and made his way over. Reaching up, he grabbed a wrist. The flesh was like Styrofoam. The tissue had been fried. The whole body was devoid of moisture. The commander closed his eyes, tightened his grip around the wrist, and pulled. The body slid an inch or two. Strathmore pulled harder. The body slid again. The commander braced himself and pulled with all his might. Suddenly he was tumbling backward. He landed hard on his backside up against a power casement. Struggling to sit up in the rising water, Strathmore stared down in horror at the object in his fist. It was Chartrukian's forearm. It had broken off at the elbow.

420

Upstairs, Susan continued her wait. She sat on the Node 3 couch feeling paralyzed. Hale lay at her feet. She couldn't imagine what was taking the commander so long. Minutes passed. She tried to push David from her thoughts, but it was no use. With every blast of the horns, Hale's words echoed inside her head: *I'm truly sorry about David Becker.* Susan thought she would lose her mind.

She was about to jump up and race onto the Crypto floor when finally it happened. Strathmore had thrown the switch and killed all power.

The silence that engulfed Crypto was instantaneous. The horns choked off midblare, and the Node 3 monitors flickered to black. Greg Hale's corpse disappeared into the darkness, and Susan instinctively yanked her legs up onto the couch. She wrapped Strathmore's suitcoat around her.

Darkness.

Silence.

She had never heard such quiet in Crypto. There'd always been the low hum of the generators. But now there was nothing, only the great beast heaving and sighing in relief. Crackling, hissing, slowly cooling down.

Susan closed her eyes and prayed for David. Her prayer was a simple one – that God protect the man she loved.

Not being a religious woman, Susan had never expected to hear a response to her prayer. But when there was a sudden shuddering against her chest, she jolted upright. She clutched her chest. A moment later she understood. The vibrations she felt were not the hand of God at all – they were coming from the

421

commander's jacket pocket. He had set the vibrating silent-ring feature on his SkyPager. Someone was sending Commander Strathmore a message.

Six stories below, Strathmore stood at the circuit breaker. The sublevels of Crypto were now as dark as the deepest night. He stood a moment enjoying the blackness. The water poured down from above. It was a midnight storm. Strathmore tilted his head back and let the warm droplets wash away his guilt. *I'm a survivor.* He knelt and washed the last of Chartrukian's flesh from his hands.

His dreams for Digital Fortress had failed. He could accept that. Susan was all that mattered now. For the first time in decades, he truly understood that there was more to life than country and honor. *I sacrificed the best years of my life for country and honor. But what about love?* He had deprived himself for far too long. *And for what?* To watch some young professor steal away his dreams? Strathmore had nurtured Susan. He had protected her. He had *earned* her. And now, at last, he would have her. Susan would seek shelter in his arms when there was nowhere else to turn. She would come to him helpless, wounded by loss, and in time, he would show her that love heals all.

Honor. Country. Love. David Becker was about to die for all three.

CHAPTER 103

The commander rose through the trapdoor like Lazarus back from the dead. Despite his soggy clothes, his step was light. He strode toward Node 3 – toward Susan. Toward his future.

The Crypto floor was again bathed in light. Freon was flowing downward through the smoldering TRANSLTR like oxygenated blood. Strathmore knew it would take a few minutes for the coolant to reach the bottom of the hull and prevent the lowest processors from igniting, but he was certain he'd acted in time. He exhaled in victory, never suspecting the truth – that it was already too late.

I'm a survivor, he thought. Ignoring the gaping hole in the Node 3 wall, he strode to the electronic doors. They hissed open. He stepped inside.

Susan was standing before him, damp and tousled in his blazer. She looked like a freshman coed who'd been caught in the rain. He felt like the senior who'd lent her his varsity sweater. For the first time in years, he felt young. His dream was coming true.

But as Strathmore moved closer, he felt he was staring into the eyes of a woman he did not recognize. Her gaze was like ice. The softness was gone. Susan Fletcher stood rigid, like an immovable statue. The only perceptible motion were the tears welling in her eyes.

'Susan?'

A single tear rolled down her quivering cheek.

'What is it?' the commander pleaded.

The puddle of blood beneath Hale's body had spread across the carpet like an oil spill. Strathmore glanced uneasily at the corpse, then back at Susan. *Could she possibly know?* There was no way. Strathmore knew he had covered every base.

'Susan?' he said, stepping closer. 'What is it?'

Susan did not move.

'Are you worried about David?'

There was a slight quiver in her upper lip.

Strathmore stepped closer. He was going to reach for her, but he hesitated. The sound of David's name had apparently cracked the dam of grief. Slowly at first – a quiver, a tremble. And then a thundering wave of misery seemed to course through her veins. Barely able to control her shuddering lips, Susan opened her mouth to speak. Nothing came.

Without ever breaking the icy gaze she'd locked on Strathmore, she took her hand from the pocket of his blazer. In her hand was an object. She held it out, shaking.

Strathmore half expected to look down and see the Beretta leveled at his gut. But the gun was still on the floor, propped safely in Hale's hand. The object Susan was holding was smaller. Strathmore stared down at it, and an instant later, he understood.

As Strathmore stared, reality warped, and time slowed to a crawl. He could hear the sound of his own heart. The man who had triumphed over giants for so many years had been outdone in an instant. Slain by love – by his own foolishness. In a simple act of chivalry, he had given Susan his jacket. And with it, his SkyPager.

Now it was Strathmore who went rigid. Susan's hand was shaking. The pager fell at Hale's feet. With a look of astonishment and betrayal that Strathmore would never forget, Susan Fletcher raced past him out of Node 3.

The commander let her go. In slow motion, he bent and retrieved the pager. There were no new messages – Susan had read them all. Strathmore scrolled desperately through the list.

SUBJECT: ENSEI TANKADO – TERMINATED
SUBJECT: PIERRE CLOUCHARDE – TERMINATED
SUBJECT: HANS HUBER – TERMINATED
SUBJECT: ROCÍO EVA GRANADA – TERMINATED . . .

The list went on. Strathmore felt a wave of horror. *I can explain!* She *will understand! Honor! Country!* But there was one message he had not yet seen – one message he could never explain. Trembling, he scrolled to the final transmission.

SUBJECT: DAVID BECKER – TERMINATED

Strathmore hung his head. His dream was over.

CHAPTER 104

Susan staggered out of node 3.

SUBJECT: DAVID BECKER – TERMINATED

As if in a dream, she moved toward Crypto's main exit. Greg Hale's voice echoed in her mind: *Susan, Strathmore's going to kill me! Susan, the commander's in love with you!*

Susan reached the enormous circular portal and began stabbing desperately at the keypad. The door did not move. She tried again, but the enormous slab refused to rotate. Susan let out a muted scream – apparently the power outage had deleted the exit codes. She was still trapped.

Without warning, two arms closed around her from behind, grasping her half-numb body. The touch was familiar yet repulsive. It lacked the brute strength of Greg Hale, but there was a desperate roughness to it, an inner determination like steel.

Susan turned. The man restraining her was desolate, frightened. It was a face she had never seen.

'Susan,' Strathmore begged, holding her. 'I can explain.'
She tried to pull away.

The commander held fast.

Susan tried to scream, but she had no voice. She tried to run, but strong hands restrained her, pulling her backward.

'I love you,' the voice was whispering. 'I've loved you forever.'

Susan's stomach turned over and over.

'Stay with me.'

Susan's mind whirled with grisly images – David's bright-green eyes, slowly closing for the last time; Greg Hale's corpse seeping blood onto the carpet; Phil Chartrukian's burned and broken on the generators.

'The pain will pass,' the voice said. 'You'll love again.'

Susan heard nothing.

'Stay with me,' the voice pleaded. 'I'll heal your wounds.'

She struggled, helpless.

'I did it for us. We're made for each other. Susan, I love you.' The words flowed as if he had waited a decade to speak them. 'I love you! *I love you!*'

In that instant, thirty yards away, as if rebutting Strathmore's vile confession, TRANSLTR let out a savage, pitiless hiss. The sound was an entirely new one – a distant, ominous sizzling that seemed to grow like a serpent in the depths of the silo. The freon, it appeared, had not reached its mark in time.

The commander let go of Susan and turned toward the $2 billion computer. His eyes went wide with dread. 'No!' He grabbed his head. 'No!'

The six-story rocket began to tremble. Strathmore staggered a faltering step toward the thundering hull. Then he fell to his knees, a sinner before an angry god. It was no use. At the base of the silo, TRANSLTR's titanium-strontium processors had just ignited.

CHAPTER 105

A fireball racing upward through three million silicon chips makes a unique sound. The crackling of a forest fire, the howling of a tornado, the steaming gush of a geyser . . . all trapped within a reverberant hull. It was the devil's breath, pouring through a sealed cavern, looking for escape. Strathmore knelt transfixed by the horrific noise rising toward them. The world's most expensive computer was about to become an eight-story inferno.

In slow motion, Strathmore turned back toward Susan. She stood paralyzed beside the Crypto door. Strathmore stared at her tear-streaked face. She seemed to shimmer in the fluorescent light. *She's an angel,* he thought. He searched her eyes for heaven, but all he could see was death. It was the death of trust. Love and honor were gone. The fantasy that had kept him going all these years was dead. He would never have Susan Fletcher. Never. The sudden emptiness that gripped him was overwhelming.

Susan gazed vaguely toward TRANSLTR. She knew that trapped within the ceramic shell, a fireball was racing toward them. She sensed it rising faster and faster, feeding on the oxygen released by the burning chips. In moments the Crypto dome would be a blazing inferno.

Susan's mind told her to run, but David's dead weight pressed down all around her. She thought she heard his voice calling to her, telling her to escape, but there was nowhere to go. Crypto was a sealed tomb. It didn't matter; the thought of death did not frighten her. Death would stop the pain. She would be with David.

The Crypto floor began to tremble, as if below it an angry sea monster were rising out of the depths. David's voice seemed to be calling. *Run, Susan! Run!*

Strathmore was moving toward her now, his face a distant memory. His cool gray eyes were lifeless. The patriot who had lived in her mind a hero had died – a murderer. His arms were suddenly around her again, clutching desperately. He kissed her cheeks. 'Forgive me,' he begged. Susan tried to pull away, but Strathmore held on.

TRANSLTR began vibrating like a missile preparing to launch. The Crypto floor began to shake. Strathmore held tighter. 'Hold me, Susan. I need you.'

A violent surge of fury filled Susan's limbs. David's voice called out again. *I love you! Escape!* In a sudden burst of energy, Susan tore free. The roar from TRANSLTR became deafening. The fire was at the silo's peak. TRANSLTR groaned, straining at its seams.

David's voice seemed to lift Susan, guide her. She dashed across the Crypto floor and started up Strathmore's catwalk stairs. Behind her, TRANSLTR let out a deafening roar.

As the last of the silicon chips disintegrated, a tremendous updraft of heat tore through the upper casing of the silo and sent shards of ceramic thirty feet into the air. Instantly the oxygen-rich air of Crypto rushed in to fill the enormous vacuum.

Susan reached the upper landing and grabbed the banister when the tremendous rush of wind ripped at her body. It spun her around in time to see the deputy director of operations, far below, staring up at her from beside TRANSLTR. There was a storm raging all around him, and yet there was peace in his eyes. His lips parted, and he mouthed his final word. 'Susan.'

The air rushing into TRANSLTR ignited on contact. In a brilliant flash of light, Commander Trevor Strathmore passed from man, to silhouette, to legend.

When the blast hit Susan, it blew her back fifteen feet into Strathmore's office. All she remembered was a searing heat.

CHAPTER 106

In the window of the director's conference room, high above the Crypto dome, three faces appeared, breathless. The explosion had shaken the entire NSA complex. Leland Fontaine, Chad Brinkerhoff, and Midge Milken all stared out in silent horror.

Seventy feet below, the Crypto dome was blazing. The polycarbonate roof was still intact, but beneath the transparent shell, a fire raged. Black smoke swirled like fog inside the dome.

The three stared down without a word. The spectacle had an eerie grandeur to it.

Fontaine stood a long moment. He finally spoke, his voice faint but unwavering. 'Midge, get a crew down there . . . now.'

Across the suite, Fontaine's phone began to ring. It was Jabba.

CHAPTER 107

Susan had no idea how much time had passed. A burning in her throat pulled her to her senses. Disoriented, she studied her surroundings. She was on a carpet behind a desk. The only light in the room was a strange orange flickering. The air smelled of burning plastic. The room she was standing in was not really a room at all; it was a devastated shell. The curtains were on fire, and the Plexiglas walls were smoldering.

Then she remembered it all.

David.

In a rising panic, she pulled herself to her feet. The air felt caustic in her windpipe. She stumbled to the doorway looking for a way out. As she crossed the threshold, her leg swung out over an abyss; she grabbed the door frame just in time. The catwalk had disappeared. Fifty feet below was a twisted collapse of steaming metal. Susan scanned the Crypto floor in horror. It was a sea of fire. The melted remains of three million silicon chips had erupted from TRANSLTR like lava. Thick, acrid smoke billowed upward. Susan knew the smell. Silicon smoke. Deadly poison.

432

Retreating into the remains of Strathmore's office, she began to feel faint. Her throat burned. The entire place was filled with a fiery light. Crypto was dying. *So will I,* she thought.

For a moment, she considered the only possible exit – Strathmore's elevator. But she knew it was useless; the electronics never would have survived the blast.

But as Susan made her way through the thickening smoke, she recalled Hale's words. *The elevator runs on power from the main building! I've seen the schematics!* Susan knew that was true. She also knew the entire shaft was encased in reinforced concrete.

The fumes swirled all around her. She stumbled through the smoke toward the elevator door. But when she got there, she saw that the elevator's call button was dark. Susan jabbed fruitlessly at the darkened panel, then she fell to her knees and pounded on the door.

She stopped almost instantly. Something was whirring behind the doors. Startled, she looked up. It sounded like the carriage was right there! Susan stabbed at the button again. Again, a whirring behind the doors.

Suddenly she saw it.

The call button was not dead – it had just been covered with black soot. It now glowed faintly beneath her smudged fingerprints.

There's power!

With a surge of hope, she punched at the button. Over and over, something behind the doors engaged. She could hear the ventilation fan in the elevator car. *The carriage is here! Why won't the damn doors open?*

Through the smoke she spied the tiny secondary keypad – lettered buttons, A through Z. In a wave of despair, Susan remembered. The password.

The smoke was starting to curl in through the melted window frames. Again she banged on the elevator doors. They refused to open. *The password!* she thought. *Strathmore never told me the password!* Silicon smoke was now filling the office. Choking, Susan fell against the elevator in defeat. The ventilation fan was running just a few feet away. She lay there, dazed, gulping for air.

She closed her eyes, but again David's voice woke her. *Escape, Susan! Open the door! Escape!* She opened her eyes expecting to see his face, those wild green eyes, that playful smile. But the letters A–Z came into focus. *The password* . . . Susan stared at the letters on the keypad. She could barely keep them in focus. On the LED below the keypad, five empty spots awaited entry. *A five-character password*, she thought. She instantly knew the odds: twenty-six to the fifth power; 11,881,376 possible choices. At one guess every second, it would take nineteen weeks . . .

As Susan Fletcher lay choking on the floor beneath the keypad, the commander's pathetic voice came to her. He was calling to her again. *I love you, Susan! I've always loved you! Susan! Susan! Susan* . . .

She knew he was dead, and yet his voice was relentless. She heard her name over and over.

Susan . . . Susan . . .

Then, in a moment of chilling clarity, she knew.

Trembling weakly, she reached up to the keypad and typed the password.

S . . . U . . . S . . . A . . . N

An instant later, the doors slid open.

CHAPTER 108

Strathmore's elevator dropped fast. Inside the carriage, Susan sucked deep breaths of fresh air into her lungs. Dazed, she steadied herself against the wall as the car slowed to a stop. A moment later some gears clicked, and the conveyor began moving again, this time horizontally. Susan felt the carriage accelerate as it began rumbling toward the main NSA complex. Finally it whirred to a stop, and the doors opened.

Coughing, Susan Fletcher stumbled into a darkened cement corridor. She found herself in a tunnel – low-ceilinged and narrow. A double yellow line stretched out before her. The line disappeared into an empty, dark hollow.

The Underground Highway . . .

She staggered toward the tunnel, holding the wall for guidance. Behind her, the elevator door slid shut. Once again Susan Fletcher was plunged into darkness.

Silence.

Nothing except a faint humming in the walls.

A humming that grew louder.

Suddenly it was as if dawn were breaking. The

blackness thinned to a hazy gray. The walls of the tunnel began to take shape. All at once, a small vehicle whipped around the corner, its headlight blinding her. Susan stumbled back against the wall and shielded her eyes. There was a gust of air, and the transport whipped past.

An instant later there was a deafening squeal of rubber on cement. The hum approached once again, this time in reverse. Seconds later the vehicle came to a stop beside her.

'Ms Fletcher!' an astonished voice exclaimed.

Susan gazed at a vaguely familiar shape in the driver's seat of an electric golf cart.

'Jesus.' The man gasped. 'Are you okay? We thought you were dead!'

Susan stared blankly.

'Chad Brinkerhoff,' he sputtered, studying the shellshocked cryptographer. 'Directorial PA.'

Susan could only manage a dazed whimper. 'TRANSLTR . . .'

Brinkerhoff nodded. 'Forget it. Get on!'

The beam of the golf cart's headlights whipped across the cement walls.

'There's a virus in the main databank,' Brinkerhoff blurted.

'I know,' Susan heard herself whisper.

'We need you to help us.'

Susan was fighting back the tears. 'Strathmore . . . he . . .'

'We know,' Brinkerhoff said. 'He bypassed Gauntlet.'

'Yes . . . and . . .' The words got stuck in her throat. *He killed David!*

436

Brinkerhoff put a hand on her shoulder. 'Almost there, Ms Fletcher. Just hold on.'

The high-speed Kensington golf cart rounded a corner and skidded to a stop. Beside them, branching off perpendicular to the tunnel, was a hallway, dimly lit by red floor lighting.

'Come on,' Brinkerhoff said, helping her out.

He guided her into the corridor. Susan drifted behind him in a fog. The tiled passageway sloped downward at a steep incline. Susan grabbed the handrail and followed Brinkerhoff down. The air began to grow cooler. They continued their descent.

As they dropped deeper into the earth, the tunnel narrowed. From somewhere behind them came the echo of footsteps – a strong, purposeful gait. The footsteps grew louder. Both Brinkerhoff and Susan stopped and turned.

Striding toward them was an enormous black man. Susan had never seen him before. As he approached, he fixed her with a penetrating stare.

'Who's this?' he demanded.

'Susan Fletcher,' Brinkerhoff replied.

The enormous man arched his eyebrows. Even sooty and soaked, Susan Fletcher was more striking than he had imagined. 'And the commander?' he demanded.

Brinkerhoff shook his head.

The man said nothing. He stared off a moment. Then he turned back to Susan. 'Leland Fontaine,' he said, offering her his hand. 'Glad you're okay.'

Susan stared. She'd always known she'd meet the director someday, but this was not the introduction she'd envisioned.

'Come along, Ms Fletcher,' Fontaine said, leading the way. 'We'll need all the help we can get.'

Looming in the reddish haze at the bottom of the tunnel, a steel wall blocked their way. Fontaine approached and typed an entry code into a recessed cipher box. He then placed his right hand against a small glass panel. A strobe flashed. A moment later the massive wall thundered left.

There was only one NSA chamber more sacred than Crypto, and Susan Fletcher sensed she was about to enter it.

CHAPTER 109

The command center for the NSA's main databank looked like a scaled-down NASA mission control. A dozen computer workstations faced the thirty-foot by forty-foot video wall at the far end of the room. On the screen, numbers and diagrams flashed in rapid succession, appearing and disappearing as if someone were channel surfing. A handful of technicians raced wildly from station to station trailing long sheets of printout paper and yelling commands. It was chaos.

Susan stared at the dazzling facility. She vaguely remembered that 250 metric tons of earth had been excavated to create it. The chamber was located 214 feet below ground, where it would be totally impervious to flux bombs and nuclear blasts.

On a raised workstation in the center of the room stood Jabba. He bellowed orders from his platform like a king to his subjects. Illuminated on the screen directly behind him was a message. The message was all too familiar to Susan. The billboard-size text hung ominously over Jabba's head:

ONLY THE TRUTH WILL SAVE YOU NOW
ENTER PASS-KEY _____

As if trapped in some surreal nightmare, Susan followed Fontaine toward the podium. Her world was a slow-motion blur.

Jabba saw them coming and wheeled like an enraged bull. 'I built Gauntlet for a reason!'

'Gauntlet's gone,' Fontaine replied evenly.

'Old news, Director,' Jabba spat. 'The shock wave knocked me on my ass! Where's Strathmore?'

'Commander Strathmore is dead.'

'Poetic fucking justice.'

'Cool it, Jabba,' the director ordered. 'Bring us up to speed. How bad is this virus?'

Jabba stared at the director a long moment, and then without warning, he burst out laughing. 'A *virus?*' His harsh guffaw resonated through the underground chamber. 'Is that what you think this is?'

Fontaine kept his cool. Jabba's insolence was way out of line, but Fontaine knew this was not the time or place to handle it. Down here, Jabba outranked God himself. Computer problems had a way of ignoring the normal chain of command.

'It's *not* a virus?' Brinkerhoff exclaimed hopefully.

Jabba snorted in disgust. '*Viruses* have replication strings, pretty boy! *This* doesn't!'

Susan hovered nearby, unable to focus.

'Then what's going on?' Fontaine demanded. 'I thought we had a virus.'

Jabba sucked in a long breath and lowered his voice. 'Viruses . . .' he said, wiping sweat from his face. 'Viruses reproduce. They create clones. They're vain and stupid – binary egomaniacs. They pump out

440

babies faster than rabbits. That's their weakness – you can cross-breed them into oblivion if you know what you're doing. Unfortunately, this program has no ego, no need to reproduce. It's clear-headed and focused. In fact, when it's accomplished its objective here, it will probably commit digital suicide.' Jabba held out his arms reverently to the projected havoc on the enormous screen. 'Ladies and gentlemen.' He sighed. 'Meet the kamikaze of computer invaders . . . the *worm.*'

'*Worm?*' Brinkerhoff groaned. It seemed like a mundane term to describe the insidious intruder.

'Worm.' Jabba smoldered. 'No complex structures, just instinct – eat, shit, crawl. That's it. Simplicity. Deadly simplicity. It does what it's programmed to do and then checks out.'

Fontaine eyed Jabba sternly. 'And what is this worm programmed to do?'

'No clue,' Jabba replied. 'Right now, it's spreading out and attaching itself to all our classified data. After that, it could do anything. It might decide to delete all the files, or it might just decide to print smiley faces on certain White House transcripts.'

Fontaine's voice remained cool and collected. 'Can you stop it?'

Jabba let out a long sigh and faced the screen. 'I have no idea. It all depends on how pissed off the author is.' He pointed to the message on the wall. 'Anybody want to tell me what the hell *that* means?'

ONLY THE TRUTH WILL SAVE YOU NOW
ENTER PASS-KEY _____

441

Jabba waited for a response and got none. 'Looks like someone's messing with us, Director. Blackmail. This is a ransom note if I ever saw one.'

Susan's voice was a whisper, empty and hollow. 'It's . . . Ensei Tankado.'

Jabba turned to her. He stared a moment, wide-eyed. *'Tankado?'*

Susan nodded weakly. 'He wanted our confession . . . about TRANSLTR . . . but it cost him his—'

'Confession?' Brinkerhoff interrupted, looking stunned. 'Tankado wants us to confess we have TRANSLTR? I'd say it's a bit late for *that!'*

Susan opened her mouth to speak, but Jabba took over. 'Looks like Tankado's got a kill-code,' he said, gazing up at the message on the screen.

Everyone turned.

'Kill code?' Brinkerhoff demanded.

Jabba nodded. 'Yeah. A pass-key that stops the worm. Simply put, if we admit we have TRANSLTR, Tankado gives us a kill-code. We type it in and save the databank. Welcome to digital extortion.'

Fontaine stood like rock, unwavering. 'How long have we got?'

'About an hour,' Jabba said. 'Just time enough to call a press conference and spill our guts.'

'Recommendation,' Fontaine demanded. 'What do you propose we do?'

'A *recommendation?'* Jabba blurted in disbelief. 'You want a recommendation? I'll give you a recommendation! You quit fucking around, *that's* what you do!'

'Easy,' the director warned.

'Director,' Jabba sputtered. 'Right now, Ensei Tankado *owns* this databank! Give him *whatever* he wants. If he wants the world to know about TRANSLTR, call CNN, and drop your shorts. TRANSLTR's a hole in the ground now anyway – what the hell do *you* care?'

There was a silence. Fontaine seemed to be considering his options. Susan began to speak, but Jabba beat her to it.

'What are you waiting for, Director! Get Tankado on the phone! Tell him you'll play ball! We need that kill-code, or this whole place is going down!'

Nobody moved.

'Are you all insane?' Jabba screamed. 'Call Tankado! Tell him we fold! Get me that kill-code! NOW!' Jabba whipped out his cellular phone and switched it on. 'Never mind! Get me his number! I'll call the little prick *myself!*'

'Don't bother,' Susan said in a whisper. 'Tankado's dead.'

After a moment of confused astonishment, the implications hit Jabba like a bullet to the gut. The huge Sys-Sec looked like he was about to crumble. '*Dead? But then . . . that means . . . we can't . . .*'

'That means we'll need a new plan,' Fontaine said matter-of-factly.

Jabba's eyes were still glazed with shock when someone in the back of the room began shouting wildly.

'Jabba! Jabba!'

It was Soshi Kuta, his head techie. She came running toward the podium trailing a long printout. She looked terrified.

'Jabba!' She gasped. 'The worm . . . I just found out what it's programmed to do!' Soshi thrust the paper into Jabba's hands. 'I pulled this from the system-activity probe! We isolated the worm's execute commands – have a look at the programming! Look what it's planning to do!'

Dazed, the chief Sys-Sec read the printout. Then he grabbed the handrail for support.

'Oh, Jesus,' Jabba gasped. 'Tankado . . . you *bastard!*'

CHAPTER 110

Jabba stared blankly at the printout Soshi had just handed him. Pale, he wiped his forehead on his sleeve. 'Director, we have no choice. We've got to kill power to the databank.'

'Unacceptable,' Fontaine replied. 'The results would be devastating.'

Jabba knew the director was right. There were over three thousand ISDN connections tying into the NSA databank from all over the world. Every day military commanders accessed up-to-the-instant satellite photos of enemy movement. Lockheed engineers downloaded compartmentalized blueprints of new weaponry. Field operatives accessed mission updates. The NSA databank was the backbone of thousands of U.S. government operations. Shutting it down without warning would cause life-and-death intelligence blackouts all over the globe.

'I'm aware of the implications, sir,' Jabba said, 'but we have no choice.'

'Explain yourself,' Fontaine ordered. He shot a quick glance at Susan standing beside him on the podium. She seemed miles away.

Jabba took a deep breath and wiped his brow again. From the look on his face, it was clear to the group on the podium that they were not going to like what he had to say.

'This worm,' Jabba began. 'This worm is not an ordinary degenerative cycle. It's a *selective* cycle. In other words, it's a worm with *taste*.'

Brinkerhoff opened his mouth to speak, but Fontaine waved him off.

'Most destructive applications wipe a databank clean,' Jabba continued, 'but this one is more complex. It deletes only those files that fall within certain parameters.'

'You mean it won't attack the *whole* databank?' Brinkerhoff asked hopefully. 'That's *good*, right?'

'No!' Jabba exploded. 'It's bad! It's *very* fucking *bad!*'

'Cool it!' Fontaine ordered. 'What parameters is this worm looking for? Military? Covert ops?'

Jabba shook his head. He eyed Susan, who was still distant, and then Jabba's eyes rose to meet the director's. 'Sir, as you know, anyone who wants to tie into this databank from the outside has to pass a series of security gates before they're admitted.'

Fontaine nodded. The databank's access hierarchies were brilliantly conceived; authorized personnel could dial in via the Internet and World Wide Web. Depending on their authorization sequence, they were permitted access to their own compartmentalized zones.

'Because we're tied to the global Internet,' Jabba explained, 'hackers, foreign governments, and EFF sharks circle this databank twenty-four hours a day and try to break in.'

'Yes,' Fontaine said, 'and twenty-four hours a day, our security filters keep them out. What's your point?'

Jabba gazed down at the printout. 'My point is this. Tankado's worm is not targeting our *data*.' He cleared his throat. 'It's targeting our *security filters*.'

Fontaine blanched. Apparently he understood the implications – this worm was targeting the filters that kept the NSA databank confidential. Without filters, all of the information in the databank would become accessible to everyone on the outside.

'We need to shut down,' Jabba repeated. 'In about an hour, every third grader with a modem is going to have top U.S. security clearance.'

Fontaine stood a long moment without saying a word.

Jabba waited impatiently and finally turned to Soshi. 'Soshi! VR! NOW!'

Soshi dashed off.

Jabba relied on VR often. In most computer circles, VR meant 'virtual reality,' but at the NSA it meant *vis-rep* – visual representation. In a world full of technicians and politicians all having different levels of technical understanding, a graphic representation was often the only way to make a point; a single plummeting graph usually aroused ten times the reaction inspired by volumes of spreadsheets. Jabba knew a VR of the current crisis would make its point instantly.

'VR!' Soshi yelled from a terminal at the back of the room.

A computer-generated diagram flashed to life on the wall before them. Susan gazed up absently, detached from the madness around her. Everyone in the room followed Jabba's gaze to the screen.

The diagram before them resembled a bull's-eye. In the center was a red circle marked DATA. Around the center were five concentric circles of differing thickness and color. The outermost circle was faded, almost transparent.

'We've got a five-tier level of defense,' Jabba explained. 'A primary Bastion Host, two sets of packet filters for FTP and X-eleven, a tunnel block, and finally a PEM-based authorization window right off the Truffle project. The outside shield that's disappearing represents the exposed host. It's practically gone. Within the hour, all five shields will follow. After that, the world pours in. Every byte of NSA data becomes public domain.'

Fontaine studied the VR, his eyes smoldering.

Brinkerhoff let out a weak whimper. 'This worm can open our databank to the world?'

'Child's play for Tankado,' Jabba snapped. 'Gauntlet was our fail-safe. Strathmore blew it.'

'It's an act of war,' Fontaine whispered, an edge in his voice.

Jabba shook his head. 'I really doubt Tankado ever meant for it to go this far. I suspect he intended to be around to stop it.'

Fontaine gazed up at the screen and watched the first of the five walls disappear entirely.

'Bastion Host is toast!' a technician yelled from the back of the room. 'Second shield's exposed!'

'We've got to start shutting down,' Jabba urged. 'From the looks of the VR, we've got about forty-five minutes. Shutdown is a complex process.'

It was true. The NSA databank had been constructed in such a way as to ensure it would never lose power – accidentally or if attacked. Multiple fail-safes for phone and power were buried in reinforced steel canisters deep underground, and in addition to the feeds from within the NSA complex, there were multiple backups off main public grids. Shutting down involved a complex series of confirmations and protocols – significantly more complicated than the average nuclear submarine missile launch.

'We have time,' Jabba said, 'if we hurry. Manual shutdown should take about thirty minutes.'

Fontaine continued staring up at the VR, apparently pondering his options.

'Director!' Jabba exploded. 'When these firewalls fall, every user on the planet will be issued top-security clearance! And I'm talking *upper level!* Records of covert ops! Overseas agents! Names and locations of everyone in the federal witness protection program! Launch code confirmations! We must shut down! Now!'

The director seemed unmoved. 'There must be some other way.'

'Yes,' Jabba spat, 'there is! The kill-code! But the only guy who knows it happens to be dead!'

'How about brute force?' Brinkerhoff blurted. 'Can we guess the kill-code?'

Jabba threw up his arms. 'For Christ's sake! Kill-codes are like encryption keys – random! Impossible to guess! If you think you can type 600 trillion entries in the next forty-five minutes, be my guest!'

'The kill-code's in Spain,' Susan offered weakly.

Everyone on the podium turned. It was the first thing she had said in a long time.

Susan looked up, bleary-eyed. 'Tankado gave it away when he died.'

Everyone looked lost.

449

'The pass-key . . .' Susan shivered as she spoke. 'Commander Strathmore sent someone to find it.'

'And?' Jabba demanded. 'Did Strathmore's man *find* it?'

Susan tried to fight it, but the tears began to flow. 'Yes,' she choked. 'I think so.'

CHAPTER 111

An earsplitting yell cut through the control room. *'Sharks!'* It was Soshi.

Jabba spun toward the VR. Two thin lines had appeared outside the concentric circles. They looked like sperm trying to breach a reluctant egg.

'Blood's in the water, folks!' Jabba turned back to the director. 'I need a decision. Either we start shutting down, or we'll never make it. As soon as these two intruders see the Bastion Host is down, they'll send up a war cry.'

Fontaine did not respond. He was deep in thought. Susan Fletcher's news of the pass-key in Spain seemed promising to him. He shot a glance toward Susan in the back of the room. She appeared to be in her own world, collapsed in a chair, her head buried in her hands. Fontaine was unsure exactly what had triggered the reaction, but whatever it was, he had no time for it now.

'I need a decision!' Jabba demanded. 'Now!'

Fontaine looked up. He spoke calmly. 'Okay, you've got one. We are *not* shutting down. We're going to wait.'

Jabba's jaw dropped. '*What?* But that's—'

'A gamble,' Fontaine interrupted. 'A gamble we just might win.' He took Jabba's cellular and punched a few keys. 'Midge,' he said. 'It's Leland Fontaine. Listen carefully. . . .'

CHAPTER 112

'You better know what the hell you're doing, Director,' Jabba hissed. 'We're about to lose shutdown capability.'

Fontaine did not respond.

As if on cue, the door at the back of the control room opened, and Midge came dashing in. She arrived breathless at the podium. 'Director! The switchboard is patching it through right now!'

Fontaine turned expectantly toward the screen on the front wall. Fifteen seconds later the screen crackled to life.

The image on screen was snowy and stilted at first, and gradually grew sharper. It was a QuickTime digital transmission – only five frames per second. The image revealed two men. One was pale with a buzz cut, the other a blond all-American. They were seated facing the camera like two newscasters waiting to go on the air.

'What the hell is this?' Jabba demanded.

'Sit tight,' Fontaine ordered.

The men appeared to be inside a van of some sort. Electronic cabling hung all around them. The audio connection crackled to life. Suddenly there was background noise.

'Inbound audio,' a technician called from behind them. 'Five seconds till two-way.'

'Who are they?' Brinkerhoff asked, uneasily.

'Eye in the sky,' Fontaine replied, gazing up at the two men he had sent to Spain. It had been a necessary precaution. Fontaine had believed in almost every aspect of Strathmore's plan – the regrettable but necessary removal of Ensei Tankado, rewriting Digital Fortress – it was all solid. But there was one thing that made Fontaine nervous: the use of Hulohot. Hulohot was skilled, but he was a mercenary. Was he trustworthy? Would he take the pass-key for himself? Fontaine wanted Hulohot covered, just in case, and he had taken the requisite measures.

CHAPTER 113

'Absolutely not!' the man with the buzz cut yelled into the camera. 'We have orders! We report to Director Leland Fontaine and Leland Fontaine only!'

Fontaine looked mildly amused. 'You don't know who I am, do you?'

'Doesn't matter, does it?' the blond fired hotly.

'Let me explain,' Fontaine interjected. 'Let me explain something right now.'

Seconds later, the two men were red-faced, spilling their guts to the director of the National Security Agency. 'D-director,' the blond stammered, 'I'm Agent Coliander. This is Agent Smith.'

'Fine,' Fontaine said. 'Just brief us.'

At the back of the room, Susan Fletcher sat and fought the suffocating loneliness that pressed down around her. Eyes closed, and ears ringing, she wept. Her body had gone numb. The mayhem in the control room faded to a dull murmur.

The gathering on the podium listened, restless, as Agent Smith began his briefing.

'On your orders, Director,' Smith began, 'we've

been here in Seville for two days, trailing Mr Ensei Tankado.'

'Tell me about the kill,' Fontaine said impatiently.

Smith nodded. 'We observed from inside the van at about fifty meters. The kill was smooth. Hulohot was obviously a pro. But afterward his directive went awry. Company arrived. Hulohot never got the item.'

Fontaine nodded. The agents had contacted him in South America with news that something had gone wrong, so Fontaine had cut his trip short.

Coliander took over. 'We stayed with Hulohot as you ordered. But he never made a move for the morgue. Instead, he picked up the trail of some other guy. Looked private. Coat and tie.'

'Private?' Fontaine mused. It sounded like a Strathmore play – wisely keeping the NSA out of it.

'FTP filters failing!' a technician called out.

'We need the item,' Fontaine pressed. 'Where is Hulohot now?'

Smith looked over his shoulder. 'Well . . . he's with us, sir.'

Fontaine exhaled. 'Where?' It was the best news he'd heard all day.

Smith reached toward the lens to make an adjustment. The camera swept across the inside of the van to reveal two limp bodies propped against the back wall. Both were motionless. One was a large man with twisted wire-rim glasses. The other was young with a shock of dark hair and a bloody shirt.

'Hulohot's the one on the left,' Smith offered.

'Hulohot's dead?' the director demanded.

'Yes, sir.'

Fontaine knew there would be time for explanations

later. He glanced up at the thinning shields. 'Agent Smith,' he said slowly and clearly. 'The item. I need it.'

Smith looked sheepish. 'Sir, we still have no idea *what* the item is. We're on a need-to-know.'

CHAPTER 114

'Then look again!' Fontaine declared.

The director watched in dismay as the stilted image of the agents searched the two limp bodies in the van for a list of random numbers and letters.

Jabba was pale. 'Oh my God, they can't find it. We're dead!'

'Losing FTP filters!' a voice yelled. 'Third shield's exposed!' There was a new flurry of activity.

On the front screen, the agent with the buzz cut held out his arms in defeat. 'Sir, the pass-key isn't here. We've searched both men. Pockets. Clothing. Wallets. No sign at all. Hulohot was wearing a Monocle computer, and we've checked that too. It doesn't look like he ever transmitted anything remotely resembling random characters – only a list of kills.'

'Dammit!' Fontaine seethed, suddenly losing his cool. 'It's got to be there! Keep looking!'

Jabba had apparently seen enough – Fontaine had gambled and lost. Jabba took over. The huge Sys-Sec descended from his pulpit like a storm off a mountain. He swept through his army of programmers calling out commands. 'Access auxiliary kills! Start shutting it down! Do it now!'

'We'll never make it!' Soshi yelled. 'We need a half hour! By the time we shut down, it will be too late!'

Jabba opened his mouth to reply, but he was cut short by a scream of agony from the back of the room.

Everyone turned. Like an apparition, Susan Fletcher rose from her crouched position in the rear of the chamber. Her face was white, her eyes transfixed on the freeze-frame of David Becker, motionless and bloody, propped up on the floor of the van.

'You killed him!' she screamed. *'You killed him!'* She stumbled toward the image and reached out. 'David . . .'

Everyone looked up in confusion. Susan advanced, still calling, her eyes never leaving the projection of David's body. 'David,' she gasped, staggering forward. 'Oh, David . . . how could they—'

Fontaine seemed lost. 'You know this man?'

Susan swayed unsteadily as she passed the podium. She stopped a few feet in front of the enormous projection and stared up, bewildered and numb, calling over and over to the man she loved.

CHAPTER 115

The emptiness in David Becker's mind was absolute. *I am dead.* And yet there was a sound. A distant voice . . .

'David.'

There was a dizzying burning beneath his arm. His blood was filled with fire. *My body is not my own.* And yet there was a voice, calling to him. It was thin, distant. But it was part of him. There were other voices too – unfamiliar, unimportant. Calling out. He fought to block them out. There was only one voice that mattered. It faded in and out.

'David . . . I'm sorry . . .'

There was a mottled light. Faint at first, a single slit of grayness. Growing. Becker tried to move. Pain. He tried to speak. Silence. The voice kept calling.

Someone was near him, lifting him. Becker moved toward the voice. Or was he being moved? It was calling. He gazed absently at the illuminated image. He could see her on a small screen. It was a woman, staring up at him from another world. *Is she watching me die?*

'David . . .'

The voice was familiar. She was an angel. She had come for him. The angel spoke. 'David, I love you.'

Suddenly he knew.

Susan reached out toward the screen, crying, laughing, lost in a torrent of emotions. She wiped fiercely at her tears. 'David, I – I thought . . .'

Field Agent Smith eased David Becker into the seat facing the monitor. 'He's a little woozy, ma'am. Give him a second.'

'B-but,' Susan was stammering, 'I saw a transmission. It said . . .'

Smith nodded. 'We saw it too. Hulohot counted his chickens a little early.'

'But the blood . . .'

'Flesh wound,' Smith replied. 'We slapped a gauze on it.'

Susan couldn't speak.

Agent Coliander piped in from off camera. 'We hit him with the new J23 – long-acting stun gun. Probably hurt like hell, but we got him off the street.'

'Don't worry, ma'am,' Smith assured. 'He'll be fine.'

David Becker stared at the TV monitor in front of him. He was disoriented, light-headed. The image on the screen was of a room – a room filled with chaos. Susan was there. She was standing on an open patch of floor, gazing up at him.

She was crying and laughing. 'David. Thank God! I thought I had lost you!'

He rubbed his temple. He moved in front of the screen and pulled the gooseneck microphone toward his mouth. 'Susan?'

Susan gazed up in wonder. David's rugged features

now filled the entire wall before her. His voice boomed.

'Susan, I need to ask you something.' The resonance and volume of Becker's voice seemed to momentarily suspend the action in the databank. Everyone stopped midstride and turned.

'Susan Fletcher,' the voice resonated, 'will you marry me?'

A hush spread across the room. A clipboard clattered to the floor along with a mug of pencils. No one bent to pick them up. There was only the faint hum of the terminal fans and the sound of David Becker's steady breathing in his microphone.

'D-David . . .' Susan stammered, unaware that thirty-seven people stood riveted behind her. 'You already asked me, remember? Five months ago. I said yes.'

'I know.' He smiled. 'But this time' – he extended his left hand into the camera and displayed a golden band on his fourth finger – 'this time I have a ring.'

CHAPTER 116

'Read it, Mr Becker!' Fontaine ordered.

Jabba sat sweating, hands poised over his keyboard. 'Yes,' he said, 'read the blessed inscription!'

Susan Fletcher stood with them, weak-kneed and aglow. Everyone in the room had stopped what they were doing and stared up at the enormous projection of David Becker. The professor twisted the ring in his fingers and studied the engraving.

'And read *carefully!*' Jabba commanded. 'One typo, and we're *screwed!*'

Fontaine gave Jabba a harsh look. If there was one thing the director of the NSA knew about, it was pressure situations; creating additional tension was never wise. 'Relax, Mr Becker. If we make a mistake, we'll reenter the code till we get it right.'

'Bad advice, Mr Becker,' Jabba snapped. 'Get it right the first time. Kill-codes usually have a penalty clause – to prevent trial-and-error guessing. Make an incorrect entry, and the cycle will probably accelerate. Make *two* incorrect entries, and it will lock us out permanently. Game over.'

The director frowned and turned back to the screen.

'Mr Becker? My mistake. Read carefully – read *extremely* carefully.'

Becker nodded and studied the ring for a moment. Then he calmly began reciting the inscription. 'Q . . . U . . . I . . . S . . . space . . . C . . .'

Jabba and Susan interrupted in unison. *'Space?'* Jabba stopped typing. 'There's a *space?'*

Becker shrugged, checking the ring. 'Yeah. There's a bunch of them.'

'Am I missing something?' Fontaine demanded. 'What are we waiting for?'

'Sir,' Susan said, apparently puzzled. 'It's . . . it's just . . .'

'I agree,' Jabba said. 'It's strange. Passwords *never* have spaces.'

Brinkerhoff swallowed hard. 'So, what are you saying?'

'He's saying,' Susan interjected, 'that this may not be a kill-code.'

Brinkerhoff cried out, 'Of course it's the kill-code! What else could it be? Why else would Tankado give it away? Who the hell inscribes a bunch of random letters on a ring?'

Fontaine silenced Brinkerhoff with a sharp glare.

'Ah . . . folks?' Becker interjected, appearing hesitant to get involved. 'You keep mentioning *random* letters. I think I should let you know . . . the letters on this ring *aren't* random.'

Everyone on the podium blurted in unison. 'What!'

Becker looked uneasy. 'Sorry, but there are definitely words here. I'll admit they're inscribed pretty close together; at first glance it appears random, but if you look closely you'll see the inscription is actually . . . well . . . it's *Latin.'*

Jabba gaped. 'You're shitting me!'

Becker shook his head. 'No. It reads, *"Quis custodiet ipsos custodes."* It translates roughly to—'

'Who will guard the guards!' Susan interrupted, finishing David's sentence.

Becker did a double-take. 'Susan, I didn't know you could—'

'It's from *Satires* of Juvenal,' she exclaimed. 'Who will guard the guards? Who will guard the NSA while we guard the world? It was Tankado's favorite saying!'

'So,' Midge demanded, 'is it the pass-key, or not?'

'It *must* be the pass-key,' Brinkerhoff declared.

Fontaine stood silent, apparently processing the information.

'I don't know if it's the key,' Jabba said. 'It seems unlikely to me that Tankado would use a nonrandom construction.'

'Just omit the spaces,' Brinkerhoff cried, 'and type the damn code!'

Fontaine turned to Susan. 'What's *your* take, Ms Fletcher?'

She thought a moment. She couldn't quite put her finger on it, but something didn't feel right. Susan knew Tankado well enough to know he thrived on simplicity. His proofs and programming were always crystalline and absolute. The fact that the spaces needed to be removed seemed odd. It was a minor detail, but it was a flaw, definitely not *clean* – not what Susan would have expected as Ensei Tankado's crowning blow.

'It doesn't feel right,' Susan finally said. 'I don't think it's the key.'

Fontaine sucked in a long breath, his dark eyes probing hers. 'Ms Fletcher, in your mind, if this is not

465

the key, why would Ensei Tankado have given it away? If he knew we'd murdered him – don't you assume he'd want to punish us by making the ring disappear?'

A new voice interrupted the dialogue. 'Ah . . . Director?'

All eyes turned to the screen. It was Agent Coliander in Seville. He was leaning over Becker's shoulder and speaking into the mic. 'For whatever it's worth, I'm not so sure Mr Tankado *knew* he was being murdered.'

'I beg your pardon?' Fontaine demanded.

'Hulohot was a pro, sir. We saw the kill – only fifty meters away. All evidence suggests Tankado was unaware.'

'Evidence?' Brinkerhoff demanded. '*What* evidence? Tankado gave away this ring. That's proof enough!'

'Agent Smith,' Fontaine interrupted. 'What makes you think Ensei Tankado was unaware he was being killed?'

Smith cleared his throat. 'Hulohot killed him with an NTB – a noninvasive trauma bullet. It's a rubber pod that strikes the chest and spreads out. Silent. Very clean. Mr Tankado would only have felt a sharp thump before going into cardiac arrest.'

'A trauma bullet,' Becker mused to himself. 'That explains the bruising.'

'It's doubtful,' Smith added, 'that Tankado associated the sensation with a gunman.'

'And yet he gave away his ring,' Fontaine stated.

'True, sir. But he never looked for his assailant. A victim *always* looks for his assailant when he's been shot. It's instinct.'

466

Fontaine puzzled. 'And you're saying Tankado didn't look for Hulohot?'

'No, sir. We have it on film if you'd like—'

'X-eleven filter's going!' a technician yelled. 'The worm's halfway there!'

'Forget the film,' Brinkerhoff declared. 'Type in the damn kill-code and finish this!'

Jabba sighed, suddenly the cool one. 'Director, if we enter the wrong code . . .'

'Yes,' Susan interrupted, 'if Tankado didn't suspect we killed him, we've got some questions to answer.'

'What's our time frame, Jabba?' Fontaine demanded.

Jabba looked up at the VR. 'About twenty minutes. I suggest we use the time wisely.'

Fontaine was silent a long moment. Then sighed heavily. 'All right. Run the film.'

CHAPTER 117

'Transmitting video in ten seconds,' Agent Smith's voice crackled. 'We're dropping every other frame as well as audio – we'll run as close to real time as possible.'

Everyone on the podium stood silent, watching, waiting. Jabba typed a few keys and rearranged the video wall. Tankado's message appeared on the far left:

ONLY THE TRUTH WILL SAVE YOU NOW

On the right of the wall was the static interior shot of the van with Becker and the two agents huddled around the camera. In the center, a fuzzy frame appeared. It dissolved into static and then into a black and white image of a park.

'Transmitting,' Agent Smith announced.

The shot looked like an old movie. It was stilted and jerky – a by-product of frame-dropping, a process that halved the amount of information sent and enabled faster transmission.

The shot panned out across an enormous concourse enclosed on one end by a semicircular facade – the

Seville Ayuntamiento. There were trees in the fore-ground. The park was empty.

'X-eleven's are down!' a technician called out. 'This bad boy's hungry!'

Smith began to narrate. His commentary had the detachment of a seasoned agent. 'This is shot from the van,' he said, 'about fifty meters from the kill zone. Tankado is approaching from the right. Hulohot's in the trees to the left.'

'We've got a time crunch here,' Fontaine pressed. 'Let's get to the meat of it.'

Agent Coliander touched a few buttons, and the frame speed increased.

Everyone on the podium watched in anticipation as their former associate, Ensei Tankado, came into the frame. The accelerated video made the whole image seem comic. Tankado shuffled jerkily out onto the concourse, apparently taking in the scenery. He shielded his eyes and gazed up at the spires of the huge facade.

'This is it,' Smith warned. 'Hulohot's a pro. He took his first open shot.'

Smith was right. There was a flash of light from behind the trees on the left of the screen. An instant later Tankado clutched his chest. He staggered momentarily. The camera zoomed in on him, unstable – in and out of focus.

As the footage rolled in high speed, Smith coldly continued his narration. 'As you can see, Tankado is instantly in cardiac arrest.'

Susan felt ill watching the images. Tankado clutched at his chest with crippled hands, a confused look of terror on his face.

'You'll notice,' Smith added, 'his eyes are focused downward, at himself. Not once does he look around.'

'And that's important?' Jabba half stated, half inquired.

'Very,' Smith said. 'If Tankado suspected foul play of any kind, he would instinctively search the area. But as you can see, he does not.'

On the screen, Tankado dropped to his knees, still clutching his chest. He never once looked up. Ensei Tankado was a man alone, dying a private, natural death.

'It's odd,' Smith said, puzzled. 'Trauma pods usually won't kill this quickly. Sometimes, if the target's big enough, they don't kill at all.'

'Bad heart,' Fontaine said flatly.

Smith arched his eyebrows, impressed. 'Fine choice of weapon, then.'

Susan watched as Tankado toppled from his knees to his side and finally onto his back. He lay, staring upward, grabbing at his chest. Suddenly the camera wheeled away from him back toward the grove of trees. A man appeared. He was wearing wire-rim glasses and carrying an oversize briefcase. As he approached the concourse and the writhing Tankado, his fingers began tapping in a strange silent dance on a mechanism attached to his hand.

'He's working his Monocle,' Smith announced. 'Sending a message that Tankado is terminated.' Smith turned to Becker and chuckled. 'Looks like Hulohot had a bad habit of transmitting kills before his victim actually expired.'

Coliander sped the film up some more, and the camera followed Hulohot as he began moving toward his victim. Suddenly an elderly man rushed out of a

470

nearby courtyard, ran over to Tankado, and knelt beside him. Hulohot slowed his approach. A moment later two more people appeared from the courtyard – an obese man and a red-haired woman. They also came to Tankado's side.

'Unfortunate choice of kill zone,' Smith said. 'Hulohot thought he had the victim isolated.'

On the screen, Hulohot watched for a moment and then shrank back into the trees, apparently to wait.

'Here comes the handoff,' Smith prompted. 'We didn't notice it the first time around.'

Susan gazed up at the sickening image on the screen. Tankado was gasping for breath, apparently trying to communicate something to the Samaritans kneeling beside him. Then, in desperation, he thrust his left hand above him, almost hitting the old man in the face. He held the crippled appendage outward before the old man's eyes. The camera tightened on Tankado's three deformed fingers, and on one of them, clearly glistening in the Spanish sun, was the golden ring. Tankado thrust it out again. The old man recoiled. Tankado turned to the woman. He held his three deformed fingers directly in front of her face, as if begging her to understand. The ring glinted in the sun. The woman looked away. Tankado, now choking, unable to make a sound, turned to the obese man and tried one last time.

The elderly man suddenly stood and dashed off, presumably to get help. Tankado seemed to be weakening, but he was still holding the ring in the fat man's face. The fat man reached out and held the dying man's wrist, supporting it. Tankado seemed to gaze upward at his own fingers, at his own ring, and then to the man's eyes. As a final plea before death, Ensei

471

Tankado gave the man an almost imperceptible nod, as if to say *yes*.

Then Tankado fell limp.

'Jesus,' Jabba moaned.

Suddenly the camera swept to where Hulohot had been hiding. The assassin was gone. A police motor-cycle appeared, tearing up Avenida Firelli. The camera wheeled back to where Tankado was lying. The woman kneeling beside him apparently heard the police sirens; she glanced around nervously and then began pulling at her obese companion, begging him to leave. The two hurried off.

The camera tightened on Tankado, his hands folded on his lifeless chest. The ring on his finger was gone.

CHAPTER 118

'It's proof,' Fontaine said decidedly. 'Tankado dumped the ring. He wanted it as far from himself as possible – so we'd never find it.'

'But, Director,' Susan argued, 'it doesn't make sense. If Tankado was unaware he'd been murdered, *why* would he give away the kill code?'

'I agree,' Jabba said. 'The kid's a rebel, but he's a rebel with a conscience. Getting us to admit to TRANSLTR is one thing; revealing our classified data-bank is another.'

Fontaine stared, disbelieving. 'You think Tankado *wanted* to stop this worm? You think his dying thoughts were for the poor NSA?'

'Tunnel-block corroding!' a technician yelled. 'Full vulnerability in fifteen minutes, maximum!'

'I'll tell you what,' the director declared, taking control. 'In fifteen minutes, every Third World country on the planet will learn how to build an intercontinental ballistic missile. If someone in this room thinks he's got a better candidate for a kill code than this ring, I'm all ears.' The director waited. No one spoke. He returned his gaze to Jabba and locked eyes. 'Tankado dumped that ring for a reason, Jabba. Whether he was trying to bury it, or whether he thought the fat guy would run to a pay phone and call us with the information, I really don't care. But I've made the decision. We're entering that quote. Now.'

Jabba took a long breath. He knew Fontaine was right – there was no better option. They were running out of time. Jabba sat. 'Okay . . . let's do it.' He pulled himself to the keyboard. 'Mr Becker? The inscription, please. Nice and easy.'

David Becker read the inscription, and Jabba typed. When they were done, they double-checked the spelling and omitted all the spaces. On the center panel of the view wall, near the top, were the letters:

QUISCUSTODIETIPSOSCUSTODES

'I don't like it,' Susan muttered softly. 'It's not clean.'

Jabba hesitated, hovering over the ENTER key.

'Do it,' Fontaine commanded.

Jabba hit the key. Seconds later the whole room knew it was a mistake.

CHAPTER 119

'It's accelerating!' Soshi yelled from the back of the room. 'It's the wrong code!'

Everyone stood in silent horror.

On the screen before them was the error message:

ILLEGAL ENTRY. NUMERIC FIELD ONLY.

'Damn it!' Jabba screamed. 'Numeric *only!* We're looking for a goddamn number! We're fucked! This ring is shit!'

'Worm's at double speed!' Soshi shouted. 'Penalty round!'

On the center screen, right beneath the error message, the VR painted a terrifying image. As the third firewall gave way, the half-dozen or so black lines representing marauding hackers surged forward, advancing relentlessly toward the core. With each passing moment, a new line appeared. Then another.

'They're swarming!' Soshi yelled.

'Confirming overseas tie-ins!' cried another technician. 'Word's out!'

Susan averted her gaze from the image of the

collapsing firewalls and turned to the side screen. The footage of Ensei Tankado's kill was on endless loop. It was the same every time – Tankado clutching his chest, falling, and with a look of desperate panic, forcing his ring on a group of unsuspecting tourists. *It makes no sense,* she thought. *If he didn't know we'd killed him . . .* Susan drew a total blank. It was too late. *We've missed something.*

On the VR, the number of hackers pounding at the gates had doubled in the last few minutes. From now on, the number would increase exponentially. Hackers, like hyenas, were one big family, always eager to spread the word of a new kill.

Leland Fontaine had apparently seen enough. 'Shut it down,' he declared. 'Shut the damn thing down.'

Jabba stared straight ahead like the captain of a sinking ship. 'Too late, sir. We're going down.'

CHAPTER 120

The four-hundred-pound Sys-Sec stood motionless, hands resting atop his head in a freeze-frame of disbelief. He'd ordered a power shutdown, but it would be a good twenty minutes too late. Sharks with high-speed modems would be able to download staggering quantities of classified information in that window.

Jabba was awakened from his nightmare by Soshi rushing to the podium with a new printout. 'I've found something, sir!' she said excitedly. 'Orphans in the source! Alpha groupings. All over the place!'

Jabba was unmoved. 'We're looking for a numeric, dammit! Not an alpha! The kill-code is a *number*!'

'But we've got orphans! Tankado's too good to leave orphans – especially this many!'

The term 'orphans' referred to extra lines of programming that didn't serve the program's objective in any way. They fed nothing, referred to nothing, led nowhere, and were usually removed as part of the final debugging and compiling process.

Jabba took the printout and studied it.

Fontaine stood silent.

Susan peered over Jabba's shoulder at the printout. 'We're being attacked by a *rough draft* of Tankado's worm?'

'Polished or not,' Jabba retorted, 'it's kicking our ass.'

'I don't buy it,' Susan argued. 'Tankado was a perfectionist. You know that. There's no way he left bugs in his program.'

'There are lots of them!' Soshi cried. She grabbed the printout from Jabba and pushed it in front of Susan. 'Look!'

Susan nodded. Sure enough, after every twenty or so lines of programming, there were four free-floating characters. Susan scanned them.

PFEE
SESN
RETM

'Four-bit alpha groupings,' she puzzled. 'They're definitely not part of the programming.'

'Forget it,' Jabba growled. 'You're grabbing at straws.'

'Maybe not,' Susan said. 'A lot of encryption uses four-bit groupings. This could be a code.'

'Yeah.' Jabba groaned. 'It says – "Ha, ha. You're fucked."' He looked up at the VR. 'In about nine minutes.'

Susan ignored Jabba and locked in on Soshi. 'How many orphans are there?'

Soshi shrugged. She commandeered Jabba's terminal and typed all the groupings. When she was done, she pushed back from the terminal. The room looked up at the screen.

```
PFEE SESN RETM MFHA IRWE OOIG MEEN NRMA
ENET SHAS DCNS IIAA IEER BRNK FBLE LODI
```

Susan was the only one smiling. 'Sure looks familiar,' she said. 'Blocks of four – just like Enigma.'

The director nodded. Enigma was history's most famous code-writing machine – the Nazis' twelve-ton encryption beast. It had encrypted in blocks of four.

'Great.' He moaned. 'You wouldn't happen to have one lying around, would you?'

'That's not the point!' Susan said, suddenly coming to life. This was her specialty. 'The point is that this is a code. Tankado left us a clue! He's taunting us, daring us to figure out the pass-key in time. He's laying hints just out of our reach!'

'Absurd,' Jabba snapped. 'Tankado gave us only one out – revealing TRANSLTR. That was it. That was our escape. We blew it.'

'I have to agree with him,' Fontaine said. 'I doubt there's any way Tankado would risk letting us off the hook by hinting at his kill-code.'

Susan nodded vaguely, but she recalled how Tankado had given them NDAKOTA. She stared up at the letters wondering if he were playing another one of his games.

'Tunnel block half gone!' a technician called.

On the VR, the mass of black tie-in lines surged deeper into the two remaining shields.

David had been sitting quietly, watching the drama unfold on the monitor before them. 'Susan?' he offered. 'I have an idea. Is that text in sixteen groupings of four?'

'Oh, for Christ's sake,' Jabba said under his breath. 'Now everyone wants to play?'

Susan ignored Jabba and counted the groupings. 'Yes. Sixteen.'

'Take out the spaces,' Becker said firmly.

'David,' Susan replied, slightly embarrassed. 'I don't think you understand. The groupings of four are—'

'Take out the spaces,' he repeated.

Susan hesitated a moment and then nodded to Soshi. Soshi quickly removed the spaces. The result was no more enlightening.

PFEESESNRETMMFHAIRWEOOIGMEENNRM
AENETSHASDCNSIIAAIEERBRNKFBLELODI

Jabba exploded. 'ENOUGH! Playtime's over! This thing's on double-speed! We've got about eight minutes here! We're looking for a *number*, not a bunch of half-baked letters!'

'Four by sixteen,' David said calmly. 'Do the math, Susan.'

Susan eyed David's image on the screen. *Do the math? He's terrible at math!* She knew David could memorize verb conjugations and vocabulary like a Xerox machine, but math? . . .

'Multiplication tables,' Becker said.

Multiplication tables, Susan wondered. *What is he talking about?*

'Four by sixteen,' the professor repeated. 'I had to memorize multiplication tables in fourth grade.'

Susan pictured the standard grade school multiplication table. *Four by sixteen.* 'Sixty-four,' she said blankly. 'So what?'

David leaned toward the camera. His face filled the frame. 'Sixty-four letters . . .'

Susan nodded. 'Yes, but they're—' Susan froze.

'Sixty-four letters,' David repeated.

Susan gasped. 'Oh my God! David, you're a genius!'

CHAPTER 121

'*Seven minutes!*' a technician called out.

'Eight rows of eight!' Susan shouted, excited.

Soshi typed. Fontaine looked on silently. The second to last shield was growing thin.

'Sixty-four letters!' Susan was in control. 'It's a perfect square!'

'Perfect square?' Jabba demanded. 'So *what?*'

Ten seconds later Soshi had rearranged the seemingly random letters on the screen. They were now in eight rows of eight. Jabba studied the letters and threw up his hands in despair. The new layout was no more revealing than the original.

P	F	E	E	S	E	S	N
R	E	T	M	P	F	H	A
I	R	W	E	O	O	I	G
M	E	E	N	N	R	M	A
E	N	E	T	S	H	A	S
D	C	N	S	I	I	A	A
I	E	E	R	B	R	N	K
F	B	L	E	L	O	D	I

'Clear as shit.' Jabba groaned.

'Ms Fletcher,' Fontaine demanded, 'explain your-self.' All eyes turned to Susan.

Susan was staring up at the block of text. Gradually she began nodding, then broke into a wide smile. 'David, I'll be damned!'

Everyone on the podium exchanged baffled looks.

David winked at the tiny image of Susan Fletcher on the screen before him. 'Sixty-four letters. Julius Caesar strikes again.'

Midge looked lost. 'What are you talking about?'

'Caesar box.' Susan beamed. 'Read top to bottom. Tankado's sending us a message.'

CHAPTER 122

'Six minutes!' a technician called out.

Susan shouted orders. 'Retype top to bottom! Read down, not across!'

Soshi furiously moved down the columns, retyping the text.

'Julius Caesar sent codes this way!' Susan blurted. 'His letter count was always a perfect square!'

'Done!' Soshi yelled.

Everyone looked up at the newly arranged, single line of text on the wall-screen.

'Still garbage,' Jabba scoffed in disgust. 'Look at it. It's totally random bits of—' The words lodged in his throat. His eyes widened to saucers. 'Oh . . . oh my . . .'

Fontaine had seen it too. He arched his eyebrows, obviously impressed.

Midge and Brinkerhoff both cooed in unison. 'Holy . . . shit.'

The sixty-four letters now read:

PRIMEDIFFERENCEBETWEENELEMENTS

RESPONSIBLEFORHIROSHIMAANDNAGASAKI

'Put in the spaces,' Susan ordered. 'We've got a puzzle to solve.'

CHAPTER 123

An ashen technician ran to the podium. 'Tunnel block's about to go!'

Jabba turned to the VR onscreen. The attackers surged forward, only a whisker away from their assault on the fifth and final wall. The databank was running out of time.

Susan blocked out the chaos around her. She read Tankado's bizarre message over and over.

PRIME DIFFERENCE BETWEEN ELEMENTS
RESPONSIBLE FOR HIROSHIMA AND NAGASAKI

'It's not even a question!' Brinkerhoff cried. 'How can it have an answer?'

'We need a number,' Jabba reminded. 'The kill-code is *numeric*.'

'Silence,' Fontaine said evenly. He turned and addressed Susan. 'Ms Fletcher, you've gotten us this far. I need your best guess.'

Susan took a deep breath. 'The kill-code entry field accepts numerics *only*. My guess is that this is some sort of clue as to the correct number. The text mentions Hiroshima and Nagasaki – the two cities that were hit by atomic bombs. Maybe the kill-code is related to the number of casualties, the estimated dollars of damage . . .' She paused a moment, rereading the clue. 'The word "difference" seems important. The prime *difference* between Nagasaki and Hiroshima. Apparently Tankado felt the two incidents differed somehow.'

Fontaine's expression did not change. Nonetheless, hope was fading fast. It seemed the political backdrops surrounding the two most devastating blasts in history needed to be analyzed, compared, and translated into some magic number . . . and all within the next five minutes.

CHAPTER 124

'Final shield under attack!'

On the VR, the PEM authorization programming was now being consumed. Black, penetrating lines engulfed the final protective shield and began forcing their way toward its core.

Prowling hackers were now appearing from all over the world. The number was doubling almost every minute. Before long, anyone with a computer – foreign spies, radicals, terrorists – would have access to all of the U.S. government's classified information.

As technicians tried vainly to sever power, the assembly on the podium studied the message. Even David and the two NSA agents were trying to crack the code from their van in Spain.

PRIME DIFFERENCE BETWEEN ELEMENTS
RESPONSIBLE FOR HIROSHIMA AND NAGASAKI

Soshi thought aloud. 'The elements responsible for Hiroshima and Nagasaki . . . Pearl Harbor? Hirohito's refusal to . . .'

488

'We need a *number*,' Jabba repeated, 'not political theories. We're talking *mathematics* – not history!'

Soshi fell silent.

'How about payloads?' Brinkerhoff offered. 'Casualties? Dollars damage?'

'We're looking for an *exact* figure,' Susan reminded. 'Damage estimates vary.' She stared up at the message. 'The elements responsible . . .'

Three thousand miles away, David Becker's eyes flew open. 'Elements!' he declared. 'We're talking math, not history!'

All heads turned toward the satellite screen.

'Tankado's playing word games!' Becker spouted. 'The word "elements" has multiple meanings!'

'Spit it out, Mr Becker,' Fontaine snapped.

'He's talking about *chemical* elements – not socio-political ones!'

Becker's announcement met blank looks.

'Elements!' he prompted. 'The periodic table! *Chemical* elements! Didn't any of you see the movie *Fat Man and Little Boy* – about the Manhattan Project? The two atomic bombs were different. They used different fuel – different *elements!*'

Soshi clapped her hands. 'Yes! He's right! I read that! The two bombs used different fuels! One used uranium and one used plutonium! Two *different* elements!'

A hush swept across the room.

'Uranium and plutonium!' Jabba exclaimed, suddenly hopeful. 'The clue asks for the *difference* between the two elements!' He spun to his army of workers. 'The difference between uranium and plutonium! Who knows what it is?'

Blank stares all around.

'Come on!' Jabba said. 'Didn't you kids go to college? Somebody! Anybody! I need the difference between plutonium and uranium!'

No response.

Susan turned to Soshi. 'I need access to the Web. Is there a browser here?'

Soshi nodded. 'Netscape's sweetest.'

Susan grabbed her hand. 'Come on. We're going surfing.'

CHAPTER 125

'How much time?' Jabba demanded from the podium.

There was no response from the technicians in the back. They stood riveted, staring up at the VR. The final shield was getting dangerously thin.

Nearby, Susan and Soshi pored over the results of their Websearch. 'Outlaw Labs?' Susan asked. 'Who are they?'

Soshi shrugged. 'You want me to open it?'

'Damn right,' she said. 'Six hundred forty-seven text references to uranium, plutonium, and atomic bombs. Sounds like our best bet.'

Soshi opened the link. A disclaimer appeared.

The information contained in this file is strictly for academic use only. Any layperson attempting to construct any of the devices described runs the risk of radiation poisoning and/or self-explosion.

'Self-explosion?' Soshi said. 'Jesus.'

'Search it,' Fontaine snapped over his shoulder. 'Let's see what we've got.'

Soshi plowed into the document. She scrolled past a

recipe for urea nitrate, an explosive ten times more powerful than dynamite. The information rolled by like a recipe for butterscotch brownies.

'Plutonium and uranium,' Jabba repeated. 'Let's focus.'

'Go back,' Susan ordered. 'The document's too big. Find the table of contents.'

Soshi scrolled backward until she found it.

I.   Mechanism of an Atomic Bomb
    A) Altimeter
    B) Air Pressure Detonator
    C) Detonating Heads
    D) Explosive Charges
    E) Neutron Deflector
    F) Uranium & Plutonium
    G) Lead Shield
    H) Fuses
II. Nuclear Fission/Nuclear Fusion
    A) Fission (A-Bomb) & Fusion (H-Bomb)
    B) U-235, U-238, and Plutonium
III. History of the Atomic Weapons
    A) Development (The Manhattan Project)
    B) Detonation
       1) Hiroshima
       2) Nagasaki
       3) By-products of Atomic Detonations
       4) Blast Zones

'Section two!' Susan cried. 'Uranium and plutonium! Go!'

Everyone waited while Soshi found the right section. 'This is it,' she said. 'Hold on.' She quickly scanned the data. 'There's a lot of information here. A whole chart. How do we know which difference we're looking for? One occurs naturally, one is man-made. Plutonium was first discovered by—'

'A *number*,' Jabba reminded. 'We need a *number*.'

Susan reread Tankado's message. *The prime difference between the elements . . . the difference between . . . we need a number . . .* 'Wait!' she said. 'The word "difference" has multiple meanings. We need a *number* – so we're talking *math*. It's another of Tankado's word games – "difference" means *subtraction*.'

'Yes!' Becker agreed from the screen overhead. 'Maybe the elements have different numbers of protons or something? If you subtract—'

'He's right!' Jabba said, turning to Soshi. 'Are there any *numbers* on that chart? Proton counts? Half-lives? Anything we can subtract?'

'*Three minutes!*' a technician called.

'How about supercritical mass?' Soshi ventured. 'It says the supercritical mass for plutonium is 35.2 pounds.'

'Yes!' Jabba said. 'Check uranium! What's the supercritical mass of uranium?'

Soshi searched. 'Um . . . 110 pounds.'

'One hundred ten?' Jabba looked suddenly hopeful. 'What's 35.2 from 110?'

'Seventy-four point eight,' Susan snapped. 'But I don't think—'

'Out of my way,' Jabba commanded, plowing toward the keyboard. 'That's got to be the kill-code! The difference between their critical masses! Seventy-four point eight!'

'Hold on,' Susan said, peering over Soshi's shoulder. 'There's more here. Atomic weights. Neutron counts. Extraction techniques.' She skimmed the chart. 'Uranium splits into barium and krypton; plutonium does something else. Uranium has 92 protons and 146 neutrons, but—'

'We need the most *obvious* difference,' Midge chimed in. 'The clue reads "the *primary* difference between the elements." '

'Jesus Christ!' Jabba swore. 'How do we know what Tankado considered the *primary* difference?'

David interrupted. 'Actually, the clue reads *prime*, not *primary*.'

The word hit Susan right between the eyes. *'Prime!'* she exclaimed. *'Prime!'* She spun to Jabba. 'The killcode is a *prime* number! Think about it! It makes perfect sense!'

Jabba instantly knew Susan was right. Ensei Tankado had built his career on prime numbers. Primes were the fundamental building blocks of all encryption algorithms – unique values that had no factors other than one and themselves. Primes worked well in code writing because they were impossible for computers to guess using typical number-tree factoring.

Soshi jumped in. 'Yes! It's perfect! Primes are essential to Japanese culture! Haiku uses primes. *Three* lines and syllable counts of *five, seven, five*. All primes. The temples of Kyoto all have—'

'Enough!' Jabba said. 'Even if the kill-code *is* a prime, so what! There are endless possibilities!'

Susan knew Jabba was right. Because the number line was infinite, one could always look a little farther and find another prime number. Between zero and a million, there were over 70,000 choices. It all depended on how large a prime Tankado decided to use. The bigger it was, the harder it was to guess.

'It'll be huge,' Jabba groaned. 'Whatever prime Tankado chose is sure to be a monster.'

A call went up from the rear of the room. *Two-minute warning!'*

Jabba gazed up at the VR in defeat. The final shield was starting to crumble. Technicians were rushing everywhere.

Something in Susan told her they were close. 'We can do this!' she declared, taking control. 'Of all the differences between uranium and plutonium, I bet only one can be represented as a *prime* number! That's our final clue. The number we're looking for is prime!'

Jabba eyed the uranium/plutonium chart on the monitor and threw up his arms. 'There must be a hundred entries here! There's no way we can subtract them all and check for primes.'

'A lot of the entries are *nonnumeric,'* Susan encouraged. 'We can ignore them. Uranium's natural, plutonium's man-made. Uranium uses a gun barrel detonator, plutonium uses implosion. They're not numbers, so they're irrelevant!'

'Do it,' Fontaine ordered. On the VR, the final wall was eggshell thin.

Jabba mopped his brow. 'All right, here goes nothing. Start subtracting. I'll take the top quarter. Susan, you've got the middle. Everybody else split up the rest. We're looking for a prime difference.'

Within seconds, it was clear they'd never make it. The numbers were enormous, and in many cases the units didn't match up.

'It's apples and goddamn oranges,' Jabba said. 'We've got gamma rays against electromagnetic pulse. Fissionable against unfissionable. Some is pure. Some is percentage. It's a mess!'

'It's got to be here,' Susan said firmly. 'We've got to think. There's some difference between plutonium and uranium that we're missing! Something simple!'

'Ah . . . guys?' Soshi said. She'd created a second document window and was perusing the rest of the Outlaw Labs document.

'What is it?' Fontaine demanded. 'Find something?'

'Um, sort of.' She sounded uneasy. 'You know how I told you the Nagasaki bomb was a plutonium bomb?'

'Yeah,' they all replied in unison.

'Well . . .' Soshi took a deep breath. 'Looks like I made a mistake.'

'What!' Jabba choked. 'We've been looking for the wrong thing?'

Soshi pointed to the screen. They huddled around and read the text:

. . . the common misconception that the Nagasaki bomb was a plutonium bomb. In fact, the device employed uranium, like its sister bomb in Hiroshima.

'But—' Susan gasped. 'If both elements were uranium, how are we supposed to find the difference between the two?'

'Maybe Tankado made a mistake,' Fontaine ventured. 'Maybe he didn't know the bombs were the same.'

'No.' Susan sighed. 'He was a cripple because of those bombs. He'd know the facts cold.'

CHAPTER 126

'One minute!'

Jabba eyed the VR. 'PEM authorization's going fast. Last line of defense. And there's a crowd at the door.'

'Focus!' Fontaine commanded.

Soshi sat in front of the Web browser and read aloud.

> '... Nagasaki bomb did not use plutonium but rather an artificially manufactured, neutron-saturated isotope of uranium 238.'

'Damn!' Brinkerhoff swore. 'Both bombs used uranium. The elements responsible for Hiroshima and Nagasaki were both uranium. There *is* no difference!'

'We're dead,' Midge moaned.

'Wait,' Susan said. 'Read that last part again!'

Soshi repeated the text. '.... artificially manufactured, neutron-saturated isotope of uranium 238.'

'238?' Susan exclaimed. 'Didn't we just see something that said Hiroshima's bomb used some other isotope of uranium?'

They all exchanged puzzled glances. Soshi frantically

scrolled backward and found the spot. *'Yes!* It says here that the Hiroshima bomb used a different isotope of uranium!'

Midge gasped in amazement. 'They're both uranium – but they're different kinds!'

'Both uranium?' Jabba muscled in and stared at the terminal. 'Apples and apples! Perfect!'

'How are the two isotopes different?' Fontaine demanded. 'It's got to be something basic.'

Soshi scrolled through the document. 'Hold on . . . looking . . . okay . . .'

'Forty-five seconds!' a voice called out.

Susan looked up. The final shield was almost invisible now.

'Here it is!' Soshi exclaimed.

'Read it!' Jabba was sweating. 'What's the difference! There must be some difference between the two!'

'Yes!' Soshi pointed to her monitor. 'Look!'

They all read the text:

. . . two bombs employed two different fuels . . . precisely identical chemical characteristics. No ordinary chemical extraction can separate the two isotopes. They are, with the exception of minute differences in weight, perfectly identical.

'Atomic weight!' Jabba said, excitedly. 'That's it! The only difference is their *weights!* That's the key! Give me their weights! We'll subtract them!'

'Hold on,' Soshi said, scrolling ahead. 'Almost there! *Yes!'* Everyone scanned the text.

. . . difference in weight very slight . . .

. . . gaseous diffusion to separate them . . .
. . . 10,032498X10^134 as compared to 19,39484X10
^23.**

'There they are!' Jabba screamed. 'That's it! Those are the weights!'

'Thirty seconds!'

'Go,' Fontaine whispered. 'Subtract them. Quickly.'

Jabba palmed his calculator and started entering numbers.

'What's the asterisk?' Susan demanded. 'There's an asterisk after the figures!'

Jabba ignored her. He was already working his calculator keys furiously.

'Careful!' Soshi urged. 'We need an *exact* figure.'

'The asterisk,' Susan repeated. 'There's a footnote.'

Soshi clicked to the bottom of the paragraph.

Susan read the asterisked footnote. She went white. 'Oh . . . dear God.'

Jabba looked up. 'What?'

They all leaned in, and there was a communal sigh of defeat. The tiny footnote read:

**12% margin of error. Published figures vary from lab to lab.

CHAPTER 127

There was a sudden and reverent silence among the group on the podium. It was as if they were watching an eclipse or volcanic eruption – an incredible chain of events over which they had no control. Time seemed to slow to a crawl.

'We're losing it!' a technician cried. 'Tie-ins! All lines!'

On the far-left screen, David and Agents Smith and Coliander stared blankly into their camera. On the VR, the final firewall was only a sliver. A mass of blackness surrounded it, hundreds of lines waiting to tie in. To the right of that was Tankado. The stilted clips of his final moments ran by in an endless loop. The look of desperation – fingers stretched outward, the ring glistening in the sun.

Susan watched the clip as it went in and out of focus. She stared at Tankado's eyes – they seemed filled with regret. *He never wanted it to go this far,* she told herself. *He wanted to save us.* And yet, over and over, Tankado held his fingers outward, forcing the ring in front of people's eyes. He was trying to speak but could not. He just kept thrusting his fingers forward.

In Seville, Becker's mind still turned it over and over. He mumbled to himself, 'What did they say those two isotopes were? U238 and U . . .?' He sighed heavily – it didn't matter. He was a language teacher, not a physicist.

'Incoming lines preparing to authenticate!'

'Jesus!' Jabba bellowed in frustration. 'How do the damn isotopes *differ?* Nobody knows how the hell they're different?!' There was no response. The roomful of technicians stood helplessly watching the VR. Jabba spun back to the monitor and threw up his arms. 'Where's a nuclear fucking physicist when you need one!'

Susan stared up at the QuickTime clip on the wall screen and knew it was over. In slow motion, she watched Tankado dying over and over. He was trying to speak, choking on his words, holding out his deformed hand . . . trying to communicate something. *He was trying to save the databank,* Susan told herself. *But we'll never know how.*

'Company at the door!'

Jabba stared at the screen. 'Here we go!' Sweat poured down his face.

On the center screen, the final wisp of the last firewall had all but disappeared. The black mass of lines surrounding the core was opaque and pulsating. Midge turned away. Fontaine stood rigid, eyes front. Brinkerhoff looked like he was about to get sick.

'Ten seconds!'

Susan's eyes never left Tankado's image. The desperation. The regret. His hand reached out, over and over, ring glistening, deformed fingers arched crookedly in strangers' faces. *He's telling them some-thing. What is it?*

On the screen overhead, David looked deep in thought. 'Difference,' he kept muttering to himself. 'Difference between U238 and U235. It's got to be something simple.'

A technician began the countdown. *'Five! Four! Three!'*

The word made it to Spain in just under a tenth of a second. *Three . . . three.*

It was as if David Becker had been hit by the stun gun all over again. His world slowed to a stop. *Three . . . three . . . three. 238 minus 235! The difference is* three! In slow motion, he reached for the micro-phone . . .

At that very instant, Susan was staring at Tankado's outstretched hand. Suddenly, she saw past the ring . . . past the engraved gold to the flesh beneath . . . to his fingers. *Three* fingers. It was not the ring at all. It was the flesh. Tankado was not telling them, he was showing them. He was telling his secret, revealing the kill-code – begging someone to understand . . . praying his secret would find its way to the NSA in time.

'Three,' Susan whispered, stunned.

'Three!' Becker yelled from Spain.

But in the chaos, no one seemed to hear.

'We're down!' a technician yelled.

The VR began flashing wildly as the core suc-cumbed to a deluge. Sirens erupted overhead.

'Outbound data!'

'High-speed tie-ins in all sectors!'

Susan moved as if through a dream. She spun toward Jabba's keyboard. As she turned, her gaze fixed on her fiancé, David Becker. Again his voice exploded overhead.

'Three! The difference between 235 and 238 is three!'

Everyone in the room looked up.

'Three!' Susan shouted over the deafening cacophony of sirens and technicians. She pointed to the screen. All eyes followed, to Tankado's hand, outstretched, three fingers waving desperately in the Sevillian sun.

Jabba went rigid. 'Oh my God!' He suddenly realized the crippled genius had been giving them the answer all the time.

'Three's prime!' Soshi blurted. 'Three's a *prime* number!'

Fontaine looked dazed. 'Can it be that simple?'

'Outbound data!' a technician cried. *'It's going fast!'*

Everyone on the podium dove for the terminal at the same instant – a mass of outstretched hands. But through the crowd, Susan, like a shortstop stabbing a line drive, connected with her target. She typed the number 3. Everyone wheeled to the wallscreen. Above the chaos, it simply read.

ENTER PASS-KEY? 3

'Yes!' Fontaine commanded. 'Do it now!'

Susan held her breath and lowered her finger on the ENTER key. The computer beeped once.

Nobody moved.

Three agonizing seconds later, nothing had happened.

The sirens kept going. Five seconds. Six seconds.

'Outbound data!'

'No change!'

Suddenly Midge began pointing wildly to the screen above. 'Look!'

On it, a message had materialized.

KILL CODE CONFIRMED

'Upload the firewalls!' Jabba ordered.

But Soshi was a step ahead of him. She had already sent the command.

'Outbound interrupt!' a technician yelled.

'Tie-ins severed!'

On the VR overhead, the first of the five firewalls began reappearing. The black lines attacking the core were instantly severed.

'Reinstating!' Jabba cried. 'The damn thing's re-instating!'

There was a moment of tentative disbelief, as if at any instant, everything would fall apart. But then the second firewall began reappearing . . . and then the third. Moments later the entire series of filters re-appeared. The databank was secure.

The room erupted. Pandemonium. Technicians hugged, tossing computer printouts in the air in celebration. Sirens wound down. Brinkerhoff grabbed Midge and held on. Soshi burst into tears.

'Jabba,' Fontaine demanded. 'How much did they get?'

'Very little,' Jabba said, studying his monitor. 'Very little. And nothing complete.'

Fontaine nodded slowly, a wry smile forming in the corner of his mouth. He looked around for Susan Fletcher, but she was already walking toward the front of the room. On the wall before her, David Becker's face filled the screen.

'David?'

'Hey, gorgeous.' He smiled.

'Come home,' she said. 'Come home, right now.'

'Meet you at Stone Manor?' he asked.

She nodded, the tears welling. 'Deal.'

'Agent Smith?' Fontaine called.

Smith appeared onscreen behind Becker. 'Yes, sir?'

'It appears Mr Becker has a date. Could you see that he gets home immediately?'

Smith nodded. 'Our jet's in Málaga.' He patted Becker on the back. 'You're in for a treat, Professor. Ever flown in a Learjet 60?'

Becker chuckled. 'Not since yesterday.'

CHAPTER 128

When Susan awoke, the sun was shining. The soft rays sifted through the curtains and filtered across her goosedown feather bed. She reached for David. *Am I dreaming?* Her body remained motionless, spent, still dizzy from the night before.

'David?' she moaned.

There was no reply. She opened her eyes, her skin still tingling. The mattress on the other side of the bed was cold. David was gone.

I'm dreaming, Susan thought. She sat up. The room was Victorian, all lace and antiques – Stone Manor's finest suite. Her overnight bag was in the middle of the hardwood floor . . . her lingerie on a Queen Anne chair beside the bed.

Had David really arrived? She had memories – his body against hers, his waking her with soft kisses. Had she dreamed it all? She turned to the bedside table. There was an empty bottle of champagne, two glasses . . . and a note.

Rubbing the sleep from her eyes, Susan drew the comforter around her naked body and read the message.

Dearest Susan,
I love you.
Without wax, David

She beamed and pulled the note to her chest. It was David, all right. *Without wax . . .* it was the one code she had yet to break.

Something stirred in the corner, and Susan looked up. On a plush divan, basking in the morning sun, wrapped in a thick bathrobe, David Becker sat quietly watching her. She reached out, beckoning him to come to her.

'Without wax?' she cooed, taking him in her arms.

'Without wax.' He smiled.

She kissed him deeply. 'Tell me what it means.'

'No chance.' He laughed. 'A couple needs secrets – it keeps things interesting.'

Susan smiled coyly. 'Any more interesting than last night and I'll never walk again.'

David took her in his arms. He felt weightless. He had almost died yesterday, and yet here he was, as alive as he had ever felt in his life.

Susan lay with her head on his chest, listening to the beat of his heart. She couldn't believe that she had thought he was gone forever.

'David,' she sighed, eyeing the note beside the table. 'Tell me about "without wax." You know I hate codes I can't break.'

David was silent.

'Tell me.' Susan pouted. 'Or you'll never have me again.'

'Liar.'

Susan hit him with a pillow. 'Tell me! Now!'

But David knew he would never tell. The secret behind 'without wax' was too sweet. Its origins were ancient.

During the Renaissance, Spanish sculptors who made mistakes while carving expensive marble often patched their flaws with *cera* – 'wax.' A statue that had no flaws and required no patching was hailed as a 'sculpture *sin cera*' or a 'sculpture without wax.' The phrase eventually came to mean anything honest or true. The English word 'sincere' evolved from the Spanish *sin cera* – 'without wax.' David's secret code was no great mystery – he was simply signing his letters 'Sincerely.' Somehow he suspected Susan would not be amused.

'You'll be pleased to know,' David said, attempting to change the subject, 'that during the flight home, I called the president of the university.'

Susan looked up, hopeful. 'Tell me you resigned as department chair.'

David nodded. 'I'll be back in the classroom next semester.'

She sighed in relief. 'Right where you belonged in the first place.'

David smiled softly. 'Yeah, I guess Spain reminded me what's important.'

'Back to breaking coeds' hearts?' Susan kissed his cheek. 'Well, at least you'll have time to help me edit my manuscript.'

'Manuscript?'

'Yes. I've decided to publish.'

'Publish?' David looked doubtful. 'Publish *what?*'

'Some ideas I have on variant filter protocols and quadratic residues.'

He groaned. 'Sounds like a real best-seller.'

She laughed. 'You'd be surprised.'

David fished inside the pocket of his bathrobe and pulled out a small object. 'Close your eyes. I have something for you.'

508

Susan closed her eyes. 'Let me guess – a gaudy gold ring with Latin all over it?'

'No.' David chuckled. 'I had Fontaine return that to Ensei Tankado's estate.' He took Susan's hand and slipped something onto her finger.

'Liar.' Susan laughed, opening her eyes. 'I knew—'

But Susan stopped short. The ring on her finger was not Tankado's at all. It was a platinum setting that held a glittering diamond solitaire.

Susan gasped.

David looked her in the eye. 'Will you marry me?'

Susan's breath caught in her throat. She looked at him and then back to the ring. Her eyes suddenly welled up. 'Oh, David . . . I don't know what to say.'

'Say yes.'

Susan turned away and didn't say a word.

David waited. 'Susan Fletcher, I love you. Marry me.'

Susan lifted her head. Her eyes were filled with tears. 'I'm sorry, David,' she whispered. 'I . . . I can't.'

David stared in shock. He searched her eyes for the playful glimmer he'd come to expect from her. It wasn't there. 'S-Susan,' he stammered. 'I – I don't understand.'

'I can't,' she repeated. 'I can't marry you.' She turned away. Her shoulders started trembling. She covered her face with her hands.

David was bewildered. 'But, Susan . . . I thought . . .' He held her trembling shoulders and turned her body toward him. It was then that he understood. Susan Fletcher was not crying at all; she was in hysterics.

'I won't marry you!' She laughed, attacking again with the pillow. 'Not until you explain "without wax"! You're driving me *crazy*!'

EPILOGUE

They say in death, all things become clear. Tokugen Numataka now knew it was true. Standing over the casket in the Osaka customs office, he felt a bitter clarity he had never known. His religion spoke of circles, of the interconnectedness of life, but Numataka had never had time for religion.

The customs officials had given him an envelope of adoption papers and birth records. 'You are this boy's only living relative,' they had said. 'We had a hard time finding you.'

Numataka's mind reeled back thirty-two years to that rain-soaked night, to the hospital ward where he had deserted his deformed child and dying wife. He had done it in the name of menboku – honor – an empty shadow now.

There was a golden ring enclosed with the papers. It was engraved with words Numataka did not understand. It made no difference; words had no meaning for Numataka anymore. He had forsaken his only son. And now, the cruelest of fates had reunited them.

128-10-93-85-10-128-98-112-6-6-25-126-39-1-68-78

Now read a tantalising preview of

DAN BROWN's

new Robert Langdon bestseller

PUBLISHED 14 MAY 2013

Fact:

All artwork, literature, science, and historical references in this novel are real.

'The Consortium' is a private organization with offices in seven countries. Its name has been changed for considerations of security and privacy.

Inferno is the underworld as described in Dante Alighieri's epic poem *The Divine Comedy*, which portrays hell as an elaborately structured realm populated by entities known as 'shades' – bodiless souls trapped between life and death.

Prologue

I am the Shade.

Through the dolent city, I flee.

Through the eternal woe, I take flight.

Along the banks of the river Arno, I scramble, breathless ... turning left onto Via dei Castellani, making my way northward, huddling in the shadows of the Uffizi.

And still they pursue me.

Their footsteps grow louder now as they hunt with relentless determination.

For years they have pursued me. Their persistence has kept me underground ... forced me to live in purgatory ... laboring beneath the earth like a chthonic monster.

I am the Shade.

Here above ground, I raise my eyes to the north, but I am unable to find a direct path to salvation ... for the Apennine Mountains are blotting out the first light of dawn.

I pass behind the palazzo with its crenellated tower and one-handed clock ... snaking through the early-morning vendors in Piazza di San Firenze with their hoarse voices smelling of *lampredotto* and roasted olives. Crossing before the Bargello, I cut west toward the spire of the Badia and come up hard against the iron gate at the base of the stairs.

Here all hesitation must be left behind.

I turn the handle and step into the passage from which I know there will be no return. I urge my leaden legs up the narrow staircase . . . spiraling skyward on soft marble treads, pitted and worn.

The voices echo from below. Beseeching.

They are behind me, unyielding, closing in.

They do not understand what is coming . . . nor what I have done for them!

Ungrateful land!

As I climb, the visions come hard . . . the lustful bodies writhing in fiery rain, the gluttonous souls floating in excrement, the treacherous villains frozen in Satan's icy grasp.

I climb the final stairs and arrive at the top, staggering near dead into the damp morning air. I rush to the head-high wall, peering through the slits. Far below is the blessed city that I have made my sanctuary from those who exiled me.

The voices call out, arriving close behind me. 'What you've done is madness!'

Madness breeds madness.

'For the love of God,' they shout, 'tell us where you've hidden it!'

For precisely the love of God, I will not.

I stand now, cornered, my back to the cold stone. They stare deep into my clear green eyes, and their expressions darken, no longer cajoling, but threatening. 'You know we have our methods. We can force you to tell us where it is.'

For that reason, I have climbed halfway to heaven.

Without warning, I turn and reach up, curling my fingers onto the high ledge, pulling myself up, scrambling onto my knees, then standing . . . unsteady at the precipice. *Guide me, dear Virgil, across the void.*

They rush forward in disbelief, wanting to grab at my feet, but fearing they will upset my balance and knock me off. They beg now, in quiet desperation, but I have turned my back. *I know what I must do.*

Beneath me, dizzyingly far beneath me, the red tile roofs spread out like a sea of fire on the countryside . . . illuminating the fair land upon which giants once roamed . . . Giotto, Donatello, Brunelleschi, Michelangelo, Botticelli.

I inch my toes to the edge.

'Come down!' they shout. 'It's not too late!'

O, willful ignorants! Do you not see the future? Do you not grasp the splendor of my creation? The necessity?

I gladly make this ultimate sacrifice . . . and with it I will extinguish your final hope of finding what you seek.

You will never locate it in time.

Hundreds of feet below, the cobblestone piazza beckons like a tranquil oasis. How I long for more time . . . but time is the one commodity even my vast fortunes cannot afford.

In these final seconds, I gaze down to the piazza, and I behold a sight that startles me.

I see your face.

You are gazing up at me from the shadows. Your eyes are mournful, and yet in them I sense a veneration for what I have accomplished. You understand I have no choice. For the love of Mankind, I must protect my masterpiece.

It grows even now . . . waiting . . . simmering beneath the bloodred waters of the lagoon that reflects no stars.

And so, I lift my eyes from yours and I contemplate the horizon. High above this burdened world, I make my final supplication.

Dearest God, I pray the world remembers my name not as

a monstrous sinner, but as the glorious savior you know I truly am. I pray Mankind will understand the gift I leave behind.

My gift is the future.

My gift is salvation.

My gift is Inferno.

With that, I whisper my amen . . . and take my final step, into the abyss.

Chapter 1

The memories materialized slowly . . . like bubbles surfacing from the darkness of a bottomless well.

A veiled woman.

Robert Langdon gazed at her across a river whose churning waters ran red with blood. On the far bank, the woman stood facing him, motionless, solemn, her face hidden by a shroud. In her hand she gripped a blue *tainia* cloth, which she now raised in honor of the sea of corpses at her feet. The smell of death hung everywhere.

Seek, the woman whispered. *And ye shall find.*

Langdon heard the words as if she had spoken them inside his head. 'Who are you?' he called out, but his voice made no sound.

Time grows short, she whispered. *Seek and find.*

Langdon took a step toward the river, but he could see the waters were bloodred and too deep to traverse. When Langdon raised his eyes again to the veiled woman, the bodies at her feet had multiplied. There were hundreds of them now, maybe thousands, some still alive, writhing in agony, dying unthinkable deaths . . . consumed by fire, buried in feces, devouring one another. He could hear the mournful cries of human suffering echoing across the water.

The woman moved toward him, holding out her slender hands, as if beckoning for help.

'Who are you?!' Langdon again shouted.

In response, the woman reached up and slowly lifted the veil from her face. She was strikingly beautiful, and yet older than Langdon had imagined—in her sixties perhaps, stately and strong, like a timeless statue. She had a sternly set jaw, deep soulful eyes, and long, silver-gray hair that cascaded over her shoulders in ringlets. An amulet of lapis lazuli hung around her neck—a single snake coiled around a staff.

Langdon sensed he knew her . . . trusted her. *But how? Why?*

She pointed now to a writhing pair of legs, which protruded upside down from the earth, apparently belonging to some poor soul who had been buried headfirst to his waist. The man's pale thigh bore a single letter—written in mud—*R*.

R? Langdon thought, uncertain. *As in . . . Robert?* 'Is that . . . *me*?'

The woman's face revealed nothing. *Seek and find*, she repeated.

Without warning, she began radiating a white light . . . brighter and brighter. Her entire body started vibrating intensely, and then, in a rush of thunder, she exploded into a thousand splintering shards of light.

Langdon bolted awake, shouting.

The room was bright. He was alone. The sharp smell of medicinal alcohol hung in the air, and somewhere a machine pinged in quiet rhythm with his heart. Langdon tried to move his right arm, but a sharp pain restrained him. He looked down and saw an IV tugging at the skin of his forearm.

His pulse quickened, and the machines kept pace, pinging more rapidly.

Where am I? What happened?

The back of Langdon's head throbbed, a gnawing

pain. Gingerly, he reached up with his free arm and touched his scalp, trying to locate the source of his headache. Beneath his matted hair, he found the hard nubs of a dozen or so stitches caked with dried blood.

He closed his eyes, trying to remember an accident.

Nothing. A total blank.

Think.

Only darkness.

A man in scrubs hurried in, apparently alerted by Langdon's racing heart monitor. He had a shaggy beard, bushy mustache, and gentle eyes that radiated a thoughtful calm beneath his overgrown eyebrows.

'What . . . happened?' Langdon managed. 'Did I have an accident?'

The bearded man put a finger to his lips and then rushed out, calling for someone down the hall.

Langdon turned his head, but the movement sent a spike of pain radiating through his skull. He took deep breaths and let the pain pass. Then, very gently and methodically, he surveyed his sterile surroundings.

The hospital room had a single bed. No flowers. No cards. Langdon saw his clothes on a nearby counter, folded inside a clear plastic bag. They were covered with blood.

My God. It must have been bad.

Now Langdon rotated his head very slowly toward the window beside his bed. It was dark outside. Night. All Langdon could see in the glass was his own reflection—an ashen stranger, pale and weary, attached to tubes and wires, surrounded by medical equipment.

Voices approached in the hall, and Langdon turned his gaze back toward the room. The doctor returned, now accompanied by a woman.

She appeared to be in her early thirties. She wore blue scrubs and had tied her blond hair back in a thick ponytail that swung behind her as she walked.

'I'm Dr. Sienna Brooks,' she said, giving Langdon a smile as she entered. 'I'll be working with Dr. Marconi tonight.'

Langdon nodded weakly.

Tall and lissome, Dr. Brooks moved with the assertive gait of an athlete. Even in shapeless scrubs, she had a willowy elegance about her. Despite the absence of any makeup that Langdon could see, her complexion appeared unusually smooth, the only blemish a tiny beauty mark just above her lips. Her eyes, though a gentle brown, seemed unusually penetrating, as if they had witnessed a profundity of experience rarely encountered by a person her age.

'Dr. Marconi doesn't speak much English,' she said, sitting down beside him, 'and he asked me to fill out your admittance form.' She gave him another smile.

'Thanks,' Langdon croaked.

'Okay,' she began, her tone businesslike. 'What is your name?'

It took him a moment. 'Robert . . . Langdon.'

She shone a penlight in Langdon's eyes. 'Occupation?'

This information surfaced even more slowly. 'Professor. Art history . . . and symbology. Harvard University.'

Dr. Brooks lowered the light, looking startled. The doctor with the bushy eyebrows looked equally surprised.

'You're . . . an American?'

Langdon gave her a confused look.

'It's just . . .' She hesitated. 'You had no identification when you arrived tonight. You were wearing Harris Tweed and Somerset loafers, so we guessed British.'

'I'm American,' Langdon assured her, too exhausted to explain his preference for well-tailored clothing.

'Any pain?'

'My head,' Langdon replied, his throbbing skull only made worse by the bright penlight. Thankfully, she now pocketed it, taking Langdon's wrist and checking his pulse.

'You woke up shouting,' the woman said. 'Do you remember why?'

Langdon flashed again on the strange vision of the veiled woman surrounded by writhing bodies. *Seek and ye shall find.* 'I was having a nightmare.'

'About?'

Langdon told her.

Dr. Brooks's expression remained neutral as she made notes on a clipboard. 'Any idea what might have sparked such a frightening vision?'

Langdon probed his memory and then shook his head, which pounded in protest.

'Okay, Mr. Langdon,' she said, still writing, 'a couple of routine questions for you. What day of the week is it?'

Langdon thought for a moment. 'It's Saturday. I remember earlier today walking across campus . . . going to an afternoon lecture series, and then . . . that's pretty much the last thing I remember. Did I fall?'

'We'll get to that. Do you know where you are?'

Langdon took his best guess. 'Massachusetts General Hospital?'

Dr. Brooks made another note. 'And is there some-one we should call for you? Wife? Children?'

'Nobody,' Langdon replied instinctively. He had always enjoyed the solitude and independence pro-vided him by his chosen life of bachelorhood, although he had to admit, in his current situation, he'd prefer to have a familiar face at his side. 'There are some colleagues I could call, but I'm fine.'

Dr. Brooks finished writing, and the older doctor approached. Smoothing back his bushy eyebrows, he produced a small voice recorder from his pocket and showed it to Dr. Brooks. She nodded in understanding and turned back to her patient.

'Mr. Langdon, when you arrived tonight, you were mumbling something over and over.' She glanced at Dr. Marconi, who held up the digital recorder and pressed a button.

A recording began to play, and Langdon heard his own groggy voice, repeatedly muttering the same phrase. *'Ve . . . sorry. Ve . . . sorry.'*

'It sounds to me,' the woman said, 'like you're saying, "Very sorry. Very sorry."'

Langdon agreed, and yet he had no recollection of it.

Dr. Brooks fixed him with a disquietingly intense stare. 'Do you have any idea why you'd be saying this? Are you sorry about something?'

As Langdon probed the dark recesses of his memory, he again saw the veiled woman. She was standing on the banks of a bloodred river surrounded by bodies. The stench of death returned.

Langdon was overcome by a sudden, instinctive sense of danger . . . not just for himself . . . but for everyone. The pinging of his heart monitor accelerated rapidly. His muscles tightened, and he tried to sit up.

Dr. Brooks quickly placed a firm hand on Langdon's sternum, forcing him back down. She shot a glance at the bearded doctor, who walked over to a nearby counter and began preparing something.

Dr. Brooks hovered over Langdon, whispering now. 'Mr. Langdon, anxiety is common with brain injuries, but you need to keep your pulse rate down.

No movement. No excitement. Just lie still and rest. You'll be okay. Your memory will come back slowly.'

The doctor returned now with a syringe, which he handed to Dr. Brooks. She injected its contents into Langdon's IV.

'Just a mild sedative to calm you down,' she explained, 'and also to help with the pain.' She stood to go. 'You'll be fine, Mr. Langdon. Just sleep. If you need anything, press the button on your bedside.'

She turned out the light and departed with the bearded doctor.

In the darkness, Langdon felt the drugs washing through his system almost instantly, dragging his body back down into that deep well from which he had emerged. He fought the feeling, forcing his eyes open in the darkness of his room. He tried to sit up, but his body felt like cement.

As Langdon shifted, he found himself again facing the window. The lights were out, and in the dark glass, his own reflection had disappeared, replaced by an illuminated skyline in the distance.

Amid a contour of spires and domes, a single regal facade dominated Langdon's field of view. The building was an imposing stone fortress with a notched parapet and a three-hundred-foot tower that swelled near the top, bulging outward into a massive machicolated battlement.

Langdon sat bolt upright in bed, pain exploding in his head. He fought off the searing throb and fixed his gaze on the tower.

Langdon knew the medieval structure well.

It was unique in the world.

Unfortunately, it was also located four thousand miles from Massachusetts.

*

Outside his window, hidden in the shadows of the Via Torregalli, a powerfully built woman effortlessly unstraddled her BMW motorcycle and advanced with the intensity of a panther stalking its prey. Her gaze was sharp. Her close-cropped hair—styled into spikes—stood out against the upturned collar of her black leather riding suit. She checked her silenced weapon, and stared up at the window where Robert Langdon's light had just gone out.

Earlier tonight her original mission had gone horribly awry.

The coo of a single dove had changed everything.

Now she had come to make it right.